The Weight of Memories

BY JAY YURTH

Order this book online at www.trafford.com
or email orders@trafford.com

Most Trafford titles are also available at major online book retailers.

Happiness is a Warm Gun
By John Lennon and Paul McCartney

Print information available on the last page.

ISBN: 978-1-4120-6091-2 (sc)
ISBN: 978-1-4122-0821-5 (e)

Trafford rev. 08/05/2020

 www.trafford.com
North America & international
toll-free: 1 888 232 4444 (USA & Canada)
fax: 812 355 4082

To my wife for letting me run and to G.O.S.
who I hope to bump into in a future life.

"WOULD YOU please stand up and read this newspaper clipping to us, Robin?"

"All right, Miss Butler," Robin said as he walked up to the front of the class and took the unevenly ripped paper from his teacher's hand. She obviously wasn't too impressed with the article. No need for scissors, a last minute thought to just grab it as she was running out the door with coffee in hand, cigarette hanging from her lips and *most* of the curriculum for the year under her arm. *Couldn't have the teacher late for the first day of school.*

Robin stood up and started reading. "Missing thirteen year olds return: Seems there's still GOLD in them thar hills!" he said as he looked up with a big smile and added, "That's the headline."

The teacher nodded and motioned him to continue.

"Robin Duvall and Jeffery Jason 'Jaybird' Young, missing for almost two weeks, walked back into their worried families' lives with what must have sounded like the biggest whopper of an excuse ever devised. Consequently as they started telling their story it seemed as if their new names would be 'Mud' and 'Pinocchio' respectively. Amazingly though, with only one look at the contents of the old traveling trunks they had brought back with them, all disbelief had dissipated. These two, now best friends, had returned to St. Joseph after successfully hitch-hiking from here to Colorado and back. Their families and the authorities were very worried after they just vanished from their lives one day, with what amounted to…"

"Thank you Robin, that will be fine right there," the teacher said, interrupting him in mid-sentence, motioning him to put the clipping on her desk, adding, "Now please tell the class in your own words about what happened with you and Mr. Young over the summer…ah…from the beginning, if you don't mind."

Robin felt cheated. He really liked that article. So much so that he had the exact same one neatly cut out and framed at home, hanging on his bedroom wall. Looking around the room though, he could see all the other seventh grade kids staring at him, nodding their heads affirmatively, eyes wide with anticipation. All except the dorky kid in the back who was busy picking boogers as if no one could see him.

"Well, I guess it all started a few days after the term ended last year at my old school. My mom had separated from my dad and we moved to another neighborhood after a week-long camping vacation. After we moved everything into the new place, she made me go next door to say hello to our new neighbors. She said that when we were moving in she saw a boy about my age taking out some garbage. I didn't want to go meet a strange kid but Mom made me. Sure enough Jason Young, you know him as um, Jaybird. He's in Mr. Henderson's home room class. Anyway, he answered the door. I reached out to shake his hand and was introducing myself, but as we shook hands I had this strange feeling like I knew him already, but I, but then I had this, well at first…"

His words faded and became unintelligible, much like what happened to him a month before their now infamous trek. He remembered that exact moment he shook Jaybird's hand. How could he forget it? Standing on the porch, his right hand clasped in a grip, he was almost frozen in his tracks by some very unusual memories. It wasn't like any other handshake. Maybe the handshake had nothing to do with the memories that suddenly surfaced. He couldn't help himself out of this particular moment as he stood in front of the class, as the whispers, giggles and muffled remarks from the children raced around the room. His thoughts were so engulfing right then that he couldn't focus on the story he was telling. He knew he was standing in front of the class but his thoughts were not there. He knew he didn't like this feeling of embarrassment, but whenever he let himself think about their first meeting, his mind reeled, so he had always tried to ignore those thoughts. *Don't want to be crazy.*

Ignoring them wasn't working at the moment, unfortunately. It was just too much for a thirteen-year-old to sort out. The places, images, feelings and knowledge all seemed one hundred percent real in his head but he just couldn't believe it. Everything was so hard to put into words that he had to often make a conscientious effort to suppress even contemplating them when they popped into his thoughts. He wasn't very good at ignoring them at the moment. Many times he would resort to just turning on his AM radio and getting into the music. This usually helped get his mind off the strange memories. He kept telling himself they were just plain old daydreams that couldn't be actual memories. Other times just going over to Jaybird's house and hanging out with him or sometimes climbing up to the tree-house would somehow ease the bewilderment. He had no idea why.

Now, standing there in front of the class, he was being laughed at, although quietly. He hated being laughed at. He absolutely hated it. This was exactly why he and Jaybird promised each other to never tell anyone about what they both had experienced during that first handshake. Jaybird had said once that he also got a rush of images and what seemed like memories that were, but a moment before, not in his head. At thirteen years old they were just young enough to make a sworn, solemn, blood brother pact of secrecy, and stand by it. They promised to never discuss that weird moment again, ever. It was just too creepy. Besides, as he was now experiencing, even attempting to verbalize what had transpired in his head then and since, was proving to be futile.

Why does being laughed at make me so mad? Robin thought to himself. In an instant he knew. He couldn't understand just how he now *knew* why he hated it, but there it was as a fact and it was providing an internal answer to his own question.

He was in front of the whole tribe it seemed. *Tribe?* It was eons ago. He knew it was before there was a way to track time as we do now. There must have been seventy-five to one hundred people from the tribe there. It was a time before names also; everyone just knew everyone else by sight. Everyone had a purpose in the tribe. His was to protect the tribesmen from any dangers, since he was the biggest, strongest and fastest. On that day he wanted to show the tribe something new. Robin remembered he was holding a handful of seeds as he stood by a big tree; this tree was a place where anyone who had discovered something, could go and show it to the rest of the tribe. As everyone continued to gather by the tree, dusk was creeping in fast. He remembered his frustration in trying to show the others that if they put the seeds in the ground they would grow into food, to be gathered later and stored for the winter when nothing grew on the land. But with no language, the charade he was acting out was not getting across. No matter how he showed them, they were not getting it. They started laughing at him and throwing sticks and rocks at him and eventually, on that day, he was driven out of the valley where they had been living. Humiliated and alone, he found a level patch of land several valleys away. There he planted his seeds. Keeping track of his old tribe, stealthily, on almost a daily basis, he saw nearly everyone who stubbornly stayed in that settlement, die. The winter was cold and long; they had no food stored and wildlife was scarce. A few got so hungry that they did actually head south for warmth and food. They may have survived but he would never know. All he knew was that he had enough to eat and no one was laughing at him. That was the first time he remembered that he hated being laughed at, especially when he knew he was right. He knew he should have planted enough seeds for everyone. He had always protected them. He could have protected them by feeding them, but they had banished him so he had just let them suffer. Robin had no idea how he could remember that particular moment in some long past life. It seemed to be a memory from a time that he *actually* lived. *It couldn't be real could it*, he wondered? *What am I, reincarnated or something? No, I am myself. Who believes in reincarnation anyhow?* It was confusing and seemed so long ago. The feeling of knowing something for sure, as a fact, is very satisfying most of the time. You just know what you know is real and factual. But knowledge was on one hand satiating and on the other quite infuriating. This is why he hated to indulge himself in his own odd memories when they popped up.

"Yes, well now, Robin, could you tell the class about some of your experiences on your way to Colorado?" Miss Butler interceded, rescuing him from his obvious confusion. She was hoping he could continue until the next bell rang so she could rush off and have another cigarette in the staff lounge with the new teacher she fancied.

Thankful this time, for the interruption, Robin nodded. He regained his train of thought enough to proceed. "Oh, sure, I...I can. Well, um... once we hitched a ride from this man in Kansas who turned out to be a drunk or maybe even crazy. He was driving fast and really bad; he was all over the road. Jaybird and I looked at each other and at the next stop sign we just jumped out as he began to speed up, after barely stopping. That's when I cut my face pretty bad. I hit the ground or scraped something on the door, I don't know for sure."

As Robin pointed to his cheek a student asked, "Did Jaybird get hurt when he jumped out?"

"No, he rolled and got scratched up, but not bad."

"Was your cut bad enough for stitches, Robin?" another student asked.

"It probably was but we were too scared to go to a hospital. My dad says that's why it looks so bad. It needed stitches. Anyhow we just held a sock to it 'til it stopped bleeding."

"Did the drunk try to back over you guys?" another one asked.

"No, he just kept going. I don't think he even knew we jumped out 'cause the car was so old and noisy. It was a piece of crap; that's for sure," Robin said, cringing at his choice of words, as he and the class started laughing.

"Robin! Watch your language," Miss Butler said authoritatively. She then quieted the class down and asked in a somewhat condescending tone, "When you finally got to Colorado, how did you know where to go? What made you look in that particular cave? Did Mister Young find a treasure map or something?"

"Well…no, but the cave was right where Jaybird said it would be. Its location was in his uh, dream. Jaybird said he was having this one dream over and over. Every night. For weeks. He was real certain that he would find these trunks hidden way back in this one cave. He also said there was gold in them and he had to get to them."

Robin had fibbed a bit on that part. Jaybird had actually told him one afternoon that he just *knew* the gold was there. He also told Robin that he had no idea how he knew but he was one hundred percent positive that he had put the trunks there himself. Robin *did* believe him, without any hesitation or doubt at all. Each of them knew what the other knew about the trunks. Remembering their secret pact, they didn't discuss it beyond that.

"And you just decided to go with him and not tell anyone?" the teacher queried, sounding just like a mother.

"Well, Jaybird had said to me, 'There are times when you just have to make your mind up and do it. Don't look back on your decisions.' For some reason I kinda felt he was telling the truth about the cave and I thought he might need some help getting there."

Robin had fibbed again. He was absolutely sure the gold was in the trunks in that very cave because he had helped put them there in the first place. Robin knew that Jaybird knew they had been there together, but neither brought it up. *No need to stick a needle in your eye for breaking a secret pact.*

"Well," Robin continued, "It just seemed like the thing to do at the time. Besides, I was mad at my mom for moving away from my dad. She gave me no choice in the matter and I had to change schools. Everything was different. I guess I had been thinking of running away from home anyway. I thought it would be cool to have someone to run away with and Jaybird had a place in mind to actually run away to. Besides, what if Jaybird ran into some bullies? I knew I could help him out in a fight."

Robin saw some heads nodding up and down. A few kids even looked at Steve, the boy Robin had yanked off a smaller kid during a fight just before the first bell rang today. That scuffle had left Steve with a bruise on his cheek and his ego. Many of them snickered, knowing that Steve was a big bad bully and deserved Robin's big, *anti-bully punch*. A pecking order had been established.

As a mischievous grin came to Robin's mouth, he continued, "Jaybird said he could see the cave so clearly and felt so strongly about it, that he was going there with or without me. He was in such a hurry to leave that I had to make my mind up right then and there. Seems like he is always in a hurry...um, anyway, I grabbed my transistor radio. We each swiped a handful of coins from our folks' not-so-secret money stashes and just took off. We each left a note that said, 'Don't worry. We'll be back. We just don't know when.' We didn't want our parents to think something bad had happened to us or anything, but Jaybird was in such a hurry that...um, maybe we could have left a longer note. Anyhow, when we finally found the cave, the entrance had been covered with rocks and dirt and weeds. Probably been like that for a long time. We couldn't even tell it was an entrance. We needed to dig our way in, but by this time we were flat broke. We decided to look for glass soda pop bottles and collect as many as we could to turn them in and collect the money. We went around the town and found many bottles. Many times, when no one was around, we went into churches and the waiting areas of businesses and grabbed all the empties they had in the return racks. At two cents for each one, we had to get a lot, but most places had full racks of empty bottles.

I know that was kinda bad, but we needed the money. When we had enough we bought the shovel and other stuff."

Robin continued with his story. Just seconds before the bell rang out for the next class, he said the words everyone was waiting to hear.

"And it turned out, Jaybird was right. There ended up being seven point three million dollars worth of gold in those trunks. The rest I guess you already read in the papers."

CHAPTER I

1977

THAT WAS almost five years ago. Today is June sixth, and it is Jaybird's eighteenth birthday. There was a little, and probably the last, party for him at his parents' house. Some of the family and a few friends had gathered. Robin, of course, came over from next door and was telling jokes in the living room. Jaybird was listening but he wasn't paying much attention, for today was a big day for him. Not just because it was his birthday. It was big because earlier in the morning they had signed all the paperwork at the bank. All the accounts and money his dad's broker had been managing for them were now legally in each one's own name. It was a day for some major decisions. Jaybird had waited a long time for today. He and Robin had made plans together and changed their minds a million times. Years ago when he and Robin returned from their little trek, Jaybird had made a promise to his mother. He had promised never to run off again, at least until he was eighteen and old enough to make his own decisions. He regretted that promise almost every day. He often wanted to just pack up and leave, to seek out and decipher the odd memories he had continued to have over the last five years. He wanted to get away and locate the places and things in his memories, which he had become used to calling his unbelievable personal facts. Somehow, validating his feelings with his own eyes, made that knowledge more acceptable to his mind. It was double validation, really. He stuck to his word. *A promise was a promise, especially to a mom.* The values he was brought up with were based around family, love and trust. He never ran off again. He made another promise to himself though, and that was to never make that kind of promise again.

Here he was, a fresh high school grad and eighteen years old at last. He could now be in control of his life and his money. Thanks to his dad and the family financial advisor, who more than doubled their investments, Jaybird and Robin had a sum that slightly exceeded eight million dollars each, if they were to liquidate everything. He had wanted this day to come for so long. So many decisions to make, so many sleepless nights spending his money in his head. Robin liquidated everything and put the proceeds in his checking account. Jaybird withdrew two hundred thousand from the bank, in cold hard cash.

He had gone to the East Valley Mall and picked up a special gift for his girlfriend Kandy. In addition he had already allowed his dad to let him know the total amount of money it would take to pay off the entire Young family's debts. It was something he just felt compelled to do. His parents were so proud of him for making that kind of decision. To Jaybird it wasn't such a hard one to make. It had made him feel very good anyway.

His best friend Robin had actually stopped talking long enough to carry in the cake. Chocolate with chocolate frosting, Jaybird's favorite. As everyone started gathering around the dining room table, Kandy was begrudgingly taking pictures. Robin set the cake in front of Jaybird and as an off-key rendition of "Happy Birthday" finally ended, Jaybird blew out the eighteen candles. Kandy snapped a picture of him just as his cheeks were puffed full of air. Laughter filled the room as he tried to blow out the one candle that just wouldn't go out. Robin was the culprit of the trick candle, of course.

Grabbing the candle and drowning it in a glass of Kool-Aid, Kandy turned Jaybird's head to face hers and planted a big kiss on his lips, as the grownups rolled their eyes.

"What did you wish for?" she asked.

"Wishes don't come true if you tell anyone. My lips are sealed forever!" Jaybird said as he puckered up and returned the favor.

Kandy sat back and watched as Jaybird cut the cake and served up slices to the others. She knew it was a special day for him; she had anticipated this day almost as much as he had. She knew that he would most certainly start to lavish gifts and money on her shortly. She had waited to reap the spoils of being with him for ten long months. She remembered what her mother had told her once when they were having one of their most important mother-daughter talks, when she had been about thirteen years old. Her mother had told Kandy all about her father and the reason for their divorce. Kandy's father was a chief of a Blackfoot Indian tribe in Montana. He was a man of few words and of little time for his wife, but plenty of time for his lover, it seemed. Her mother told her that his fooling around was the reason she divorced him. She stated during that conversation that Kandy should pick the richest, the smartest and the best-looking man, or two out of the three. She said to never compromise on the money issue, when planning for her future. "Men aren't permanent fixtures," she said, "so you have to look beyond the relationship. It's all a game anyway; understand the rules and play to win...Things will eventually change, so you must set yourself up. Love will come later. After you get what you need to survive, then and only then should you go looking for love. All men will leave you sooner or later; they just get tired of the same thing, so get what is coming to you. Don't be left out in the cold, uneducated and poor like me. I got nothing out of my marriage and both you and I suffered for that. You can do better for yourself. I should have done better for you. Play the game and win it."

Whether or not Kandy's mother really meant what she said that day or if it was the alcohol and marijuana talking, didn't matter. It wasn't something any normal mother should be telling her thirteen-year-old daughter, but Kandy took it to heart. Something clicked in her head at that moment that would start her on a quest. A quest to search for the perfect male, perfect only in her warped little mind. It was as if that brief talk set her on a path...her own special life-game. She vowed never to veer from it until she won.

When the perfect chance presented itself to her, she latched onto the soon-to-be-the-richest-young-man in high school. He had money, that was one of her requirements. He was not bad looking. Seems many of the other girls at school thought he was cute. Not really her type in the looks department though. A little compromise but those were two of her requirements. He was a bit on the smart-alecky side. Rumor had it that he never ever studied and still got "A"s. Smart. The third requirement had also been met. At six feet with light brown hair and hazel eyes, she figured he was just cute enough to make up for his smart-ass flaw. She actually had all three of her requirements in one package. *What luck*, she thought. But she had one goal in mind: Marry him. All she had to do was *act* like she cared for him and make him fall in love with her somewhere down the road. Since she believed that he would eventually leave her, as Mommy had preached to her, she played along with whatever he wanted. Sometimes she felt he was actually a nice guy. She might like those kinds of things in a *real* boyfriend, if she could ever let herself care for a man. Maybe someday when her quest was over and she was set for life. But not now. She had to get set up. The game had started. Her mother had spun the dial and Kandy was moving the pieces. She wouldn't be cheated out of a good life, like her mother had been, no matter what. She would marry him, wait till he dumped her and then get a nice settlement. First she had to be as nice to him as she could so that he would ask her to marry him. Her act was very believable, at least to Jaybird. Many of the family had always thought of her as a gold-digger, digging for the gold Jaybird had already dug up.

Kandy Kane Norton was a slender young woman, barely seventeen years old, having just finished her junior year of high school. She stood five foot five and had long straight jet-black hair reaching all the way down to her waist. Her high Indian cheek bones made the perfect cradle for her big brown eyes to hover over. Jaybird thought she was exotic looking and he was blindly in love. He had told Robin that he fell in love the first time he laid eyes on her. He just didn't tell Kandy for a whole month.

Kandy had met Jaybird at a car wash fund-raiser for school. They had "hose duty" together and Jaybird had struck up a conversation after accidentally spraying her with the water hose. This would be the start of their tenth month of dating. Kandy had never had a boyfriend before Jaybird. No guy had ever fit into her twisted qualifications, not to mention she was still very young and wasn't allowed to date until she was sixteen. She knew he was the boy who had found all that gold years ago; she knew instantly that he was her ticket out of the poor house. She put on her best behavior and the facade had begun.

"Why don't you open your birthday cards, Jaybird?" Nan asked, handing her son a small pile of envelopes.

Jaybird shuffled through them and then quickly started to open a bright yellow one, exclaiming, "This is the one I always open first. Although…funny, this year it won't be as exciting as all the other years."

This prompted Robin to ask, "And why is that; are you too big for birthdays now?"

"Well, no, it's because it's from my favorite uncle whom I have never met: Uncle Nicholas. He always sends a hundred bucks. But that just won't match the eight million bucks I got today."

"Say, I don't remember ever hearing much about him. What does he do?" Robin asked.

Jaybird looked at his dad, Harry, inquisitively, with raised eyebrows.

Harry managed a forced laugh and said, "Well, you did meet him once when you were about four years old. Anyway that damn hippie is off trying to save mankind or something noble like that."

"Where does he work again, eh…Dad?"

"Um…some bio-science company called–Nan, a little help?" Harry yelled to his wife, cocking his head around towards the kitchen.

"Intertwine, Hon," Nan called from the kitchen, lovingly mumbling, "gee whiz, his own little brother," to herself.

"There you have it. He turned out to be the smart one in the family. Got his doctorate and all, yet never tells us what the heck he does, or maybe I just don't understand fully. But seriously, even though he has long hair and is still into all that hippie crap, I think he does very important work on the human DNA or genes or both or you know, scientific stuff. He wrote some books, too. I just never picked up another one after trying to read the first one."

"So, no clue as to what your brother does, eh Harry?" Robin teased.

"Not really, but I do know he writes boring scientific books. Well, boring to me. Yet he always had…well, quite an imagination so when he finally settled down and put his nose to the grindstone he made some money with all those brains. Got a big house out in New Jersey somewhere," Harry said, laughing but still feeling a bit embarrassed inside at having to always withhold some personal information about his little brother.

Harry wasn't about to tell his kids, wife or anyone else in the room for that matter the truth about the problems Nicholas had when they were younger. Seems their parents thought Nicholas started acting funny at around the time the family went on a big vacation to Disneyland in 1958 when Nicholas had just finished his junior year of high school. Harry was twenty-three at the time, still living at home even though he had just married Nan. He remembered that Nicholas spent two or three days a week at the doctor's office for almost a year after they got back from Disneyland. Turned out the doctor was a shrink. Eventually Nicholas either got better or said whatever they wanted to hear. He remembered Nicholas telling him once that he *did* know the difference between reality and make-believe, unlike what everyone thought about him. But Harry mostly remembered the social embarrassment the family endured with having a *crazy* child. At that time if you needed a shrink, you were nuts and everyone would tease you. Plus how could he ever forget the many nights he would wake up to Nicholas screaming, "Minnie Mouse is my wife!" at the top of his lungs.

Jaybird opened his card and the hundred dollar bill fell out as expected. He speed-read the card and stuffed the bill in his wallet, thinking to himself, *I always liked getting those hundred bucks from Uncle Nick. I should go see him sometime. Genes and DNA? I never heard that from my dad before. I thought he was just a novelist. Maybe he can clue me in on where I get these damn memories from. Maybe it's a hereditary thing.*

After all the cards were opened and a quiet lull came over the room Kandy leaned into Jaybird's ear and whispered, "What are we doing tonight?"

"Well, we are going to watch the video of Robin's fight, I thought I mentioned that?" he replied. He was actually bursting at the seams to tell her what he had decided to do. He wanted to skip the whole party and be alone with Kandy, but he also knew he had to pick the perfect moment. This wasn't it.

"I know *that*. I mean after the fight?" Kandy said snobbishly.

"Let's play it by ear, OK?" He was about to explode trying to hold in his little secret.

"Are you mad at me?" she asked, tilting her head to the side and batting her long eyelashes at him with that puppy-dog look in her eyes.

Jaybird shook his head and stated bluntly, "You know I never get mad. C'mon, let's watch the fight."

"But I don't want to watch it. Can't we go somewhere and buy something?" she asked, whispering in his ear, trying to sound like she was joking.

"You know this fight is very important to Robin and we are already here. I'm not leaving now. It shouldn't take too long. None of his fights do anyway," Jaybird said, not understanding her desire to leave the party so early, that is, unless Robin had told her what he had planned for the evening.

The fact was that Kandy couldn't stand his family or his friends, especially Robin. She had made up her mind to not get close to any of them. She always had a fake smile on her face but nothing important to say to them. Little did Kandy know that they could see right through her, as any caring family would. But Jaybird was blind to her game and deaf to his family's concerns about her.

As seats were taken around the TV, Robin pushed in the Betamax tape and turned around. The room got quiet. Everyone knew he was going to make an exciting intro. He did.

"I want to thank you all for coming to my fight preview, oh, I mean Jaybird's birthday party. Actually you know he has had eighteen of these birthday things and this is my first pro boxing match. Gosh…what's really important here, folks?"

Jaybird laughed along with everyone. He knew Robin loved to work a crowd. A true class clown in school who thrived on attention and always stood up for the underdog. Jaybird just sat back and watched Robin work the party. Forever being the straight man to Robin's punch lines, he was very content to let Robin have the floor for as long as he wanted it.

Robin looked at Jaybird and continued somewhat uncharacteristically, "Actually I want to be serious for a minute here. I would like to thank Jaybird for some things. Thanks for splitting the gold with me in the first place. Thanks for helping to get me into the gym and the boxing ring. You gave me that little push in the right direction, which I needed. Oh yes, and thanks to Harry for overseeing the money so well. What a huge pile I have now. And thank you all for putting up with this preamble. Enough said?" He looked around the room at all the smiles and said, "Good, then I hope you will enjoy watching me on my first step up the ladder to becoming the Heavyweight Champion of the World. Please pay attention as I kick this guy's ass!"

The room filled with clapping and laughter as Robin pushed the play button. All eyes were glued to the huge fifteen-inch Zenith TV screen.

Robin Stanley Duvall was a stocky, muscular 185-pound young man who stood five feet, eight inches tall. He had turned eighteen years old on January first. He had been born with a tremendous genetic gift of strength. This, along with his dedication in the gym and a burning desire to become the heavyweight champ, as well as his sense of humor, made him an extremely powerful and engaging young man. His broad shoulders, small waist and thick legs gave him somewhat of an awkward-looking gait. Jaybird had always called him "Monkey" because he was so bowlegged. No one else could get away with that nick-name though. The scar Robin got from jumping out of the drunk's car years earlier made him look mean, verging on menacing. The scar curved along from the outside corner of his right eye forward over his cheek then back to the base of his right ear. It looked like an inverted letter C. He had learned to use that menacing look to his advantage when he wanted to psyche-out an opponent in the gym before all his amateur fights. It had also worked well during all his childhood scuffles. Yet he had a completely humorous demeanor. His quick wit made him a very likable person when you got to know him, if you could drag him away from the music that he always listened to. It just wasn't very smart to tease him about his first name. That, as many a schoolboy found out, was not a very good idea.

Robin had always loved watching Ali, Frazier and Foreman fighting on *Wide World of Sports* but Jaybird was the one to put the bug in his ear that got Robin to thinking, then dreaming about a career in professional boxing. As soon as he started to learn the fundamentals of boxing in the gym, he could tell it was going to be something he would love to pursue. He figured that when his boxing career was over he could be a personal bodyguard or a policeman. He never really understood that the multi-millions of dollars he was going to get when Jaybird turned eighteen was quite enough to live on for the rest of his life without ever needing a real job.

Robin knew he had been a musician and a fighter many times before as well as having many lives where he just protected people. After creating music at home he might have to go out and demolish one person as he was protecting another. His lives had been filled with extremes. It seemed that he was almost always born to do those types of things in life, yet he could never tell anyone why or how he knew it. No one would believe him, that's for sure. Yet he could distinctly remember one life where he had been a longtime winning, very popular *free* professional gladiator in Rome named Dudlius Railmanus. He had lived from what he calculated to be around 211-116 BC in Rome. People at that time had thought he was crazy for wanting to be a gladiator; most gladiators were slaves and criminals who were used for the "entertainment of death" value only. But the Coliseum was a magical place at that time for him. He was semi-famous, wealthy beyond his dreams and enjoyed his life. Much of that was due to the wealthy lanista or manager who had befriended him. He was one of the few honest lanistae of the times and provided everything that Robin needed for a grand life. They were both showmen and each basked in his own limelight. Robin remembered starting out as a performer in the *Munus* Games. These were rituals presented annually as gifts for descendants, designed to keep the dead person's memory alive. From this, the Dudlius Railmanus reputation had grown. From his acute sense of duty and honor to the *Munus* came other opportunities. Along with the fame came a great sense of loss. He had outlived all of his contemporaries; he was ninety-five years old when he finally died. This was an extremely long life for the times. He had made many friends over his long fighting career, as he fought well into his fifties. Toward the end of his career it seemed that every young warrior wanted to fight him and have the honor of killing the great gladiator Dudlius Railmanus. After one arduous fight which he nearly lost and, having felt his mortality challenged, he decided to stop fighting at the impressive age of fifty-eight. It was in his later years of luxury that he saw all his friends eventually meet their deaths in front of the crowds at the Coliseum or in other less prestigious ways. It was hard to lose everyone you knew and then die without family or friends at your side. That kind of pain was hard to forget.

Currently in this present life, Robin enjoyed being the focus of attention. He always wanted to push himself to the limits. One more lap, one more round, one more sit-up or one more rep on the barbells. He could see the end product of his hard work. The Heavyweight Championship of the World. He knew he wouldn't be happy if he were anything less. All he needed was a little prodding. Now it was show-time.

The taped fight was getting good. Robin's opponent had a winning record. He was big, tough and five years older. Robin was tough also.

As Jaybird watched the fight, he remembered that he had always seemed to be with Robin when there was a fight, whether it was after school, during lunch or at a mall. Jaybird was always there, watching in amazement as a situation would escalate into more than it should have been. The incident would inevitably start over some bigger guy making fun of Robin's name. Never failed. Plus, bullies only pick on people smaller than themselves. Put Robin's size and his name together and you had a fight waiting to start. Robin would always start off smiling, ignoring the punk or even begin walking away, but it seemed that young boys needed to be taught a lesson the hard way more often than not. They just weren't going to learn anything if it didn't hurt or embarrass them. So, of course, someone would call Robin a girl or a wimp or worse; another would yell out a time and place to meet and fight or else that would prove that Robin was a chicken. Jaybird remembered a few times that Robin would even stand up for him if someone were picking on him.

It didn't matter how the fights got started, Robin never missed a set meeting time to fight. And he never lost. *Never*. He would play around with some of the poor fools, prolonging the inevitable. He would even take a few punches if Jaybird wasn't there yet and Robin knew he was coming, just so Jaybird could see him end it.

Jaybird mused about the secret signal they had developed somehow, which told Robin it was time to finish the fight. Jaybird would look at his watch, turn his palms skyward and shrug his shoulders and then tap his watch again and frown, as if he and Robin had an important meeting to run off to. Sort of like saying, "Well, you coming or what?" Once Robin saw him do that it was like a challenge for him to see how fast he could bring on the end of the fight. Jaybird called it getting him into the "da, da, da, dum" mode. Robin would usually be able to connect with three left jabs and a right cross that would end the fight. A quick 1-2-3-4, or da, da, da, dum combination. When Jaybird was telling everyone about the fight afterwards, he would always tell the story while using that famous Beethoven sound bite: "da, da, da, dum." It stuck. It became somewhat of a local urban legend. Then of course all the big bad bullies from other schools would come seeking out Robin after classes and on weekends at the park hang-outs, etc., with no real reason to fight except to hopefully be that one guy who would beat him. But no one ever beat Robin. Not even the mid-twenty-something thugs who couldn't understand that high school had been over for five years and street fighting was a childish thing. It didn't matter. No one beat Robin, *ever*.

Robin thought that it was quite an unusual coincidence that Jaybird had picked a bar from a Beethoven symphony as his moniker. *Or was it?* No, not really, it seemed. Robin knew Jaybird had been Joseph Haydn who worked with him back in the early 1800's but died in 1809 after a few years of collaboration and even admiration. Robin remembered penning that very piece himself back in 1804. Robin knew he had been Beethoven; he remembered it so clearly. But remembering the blood brother pact, he would never mention that to Jaybird. Or to anyone else. Robin decided to take a variation of what Jaybird had thought up and used it as his ring name when he first started his amateur boxing career. He was now Robin "4-D" Duvall. He never lost a single amateur fight in two years. As his winning streak had increased, he had to explain that "4-D" less and less with the smattering of local media that turned out to cover the events. All fifty-five fights were won by knockouts or the referee stopping the fight, or the opponent running away asking his corner to throw in the towel after some of Robin's hard punches connected. He had won the Missouri State Golden Gloves title two years straight. He would make a great pro boxer if he wanted to box for a living. Every major manager in the region was keeping an eye on him to turn pro. As it turned out Robin wanted only one person for the job: his YMCA coach, Adam Ellwood, who had been for him from the start.

Suddenly Robin told everyone that the second round was the last round. All eyes were glued to the TV. All but Kandy's. She was watching Robin's new female friend, Julie, who had just happened to sit next to Jaybird on the couch. Kandy had decided to keep an eye out for any touching that she might deem unacceptable. She knew how lucky she was to have found Jaybird, so she wasn't about to let any female get too close to him and ruin her plans. Those actions always came across as jealousy in everyone else's eyes but it seemed to make Jaybird feel good for some reason. It *was* jealousy, but it was Kandy's very own skewed kind of jealousy. She truly thought every woman was playing the same game with every man as she was.

As Robin watched the fight he realized that he had never seen himself fight before. He noticed he was quite a bit shorter than his opponent. Now that he thought of it, he couldn't remember any opponent being shorter than he was. Funny. But this wouldn't get in the way of his dream of becoming the Heavyweight Champion of the World someday. Even though he was more of a cruiserweight size, he would only fight other heavyweights. Joe Frazier was small but he was a champ. *No sir; he would beat them all,* he thought, *just bring them on.* This was the start of his dream come true and it had gone very well. He thought about how often he dreamed about what he would say when they finally gave him the Championship Belt. He could picture himself: sweat pouring off his body, hands up in the air, cameras in his face, the young round-card beauty on his arm.

"Hi, Mom." No, that wouldn't be cool. Besides all the college football players said that.

"It feels groovy." No, that was too 60's. He decided to keep working on what to say at that moment.

Robin looked up and leaned forward to the edge of the couch and yelled, "Here it comes!"

With the first left jab, everyone started chanting, "da, da, da, dum!" ending with a "dum" and a punishing right cross.

That was the end of the fight. Another knockout. But this one meant much more; this was his first knockout in his first professional fight. Robin's coach, Adam, had told Jaybird once that he had very high hopes for Robin. He stated many times that this kind of natural fighter doesn't come along very often. He was a rare find. It was if Robin was special-ordered to do one thing and do it perfectly, from instinct. Adam didn't have to coach him; it was more like Robin was coaching him. He said Robin would, in all likelihood, be on a fast track straight to the top of the boxing world if he only wanted to go in that direction.

Robin jumped up and started to take the tape out of the Betamax then stopped and asked, "Does anyone want to see it again?"

"What's the big deal? I've seen it all before," Jaybird said, teasing him.

"What's the big deal? Are you serious, man?" Robin straightened his collar, cleared his throat and said, "The big deal is how some poor child from a broken family whose cat died from what I now call "tumble-dry shock syndrome", could pull himself up from the bottom of the barrel and rise to such a prominent position in the community!"

"What position would that be?" Harry asked, egging him on.

"Well, I'm not poor anymore of course. My family isn't broken anymore cause my parents got back together. I stopped putting our pet cats in the dryer to dry them off. My position, well my position is one win, no losses and no draws. Man, I feel like a hometown hero, thank you very much. And remember, if you all can make it next Sunday to Kemper Arena, I am fighting another sucker."

Everyone was laughing as they got up. Robin turned around and took the tape out of the new machine and as the news came on he commented, "Hey, there's that male ex-model dude, what's his name?"

"Edward Bloodhead," Jaybird said leaning towards the TV to catch the segment.

"Yeah, that's him," Robin said,

"He's the guy who won't shake anyone's hand. But hey, he is a billionaire. He can do whatever he wants. He must have the Midas touch. That's why he won't shake hands, huh, Jaybird?"

Jaybird nodded, "You're probably right."

"He's just eccentric. Anyone with that kind of money usually has some sort of a quirk," Harry said.

"What kind of a name is Bloodhead anyway?" Kandy asked.

"Scary, eh? Kinda scares you, huh, Kandy?" Robin answered, as he lurched towards her, laughing.

Kandy just rolled her eyes and looked away. *Sit on it dude.*

"Well, way back when, most last names came from something the family did or maybe colors, animals and what-not," Harry interjected.

"So his family bloodied heads, Mr. Young?" Kandy asked, trying not to sound sarcastic.

"I'm just saying that's where some names came from. You can infer what you want," Harry said as he quickly shuffled off to the kitchen. He wanted to get out of the room before he acted on the urge to smack the smirk off her face. *It's your son's girlfriend,* he kept telling himself. *Be nice.*

"Say, Jaybird, didn't you tell me that you wanted to do what he does?"

"Well sort of. I mean he used to pop up all the time in magazines and like um…on *Dick Cavett* or the *Tonight Show* and stuff on TV. He is always giving interviews in different places all over the world. Quite the playboy jet-setter. Whenever they interview him it looks like he is living it up. Exotic places and all, you know," Jaybird replied.

"You want to do *that*?" Kandy asked not understanding his desire at all, but hopeful that she would be with him if that's what he wanted to do.

"Sure, wouldn't you? You know, for the travel, adventures, meeting people and making friends. I guess I can do that now, huh? I have my money!" Jaybird said with a grin.

"Sure, that sounds like fun," Kandy agreed.

She figured that if he wanted to go to far-off exotic places, then she should help cultivate his desires in that direction. *Getting all she could out of the relationship before she pulled the plug was just what her mother had told her to do,* she thought.

Trying to find a place to jump into the conversation, Julie pointed at the TV and said, "Look, he's on a huge yacht out in the South Pacific somewhere, they said. I bet he gets hounded everywhere he goes. Ooh, I wish they would get a close-up; he's so gorgeous."

Jaybird shook his head, saying, "I don't know about him being gorgeous but I'm sure he gets hassled a lot. I'd hate that part. I bet he's cool, although they say he is very reclusive now, like Howard Hughes, you know. He won't give interviews anymore and lives on that yacht or something, I guess."

"Yeah, Howard was pretty screwed up. He was too eccentric. Kept his pee in bottles, you know," Harry said from the kitchen doorway.

"Robin, did you know that?" Julie asked, trying hard to interact with everyone.

Robin was still worrying about her comment about the guy on TV being gorgeous but managed to respond,

"Well sure, everybody found out about Howard after he died, from books people wrote. Say, are there any unauthorized autobiographies out on this Bloody-headed guy, Jaybird?" Robin asked as he motioned to Julie that they were leaving and held open the screen door for her.

Jaybird followed them, laughing, then said, "I don't know, but I saw a news report on him once when he had found some sunken ship that had some valuable cargo on it. He recovered the stuff and it seems that Spain was trying to claim the ship for herself, along with all the cargo. He was fighting their government or something for the rights to the stuff he found on the wreck."

Robin really wasn't listening to the answer. He was watching everyone admiring his new car.

Robin looked at Jaybird and asked, "Do you want to take my new wheels around the block or what?"

Jaybird turned around to see Kandy shaking her head no, so he just repeated the motion, even though at that moment he truly wanted to get behind the wheel of any car and get going. *I could always drive it another time. No big deal,* he thought. Besides, he liked to make Kandy happy whenever he could.

Robin unlocked the door to let Julie in and then remembered he had set up a drag race for that evening. He always had a penchant for winning and to win you had to have a fast car. Now with tons of money readily available to spend on a fast car, he was out for pay backs on all the other cars that had beaten his '70 GTO. Now he could afford to build this new Maserati into one mean street machine. He had special-ordered it with a massive, barely street-legal, racing engine. He had always wished he could have fixed up his hand-me-down 'Goat' his father had given to him, but since he hit that pole over on Jules Street, on his father's birthday no less, it had been immobile, just sitting beside their house. So now with his Maserati, even if he got caught for speeding, he figured he had the money to pay for any size ticket. There was no reason to go slow. He was so competitive.

He laughed to himself at the reason he just had to have a Maserati. It was a simple reason, really. He, Jaybird and a few friends all had their favorite electric miniature H/O slot cars when they were fourteen years old. They were all just starting to really get into cars and his favorite one was a blue convertible Maserati. He always told everyone that when he got older and had his money, he would buy one, and last week the car had arrived at the dealership over on the Belt Highway. His post-dated check held it until today. He had been waiting at the dealership fifteen minutes before it opened this morning.

Robin pushed play and The James Gang resumed playing on the

cassette deck as he and Julie pulled away. Waving goodbye, Robin remembered something Jaybird had mentioned to him, so he stopped, backed up and yelled out the window over the throaty rumble of his car, "Good luck tonight man. Hap and peaciness."

With that he took his foot off the brake, let the car roll back a bit, dropped the clutch and hit the gas, laying down some burnt rubber which looked like two huge black double 'J's that stretched thirty feet up the now smoke-filled road. Jaybird wanted to yell out a big "Thanks!", but he put on his best "I can't believe he just did that" look for his parents and the other adults as they shook their heads and headed for their own cars, one of them mumbling, "Someday he will get in a wreck, driving like that." *Don't all parents say that anyway?*

Somehow Jaybird knew that every male standing there really wanted to take off in a car *exactly* like Robin had just done, but having been domesticated by their better halves, they jumped in their station wagons and slowly drove away. And he figured all the women were thinking, *Silly little immature kid.*

Julie got big grin on her face as they sped away. She had no problem with his driving. Grateful that they were finally alone, she knew she would be having a much better time with Robin now. Being in a room of people you have never met before was difficult enough, but add on a first date –that would make anyone nervous.

"Robin?" She asked.

"Yes, Julie."

"What is hap and peaciness?"

"Oh, did I say that? It is like peace and happiness, only…different."

"You're a bit on the strange side, Mr. Duvall. I think I might just have to get to know you better.

With that, Robin got a big grin on his face. *There's a first,* he thought.

Kandy hated it whenever Robin said hap and peaciness but she smiled and put her arm around Jaybird's waist and pointed to the street saying, "Look, the marks he left look like your first two initials. Anyhow what did Robin mean by "Good luck tonight, Jaybird?"

Jaybird squeezed her and said, "I'll tell you about it later. We should help clean up the mess inside."

As much as Kandy didn't want to say it, she managed to get out an, "Oh, you go watch TV. I'll help your mom. Besides it's your birthday. You just relax."

Kandy went in the kitchen and picked up a towel to dry the dishes that Nan had just started washing. She really had a hard time holding a conversation with Nan, yet begrudgingly answered all of her questions with a plastic smile on her face. Nan liked to just ramble anyway. Nan normally liked everyone without reservation, but she had had an uneasy feeling about Kandy from the start and was really trying hard to ignore it.

Jaybird sat down beside his father, Harry, on the couch. Harry was just thinking this was a perfect time for another father-to-son talk, since the other family members had all left.

Harry slapped Jaybird on the thigh and said, "Well, Jaybird, it is a big day for you. I just want to impress upon you the responsibility of having so much money. I know we set it up so you and Robin could get control of your money on your eighteenth birthday but that shouldn't stop you from continuing to invest for the future. If you get wild and crazy with it you will soon see how fast it will be gone. You can never predict future events, you know.

"I wont go crazy with it, Dad."

Harry raised his eyebrows and said, "You are prone to doing things on the spur of the moment. Remember when you coaxed Robin into running out to Colorado with you? And when…"

"Dad, that was years ago. I'm eighteen now."

"That won't mean as much to you ten years from now as it does today. Eighteen is actually a strange age. You are old enough to go to war and kill or get killed but you aren't old enough to drink alcohol in some states. And eighteen-year-olds think they know everything. They think they have all the answers at this age. Well, I mean, you *are* smart, and who would have thought you would start getting straight "A"s from seventh grade on? Anyhow, I know my brother was a know-it-all at eighteen. He just kinda disappeared after high school. Kinda like you did. Only he didn't get in touch with anyone for some four years. Turns out he went to college on his own dime. Sure he turned out OK, but he worried our parents something fierce."

"Really? Uncle Nick?"

"Yes, your Uncle Nicholas. Of course, he really thought he knew it all, too. He was pretty much a smart-ass, if you ask me. And son, I love you but you have been known to lean in that smart-ass direction. It's OK to be smart but don't rub it in, especially to the less intelligent. Anyhow, I guess I just want you to know that your mom and I are here for you. Try not to rush things. You can always ask us for advice."

"I know that, Dad. But since I know everything…never mind, I'll be serious. I want you and Mom to remember that if you need anything just ask me."

"Now that sure sounds funny coming from my son."

"Well, you know what I mean. Money-wise, that is," Jaybird said, laughing along with his dad.

"I know I have been working a lot lately and I may not have been paying much attention to you and all, what with you being the youngest and leaving the old nest soon, Nan and I are gearing up for some time to ourselves. We sure appreciate your letting us pay off the mortgage. That makes our retirement look brighter, not to mention earlier."

"No problem, Dad. You made the money grow to where it is now."

"Well my broker did. So tell me, what are your plans for the future *today*, son?"

Whispering, Jaybird leaned over and said, "I think we are going to take a trip to Atlantic City or Reno, I haven't really…"

"No, what I mean is, for the rest of your life, you *have* been changing your mind a lot lately."

Jaybird thought for a second and said, "I guess I really haven't decided for sure yet. But I know I don't want to go to college. I don't need a piece of paper to help me get a job. I don't need a job."

"You should never stop learning, Jaybird. Knowledge is valuable. You may rethink the college idea later in life. There is a lot to know out there. You can afford any college you want. Plus, I know you have five colleges that want you to attend, Mr. Honor Roll. But if you want to relax for a while I can understand that. Just take it slow and easy. If you rush things without thinking them through, it seems they always come back to haunt you later on," his father said, trying not to preach.

They talked about a lot of things, it seemed, while the ladies did the dishes. Jaybird was about as attentive as most any millionaire teenager would be. He tried to listen to his father and stay with the conversation, but right now he just wanted to be on his own and to do as he pleased. To do things when he wanted to and how he wanted to. Plus, he needed to be alone with Kandy.

After Kandy emerged from the kitchen, Jaybird told her they were going for a ride. This pleased her to no end, as she had wanted to get out of the house since she arrived.

As they drove down the boulevard to cruise around with the after-factory air blowing cold in his '65 Ford Falcon, Jaybird pushed in the 8-track tape and clicked to track two. His favorite group, The Beatles, came on. Everything was just about right so he reached for Kandy's hand just as the song "I Want To Hold Your Hand" began playing. *I just have to wait for the next song. Almost perfect* he thought, *almost there.*

CHAPTER II

THE OFFICIAL part of the meeting was almost over for the members of 'The Calm' and Dr. Nicholas Young was having a great time answering questions from the newest member. He was accustomed to explaining many things over and over again and it never got old.

"Why do we call this group 'The Calm'?" Dr. Young said, repeating the question, "Because when new 'Knowers' like you, finally get an answer or two about what has happened to him or her and they understand that they are not alone with their feelings, nor crazy, they seem to calm down. I guess I could have called the group 'The Mellowers' or the 'Understand-erers' but hey, I started the group so I went with 'The Calm'!'"

"Oh, OK. You know, I think it is a neat name, I was just curious, Thanks!" the new woman stated.

"Groovy, then. Are there any other questions before we adjourn for some pie and coffee?" Dr. Young asked the small gathering of people.

One man raised his hand and asked, "Could you tell me why you weren't or aren't…well, an archeologist or anthropologist or something? 'Cause there is some controversy over a chapter in your last book about the Emperor Ashok. Seems that some scholars want to know where you come up with your so-called facts."

Dr. Young got a wide smile on his face and said, "Controversy is like...or should be...my middle name, I think. Even the literary estab-lishment wants to categorize some of my books as fiction instead of non-fiction. As you know, I don't think the general public is ready for us 'Knowers' to just start rewriting history or to be more exact, correcting it with the truth. Just because we actually were that someone in history and actually know the true happenings at that particular time, even though we have recalled those memories, we can't...just yet...come out of our little closets and tell everyone, "you're wrong here, here and here and oh, here!" But every now and then those big-time scholars just interpret things a bit too wrong. They get off on the wrong tangent. As you well know, Greg, I don't do it too often, but every now and then I allow myself to set the real record straight. It is somewhat easier to do that with very old lives I have lived, because reading the language or pictures of their time in today's scientific circles, really is truly an interpretation, and not a science. I mean really, there weren't any dictionaries back in Ashok's days in the third century BC. So even though I try to present the facts using available documentation, sometimes I just put a piece of real fact in there that can't completely be corroborated like...anywhere else but in my head. I suppose this is where I get branded controversial. Um...so...what was the question again, Greg?"

Greg laughed and said, "Could you just let us know a little bit about what the history books state about Ashok and what you know to be true?"

"Think I can't? OK, right...be glad to. I think what you are referring to is the part of the historical community's common acceptance that Ashok was an emperor from India who built a Buddhist monastery in Kath-mandu, Nepal, because his daughter was married to a prince from there. It is written that Ashok was India's greatest ruler whose empire covered like...two-thirds of that subcontinent. Then he suddenly renounced violence and converted to Buddhism, built the temple there for his daughter and stopped warring. They think it was Buddhism that made him see the light, as it were. Whew, did I say that all in one breath?"

"So what really happened?" Greg asked, knowing the newest female member would enjoy the way Dr. Young would tell the story.

"Thought you'd never ask. Well, as I remember it, I was going to Nepal to talk to or, well okay, kill the prince who had actually enslaved my daughter. As I was riding through a village, a woman bowed down to show her respect after I was returning from the bushes during a short um…bladder evacuation stop. When she took my hand to kiss the back of it, boom! It happened. I had these memories. All my memories. I was complete. I knew all my past lives. I was a 'Complete Knower' at that moment. Shortly after that moment, I lost all desire to kill the prince who had taken my daughter, but I did persuade him to return her to me; it didn't take much. I was a great and scary ruler! On our return to India, I decided to visit some of my family in a village that is called Balasore today. This was actually a coastal village way back when, but they moved inland. My royal procession learned that a violent earthquake and ensuing tsunami had wiped out the entire seacoast. Along with the huge upheaval of the sea floor from the bay, there came a vast hoard of diamonds. The ground shook and moved so much that it left the area literally covered with diamonds. It must have been a mother lode. Of course the diamonds were collected and presented to me, as I was the Emperor. The survivors who were out hunting or otherwise not around when the waves hit, all thought I could use the diamonds to appease the gods. That's just what the mind-set was at that time. Keep the gods happy. Anyhow it was that day that I decided to build the monastery or stupa, for myself! Well, for my future selves, as it were. Basically I had all these memories of being aware of my previous existences…in other past lives and I knew I would be back again in another body and would probably remember myself again as I had done so many times before. Anyhow, to make a long story short…I hid quite a large number of bags full of diamonds."

"In the monastery!" Stated the new woman, sure that she knew the ending.

"Actually, no!" Dr. Young said, surprising the few members who hadn't heard the story before.

"I used the wonderful idea of building a stupa as a cover for me to take long personal walks alone in the hills to find caves where I could hide the diamonds. I mean, here I had my subjects building a Buddhist temple that we called at that time an "Enlightenment Monument" and I was really the only one who had been enlightened!"

"So you knew your 'O' had been around for quite a while after you touched that woman; right, Doctor?" another member asked.

"Think I didn't? My first couple of books didn't make very much money, but when I went to Kathmandu for a book signing well, let's just say I had to go for some long hikes in the hills...again! Now you know what paid for this big ol' mansion," Dr. Young said, adding, "Now, I will anticipate the next question from the new lass, but since I am getting hungry, let's head on over to my dining room and get some munchies. Greg, do me a favor and let her know what the 'O' is. I need to get some rhubarb pie and one-hundred-percent Kona coffee in me!"

"Not a problem, Doc, and her name is Carol," Greg said chuckling, as the 16 or so folks got up and meandered out of the Great Room.

Most of them knew that the conversation would continue for hours in the dining room once Dr. Young got some coffee in him. They would swap stories of their memories and see if any of them had known the new woman in any of their past lives, as Greg had. Greg was one of her 'Rendering Parents' way back in 785 AD. It was always interesting to have a new 'Knower' come along to get things going. New stories were always fun to hear.

CHAPTER III

"*SOLD*" *WAS always a fun word to hear,* thought Edward, as he reached for the chilled bottle of champagne. His yacht was anchored off a 1200 acre circular island about a half-hour by air from the small, unpaved airport in Bora Bora. He had just closed the island deal three hours earlier. He poured glasses of a 1958 Dom Perignon champagne for himself and Elizabeth, his current girlfriend and toasted his good fortune.

"I outbid them all again," he said, as he downed his entire glass. "Come on Liz, drink up, we're celebrating."

"Sure, Eddie," she said, as she took a drink.

Edward motioned her closer to him. Then he entwined his arm around hers as she followed his lead and did the same. They looked into each other's eyes and sipped from the crystal glasses.

"It's mine; everything is mine. Kiss me again. Quick!" Edward ordered.

He stood up and walked over to a porthole. He gulped his Dom and looked over the sun-drenched waters. The sunlight quivered along the ripples of water that slowly moved away from the yacht yet never really seemed to go anywhere. *It was like a magazine cover job he had done once,* he thought. How good he felt to have acquired this little piece of earth. Soon he could begin the task of searching the inland lagoon for its contents. He knew what he was looking for and finding it would more than make up for the price of obtaining the island. He beckoned Elizabeth over to look out the porthole.

"See that out there? All that land is mine. I own it. The beach, the trees, the crabs, coconuts and whatever else is there. This is my island. What a steal at six-and-a-half million."

Edward stood there basking in his glory. He put his arm around her as she leaned her head on his chest. He kissed the top of her head lightly. He rambled on about there being only seven out of the one hundred twenty islands in Tahiti that can be sold to private citizens and those can only be sold once every five years. *Got to keep the riff-raff at bay,* he thought to himself.

She wasn't really listening to him. These seemingly happy moments were rare lately and she wanted to make this one last. She knew this mood. She knew what to expect from him now that he had triumphed. It was when he was bored and looking for his next challenge that she didn't know what he would do next. That moody, mysterious side of him was at times appealing to her and at other times it made her very uneasy.

Elizabeth Lewis had light blue eyes, blond hair and stood five feet, five inches tall. She had been a Playboy Playmate of the Year two years ago when she was twenty. Gorgeous was the only adjective needed after seeing her. She was recognized almost everywhere she went after gracing the covers and a dozen pages inside of the world's most renowned men's magazine. She had done the talk show circuit also, including a brief evening answering all of Johnny Carson's silly questions.

Her looks alone had created in Edward a desire to make her his possession. A prize, a trophy. He wanted her and he had gotten her. They had been sailing all over the world together for about a year and a half in his 150-foot luxury yacht, hop-scotching from country to country. Doing little projects here and there, but mainly just spending money as far as Elizabeth could tell. They truly made a perfect-looking couple whenever they ventured out in public, but in private the relationship was strained.

Edward Bloodhead was a thirty-year-old Greek God type. He stood six feet, three, with long dark brown hair that he always kept in a ponytail. His broad shoulders accented his perfect V-shaped torso. His Olympian face had also graced many a magazine cover and had been seen in countless commercials before he abruptly quit the burgeoning male super-model business eight years ago to embark upon his eccentric lifestyle. His absence from the full-time limelight of modeling guaranteed him an even larger fee when he did decide to do a special appearance. At this point in his life he didn't really *need* money anymore, he just *wanted* it. He thrived on getting more of it, but he gathered it on his own terms. He wanted to be the richest man in the world no matter what it took to get there. Then he could mold the world around him to his liking. He would be in control of everything. Getting money was paramount and he had a clear idea of how to achieve that goal.

The soft sound of the jazz great Miles Davis filled the air as Edward slid his hand slowly down Elizabeth's back and started to caress her perfect rear. He whispered in her ear in-between flicks of his tongue,

"Why don't we get in the Jacuzzi and steam up the place? Hell, we don't even need hot water. We can make it boil ourselves, if you know what I mean?"

She squeezed him tight and then moved slowly toward the bathroom, leaving a trail of clothes behind her. Arriving at the door naked she turned around, giving him a devilish smile as she put her index finger into her mouth and seductively pulled it out. Edward raised his glass up to his lips and downed the last drop of champagne as he headed towards the bath for a little afternoon delight. On his way there he stopped and looked out at *his* island just one more time and thought to himself that these were the rare moments of the present that he must try to enjoy, the moments that could block out all the anger and the hate that were constantly in his mind, haunting him, reminding him and pushing him in directions that just eight years ago he would have never imagined. He savored any fleeting minutes or hours of happiness, for he knew it would be short-lived and he would succumb to the overpowering desire to find a way to have–everything. It took over his thoughts like a disease. He had to have things his way. Having his way all of the time meant he would stop at nothing. If it took yelling, kicking, maiming or even killing, he *would* get his way. Whatever it took. It was the only way to reach his goal. He was becoming increasingly good at getting everything he wanted through money and manipulation. But first he had to act on this newly recalled memory. He knew this island was but just one of the many old memories that would provide him with even more wealth. He knew what he had placed there in the lagoon. He was growing used to the intriguing ways he had left items all over the world only to be collected at a later date in time. Most items were so old that they were almost always worth a hundred-fold more than when he had hidden them in the first place. He wasn't quite sure why or how he had these memories but he really didn't care. He had them, so he would use whatever means were provided to him to better his situation. Since he had consciously meant to set himself up in a later life then he undoubtedly needed to make the most of it. He wondered if anyone else could remember being someone else, from long ago. He couldn't imagine being the only one able to have these retro-thoughts, but he had never heard or read about it anywhere. It was much different from a reincarnation. It didn't matter right now; Elizabeth was beckoning him from the bathroom to hurry up and join her in the Jacuzzi.

CHAPTER IV

AT COUNTY Line Road, the flagman was beckoning both drivers to stage their cars at the start line. Robin reached for the stick shift. He revved the engine and inched forward as he glanced slowly over his left shoulder at the 1969 SS Chevelle that was just finishing up its burnouts. The deep glossy black metallic paint reflected the streetlight well enough that Robin could see himself in the door panel of the Chevelle. He caught the driver's eye and said over the rumbling machines, "Am I live or am I Memorex?"

The driver just ignored him.

The flagman, as was customary, came over to shake each driver's hand. This person was usually someone neither driver knew. Not that it made any difference but it was some street-race rule everyone followed. As the rear end of his opponent's car started rising up in the air and became enveloped in smoke from the guy power-braking, Robin looked at the flagman standing between the two cars as he turned down the radio. He couldn't have the radio on in a drag race because he needed all his concentration. *Like when you are looking for a street to turn onto that you have never been on before, you always turn down the radio,* he thought.

The flagman pointed first to one car then the other. A split-second later his hands went straight up over his head. A rush of adrenaline shot through Robin's body as he slammed the gas pedal to the floor, sidestepping the clutch. The Maserati's wide tires gripped the asphalt and sent the car lurching forward. Julie was yelling, "You got him outta the hole!" as Robin quickly jammed the car into second gear.

With a white-knuckle grip on the shifter, he glanced at the tachometer. As soon as it hit 6800 RPMs he would ram it into third. A quick audible screech was heard as third gear caught rubber.

"We're pulling away!" Julie screamed while looking over at the Chevelle as Robin's speedometer approached triple digits. 6800 RPMs again; fourth gear. With the gas pedal never leaving the floor, they roared toward the large road sign that acted as the finish line, a quarter mile from the start.

"You got 'im, Robin, you got 'im! Yes, we won, we won!" Julie yelled as she grabbed his right hand that still had a death-like grip on the stick shift.

Robin let out a primal victory scream himself as he applied the brakes that slowed the car down unexpectedly fast. *This car far outperformed the GTO,* he thought. *Lighter and faster, for sure!* He was most impressed with the braking though, which seemed stop the car on a dime.

"I love speed. I love these brakes and I love this car, man; I love to win. Being first feels so good!"

Julie laughed and asked, "What if you had lost the race? You would have been second?"

"I've been second before and you know what? It sucks. Being first is a far better feeling."

"Robin, you crack me up."

Almost on cue the song "Little GTO" came on the radio. Robin reached down to turn the volume up, saying, "Hey, Julie, this is my old car's name-sake song. How cool. I guess I'll have to find a song with the name Maserati in it now."

Robin turned the car around and headed for the starting line where some onlookers were waiting to congratulate the winner. Smiles and high fives were in order as he and Julie got out of the car to bask in the illegal victory. The losing car drove up and the driver leaned out his window to shake Robin's hand. He shrugged his shoulders and gave Robin the dollar they had bet. That's how it was in street-racing on the first race. The bet didn't matter as much as the bragging rights did and the lane choice for the next race, if the loser wanted to try again. Robin never knew, when he won, if the loser was sandbagging. That particular trick was to lure the other driver into upping the ante. A bluff to entice him into racing again and betting more. Robin never bluffed though. He raced to win every race. That didn't matter right now. It was time for Robin to brag. Big time. Now all he had to do was find every driver that beat his old GTO and ask them to race his new car. He knew he'd win. He had ordered enough custom racing parts into this car to make it one mean machine. He would have to do a lot of cruising down St. Joseph Avenue or around town to find all his old racing nemeses though.

"Hey, Robin, do you have that new Fleetwood Mac cassette?" Julie asked after things settled down a bit.

"Sure, look behind the seats in those tape cases."

Looking in the car, Julie was surprised to see five music cases full of cassettes. *My goodness,* she though to herself, *this guy loves his music. There must be seventy-five cassettes in here. Hmm, and to think I only have ten.*

Later in the evening as he drove towards Julie's house, he was thinking how nice it was to have found a girl who liked to go fast in a car like he did. He had a really great time with her tonight and his favorite song had come on while he was with her. What timing. He hadn't had much time to think about her until now, just as the so-called "date" was over. It felt like they had been friends for a long time already; it didn't really feel like a date. He decided at that moment that he was going to ask her out again.

Before he got the nerve up and after a short lull in their conversation, Julie asked, "Did you get the feeling that Kandy was, I don't know, sort of watching me at Jaybird's house?"

"Yeah, but she has been like that ever since she and Jaybird started dating. I think she is jealous of everyone. Even me."

"That's the impression I got...and she seems so superficial. She seems creepy and fake to me," Julie added.

"Well," Robin said as he turned up the driveway, "It's not the first time I've heard that from anybody. A few others in Jaybird's family feel just like you do. Just tell me if she ever says or does anything strange to you. I'll tell her to cool it. He is the kind of guy who makes up his mind and goes off and does it or whatever. Then he will change his mind and head off in a totally different direction on a whim. But that's just Jaybird. Right now I'd say he is so whipped that he can't even see what she does. He is totally in love. It's his first real love, you know, like Lucy loved Desi?"

As the words came out of Robin's mouth he realized that he had never been in love and really had no room to talk. He felt confident that he would never get as wrapped up as Jaybird seemed to be.

Julie started to open her door but Robin let out a loud, "*Stop!* Don't move!" His words really surprised her, so she just sat there frozen in her seat.

He ran around the car and like a perfect gentleman opened the door for her as she smiled appreciatively and thanked him.

Robin quickly mustered up the nerve to ask her out again as he walked her up the steps.

"Say Julie, do you want to ride around next Sunday? No, wait. I'm fighting that day. Saturday? No, wait, I should be in bed early Saturday. OK, how about Friday night?"

"Sure. I had a blast tonight. Pick me up at say...six PM?"

"Great. I'll be there with toes on my bells." Robin said with a straight face.

"You mean with bells on.... oh, Robin, you just kill me," she said, smiling as she walked into the house.

Inside, she placed her purse on the hallway table and peeked around the corner at her mother sitting in front of the TV. She decided to sit and talk to her. She told her mother how much fun she had had that evening with Robin and that he had asked her out again next weekend. They talked for about an hour and her mother, as always, was impressed at the level of maturity Julie had, even though she was only eighteen. Julie explained that Robin made her laugh all the time; he had a wonderful sense of wittiness about him. He always seemed happy; always had a smile. She told her mother that he was not the best-looking guy around, due to the scar on his cheek, but she thought it gave him character and she could see herself in a long-term relationship with him if he wanted one. She felt like she definitely wanted to get to know everything about him. She liked the fact that he even had a long-term goal of being a champion boxer. Julie knew she was flipping for him as she went on and on about him. Her mother just listened; she was happy for her only daughter.

As Julie walked up the stairs toward her bedroom she heard her mother call out, "So I take it you had no need for the dime I gave you?"

"No, Mother," she said. "He was the perfect gentleman."

Julie laughed as she felt under her blouse and retrieved the dime from her right bra cup. Her mother always gave her a dime to place there when she went on a date. It was a little tradition. Her mother said, "If the guy's hands start to travel onto parts of your body that you are uncomfortable with, just get out of the car and run to the nearest pay phone and call me for a ride home." Julie knew that Robin was an honorable man and she was sure she could do without the dime on their next date.

As Robin drove home with the speakers straining to handle all twenty-five watts of distorted music, he wondered if he should have tried to kiss her. He always hated first dates. It seemed like that's all he had ever had. Eleven first dates in all. No repeats. Yes, he was keeping track. But this was the best date he had ever been on and he had a second date already set up. He mused at how he really wasn't nervous after they started talking but he was sure he had put on one too many splashes of Hai Karate cologne while getting dressed for this date. *Maybe it was better to have saved that first kiss for another time*, he thought. *Why ruin a good time?* Maybe that's why he never got a second date. He had always tried to slip in a kiss on his other first dates. Maybe girls in this day and age didn't like to be rushed into kissing so soon. This was definitely something that needed more contemplation. He jumped out of his car and headed to his room where he started re-living every minute of his date with Julie. At least tonight he had something else to dream about. Hopefully his usual dreams, which regularly seemed to be strange and off-the-wall, yet familiar, would take a back seat to his infatuation. Just then he had a thought for a poem. He grabbed a pencil and paper and started to write down a few of his feelings for Julie. He quickly molded these into a poem. He knew he should give it to her on their next date.

After he was done writing he remembered that he had given his parents a twentieth year anniversary present with the money he had received. They were booked on a cruise ship and would be gone for the entire week, starting Wednesday. Upon their return, they would be moving into the new house he had also bought them. He decided to make plans for one last cozy evening in front of the fireplace; this time with Julie. He hoped she liked and trusted him enough to be alone with him in his house. He definitely didn't want her to vanish, as had all the other girls.

CHAPTER V

THE LATE afternoon sun vanished as the day morphed its way toward dusk. Kandy and Jaybird had been cruising around all the hangouts for about twenty minutes. All the while, Jaybird was trying to pick the perfect moment. At the same time he was straining to capture a feeling of familiarity he was having. He felt he had been at this exact moment and place before. He couldn't grasp it though. He had always had these kinds of feelings, well, at least since he had met Robin. Sometimes it was like a deja vu or a half memory and other times just complete knowledge. Often, when his mind was not engaged in an action of the moment, he got these odd thoughts. *How come?* he wondered. *Why do they seem so real, like true memories?* Try as he might to ignore them, it was getting so hard to just brush them aside. Finally he noticed the song he had been waiting for. "I hope this is the right time to ask you this," Jaybird said, as The Beatles' song, "Please, Please Me" started playing.

"Well, here goes......will you marry me?"

The look on Kandy's face was most certainly a Kodak moment. It was of complete and total shock. Her eyes opened wide as she turned quickly toward him, sliding as close to him as possible, grabbing his neck, kissing him all about the side of his face as he tried to keep the car in a straight line. She had always hoped they would get engaged after she got out of high school or sometime soon after. But this wonderful surprise would really push her plans into action faster.

"Weeeell…?" Jaybird asked, laughingly.

Still with a death grip around his neck, Kandy managed to squeak out, "Yes, oh yes, I most certainly will!"

"Great. Now that I have your 'yes', why don't you look in the glove compartment and…"

Before he could even finish, Kandy was trying to open the latch.

"I can't open it; it's locked. Where's the key? The key, Jaybird!"

"Oh, sorry my little candy cane, it's on my key chain here," Jaybird said as he jangled the keys in the ignition.

"Pull over, I am dying to see what's in there! Oh, how I hope it is what I think it is!"

Jaybird pulled over and put the car in park. He unlocked the glove compartment as fast as he could. Kandy reached in and found the small box that was there. As she opened it she almost fainted. She was staring at a two-carat diamond ring. She put it on and leaned over to kiss him. *This ring will never come off, well at least until I pawn it,* she thought to herself as she kept her lips pressed to his as long as he wanted. Usually she would pull away but she knew it was a special moment for him and for her also, although for two totally different reasons.

Breaking the silence, after the kiss, Kandy sat up in her seat, looked around and asked him, "Where are we? I want to remember the exact place where you asked me to marry you." She knew Jaybird remembered everything. Every little *first thing* they ever did. She knew he was a sentimental kind of guy and she should play this moment up to the fullest. That way he would have no doubts about her love for him. Although she knew beyond a doubt that he loved her madly, she didn't love him. Pretending had actually become fun for her.

Jaybird eyed the street sign saying, "Second Avenue. It figures."

Pulling a piece of paper out of the glove box, Kandy asked, "What is this? Looks like a form. Is it car papers or something?"

"Nope, it's a consent form."

"For what?"

"For your mom to sign, 'cause you're only seventeen."

Kandy thought for a second and then asked, "Does that mean you want to get married soon?"

"Yes. I was thinking about next weekend actually."

Kandy couldn't believe her ears.

"OK," was all she could mutter.

Jaybird took the form and put it in her purse.

"Now remember," he said, "have your mom sign this before next weekend. Monday we will get you a blood test, too."

"Who should we invite?" Kandy asked.

"No one."

"No one? What are you talking about? I want a big wedding. In a church. And Fleetwood Mac should play, you know, and everything! Wouldn't that be so cool?"

Jaybird patted her hand, "Well, sure, but I doubt I could get them to come rushing to our wedding on such short notice. It's not like I know them or anything. So…I thought we would go to Topeka, Kansas, and get hitched. All we need is one witness. I was thinking your friend Joan could be our witness."

"You want to tell me the whole plan or what?" She knew she had better let him play the guide at this point. *But Topeka? What was the deal with that?* she thought. It sure didn't sound glamorous or extravagant.

"If anyone asks what we are doing next weekend, tell them we are going to gamble some money away up at the Aksarben race track in Nebraska. We will really be down in Topeka getting married," Jaybird said.

"But why do we have to keep it a secret and why ask Joan to go with us?"

"I don't want anyone to try and talk us out of it. I'm eighteen now. I can do what I want. This way they will have to deal with it after the fact, you know. Besides I want to get married but I don't know if my parents would think it's a good idea so soon after high school. Plus you're not even out of school yet. My dad was talking to me about going at things slowly and stuff, just tonight as a matter of fact and…"

"OK, OK…I guess I understand that part, but why Joan and not your best pal, Robin?" she asked sarcastically, but very relieved he hadn't invited Robin.

"Robin would tell someone. He could hardly keep it to himself when he found out I was going to ask you to marry me. Remember when he said 'Good luck' and you asked me about that? Well, that proves once again he just can't keep a secret and Joan is basically the only friend you have, right?"

"Yeah, you're right. I just don't make friends that easily. I'm shy like that. I should try to make some friends, I suppose. But answer me this; you don't have the hots for her do you?"

Jaybird looked at her bewildered and said, "Are you joking? You are the only woman for me in this whole world. I love you!"

Kandy sat back in the seat as she looked at the consent form and the ring for a few moments, knowing that he meant every word he said. "Well, I guess you have thought of everything; how about driving me over to 'Two Scoops' for an ice cream sundae?"

"Sure thing, Mrs. Young!" Jaybird said, smiling as he started driving away. He then added, "You know I asked you to marry me when 'Please, Please Me' came on. I think that should be our song now."

Kandy half nodded, leaning back in the seat. She could really not care less about things he thought were sweet or romantic. All she wanted to know was how much the rock on her finger would fetch her at the pawnshop. They were both equally engrossed in the moment, but each one for dramatically different reasons. Jaybird drove silently with a big smile on his face as Kandy held her left hand up to see, with every passing street light, the diamond reflect its sparkle with tiny flashes of brilliance

THE MASERATI was performing brilliantly and the butterflies in Robin's stomach had begun fluttering, as always, before each race. Once again it was the weekend on County Line Road. Robin was staging his car for yet another race. He and Julie had been through seven already that night and his car was unbeatable. To Robin's delight, Julie had given him a kiss on the cheek prior to the start and end of each race. He hoped he could find cars to race all night just to keep the kisses coming. He really liked it when she kissed him; it gave him some kind of a feeling he couldn't put his finger on. Strength, manliness, coolness? Whatever it was, he wanted more. Plus now, he mused, he didn't have to worry about that first kiss at the end of the date.

The driver in the other car was a few years older and looked to Robin like he was one of those guys who hadn't figured out that high school was over with, some four years ago for him. Probably had that "Glory Days" complex, along with a $2.35 an hour job washing dishes at a restaurant or something. *Well, no need to be high and mighty just because you have money now,* he thought to himself instantly.

As Robin waited for another kiss from Julie, the other driver was laughing and trying to tease Robin about his foreign car.

"Hey what kind of a sissy car is that? Maz er ah tay tay? And I hope you know the girl has to go with the winning car also, Bud?"

Julie nudged Robin's hand as it rested on the custom Hurst shifter handle, "Robin, could you turn the music down a bit, that guy is saying something to you, I think."

Quickly Robin turned the volume down and said, with quite a bit of ire in his voice," Are you making fun of my girl, my car and me? 'Cause I hate that and I'll kick your..."

Just then Julie placed a nicely-timed kiss on Robin's check and said softly into his ear, "Just wait, he won't be laughing at the end of the race."

Julie had Robin's number down pat. She was going to be very good for him. Robin just smiled and bit his tongue without finishing his sentence. But he did love his music, so he turned it back up full volume.

The flagman reached in to shake the other driver's hand first and then came around to shake Robin's. Suddenly as they shook, Robin experienced the same strange and totally engulfing rush of feelings he had when he first shook Jaybird's hand some five years earlier. Sudden feelings of immense knowledge, seemingly forgotten memories and painful losses ricocheted through his whole body. He felt almost light-headed. He tried to say something to the flagman but he couldn't. His mind was being flooded again. Waves of memories. Sorrow, pain, laughter. Familiar names and places. Some names and places were out of reach, just barely there. It felt to him like so many other times when he had wakened from a dream. He had known everyone in the dream, but once awake, all the names were gone. He knew he knew the names and where he was but the details just instantly disappeared. It would bother him all day. Now he was gazing ahead at the flagman, who had sort of stumbled into his position between the fronts of the two cars, looking as if he maybe had had too many beers. Somehow the flagman managed to point to one car, then the other. As soon as both of his hands rose straight up in the air, a squeal of tires and roar of horsepower was heard. The flagman stumbled over to the side of the road after the cars flew by him.

Robin, by sheer instinct, had pressed his foot on the gas and side-stepped the clutch as his car accelerated forward. But he wasn't fully there mentally. He was overpowered by these new feelings and certainties. His thoughts were not where they should have been at that precise moment; they should have been on the race at hand. He started half-remembering things at light-speed that just moments before he had no memory of. It inundated him.

Julie watched the yellow lines in the middle of the road blink by; she waited for the shift of gears that always coincided with a familiar sound of the engine hitting the peak of its power band. But Robin was trying to embrace the suddenly unlocked memories that were speeding through his mind, unaware that he kept the gas pedal pressed to the floor. He barely had time to realize what Julie was screaming. She was screaming "Shift! Shift! Robin, shift!" at the top of her lungs.

The sound of the metal rod blasting its way through the cast iron engine block on its way through the hood of the car made Robin unconsciously yank the steering wheel to the left as he became semi-aware of his surroundings at about ninety miles an hour. But it was too late. The car careened off the shoulder and he lost control completely. It bounced violently from left to right before it caught an edge and flipped over and over, rolling down a forty-foot embankment. The crushed car finally came to a rest upside down.

As Robin sat disoriented and cross-legged atop the dome light with the seat pressed against his head, he tried to look around. The eerie glow of the light and the condition of the car prevented him from seeing anything. He had a brief moment of lucidity, saying, "Julie, are you OK?"

But he fell unconscious before he heard any answer.

It didn't matter. She couldn't hear him. The sparkle had left her eyes.

CHAPTER VII

THE SPARKLE in Kandy's eyes as she got in the car, was not of love for the man she was about to marry; it was for the feeling that she was finally getting closer to fulfilling her private mission in life. A week had passed. Now, with the consent form signed, blood test in hand, an appointment with the Justice of the Peace and Joan in the back seat of Harry's Oldsmobile Ninety-Eight, they headed for Topeka, Kansas. Jaybird was thankful that his father let him borrow the "big boat." His own Ford Falcon wasn't too reliable over long distances. Jaybird hadn't bought a new car for himself yet. He couldn't decide on anything. He had almost bought a dozen different cars during the past week. Kandy reminded him of his spur-of-the-moment tendencies, so he decided to think about it. After all those years of dreaming about the millions he would soon get his hands on, he still couldn't make up his mind about what to do first. He hated waiting for anything but he listened to Kandy this time. He wanted to be the kind of guy who listens to his lady.

It was a beautiful, warm, clear Saturday. Just right for a drive into Kansas in your father's car. Jaybird was telling the girls about how Robin had let him know that he was in love with Julie. He told them he thought it was about time Robin found someone who would stay with him for more than one date, not that Jaybird had a lot of experience to draw from. Joan stated that he would be cute if he didn't have that scar on his face. Kandy mentioned that he walked like a monkey. She never had a pleasant word to say about him except that he was Jaybird's best friend. That was her "pat" statement. She put up with Robin's presence only for her own perceived greater purpose, which was to keep Jaybird happy.

Once in Topeka, they found the courthouse from directions a gas station attendant gave them. Jaybird probably would have driven around all day lost. *You know, it's a guy thing,* Kandy thought. But at Joan's insistence she made Jaybird stop to let her go to the rest room.

After filling out the request form, the three of them stood in line to wait their turn. A yellowing sign over the counter read "Marriage Licenses." Kandy grabbed hold of Jaybird's arm and held him closer, "This is like a dream or something. I am so excited!" She looked at Joan and they both giggled like little girls. Then Kandy looked away and rolled her eyes. *This is so easy,* she thought. *Maybe after I get my settlement I will go out to Hollywood and pursue an acting career.*

At the counter a woman clerk asked if she could help them. Jaybird laid the paperwork down on the counter and said, "We have come all the way from St. Joseph, Missouri, to get a marriage license to get married in this fine city."

The clerk picked up the papers and shuffled through them with a 'who cares where you're from' look on her face.

"Is Jaybird your given name, sir, or a nickname?"

"Oh, it's a nickname. My real name is Jeffery Jason Young."

"And does Kandy have a middle name sir?"

"Yes, it's Kane."

"Kandy Kane? Really?"

"Yes!" all three of them said in unison.

"OK. Thank you-all." *What kind of a parent would name their kid that?* the clerk thought to herself, although she had seen quite a few humdingers in her stint at this office branch.

She made the corrections and had them initial the changes on the form. She stopped again when she came upon the Missouri blood test results. She informed them that they would still have to go across the street to the Department of Heath to transfer the results over to a State of Kansas certificate. Disgruntled, the trio started walking across the street. Halfway across Jaybird held up the blood test paper and said, "Hey this form has your birth date on it, Kandy."

"So?" Kandy said, shrugging her shoulders.

"So, if we just change your birthday here to a year earlier, we won't even need this consent form."

"That's a good idea," Joan said.

Kandy gave him a pen from her purse and he proceeded to change the year to 1959. He then looked at Kandy and asked, "What's your birthday, ma'am?"

"March 11, 1959, sir," she said adding, "Do you think they will question the date?"

"They probably run so many people through here in a day that they won't even notice."

They got the blood test transferred without a problem and headed back to the courthouse. Once inside, Jaybird asked Kandy and Joan to sit in the waiting chairs. He said he would stand in line and handle getting the license. Finally, after waiting his turn, he stepped up to the counter. The same woman was there to help him. Looking at all the forms she said, "Everything looks in order here now. You'll have to get Ms. Norton; I need to see some identification from both of you."

At that second Jaybird realized that the only ID Kandy had was her driver's license and that would have her real birth date on it. Without much thought he pulled the parental consent form out and handed it to the clerk along with his ID.

"What's this, sir?" the clerk asked.

"A parental consent form. Kandy doesn't have any ID."

"You don't need a consent form in this state if she is over eighteen. Doesn't she have a driver's license?"

Jaybird shook his head no and stated, "Well, not yet. Kandy is only seventeen and she hasn't learned how to drive yet."

The clerk was scanning the forms with a puzzled look and stated, "From the birth dates on these forms, I believe she would have just turned eighteen a few months back. But it does look like the date here used to say 1960. It looks to have been written over."

"Oh, you know what. That is my fault. I must have put the year I was born instead of hers by mistake."

Handing the papers back to Jaybird, the clerk said, "Here. Take these, and get the corrected date put on the blood test certificate then fill out a new request form with the correct date on it. You might as well have her fill it out. I'm sure she knows her own birthday."

Jaybird noted the tone of sarcasm in her voice. It went along with the smirk on her face. As he backed away from the counter he asked her if Kandy would need an ID before she would give them a marriage license. The clerk said no ID was needed for anyone under eighteen, only a valid consent form.

Back across the street they went to get the date corrected or uncorrected, as this case was. They then stopped by a phone to call the Justice of the Peace to say they would be running late. Once again Jaybird filled out the request form in the license office, as Kandy and Joan stood by. From the corner of his eye he could see the clerk watching them. A feeling of confidence come over him as they all got back in line. After waiting for what must have been only a half-hour, they approached the counter. The same clerk once again took the paperwork from Jaybird. She looked at the consent form and promptly said, "Sir, you don't have the parent's signature notarized on this consent form. I don't think you'll be getting a marriage license today. "

With that she handed him back all the papers and called the next person in line.

Jaybird wondered how he could have been so stupid as to overlook that. Sure enough, directly under the signature line were the words "Not valid without Notary seal."

The three of them walked away in silence to the car, stopping at a phone to cancel the appointment with the Justice of the Peace. The day was sunny but it might as well been pouring rain. Kandy was fuming. It seemed her plans were falling apart all of a sudden. She was almost in tears. It felt like the end of the world to her. Jaybird was also upset, but he was only upset at himself. He hated doing stupid things. He wanted to get married now, today. He knew he had let Kandy down. Joan felt bad for both of them. No one said a word as they got in the car and headed home. Neither of the girls bothered to tell him to slow down.

Jaybird seemed to remember a time when he had this very same feeling in his gut, maybe in his heart. He couldn't put his finger on it but he knew this feeling. If only he could grasp it. Something told him that it would work out in the end, though. How he had that knowledge was beyond his understanding. How could he know that this would work out? He tried to ignore the thoughts. They were confusing him. Maybe he was just wishing it would all work out. He had had these kinds of strange feelings countless times over the years. He had always found a way to suppress them.

They had been driving for only a few minutes when Jaybird suddenly slammed on the brakes and pulled to the side of the road.

"What the hell are you doing?" a surprised Kandy yelled.

"Turning around," Jaybird said as he started to make a U-turn.

"What on earth for?" Kandy asked as she reached down to grab her purse, the map, and everything else that had slid onto the floor when the car slowed down so abruptly.

"I want to get married *today*! I don't want to wait, so I am going to pull into that accounting and tax preparation place back there.

"Why, Jaybird?" Joan questioned.

Jaybird got a big grin on his face and said, "Because I bet there is a CPA in there with a notary stamp."

"Wow! Good thinking," Kandy said, as a smile came quickly back to her face. Her hopes of getting married were renewed once again.

A minute later as Jaybird sat back down in the car, he told the girls that the lady at the door had given him the phone number of the man to whom they sent all their documents for notarizing. Jaybird found a phone booth and called the number. After explaining their plight, he got directions to the man's house.

As the girls yelled out "left" or "right", Jaybird couldn't help but wonder how he was able to put a tax office and notary together, he had never dealt with the accountants; it was always his dad who took care of that. *It didn't matter,* he thought. *It will work out.* Then he had a strange memory surface. He remembered a time when he was about twenty in 1468 in China. He was about to start his first day as the local tax collector. It was a somewhat noble position that he was taking over from his father. He had his abacus and a list of all the villagers' homes that he had to visit that day. *An abacus* he mused, *now there was a really inventive tool for its time.* He had been very quick with it and he enjoyed even the hardest calculations. *Odd memory*, Jaybird thought to himself.

"We're here! Pull in the driveway with the red mailbox," Joan said, snapping Jaybird out of his thoughts.

Once inside the old man explained, his just as old wife translating sometimes, that it would be illegal to notarize a signature that he hadn't actually seen being written. The ramifications would be an invalid document. After a few minutes of pleading and teary eyes from the girls, the kind old man just was not budging. Then Jaybird reached over and clasped onto the old man's hands and started to beg for himself. As they touched hands, Jaybird got a jolt of feelings in his head that seemed to just come out of nowhere. He was flooded with a sudden familiarity for this man. Jaybird knew that he had been acquainted with him before. *Before what and before when? But how could that be?* he thought. He sat back in his chair for a moment, seemingly in a daze. The old man looked at his wife, gave her a wink and patted her knee, saying, "Oh, well, what in the dang tarnation do I care about this little problem? Hell, I'm eighty-four-years old. What would they do if they found out, put me in jail for ten years? Shoot, who's gonna know anyways?"

Kandy and Joan thanked him profusely for a few minutes as they all decided upon a way to proceed. The deal was that if the old man's wife called Kandy's mother and she could offer up the whereabouts of her daughter without any prodding, and then describe the three of them, he would notarize the consent form.

As the women got the phone call going, the old man thought to himself that he wasn't going to gain anything keeping two lovebirds from getting hitched. Plus he *knew* that he had been Jaybird's son once before. It was a long time ago in the early 1200's. It had been over two decades since the last time he had felt that from another person's touch, but he always found it to be exhilarating. The only other person he ever told about those old memories and past lives was his wife of sixty-five years. He honestly still didn't know if she truly believed him. But she loved him and she was always by his side, so it really just didn't matter.

The phone call worked as planned. As soon as the old woman said that she was calling from Topeka, Kandy's mother started emphatically rambling on, with an occasional slur, about her daughter who was getting married that very day in Topeka, Kansas. That few minutes of conversation had saved them from having to drive home totally disheartened. The old man signed and notarized the consent form. Jaybird then tried to give him fifty dollars but he would only accept his normal fee of two dollars. Jaybird couldn't understand why he would only take two dollars, but he begrudgingly handed him one of the two-dollar bills he had stashed in his wallet. Jaybird had grabbed a dozen of them when they were first re-issued in 1976. He just liked those bills.

What a nice guy, Jaybird thought. *But then he was always a nice guy.* Jaybird couldn't fathom how he knew that about the old guy or why. He just *knew* it. He had been a good son to Jaybird. He had always made him proud. He had followed in Jaybird's footsteps as a stable master as he was Jaybird's oldest son at the time, such a long time ago.

On the way out the door Jaybird tossed a crumpled up fifty-dollar bill behind the couch without anyone noticing. It made him feel much better inside. He thought to himself, *How cool it would be to live so long and have accumulated so many memories that you could bend the rules just enough, enabling two people to be so happy in the process. What harm could come of it?*

Kandy again called the Justice of the Peace from the first pay phone they came across, and rescheduled another appointment, believing this time they would surely get the marriage license.

Back to the courthouse they went with renewed hope. After another stint in the line, they were once again helped by that same clerk. Jaybird wondered to himself if she ever took a break. She rolled her eyes as she saw the three young adults approach the counter. As Jaybird presented the papers to her he received a very condescending look from her.

With her lips pressed tightly together she blinked slowly three times, saying, "How did you get this notarized in such a short time? Didn't you say you all lived in St. Joseph, Missouri? I seriously doubt that you could drive from here to there and back in less than, what's it been, about an hour?"

"I never said we drove here," Jaybird replied calmly.

"Well, sir, how did you get this notarized in such a short time then?"

Jaybird didn't even flinch as he looked her right in the eyes and told her a big fat lie, "We chartered a helicopter, if you must know."

Now the other people in line had something to pay attention to, instead of just being bored standing in line.

The clerk started to laugh and shake her head saying, "Now you really don't expect me to believe that, do you?"

"Is there a problem with my paperwork, ma'am?" he asked as sarcastically as he could. He felt a strange strength welling up inside him. He wanted to race past this moment, so he decided to just go for it.

The clerk snorted and snatched the papers, saying, "I'm going to get my supervisor, sir; just a moment." And with that she turned and walked over to a desk that had another yellowing sign hanging over it that read "Supervisor."

Jaybird felt the power of that sign. It must have been hanging there for thirty years. He felt the proverbial red tape start to gather steam, but he held his stoic look. The others standing in line were now choosing sides in their own heads about these exciting little soap opera events unfolding in front of them.

After a minute of discussion and a few glances over the clerk's shoulder, she and the supervisor came back to the counter.

The man held up the paperwork and said in a very authoritative voice, "My clerk here tells me that you were in here about an hour ago with this form and it wasn't notarized, not to mention the date problems you had earlier in the day. Could you explain that to me, please?"

The clerk stood there with a look that you could just read from her face. It surely meant, "So there. Take that, I win, you little snot-nosed kid."

It also seemed that every person in the place was waiting to hear Jaybird's response. No one was uttering a word. Kandy and Joan were clutching each other's arms hard enough to cause pain with their fake long fingernails. It was as if time stood still.

Jaybird looked at his watch; it showed exactly two o'clock. He took a deep breath, exhaled loudly saying, "I was told to get this notarized and I did. We chartered a helicopter and had my fiancée's mother fly down here and sign this *new* form in front of a notary. Then we brought it back here just like this lady said to do."

With his voice now rising to a full crescendo he added, "So what is the problem here? I did exactly what she told me to do and now there is still a problem? I suppose there is something else wrong with the paperwork again? Or is she insinuating that I am a liar? I am getting pretty tired of this clerk giving me such a hassle. As a matter of fact I would like to file a complaint on her!"

Kandy and Joan looked at each other in utter amazement. Neither of them had ever heard Jaybird even raise his voice. This was almost a yell they were hearing from him.

The supervisor glanced quickly around the room at the small crowd of people who were now talking amongst themselves and yet paying close attention so they would not miss the supervisor's response. He handed the clerk the consent form and told her to check the notary number to see if it was still valid or if it had expired. He explained to Jaybird that is would only take a few minutes for them to look it up in the "active" list.

Jaybird turned around and looked at Kandy. He noticed quite a few people smiling at him as he caught their eyes. One man even mumbled something about "municipal employees thinking they were doing us a favor or something." Jaybird suddenly wondered if the old man had kept his notary dues up to date. That would just be par for the day if his notary certificate number had expired. *Just another obstacle to overcome.* After a short time the supervisor himself tapped Jaybird on the shoulder and promptly handed him a marriage license. This was accompanied by many grins and a round of subdued applause from the other patrons in line.

As they got in the car, Kandy just had to ask, "Jaybird, were you *mad* at that man? I can't remember you ever raising your voice before."

"Yeah," Joan said, "but you were very effective."

Jaybird moved his eyebrows up and down and said, "Nope. I was acting. I figured that if those two jerks, I mean clerks, got embarrassed enough, they would hurry up and give us what we wanted just to get us out of their hair. Plus they surely couldn't spend too much time on us. I mean there were a dozen or so people behind us and they were getting grumpy."

"I guess you're right there; it sure worked out for us," Kandy said, ever so thankful for his resourcefulness.

"Besides, "Jaybird added, "I never get mad."

"We know!" the girls said almost in unison.

As Jaybird drove and the girls talked to each other, he remembered that he had been a pretty good actor once before. That knowledge just leapt in to his mind as he himself was wondering where he mustered up the gumption to put on an act like that. And just like that, he knew. He had been Lionel Barrymore and had earned one of the first Academy Awards for best actor in the movie "A Free Soul" The fourth Best Actor Oscar given, actually.

Shortly after the "I do's" were exchanged, Joan was throwing rice at them with one hand while attempting to hold the eight millimeter silent movie camera steady with the other as she walked backward down the steps and out the door. The secretary there had given Joan directions to a restaurant called the Two Joshua Trees while Kandy and Jaybird were smooching after the congratulations. The secretary claimed it was a very nice place to eat with a wonderful atmosphere. Driving a short distance up the road, they found the restaurant. It was nearly dinner-time, so there was a long line of people waiting to get in. Jaybird had an idea. He was tired of lines. He wanted to get seated now. So he walked up to the hostess desk and as he was explaining to the woman how he had just gotten married, he subtly slid two one-hundred dollar bills on the reservation pad. She looked at the tuxedo he was wearing and took the bills as she walked outside to see his new bride. After he pointed Kandy out, the hostess asked the people in line if anyone minded if these two brand-new newlyweds of only about fifteen minutes, and their friend, could jump to the front of the line.

As smiles, claps, ooh's and aah's reverberated up and down the line; there seemed to be no resistance to that initiative. Not even from the very large man who looked as if he could have eaten a whole cow right then and there. They sat down to a fabulous steak and lobster dinner and the owner even brought a bottle of champagne to their table, on the house. Kandy kept asking Jaybird who he thought he was looking at, every time he wasn't looking at her. He thought it was cute the way she always wanted to be the focus of his attention. Joan filmed periodically, catching special moments like toasts and specks of food on the side of Jaybird's mouth.

The hostess came back to take a Polaroid of them for the restaurant's "Celebrity Wall." They may not have been famous but it was a very special occasion.

As they downed the second bottle of champagne, Jaybird decided to pay the bill for every table in the place, as long as he was still in the restaurant. The waiter sent the owner over to their table to question Jaybird's ability to pay for such a grandiose gesture. His reservations were quickly squelched as a wad of hundred-dollar bills was placed in his hand. Jaybird was learning to use his money to get what he wanted. He never thought twice about spending it. Somehow it didn't feel real. Yes, he had millions to spend if he wanted to. Getting used to having it was starting to grow on him. He chuckled to himself and thought, *Everyone says you can't take it with you. That was true but you could hide it in a cave.*

After phoning a taxicab to come and get them for a ride over to the hotel, Jaybird looked at Kandy and said,

"I love you, Mrs. Young. Please remind me that we left the car here when we get up tomorrow."

"I will if I remember and I love you too, Mr. Young!" Kandy said, with her best coo. She was extremely happy with his perseverance. Without his knowing it, he had brought her one step closer to her goal. She laughed at the thought of him being such a sucker.

Joan just kept filming as best she could. With five glasses of champagne in her system and all the laughing, much of the action was not in the center of the frame. But Joan didn't care; her head was floating in the clouds.

CHAPTER VIII

LATE THAT Sunday afternoon the two newlyweds floated in through the front door of Jaybird's parents' house, each on completely different clouds.

"I didn't hear you, Ma. What?"

Jaybird's mother, Nan, repeated the news of Robin's car wreck as she hurried in from the recreation room. Even before Jaybird could tell his mother about his own exciting news, which didn't seem so exciting now, he decided to go straight to the hospital. Kandy wanted to tell her mother she was married. She didn't much care to see Robin. There was no warmth in her heart for him. So she persuaded Jaybird, who should have been extremely mad at her, but was too freaked out to worry about it, to drop her off first at her mother's house. Jaybird then rushed to the hospital. Once inside, he assumed that the man standing by the counter in the light blue smock with an arm full of charts was a doctor.

"I am looking for Robin Duvall. I'm his best friend. Could you tell me what room he's in, please?" he asked.

The doctor looked up, waved off the attempt from the nurse behind the counter to field the question, answering, "And your name is…?"

"I'm Jaybird Young."

"OK, Mr. Young. Mr. Duvall said it was all right to tell you about his situation. I just came from his room, as a matter of fact. He is just getting done with supper. He should be awake for a while now, but he may begin to get groggy from the painkillers he had earlier. He has some stitches and a bad knee injury."

The doctor explained Robin's condition and the circumstances surrounding the accident. With that information Jaybird asked, "All right, thank you, sir. So what room is he in?"

"Room one. Right here," the doctor said as he pointed over his shoulder.

Jaybird walked about ten feet and stood outside Robin's door; he took a deep breath as he glanced up and down the hospital hallway. He thought how strange that the sight of cleanliness and smell of disinfectant which usually made you feel good, seemed to be overpowered by sorrow, pain, and death in a hospital. He actually wanted to get out of there. He was feeling very uneasy, and then he remembered that he had never set foot in a hospital before. He now knew he didn't like it much.

Robin waved him over as Jaybird opened the door and poked his head through. Jaybird managed to put on a smile saying, "What's on TV?"

"Oh, just some show about how to drive your car," Robin said, rather cheerfully, considering the circumstances. He had a shattered knee held together by pins and forty more stitches below his lip on his chin. Those were eventually going to scar over and complement the other scar on his face, but without symmetry.

"How's the leg?" Jaybird asked.

"Well, it's amazing how many pins you can put in one bone and how many stitches a face can hold. I guess I really lived up to my name, huh?"

Jaybird tried forcing an obligatory laugh, saying, "Yeah. Da, Da, Da Dumb, is probably what my mom would say."

Suddenly a serious look came over Robin's face. He turned down the TV using the controls by his bed and put his hands behind his head. It was a look that Jaybird had never seen on his best friend's face before.

Robin began, as he shook his head, "What was I thinking about? I don't understand it, man. I couldn't concentrate. Everything hit me all at once. I don't even know what it was that hit me."

Jaybird looked at him a bit puzzled, "What hit you? What are you talking about? The steering wheel?" Jaybird said, moving a chair closer to Robin's bed and sat down. He figured the sedative or painkillers were making him lose his train of thought.

"No. Not that. Listen," he stated. "I was all ready to race this Corvette when the flagman came over to shake my hand, you know, and out of nowhere I had the same sort of thing happen to me like when…well, like when I first shook your hand way back."

Jaybird was pleasantly surprised that Robin had decided to break their long-held blood-brother pact and talk about their strange encounter. Over the years he had often thought about bringing it up with Robin but he figured that he should honor their promise to each other. It was a relief to finally be able to have a conversation about it.

"Oh, man! Really! It happened to you again, too? Boy, you must have not been paying much attention after that moment, huh?" Jaybird said emphatically.

"Hell, no, I wasn't. I don't even remember actually starting the race. Yet when I think of it, the whole thing is like…it seems to all be in slow motion, right from the moment I heard this loud noise. That kind of brought me back to reality. But by then I couldn't hold the car on the road. It seemed like I had enough time to correct the direction of the car, when I think back on it now. But I didn't. In my mind it's like one of those books that had a picture on the corner of each page and you could fan the pages and make it go fast or you could make it go real slow, you know. Each frame in my mind took so long to click to the next one. But that just can't be. It must have only taken a second or two to go off the road and roll. Those few moments seem like a bow tie now."

"A what?" Jaybird asked in bewilderment.

"A bow tie. It is like my life is wide open like at the edge of a bow tie.

Everything is big and bright, I see all around me and take everything in all at once. Then my field of vision started zooming at light speed, getting smaller and smaller towards the moment of the wreck. The wreck is the compressed middle of the knotted area of the bow tie, like a singularity where time sort of stops for a moment, and then starts to begin going fast-forward toward the wide part of other side of the bow tie, only I am turned around watching the wreck behind me. And even though I went through the wreck so fast, I can still see every single millisecond of it. It seems like a dream but I know it isn't."

Robin stopped for a second and then asked, "It happened again to me, too? You said "too." Did something like this happen to you, Jaybird?"

"Oh, yeah…I mean I didn't wreck a car or anything. Never mind about me, I'll tell you about it later. First, tell me what else you remember of the wreck?"

"I don't remember much after I started rolling down the embankment, except waking up here."

"The mind can play funny tricks on you, huh?" said Jaybird.

Robin motioned Jaybird to lean closer, "I believe you're right, but it wasn't a trick; it was a memory. I had this memory all of a sudden just pop in my head after that dude shook my hand. It hurt somehow, initially. Not physically, but the feelings I got were so…so unnerving to me. I remembered standing somewhere…somewhere else with that flagman dude…or I was watching him…it's not completely clear. I don't know. Oh, I'm just going to say it. He was my father once before…a long time ago. I was remembering…something very important, but sad, when, um…I guess the race started and I took off, from instinct. Then in the next second I felt like I had actually known him…well like way back in some long lost past life. That memory felt good, as well as sad, though. Any idea as to what it all means? Um, I know we promised each other. We swore never to mention this kind of thing again but…."

"Oh, hell, forget that old promise, we were just kids when we made it. I was going to talk to you about my memory encounter also, sooner or later. So, no, I don't really understand what it all means either…for sure, but it really feels good to finally say something about it to you."

"Take a guess though, please, Jaybird. I want you to tell me if you think I'm going crazy or nuts. What the hell are all these weird feelings and memories and…and stuff. I can't remember other lives, can I? Oh, I give up, I must be nuts!"

Jaybird slowly shook his head and stated, "First of all, you're not nuts. I have strange memories like that, too. I don't know what you felt, but for me, when I shook your hand that first time years ago, I had so many weird things flood my mind, man. It was like thousands of other times and places. As though I had lived somewhere else in history or in my mind. And also with this old guy the other day. I…I had some of the same weird feelings and memories when I grabbed his arm. It's like I know some things for a fact, yet how could I? It seems too far out there. I mean this guy was old but I…I just know I was his dad!"

Jaybird pointed to the window as he continued, "I always feel like I have to get there, somewhere and do something when I get there. I feel an urgency to…well, everything. Everything seems so damn urgent. But I don't know how these feelings or memories got there. And the strangest thing is, you know when we hid that gold back in 1849, I know that you and I were…"

"Brothers!" Robin blurted out before Jaybird finished his sentence.

"Yep. Brothers," Jaybird agreed. "But that was over a hundred years ago!"

"You're right, man. I knew it, too. I just never let myself say it. I always felt that you were…um, going to die or something so I needed to protect you while we were growing up. Man, that's just so weird. How could we know that kind of stuff? How could I *know* it?"

"I don't understand either," Jaybird said, "but I do know that you and I put those trunks of gold in that cave a long time ago. It was like when we shook hands, I was filled with a few other memories of you and me being acquainted with each other from before. That particular time was very clear. Then I kept having daydreams of exactly where those trunks of gold were. They weren't dreams, you know? I really did know where they were. I also felt that we had to go get them as soon as possible. It was like I was going to die if I didn't get them. Or maybe I had to get them before I died. Man, it was a lot for a kid to handle."

Robin gave Jaybird a look of empathy. He thought for a few seconds, reaching back to that very strange moment when they had first met five years earlier, then stated, "Well, I also had a rush of memories when I shook your hand; but let me tell you I was scared of it. It was like I had always known you. And then it was like I was going to…somehow lose you. It was like how a person feels when someone in his family dies. The feelings were…that strong. I felt like I had to go with you after you told me about the cave in Colorado, for fear of something happening to you. I really didn't understand that feeling, you know, but I just knew that you and I had hidden that gold together there. After you told me about the cave did it become much more clear in my mind. Yet I shouldn't have known that. Hell, I even know that my name was Sam Brannan. I got all that gold from my businesses out in San Francisco."

Jaybird thought for a second and said in a matter of fact tone, "Yup, you were the richest man in California. You were California's first millionaire. You built a fortune from the gold rush by creating a bunch of little businesses that kept the miners supplied with all the goods they needed to live, as they ravenously looked for more gold. Not to mention all the land you bought and the paper you published. You basically founded the town of Calistoga around the hot springs. I was your brother. I remember that I suggested to you, more than a few times, that you should hide some of the gold out of state so that if something ever happened to you, you had something to fall back on. Right after we hid the gold, I headed down to Nevada to get a jump on the next big thing."

"Right," Robin said. "Wow, I don't know how I remember this but many of those miners were paying in gold nuggets and gold dust. I had enough real money at that point to just hoard a bunch of the gold that was flowing in. I think the big moment during that life was when we both met that Pony Express rider who was on a break before heading back to the Midwest for another mail delivery."

Jaybird looked at him and nodded his head affirmatively, saying, "You know, you are right! He was on a drinking break as I remember it though. Yup, that was the guy that made us remember our past in that life. Man alive. That's what started the big change in your lifestyle, Robin. Before meeting him you were a prominent elder in the Mormon Church, doing good for the community and everything. Then you quickly took a dive into the evils you were catering to: whiskey, gambling and women."

"Oh, my God! You're right! Shortly after getting those memories I kinda fell off the religious wagon. That produced a nasty divorce and my wife took most of my money and holdings. I frittered away the rest over the next few years," Robin said, then added, "Man, I sure got confused about how to live my life."

"Divorce? Hmm...I don't remember that. I think I...I died before you were divorced. But you were having a hard time being loyal to your wife before I headed out to Nevada," Jaybird stated.

Robin sighed heavily, saying, "Yeah, you did die. I got a letter in the mail one day and it told me you had died. I was never the same. That letter came a week after my divorce was final in...1878. Bad timing, I guess."

"Friday though, Jaybird, with that flagman, I had a memory where I was staring at him. I was somewhere else, feeling so sad. I remember he told me to never forget this scene."

"What scene, Robin?"

After a long pause where Robin seemed to be searching his memories very hard, he slowly said, "There was this pillar or a tree with no branches or something else tall and sturdy like that, positioned a few feet in front of me. I was standing in the shadow of this tall thing and the guy was saying, 'Never forget this'," Robin said, extending his arms over his head.

Jaybird stared at Robin's raised arms. An image was forming in Robin's mind but he couldn't quite get hold of it. He kept his hands in the air. "The flagman," was all he could say in a whisper.

Robin looked at Jaybird as a chill ran down his body. With his hands still over his head, he looked up between them.

"This means something, doesn't it, Jaybird?" Robin asked, as he dropped his hands. "Do you think the image I saw before I crashed was of a man holding his hands up in the air, maybe? What could it mean? Oh, man, I almost have it. But it's just out of reach."

Jaybird shrugged his shoulders saying, "I don't know, but I think it most certainly does mean something important. Why else would you remember it? Did you recall anything else? Sounds, smells or colors? Anything weird like that?"

"No, I don't think so."

There was a long silence as each reflected on separate memories. For years they had been ignoring and discounting the validity of their strange knowledge. They had refused to accept the reality of those thoughts. They had suppressed even the idea of it being a truth with child-like fervor. It was the "cross your heart and hope to die" attitude. Now, as the two friends came upon this impasse, maybe they could, together, reach some level of understanding. Maybe they could begin to talk to each other about what had been kept locked up inside each head.

"Totem pole," Robin blurted out, scaring Jaybird somewhat.

"What?"

"That flagman guy was standing in front of a totem pole. He was my father and his name was…hmm. Just can't grab that, but we were definitely…Indians."

Jaybird just nodded.

"Jaybird, can I tell you something that I never have before, and only 'cause I figured you would think I was crazy?"

"I'd never think you were crazy. Come on; you're my best friend. Besides, look what we have been through. Out with it," Jaybird demanded, imperatively.

"OK, here goes…I can remember so many different times that I have lived in or used to live in, sometimes remembering even my names, other times not. Basically, I know I have been alive more than just once before!"

"Robin, I know exactly what you mean, man. Me, too! It is all so strange; I have tried not to pay any attention to it. Maybe I should start thinking about this more. Lately the memories have been getting really vivid. Or maybe I have been trying to come to grips with them more as I get older, you know, allowing myself to think about them more."

Robin pondered on Jaybird's comments for a moment and then said, "Maybe we should pay attention to the memories. You know, it's like we were reincarnated or something. And…hell, I don't even believe in that. With every passing day the memories in my mind and the images in my dreams are getting clearer and clearer also. Somehow something tells me that I could know more, if I would just concentrate on it. Sounds crazy, huh?"

Jaybird just shook his head from side to side.

Robin flatly stated, "Exactly. It isn't crazy, at least not anymore. I think me and that flagman or whoever…were never going to see each other again. I think he was about to die! Or I was about to die! Boy, oh, boy, you know something, Jaybird? If we ever tell anyone else about this they would surely commit us."

"I'm sure you're right, there, man. You know I even thought that when we talked about it on our way to Colorado, way back, that you might have thought I was nuts. So I never brought it up again."

"Hey, I remember that. That was when we promised each other to never talk about the feelings or mention it to anyone else. Of course, I tried once in from of my seventh grade class. I got laughed at."

"Uh, oh; you hate to be laughed at, huh?"

"Sure do. Laughed *with* is fine but not laughed *at*," Robin said, adding, "You know, I think I just couldn't deal with all that back then. My parents just split up and we moved, a new school and all that stuff. I think I just sort of ignored all the memories and feelings and knowledge I had instantly recalled after I shook your hand. I tried to just block it all out. And as I got older I could only think about one thing and one thing only: winning the heavyweight title."

The two of them sat there in silence for a few minutes. Each one immersed in his own thoughts again. Jaybird, thinking to himself that he too had felt the need to be funny as a way to deal with the abnormal feelings he was having. He just wasn't good at being funny; he just knew he wasn't as quick-witted as Robin. Eventually Jaybird got up and looked out the window. Turning around, he asked Robin if he wanted to hear his theory about their whole situation.

Robin gave him a wave-off with his hand, saying, "No. It's of no concern to me."

Jaybird looked surprised. When Robin could no longer hold back his smile, he said, "Of course I do. What's your theory, Doc?"

"Well, I had to read this book in Psychology class once about the two halves of the brain and how schizophrenics are like, maybe, less developed, evolution-wise, in the brain and all. They hear voices, only it is really just themselves thinking. But they can't tell the difference. They can't figure out that what we call talking to ourselves, really isn't coming from an external source They think some invisible person is telling them to do stuff when it is really themselves telling themselves to so stuff."

"Oh, how weird. That must drive them *crazy!*"

"Very funny, Robin," Jaybird said, laughing so hard that his stomach hurt.

After they both got over it Jaybird said, "Anyhow, that's why they answer themselves and talk to hallucinations and act, well, like you said, crazy. They just have a hard time figuring everything out. Anyway this author has a hypothesis about mankind as a whole. He believes there are, and have been, certain phases in the evolution of humans and that some family lines have evolved faster than others. He thinks there may be three or four different phases of consciousness. But the people in each phase are all living among the others. You know, it's like the Indy 500 car race. There is always someone in the lead and someone in the middle and others behind. But they are all in the same race."

"Well, we are in the human race, you know," Robin said, not meaning to make a joke.

"Hey, I'm being serious here, man! And if you make me laugh again, I might cry, 'cause my stomach hurts so bad!"

"Sorry, it just came out," Robin said. He assumed the painkillers were somehow making him feel a lot funnier than he was.

"So anyhow, this guy thinks it is all a learning process and some folks aren't evolved enough to use certain areas of their brains, but that other doctors treat their patients with drugs because they believe the problem is just a chemical imbalance."

Robin sat up in bed and said, "Let me paraphrase here, if I may. You're saying that maybe I am using more of my brain than other people, yet I still make an idiot out of myself by wrecking my car! Or, no; maybe I'm "under-evolved." Very interesting...Mr. Spock."

Jaybird smiled and continued, "All I'm saying is that I can remember different stuff than you do. It seems we both lived in that one particular time together, way before this time, in the mid 1800's. And you have known this flagman dude in another time also, right? And I think you were like Beethoven!"

Robin thought for a second then said, "Yes, I was Beethoven, way before the gold rush time and you were someone I looked up to like a mentor, named um...Haydn. Why are some memories so clear and others somewhat fogged over?"

Jaybird shrugged his shoulders and said, "You know, I have heard about those hypnotists regressing people to past lives. That memory had to come from somewhere. You certainly can't remember something that didn't happen, can you?"

"Exactly. But after you're dead? How could that carry over to any other life? There must be something to all this stuff. Somebody has got to have an answer," Robin said rhetorically. "You know, Jaybird, sometimes when I am watching TV I get a feeling that I know or should know something about a place I see, or even a photograph or picture, can conjure up a powerful feeling. But I can't understand why. Sometimes it just never gels. Other times I hear myself saying, "Hey I've been there, only not in this life." Does that ever happen to you?"

"All the time man, all the damn time."

Robin turned up the TV and said, "Listen to the news here. They found some dinosaur bones in Montana, I think. It caught my attention earlier today. See if you get anything from it."

Jaybird looked at his watch and said, "I would love to stay and watch but I should get back to my wife and then…"

Robin's eyes opened wide and he about fell out of the hospital bed, saying, "Wife! Wife! Holy moly! You got married? When the hell were you going to tell me you got married?"

"Sorry. I guess your situation kind of took precedence. We just eloped and got married in Topeka. Believe you me, it is a long story. I'll have to tell you later. I really should be helping Kandy. She is changing the reservations. We were going to Tahiti for a honeymoon but I am going to stick around here for a while."

"What? No! You're not sticking around here! You get your ass back home to your wife and get packing. Hell, my parents will be back in a few more days, so what do you need to hang around for? And hey…where are you two going to live?"

"Well, I don't know. Hadn't thought that far ahead. Look, it just feels weird to leave my best friend in a hospital, alone," Jaybird quipped.

"Get out of here!" Robin said with a wave of his hand, "I'm a big boy now. Just one that can't drive too well."

Even as he was telling Jaybird to go, Robin had the strangest feeling that he really should be hanging around *him*, to protect Jaybird for whatever reason. He couldn't figure out why. It didn't matter; he couldn't go anywhere. The knee was shattered.

"Are you sure, Robin?" Jaybird asked.

Robin then held out his hand and shook Jaybird's hand, saying, "Congratulations, man, now get out of here or I'll call the mean old nurse to throw you out. Hap and peaciness dude, hap and peaciness."

Jaybird laughed, as Robin held up his right hand, splitting his fingers, as Spock always did. Leaving the hospital room he thought to himself how much he missed *Star Trek*, but the reruns were always on some channel. He knew he was not going to leave for Tahiti. It wouldn't be right. Just before the door shut he heard Robin call after him.

"Say man, what room is Julie in anyhow, I gotta see how she is doing?"

Jaybird froze in his tracks. Had no one told Robin?

CHAPTER IX

"**NOOOO, NO** one told me. Dead! Oh, my God. No. No. No. This can't be. I had no idea. What have I done?" Robin said, slamming his clenched fists beside him on the bed over and over again as Jaybird walked back into the room. Robin's mind was reeling. He couldn't fathom what Jaybird had just told him. It was like a bad dream. He pulled the pillow from behind his head to cover his face. He felt like crying but he didn't know how. He was Robin, the tough guy who could always find a joke for every situation, for any event in his life. For every bit of bad news, he could see the light on the other side of it. But this was too much. His heart was pounding. He kept his face buried in his pillow. No joke found its way to his lips. Everything suddenly was stuck way down in his stomach. He wanted to vomit.

Jaybird tried to think of something to say to comfort him but he had no words either. He just stood there by his friend and waited for him to get it all out. After a few minutes Robin looked up at Jaybird. The sorrow in his eyes said it all. Robin finally asked in a half-cracked voice, "You weren't going to tell me, were you?"

"Actually, I thought the doctor or somebody would have already done it."

"Yeah, I suppose it would have been easier on you if they had."

"Don't worry about me, Robin. Are you going to be able to handle this? Is there, um, anything I can do for you?"

Robin looked at his leg, felt the bandage on his chin and started shaking his head from side to side. As terrible as the whole situation seemed, he had an unusual feeling of having being through these depths of sadness and loss before. The feeling he had was like an acknowledgment of the situation, an acceptance of the circumstances, as if something just like this was bound to happen. When that feeling engulfed him, he felt ashamed. He thought to himself, *this always happens to me. Everyone around me dies before I do. That shouldn't lessen the horrible feelings of the situation, though.* Somehow he knew he should feel worse than he did.

After another long, awkward, silent moment, Robin asked, "What else should I know?

"What do you mean what else?" Jay asked, perplexed by his question.

Just then the doctor walked in with all kinds of gadgets hanging on and off his smock. He took the chart from the end of Robin's bed and looked it over, never acknowledging either of them.

"Doctor," Robin said, "is there anything else I need to know about my situation? Anything you need to tell me?"

The doctor looked up from the chart. It was obvious that he didn't hear the complete question from the bewildered look on his face.

"Doc, am I going to live? Any internal hemorrhaging or whatever they call it?"

"No. Just a plethora of stitches and a badly compound fractured leg, held together by titanium pins. You'll live all right. We'll take good care of you here."

"Sure, like you did Julie!" Robin retorted. He was angry with himself, extremely angry with himself, so he lashed out.

"If you are referring to the young woman in the car wreck with you Mr. Duvall, she was DATS, son. I'm very sorry." His demeanor never changed. Obviously he was used to patients who were under extreme stress, with emotions running high. Robin's insinuation didn't faze him a bit.

Jaybird tried to defuse the moment and asked, "Yes, Julie is, um, was her name, but what is DATS, doctor?"

"That's dead at the scene. Her neck was broken. She died instantly, I would imagine. I'm very sorry for your loss, Robin. Was she your girlfriend?" he asked as he started working with some knobs on the machines next to Robin's headboard.

Robin and Jaybird looked at each other for a second. Both were visualizing the gruesome scene of a person with a broken neck. Neither had a reply. It was too hard to think about it. Jaybird just watched the doctor fiddle with the equipment, as Robin gazed out the window.

As the doctor was leaving, Robin called out, "Is there any way I can get something for the pain in my leg?"

"Yes, of course. I'll send in a nurse," the doctor replied.

"Look, Jaybird, I think I need to be alone, you know?" Robin said softly, with a tremor in his voice.

"Sure, I understand," Jaybird said as he backed up toward the door.

Jaybird couldn't think of anything to say anyway. He just quietly left. He had never seen that kind of look on Robin's face, nor heard that kind of weakness in his voice before. He knew Robin was in pain, internal and external.

Robin looked out the window. He noticed that it was a bright and clear day outside but it could have been snowing cow piles. He didn't see the beauty of it. His thoughts were of Julie and his eyes were now tearing up as he was overcome with emotions. He went back in his mind to the first time he ever talked to her. There was only a week or so left of the school year. Her mother had just moved to town a month earlier due to a job promotion and Julie had to finish up her senior year at a new school. Robin had walked into the library for study hall one day and there was a new cute red-headed girl sitting at *his* table by the window. No one ever sat down there, only Robin and a few choice friends. That was just the way it was. Everyone knew it. He was a senior and that was *his* seat. He walked up to the table and jokingly told her that she could continue to sit there if she would go out with him. He assumed she would get up and leave. Not Julie. She turned and looked at him as he slowly eased himself into the chair. After she gave him a quick body scan, she replied that his offer seemed to be fair enough. Robin laughed and said he was serious and Julie said that she was also. So after some playful conversation they set up a date, to cruise around town one evening. It just happened to be Jaybird's birthday.

Robin remembered how excited he was, thinking about going out with her. He kept thinking up things to ask her on the phone those seemingly long days before the date. They were stupid little things. He liked to talk with her and she seemed to enjoy their conversations. At least that's the impression he got. He had hoped he wasn't bothering her. Every day he would call her up while stretching the thirty-foot long phone cord from the kitchen wall around the corner and down the steps to the basement so no one would hear him, as they talked for hours.

He could even recall the color of the dress she had worn on the first date. It was blue with white flowers on it. How beautiful she looked as he watched her come down the stairs of her house when he went by to pick her up. He had brought flowers for her. His mother had always told him to bring flowers on the first date. A bouquet for the date and a single flower for the mother.

You need to win over the mother from the start. Not red roses, his mother had said, *anything else but red roses.* Robin had listened. He saw Julie blush as she took the flowers, thanking him quite a few times and asking her mother to put them in water. Her mother beamed. He was nervous, but only for a few moments. Once they were in his new car she was asking all kinds of questions about the car and its capabilities. They had a great time from then on. He knew they were going to be friends, if nothing else. She liked his car. That was so important to an eighteen-year-old male. Robin couldn't remember ever liking a girl as much so fast. She even liked to street-race. He had been out with other girls who just wanted to get out of the car and watch from the side of the road. Oh, how he wished *now* that she had got out, just like the others had. She wouldn't have been killed. Why did this happen? How could he have been so distracted at the start of a race? He knew he should have been more focused. He was just so surprised to have felt that strange rush of feelings for a second time. *Why then?* he thought. *Why with Julie?* He decided he would never race cars again. He also felt that he could never let Julie out of his heart. He would never forget her. He was sure that he could have loved her. Maybe he was already in love with her, he contemplated. But he had only known her for a short time and had only two dates. He just lay there trying to understand why Julie had to die, reliving their short-lived relationship over and over again. He couldn't help but think about the poem that he never had a chance to read to her. He had it memorized.

Maybe it wasn't done or maybe it was. It didn't matter; it was there, repeating over and over in his head:

The sound of your voice can make me calm

When you laugh at something simple coming from this silly dope.

But you'll put your little hand in my big palm

And the softness of your touch fills my heart with hope.

I never had a friend such as I found in you

One who cares about me and others too.

If I could hang out with you all day, that's what I'd do.

You're so smart, attentive and refreshingly true.

My wish is to always have this feeling so real

But if there ever came a terrible time, a bad time or worse,

One that left you hurt or your heart unable to heal,

I tell you right here and now that I vow to talk only in song or verse.

The nurse came in and gave him a shot of morphine and very quickly the throbbing pain in his knee subsided, but he knew there was no drug to take the pain out of his heart. Julie was still there and it hurt. As he contemplated the last line of his poem, an immense feeling of loss came over him. He felt it deep inside. Somehow again, it felt familiar. He just couldn't grasp why.

As he drifted into a stupor, he wondered if what he had written had resulted from a premonition. Was he making bad things happen by putting thoughts in a poem? *It couldn't be*, he thought. Along with his feeling of loss, there was fear. Fear of the knowledge that he had, of the truth. The truth was creating the fear. The truth was that he knew he should be used to this feeling of loss. He still couldn't understand why he should be used to feeling such pain. As that thought crossed his mind, he suddenly *did* know why he should be used to the feeling. It was because his family and friends always died before he did. He knew he had usually outlived everyone close to him in his past lives. There were a few lives that were short but he knew he was very old in the vast majority of them. That is where the sorrow and loss feelings came from. He also knew that *everything* had been said before. Every feeling had been explored. Every mood had been defined. He thought of how much he loved to listen to music. He knew why. Music captures every nuance of love, pain, happiness, and moments in time. The personal interpretation of any music heard at the same moment in time could mean something entirely different for each individual person hearing that same piece of music, even if a whole crowd at a concert heard it at the exact same time. He felt that music, including *his* music, was the keeper of every essence of emotion for any given instant in time as perceived by the composer and interpreted by the listener. He mused that there are only a finite number of words available to any language but they can be rearranged in infinitely different ways. There were only so many musical notes as well. Music was just a matter of rearranging the finite notes in a different order. Suddenly he felt his heart become colder, harder, locked down tighter. He knew this feeling. He just didn't like it. Robin could only imagine the pain Julie's family was going through. He knew that no words could say enough to ease their pain. Just before he fell into a deep drug-induced sleep he made a pledge to Julie's memory. He decided that he would do everything he could to ease her family's pain. Jaybird had said many times to him, "Just make your mind up and don't look back." He contemplated talking only in song or verse just like the last line of his poem said. That surely would enable him to remember her, forever. He just didn't have the mind-set at that moment to make a commitment to himself. He faded into a deep sleep.

CHAPTER X

ELIZABETH WAS fading in and out of little cat-naps because of the boring book she had been reading. She decided to stop reading and stood up to stretch. She looked aft of the yacht and called out, "Eddie. What exactly are you going to do with this island? There is absolutely nothing on it. No buildings, no people, nothing but sand, water and a little jungle."

"What?" Edward asked, somewhat annoyed.

"What is your big plan for this island? Are you going to develop a resort on it or what?"

"Don't worry your pretty little head about that. Just be assured that I will make a lot of money from some aspect of this little rock."

"How, Eddie?"

Edward wasn't much in the mood for talking. He knew he had to tell her soon that she wasn't coming with him. He knew she would be upset. He would have to try and make it sound as if his idea was the best for the both of them. He was growing so tired of her. The challenge was gone. She was his now, but like a toy two weeks after Christmas, he wasn't thrilled by her anymore. He *knew* this part of the relationship was coming. All his relationships ended exactly the same. When he was done with them he just threw the women away. He knew there were plenty of other fish in the sea. His ego was too much for monogamy. Everything was about and for himself. A long-term relationship would be useless to him since the boredom of domestication would not provide the needed excitement and adulation he was accustomed to, and which, as far as he was concerned, only happens in the beginning of a relationship. For Edward, when it came to women, it was always about the challenge, never the follow-through. Besides, he had way too many bones in his closet that didn't need to be discovered.

He looked at her and offered an explanation out of sheer boredom, "I am first going to explore the lagoon, just to see what is lurking in the waters there. You never know what is there 'til you look," he said. But he knew what was there. He knew exactly. He had put it there many hundreds of years ago.

As he walked toward her he could see the look of dismay cross her face.

"And what am I going to do?" She asked, very certain she knew the answer.

"Well," Edward said, as he motioned the captain to weigh anchor, "You are going to be at the best hotel in Tahiti. Spending my money, I presume."

"So you *are* dumping me off again? How long this time?"

"I don't really know. Not more than two weeks, I would guess."

"Eddie, I want to stay with you this time. I get so bored when you leave me alone."

Edward sat down by her and tried to sound understanding, "You know I will be back to get you as soon as I can. It just doesn't make any sense for you to hang around when I am working. I get dirty, tired and mean. I don't want you to have to deal with that."

"But I want to, I want—"

"No! You're not my wife, you know. You don't have to be everywhere I am all the time. I could just put you ashore anytime and be done with it. Anytime. Now that's the end of it." Edward stood up and walked toward the bow of the yacht. Turning around as the wind blew his ponytail across his face, he waited for her response.

Elizabeth didn't give him the satisfaction of a fight. She wouldn't play his game. Not this time. She grabbed the book and laid it back down. This was not her idea of fame and fortune. She had expected more from being Playmate of the Year. She felt like her best years were slipping away. She wondered why she put up with his wild mood swings. Was it love? Desire? Maybe something else? She didn't want to think about it. She picked up the book and again began reading, then flipped another page even before she was done with it.

Edward knew she was mad but he didn't care. He had other plans. They didn't include her.

After a smooth ride to the Bora Bora Islands, the yacht anchored in a small, beautiful secluded bay. Dusk was casting a purple hue on the clouds as the last slivers of sunlight faded behind the horizon. Edward waited for Elizabeth to emerge from the yacht's master suite. She finally came out, pushing two suitcases through the door. A deck-hand quickly grabbed them and carried them down to the waiting launch as she followed. After a short, silent and somewhat tense boat ride to the docks, Edward's first mate hailed a taxi and told the driver to take her to the Hotel Bora Bora, just as Edward had ordered him to do. Elizabeth got in the back seat without looking at Edward.

"I'll see you when I'm done, Liz. Remember, if you need anything just ask for the concierge, Mr. Brown. He can take care of anything you need," Edward said, as he started to wave goodbye, but she had already told the driver to proceed. *No matter,* he thought. Now that she was out of his hair he could have some fun. First he had to get a working party together.

"Back to the yacht. We're getting out of here," Edward barked at the first mate.

They headed around Matira Point then North East toward Aratika.

Once pier-side in Aratika, Edward took his personal secretary, Duke, with him on a little excursion. Duke was no secretary but Edward liked to call him that, since his real occupation would draw too much suspicious attention. They went to a nearby marina bar. Inside, Duke started checking around with the locals. After a while he was quite sure his boss could get what he needed from a man named Voodoo. They would meet Voodoo at his favorite watering-hole later that evening.

What a name, Edward mused. He was quite sure the man's mother hadn't given him that name. *I'll bet he has everyone scared of him. Just the kind of person I am looking for,* he thought.

"Duke, I need you to find a phone and call the Switzerland office and see if there are any messages I need to address," Edward ordered.

Later that evening over a few beers Edward reiterated the specifics of the deal he and Voodoo had hashed out.

"So are we clear on the terms of this?" Edward asked. "Five experienced divers at 500 dollars a day with a fifteen day guarantee. Down to 250 dollars a day if we go past fifteen days. That will ensure the work gets done fast."

"Yes, sir, Mr. Bloodhead, mon. I have it all right here," Voodoo said, pointing to his temple. "I was ah, wondering, would you like to get some women also then?"

"Damn straight. I was just going to bring that up. Eight of them, as a matter of fact. One for each of the divers and three for me. Good clean ones now, only the best, you got that?"

Voodoo slowly nodded his head affirmatively and said, "Only the best for you, Mr. Bloodhead, only the best."

"Great. Have them at pier three at 0700 tomorrow. The ship's name is the *3 CANES* That's spelled C-A-N-E-S."

"What does that stand for?" Voodoo asked, looking at Duke for an answer.

"What do you think?" Edward snapped impatiently.

"Well, sir, I have no idea but I could guess maybe that three old people with canes first named the ship.

"If that's what you think then it is probably correct."

With that Edward stood up and laid a hundred dollar bill on the table and told Voodoo to enjoy the rest of the night on him. But when Voodoo extended his hand to shake, Edward just turned for the door, saying, "0-700 sharp," and walked out. Voodoo laughed at Bloodhead's pompous attitude. He grabbed the bill and bought a round of drinks for everyone still in the bar.

Early the next day Edward was reading a message from his accountant; it was making him feel very good about his trio of patents, along with the revenue they were generating. The message stated that the net profits from the North Dakota refinery had just eclipsed five million dollars for the last month.

Edward had won a bid to buy a huge tract of land in Canada. It was brought to his attention that Amoco Canada Petroleum Company was selling about eight percent of its properties, some 1.75 million acres of land. Edward put a bid in for a quarter of that. His bid was for thirty-five million dollars and they accepted it. His company, 3 Canes Unlimited, now owned 450,000 acres of undeveloped land in the Athabasca wilderness in Alberta, Canada.

As it turned out, the land had some of the richest tar sand oil deposits in the world. After more than a year of getting the business off the ground and the entire infrastructure in place, etc., his company had actually started turning a profit. The company extracted oil from the tar sands, which basically look like black, sticky, sandy mud. The oil had to be separated from the sand somehow. Edward had his engineers study the recovery process and they reported to him that it wasn't profitable. No one in the industry could recover the oil economically with the "hot recovery systems" currently in use. But Edward had an idea and he had the money to put the idea in motion. Consequently he filed for three patents for a new invention he dreamed up and had his small team of highly paid engineers develop it. The process made use of refracted laser beams that cut through the cold tundra to the exact measurements of the container that would transport it. The chunk of frozen tundra was pulled back into the container, solid and whole. The container was then placed on a semi-trailer and driven out of Canada to his North Dakota refinery and melted down. From there the liquid crude oil was separated from the various byproducts, which included gold, silver and copper. On the border of Canada and North Dakota there were two towns named Portal and Northgate. Edward had his company build a refinery on a large tract of land between the towns. He also started buying up all the available land around his refinery. He had Duke put out that 3 Canes Unlimited would pay triple the assessed value for any property in Divide or Burke counties. He had a few long-term goals in mind for that area and his burgeoning business ventures.

Later that morning, Edward and Duke watched from the starboard side of the yacht as a small, old, beat-up bus coughed and choked toward the after-brow. He saw Voodoo get out and take charge of the mini-operation. The divers grabbed all their gear and placed it in front of them as they stood in a row like military men waiting for an inspection. The women were meandering around, primping, tugging at their tight skirts and pulling up on their tube tops. Each one had a distinctive beauty all her own. Much to Edward's surprise he counted fifteen women. Voodoo corralled everyone together and told them to stay put as he headed up the after-brow.

"Good morning, sir," Voodoo said, smiling as he removed his hat.

"Morning. I'm sure I said eight women," Edward stated, putting his arms across his chest.

"I thought you would enjoy picking your own first, sir. I know not your taste."

"Well, now, that is a good idea. Why didn't I think of that?"

Edward snapped his fingers and started down the after-brow, with a weary Duke a step or two behind him. After Edward chose his three women, he instructed the divers to pick one each for themselves. The grins on their faces were his assurance that this idea appealed to all of them. They carried their gear up the after-brow as the three men watched from the pier. With that done, Voodoo proceeded to ask for payment up front for the fifteen days the divers were guaranteed and for the women's services as well.

"We agreed on half now and the rest when we come back. That's how I remember it," Edward told Voodoo as he turned to get the cash from an envelope Duke was holding.

"Well, yes, sir, but I must insist that it be full payment now," Voodoo said, with an air of confidence. He then threw six small bones down beside Edward's feet, looked up at the sky, clapped his hands together twice and stomped his left foot twice.

Edward turned around while kicking the bones aside and stated in a matter-of-fact tone, "You do not *insist* anything to me! We never agreed on full payment up front. That's not how I do business and that's not what we agreed on. Besides, I'm sure I am paying double what any semblance of a normal rate would be."

The divers and the women were watching wide-eyed from the deck of the yacht as the two men argued. A couple of them started to snicker. They knew no one got the better of Voodoo. *What did this pretty white boy think he was doing?* one diver thought to himself.

Voodoo then reached into his pocket and pulled out a small chicken foot on a string. He started to dangle it in front of Edward's face and mumble some incomprehensible words.

Edward grabbed the foot from him, threw it to the ground and crushed it as a surprised Voodoo stepped back in disbelief.

"Listen," Edward said, "I don't believe in that voodoo crap any more than you do. I said half and that's what it will be unless you want to call the whole deal off, which means I'll just have to find someone else to supply my needs. Are we clear on this, Mr. Voodoo?"

"I think you make big mistake, Mr. Bloodhead. Big mistake. You no live long."

"Look, you misplaced Haitian black magic clown. You do this my way or not at all."

With that Edward shoved the envelope containing $18,750 in cash into Voodoo's chest. Voodoo took the money reluctantly and headed toward the bus, still mumbling and flailing his arms.

Edward laughed to himself as he walked up the after-brow. He couldn't understand how anyone would put any belief in black magic in this day and age. He knew that Voodoo's act was an old shaman ploy to scare the weak-minded into doing virtually anything out of fear. He wasn't afraid of anyone or anything, least of all any old outdated cult religion. *These guys are a dime-a-dozen anymore,* he thought.

As he stepped off the after-brow onto the quarterdeck an old memory came to mind. He still couldn't understand exactly *why* he had them. Although a good many of his memories had made him richer, most were painful. He just accepted them as facts and never told anyone how or why he knew what he knew. He just barked out orders. Since he paid extravagant salaries, everyone just did what he demanded, never expecting explanations. This situation with Voodoo was making something surface in him. He remembered back a long, long time before this life, during the Spanish Inquisition. He rode into a small town where a group of people were embarking on what they collectively thought was a fair trial. A young man was charged with being in league with the devil. They were going to test him by submerging him in water for ten minutes. If he survived then he surely had God inside him. If he drowned then he was obviously an evil man. Edward remembered challenging the priest who was overseeing the trial, to show everyone what it meant to have God inside himself by taking the ten minutes under water *first*. After much bantering from the townspeople, the priest was forced to prove his own faith in the test. Edward watched with glee as that priest drowned, as would any man. His true happiness came in knowing that another priest or soothsayer's life was extinguished, and could no longer mislead or rule the lesser-minded with their promises of an almighty being that would always save them if they would just truly believe. They were never saved when they pushed the limits of reality and the human body. *When would religion become just a forgotten footnote in history, like the notion that the earth was flat?* Edward thought to himself. *Why has it lasted so long?*

On deck, one of the divers asked Edward what Voodoo had held out in front of him. Snapping out of his daydream, Edward told him it was something that would have had more use in soup than what Voodoo had in mind for it. The diver's eyes opened very wide and he wondered to himself when Mr. Bloodhead would succumb to the curse Voodoo most certainly was conjuring up to put on him right now. He prayed to his God that the ship wasn't the target of an evil spell. He knew the Voodoo was the wrong man to have angry with you.

Once at sea Edward gathered everyone around and tried to make them as happy as he could. He knew they would work harder if they were happy.

"Now I want you all to enjoy yourselves as long as you are here. Ladies, I want you to treat these men wonderfully. Please ask any of the deck hands for whatever you need. The work during the day may be hard but the night will be a time for relaxing and celebrating. Oh, by the way, tops are optional. Feel free to remove them."

With that, a few of the women started to get topless, then the rest followed suit. They knew they were being paid well, just doing their jobs. Everyone started to mingle and explore the yacht as it weighed anchor.

It was a beautiful morning. The sun was peeking through the sparse cotton-ball-like clouds and a pod of dolphins leapt alongside the yacht as if they were playing a game of follow-the-leader, and they were the leaders. They headed towards *Edward's* Island.

CHAPTER XI

JAYBIRD HEADED home after he left the hospital and tried to explain to his parents why he and Kandy had eloped. His parents both sat down slowly, still a bit stunned by the news. Harry didn't really understand why Jaybird wanted to get married at such a young age and to a seventeen-year-old whom no one even liked, at that. She still had another year of high school to complete. Not to mention the fact that neither he nor Nan had ever really warmed up to her. As Harry and Nan started to talk to him Kandy came back from the bathroom. With her right there, it was awkward for them to be totally honest. They put on smiles and gave her a hug, welcoming her to the family. They were totally surprised to say the least, but what else could they do? At this point it was too late to stop them from getting married. Harry looked at his wife and rolled his eyes when neither Kandy nor Jaybird was looking his way. They would definitely have a lot to talk about when the kids left. Harry knew it was another spur-of-the-moment decision. This one, though, had a 'til death do us part clause in it.

Kandy was so excited about going to Tahiti that she hadn't changed the reservations like Jaybird had asked her. She could only see herself spending gobs of money there. Jaybird knew he should stick around. Going away at this time just made him feel funny. His best friend was hurting in more ways than one. Robin had insisted that he was fine and really needed to be alone anyway, at least until his parents got back. Jaybird decided that he should honor his wishes. So it worked out well that Kandy hadn't canceled their flight.

The following day, Jaybird and Kandy both went to see Robin again. When they got there, the doctor was attending to Robin.

Jaybird noticed the faraway look on Robin's face so he asked the doctor, "Doc, will he walk again?"

"Yes, by all means. We should be able to get him out of here with only a limp in most likelihood, even though he has smashed his knee pretty badly," the doctor replied.

"A limp! But he will be able to box still, right?"

"Oh, I think he better just plan on walking first as a goal. This kind of injury will require lots of rehabilitation."

Jaybird looked over at Robin. Robin didn't have to say anything. Maybe he should have asked that in the hallway. It looked to Jaybird as if the last breath was leaving Robin's body. His eyes slowly closed and he turned his head toward the window.

Jaybird knew how much boxing meant to Robin. It pained him to see the hurt in his face. But he didn't say a word. Kandy just stood there, silent.

"I will check back later," the doctor said, hanging up the chart after making chicken scratches in a few areas.

Robin just looked ahead and said,

"No, wait. My leg really hurts. I mean, it is throbbing. Could I get some painkillers or something, please?"

"I'll send the nurse around shortly. Hang in there."

With that, the doctor walked out the door.

Jaybird wanted to come up with something comforting to say but he couldn't. He was at a loss for how to act. Robin looked groggy and seemed like he really wasn't in a talking mood, so Jaybird asked, "Robin, is there anything you want or need from me before we head out for Tahiti?"

"I can't think of anything at the moment. I'm kind of fuzzy."

Kandy piped up, trying to act concerned, saying, "How about clothes or eight-tracks? Cassettes maybe?"

"No. I got a TV here with a remote control channel changer. I think I'm good to go," Robin said. He really wanted them to leave. He didn't want to talk to anyone right then. All he could think about was Julie and now he could also worry about not being able to box. He was certain he would never win the heavyweight title now.

After a long silence Jaybird said, "Oh, there is one thing I need to do for you. Where do you want to have your car towed for repairs? Major repairs will be needed. What was the name of your insurance company?"

Robin frowned as he gave Jaybird a serious look, then said, "Insurance!"

"Yeah, insurance coverage."

The look on Robin's face said it all. Jaybird could tell Robin had no insurance.

"Oh, man. They will probably take my license away, huh?"

"Who cares about that. You didn't have insurance and Julie is dead! That sounds like a lawsuit. I'll have my dad send over his lawyer. What were you thinking? No insurance on a Maserati. With the way you drive?"

He didn't mean to chastise him; it was just something Jaybird's father had burned into his head over the two years he had been driving. Never drive anything without insurance. Harry had been in a car with a friend once who had no insurance. His friend had died and the family lost just about everything because of it.

"I just bought the car. I forgot. I never expected…"

Robin turned his head away from them as yet another problem was added to his torture. A moment later a nurse came in and started getting a needle ready for Robin's shot of morphine. Kandy pulled Jaybird up by the arm and they headed out the door. Jaybird waved goodbye, telling Robin he would make sure a lawyer came to see him as soon as possible.

Robin said, "Thanks, now get going. Enjoy your honeymoon."

He never looked in their direction.

As they headed out of the hospital Jaybird imagined how awkward Robin's walk would look with an added limp. He couldn't believe he had neglected to secure insurance coverage. Robin had heard Harry's story about the wreck his friend had just moments after Harry got out of the car. Harry's friend was driving crazily. Harry said, "It's a good thing you have insurance." When the driver laughed about not having any, that's when Harry got out. His friend died a block down the road and it hurt their family emotionally as well as financially. Seems that the car jumped the curb, killing a pedestrian before slamming into a tree and killing the driver.

Back in the room, Robin was again given a shot of morphine. He didn't enjoy getting shots but he felt much better after it hit his bloodstream. He knew this was his mess and he would have to deal with it his way, the best he could. He thanked the nurse for the morphine and tried not to think of all the repercussions that being uninsured would add to his turmoil. But it was no use; that was all he could think about until he fell into a drug-induced sleep.

That afternoon Kandy and Jaybird climbed in the back of the Young family car. Jaybird was still feeling uneasy about leaving while his best friend was in a hospital, but then again, he felt a pull to get away, too. He felt like he had to keep moving or something would catch up to him. What was he running from or to...he didn't know. *Well, just how many honeymoons does one man get?* he thought, trying hard to find some rationalization for his situation. He didn't like the hospital and he never knew what to say to Robin while he was there. It was too surreal to see Robin in a weakened position. It wasn't normal. He knew Robin would pull through. He was tough. He would win in the end. Jaybird had never seen him lose. How could Robin lose?

"Penny for your thoughts," Kandy said, nudging Jaybird's arm.

"I was still contemplating whether or not we should stay here until Robin gets out of the hospital."

"Jaybird," Kandy interrupted, "you know Robin will be up and walking long before he should be. The doctors will yell at him and he will prove them wrong. He will be just fine without you. He will probably be out when we get back. His parents will be there to help him, you know. Besides, he always has a positive attitude about everything. He's pretty strong-willed, you know?"

Although Jaybird had no idea that Kandy had any insight this clear on Robin he replied, "You're probably right, Kandy. I have thought of that, too. This is our honeymoon we're talking about here. Besides, Robin is usually the epitome of positive attitude. He is as solid as a rock. Although I have never seen him so down as he was yesterday, it is understandable."

"He seemed to be handling everything all right to me," Kandy said. She was hoping that he wouldn't delay the trip. She was ready to leave. She would say whatever it took to get him out of Missouri.

"Really? Yeah, I guess you're right."

"Plus he told us to enjoy our honeymoon, didn't he? You shouldn't worry or go against his wishes. He is in good hands at the hospital. The only thing you can do for him is let him work through it himself."

Jaybird drew in a deep breath, then exhaled, saying, "OK. Let's get out of here."

Harry dropped them off at the airport curb and they checked their luggage through with a skycap. The look on the skycap's face when Jaybird tipped him a fifty-dollar bill was a Kodak moment. As Harry was getting back in the car he assured his son that their lawyer would be getting in touch with Robin no later than Tuesday of next week.

During the plane ride, Kandy asked Jaybird what hotel they were staying at.

"The Hotel Bora Bora. It's supposed to be the nicest one there," he said.

"Great. I can't wait to get there and well, you know…get started," she said, holding his hand even tighter. She was sure he wanted to hear that, even though she wasn't looking forward to it as much as she knew he was. *The things I am putting myself through are so hard*, she thought. But she had a master plan, and it was full speed ahead now finally.

"Yes. I do know!" Jaybird said closing his eyes, trying to visualize the moment, like he had done a million times before.

After the long flight Kandy and Jaybird headed across the wooden walkway leading toward their room. The bellboy handed Jaybird the key to the room after he unloaded their luggage. Jaybird was looking at the room number for a second when he noticed the bellboy's hand. It was outstretched, waiting for a tip. Jaybird obliged with a $100 bill this time.

The bellboy said, "Thank you very much, sir!"

"Sir! Did you hear that, Mrs. Young? I just got called sir."

"Great, but don't expect me to be calling you that," Kandy said. *Like that would ever happen*, she thought to herself.

He looked at the room number. It was number two. He had a strange feeling, as if he should be remembering something or that there was something he should pay attention to. But he couldn't explain it. Kandy went straight for the rattan chairs on the veranda of the "fare", which is what the hotel employees had been calling the little cottages. She plopped down and sank deep into the cushions with a heavy sigh. The hotel had built many of the fares over the water, directly atop the magnificent coral reef that was teeming with tropical fish. It was a perfect place to be on vacation.

After Jaybird ordered their dinner, they started browsing the numerous brochures of activities available in and around the hotel.

"What do you think? Para-sailing or snorkeling?" Jaybird asked.

"Massage or the Spa?" Kandy responded.

"Boating or skiing?" he asked.

"Moped or ATV?" she asked.

"Fishing or scuba diving?" he asked.

"Eating or drinking?" she asked, trying to get herself in a good mood.

"Biking or hiking?" he asked, laughing.

"My, there sure is a lot to choose from," Kandy said, laughing along with him as she held up a handful of brochures. Secretly hoping she could do these activities by herself.

They spent a good portion of an hour just examining all the little things placed purposely around the room. The TV movie selections and directions. The room service menus for breakfast, dinner, lunch, brunch and drinks. The hotel stationary and pens with their phone number and address on them. The directions for using the phone, a local paper and how to use the small coffee maker. The handy-dandy dry-cleaning bag in case you needed your swimming trunks or underwear pressed and the iron and ironing board if you were too cheap to get anything dry cleaned. The outrageous prices for anything in the mini bar and of course the Gideon Bible. *Being in a hotel can be so much fun*, Jaybird thought.

At one point Jaybird held up his stack of brochures and suggested that they do everything twice, when there was a knock at the door. Jaybird opened it and the food cart was rolled in. He tipped the man way too much and in return the man thanked Jaybird way too many times, as he left the room. Jaybird looked at Kandy and said, "After we eat, there are a few things you and I should do more than twice also. What do you think?"

Kandy had come in from the veranda so Jaybird wrapped her in his arms. They fell back onto the oversized bed, knocking the fresh flowers off each pillow.

Their honeymoon night had finally began right then and there. Kandy was hungry but knew she had to act like she was enjoying everything he did to her from that moment on. It certainly would be an interesting night of acting, whether she wanted to make love or not. It would definitely be memorable. They were both virgins.

CHAPTER XII

THE VIRGIN sand was hot, deep and untouched by humans for a very long time now. The divers struggled to carry their gear up the beach. They had underwater metal detectors, six large coils of rope, air tanks, coolers and lots of other gear they had to unload from the launches. Someone asked Edward how far it was through the jungle to the lagoon. He told them it wasn't very far. He explained that two of his crew would cut a path and come back after they had broken through the foliage exposing the lagoon. With that said, Edward motioned his two machete men to get on with the defoliation. The two young men headed up the beach as the multitude of crabs quickly scurried away, each somehow finding its own secure hole to hide in. Stopping at the end of the sand the two crew members momentarily surveyed what looked like an impregnable fortress of trees, vines and other tropical underbrush. Realizing their pay would be well-earned today, they began wielding their machetes and commenced to clear a path.

The others sat down to wait under the shade of a huge palm tree whose limbs hung precariously close to the ground. They could hear the slashing of branches slowly fade, as the ocean breeze carried the sound away from them back into the confines of the dark jungle.

Within an hour the two men emerged from the bushes completely drenched in sweat. They informed their boss that the lagoon was not more than one hundred yards inland. Edward told the divers to grab their gear and follow him through the brush.

It was a pleasant walk. The foliage was so thick that the sun couldn't penetrate and there was an abundance of moisture on the leaves that dampened their bodies, subduing the heat even more.

As Edward came up to the clearing his dubiety decreased as his heart-beats started to quicken. He slowed his pace down, almost stopping. Like a child peeking around a corner with uncertainty but anticipation on Christmas day, truly hoping that everything he had been promised was actually there, he broke out into the open. There in front of him was about a two-acre body of water with barely a ripple on its surface. It was such a beautiful light blue color, he could see down twenty feet. The sunlight glistened off it, almost blinding to the un-shaded eye.

Edward knew this was the place. What his eyes were viewing now matched exactly the images from another time. Same place, same soul, different time. His heart began to pound as he remembered.

He instructed the others to take in some fluids first and then get into their scuba gear.

"What are we looking for, Mr. Bloodhead?" a diver asked.

"Out there, about in the middle of the water, will be three metal trunks of valuable…well, let's say…trinkets," he replied, pointing toward the lagoon.

"Do you know how they got there, sir?"

"Yes, I do. They fell out of an alien space ship. Now enough of the questions," Edward snapped.

"You will look for those trunks and when you find them, you'll bring them back up and we will get out of here. It's really that easy. If we don't find them by nightfall, we will come back tomorrow and the next day and the next. Understand this, everyone: I am not leaving without those trunks. All three."

One diver wished to himself that the curse Voodoo had surely placed on Mr. Bloodhead wouldn't affect the whole diving party. He double-checked all his gear just in case. He was sure all the divers were doing the same thing, and he was right.

By the end of the day they had failed to locate any trunks. Edward was disappointed but he realized there was a lot of water to search. They erected tents to house all the gear overnight. The only thing they would need to bring with them the next day would be air tanks. There certainly wouldn't be anyone around to steal anything, so no guard was posted. Edward then ordered everyone back to the yacht. Tomorrow would be a full day of diving. He wanted to get to the trunks as soon as possible.

The moon lit up the deck of the *3 CANES* where the girls were all rubbing their men down with cool lotion to help ease the effects of the hot sun. The music was playing and the wine was flowing. Edward's three women were flirting with him as he got out of the shower and one started tying up his ponytail. The crew had laid out food enough for twice as many people. The crew had grown accustomed to his strange habits. They knew Edward didn't pay any attention to money spent on food and drinks, but he was cheap on things like pay to any part-time help or contractors, although he paid his permanent employees quite well. Consequently the ship's crew had learned to be a little overly generous to guests to ensure everyone had his fill.

One girl asked Edward if he was sure he knew what he was doing by crossing Voodoo. He responded by telling her that he wasn't spooked. He didn't believe in religion in any shape or form: good, bad or magic. They all laughed and one called him a tough-headed man with a pretty face. Another man didn't agree. He thought Bloodhead was just a stupid man, with no idea of who he was dealing with.

As the night wore on, Edward retired before the others around ten PM. He was prepared for the women. He wanted to have sufficient time to play with them. Before heading to the master cabin he reminded the men that they had a full day of searching and it would start early in the morning, regardless of anyone having a hangover. There would be no excuses.

The divers knew their limitations relative to drinking and diving and bid him good night. After Edward left, the party started to pick up a bit. Now that he was gone, many of the remaining inhibitions were dropped. The dancing and drinking went on until about midnight. At that time everyone started to head for his own bunk, ready for some much-needed sleep.

The next day Edward Bloodhead watched the divers submerge into the lagoon. His hopes were once again renewed at the thought of what a full day of diving could bring. He tried to get comfortable in the chair under a large umbrella. He drifted off into a half-sleep while he remembered how he had contracted the metal trunks to be made. He still didn't know how he could remember these things, but he could not care less at this point in his life. He used his strange knowledge to his advantage and never told anyone. He remembered that the blacksmith couldn't understand why he wanted three large empty trunks of metal, each with only a small three inch slot in the top and a thick handle welded on each of the four sides. The blacksmith even laughed at Edward when he had been told that these three foot square trunks were going to be filled all the way to the top with gold coins. But that was exactly what Edward would do. Over a number of years he and his ship of thieves would board other vessels and take everything of value. Edward, whose name during that time, from 1533 to 1566, was Manual de Guzman, was a ruthless pirate. Being the captain of his ship, he would only take the gold coins. Everything else like jewelry, paintings or silverware, was split up evenly with the surviving members of the high seas raid. Ship after ship, year after year, he would put only gold coins into his trunks. They were full of doubloons, double escudo pieces and excelente gold coins, denoting every different denomination of the day. All would be rare to a modern numismatist today, but plentiful in Spain and Europe at that time, especially to anyone who could afford to travel by ocean vessel. The raids were usually very bountiful.

When a trunk became full of coins de Guzman would fill the lock with candle wax, and have the slot sealed up with a metal plate and brought to this lagoon. This would protect the coins until they could be retrieved at a later time, much later, indeed. He knew exactly what he was doing. While Bloodhead had lived as de Guzman he had also been able to recall many lives before that. With that knowledge he concluded that he should be able to remember his past lives once again in the future. He knew he should set himself up for the future if at all possible, so he came up with hiding his stolen treasures. He waited for all the trunks to be filled and then he had his crew drop them into the lagoon of this very island, which was uncharted at the time. After he was back at sea, he had his map depicting the island destroyed. It was a long journey across the ocean just to hide the treasure, but the new lands seemed like the perfect hiding place. He vowed that if anyone ever attempted to locate the island they would suffer a fate worse than being keelhauled. The Captain vowed that any man caught stealing his pilferage, would be flogged or caned with a whip of nine tails, three times. Many a man did suffer that very torture, whether he deserved it or not. That's why Bloodhead had bought the yacht he had now; for the name and what it meant to him and him alone.

The pirate crew dared not cross Captain de Guzman. Never mind any fate he decreed. They both feared and exalted him. He had killed men for much less than just stealing from him. There was no reason to take the Captain's portions anyway, since they were compensated quite well during their pirate raids.

De Guzman knew, even in the 16th century, that gold would be worth much more at a later time than it was then. Gold had always retained its value. Mankind had valued it for eons due to its visual appeal and the fact that it is basically indestructible. It can be melted down and reshaped or recycled over and over again, forever.

Even as Edward cringed at the memory of the horrible death he suffered as de Guzman, he figured this find would make up for it a thousand-fold. But the memory of looking down at the long blood-covered sword protruding from his chest cavity as he watched the light fade to black was enough to make his body shudder, even now. He wasn't able to turn around to see the face of the man who killed him although he had tried. *So much for that old theory of not being able to remember the pain of your own death,* he thought.

Wondering if the trunks would actually still be there after more than 400 years, he opened one eye and scanned the lagoon. He didn't see any divers so he just sat there, anxiously waiting and hoping.

CHAPTER XIII

JUST BEFORE Jaybird opened his eyes he waited, hoping that the night before would be repeated again and again. Something told him it would. As he slowly lifted his lids he could see the morning sun creeping through the window, splitting the room in half two feet over the bed. Jaybird looked at the strange separation of hues, raising his left foot, piercing the stream of light, creating a shadow of his foot on the far wall. He laughed to himself for a second as he tried to create an animal. But it didn't matter; his foot just couldn't contort into anything remotely resembling an animal. A chain-sawed tree stump maybe. Suddenly he realized that his right arm was under Kandy's body and it was completely numb. He tried to pull it out from under her without waking her, but she groaned and started to open her eyes. He told her to go back to sleep and she rolled over and off his arm. He sat up and looked at the uneaten tray of food and started laughing to himself until the tingly sensation of blood corpuscles rushing back into his muscles made him get up and shake his arm vigorously. After that torment was over, he plugged in the small coffee-maker and stepped out on the veranda to inhale the fresh Tahitian morning air. Smiling as he looked down at the swarms of multi-colored fish darting around the reef, he remembered the night before and wondered if making love came naturally to all men the first time. He fancied himself to have done just fine. *It must be the same for everyone,* he thought. Funny how nervous he was until he actually started. The ten months of waiting to make love to Kandy were finally over. No more locker-room lies to cover up the fact that he was still a virgin. Everything seemed new and alive. *It is going to be a wonderful day,* he thought.

Kandy smelled the coffee and opened her eyes, positioning her head so she could see Jaybird leaning over the wooden railing. She reached down between her legs to gently massage that now very tender area. Grinning, she thought to herself how funny it was that she had never imagined in her wildest dreams the pleasure she had experienced the night before. Especially with Jaybird. She had been so consumed with how she *should* act that she couldn't tell where her act stopped and some heat-of-the-moment emotions started showing through. After the first initial pain, she had actually enjoyed the evening. *Maybe love does come later, after you play the game and get what you want first?* No, on second thought, she couldn't allow herself to *really* fall in love with Jaybird. He was merely the prey and she fancied herself winning the hunt.

She remembered that they had groped each other often and seen one another nearly naked a few times before, but never completely naked. She always told him that her religious beliefs wouldn't allow her to have sex till she was married. It had kept Jaybird in constant pursuit. He said he respected that in her, though he would always ask if she had changed religions yet. *Last evening's events make it all seem worth the wait,* she thought. Lying there, trying to decide whether to fall back asleep or get up and pour herself some coffee, a thought flashed in her mind. *Where did Jaybird learn how to make love? How could he know just what to do to make her feel so good, even though she didn't really even want to enjoy it? Maybe it is an instinct that men have,* she mused. *But, maybe it wasn't his first time!* She *had* felt like she was being led the whole night. Not that she really minded much after they had started, but it never occurred to her to take the lead; she had no ideas or inclinations to offer in love-making; she was a virgin. She had been very content with whatever Jaybird suggested they try. She blinked her eyes a few times. She didn't want to think about that right now. She was famished. No time for jealousy.

"Let's go to the beach and order breakfast," Jaybird said from the veranda, almost reading her mind.

"Just what I was thinking: food!"

With that she rolled off the bed and tried to stand but her lower body was very sore so she flopped back down on the bed, groaning, with a smile on her face. It was one of those feel-good pains.

"Mr. Young, could you come over here and explain these pains to me, please?"

Jaybird went to her side. Gently he brushed her long hair away from her face and started kissing her. He then whispered how he would take care of her forever. As they lay there slowly moving their hands to now-familiar places, Kandy felt something starting to swell. She stopped kissing him and held him back at arm's length and said, "Oh, no! No way. Not again. Not so soon."

"No, what?" Jaybird asked mischievously.

"You *know* what. I don't think I will be able to enjoy that for a while. I'm too sore from last night."

He looked at the disheveled bed and knew there would be a lifetime of lovemaking. Now was a time for understanding.

"So it's off to the beach for breakfast then, my little Kandy Cane," he said, adding, "You're all right, aren't you?"

"Yes, I guess so. I'm just a little sore. Let me shower first, then we can go to the beach and eat."

Jaybird held her arm as she rose out of the bed and wobbled towards the bathroom. After a few steps she let go of him. He laughed as he watched her and said, "You walk as funny as Robin does; now hurry up, let's get going!"

They spent the whole day at the beach recovering from the experience of their honeymoon evening, along with their jet lag. In between the many cat-naps and a few rum and cokes, Jaybird told Kandy that he wanted to travel around the country. He wanted to see every historical place in every state. Kandy was up for whatever he wanted. Appeasing him had become easy for her. She just agreed with whatever he wanted. She even mustered up enough gumption to suggest that they pay a visit to every family member on both sides of the family during the vacation. He had agreed with that idea 100 percent.

The sun started to slide down behind the horizon it left what looked like a golden walkway right up to the beach. Dusk was going to be upon them soon. Minutes later the round orange ball disappeared as if the water had quenched its burning embers without a sound.

"You know, the sun isn't really there; it has already set but it takes eight and a half minutes for the last of the light to actually get to earth," Jaybird said, matter-of-factly.

"Great. So how long do you think it will take to see all the lower forty-eight?" Kandy asked, unimpressed with that little bit of info.

"Oh, I don't know; probably four months, but I think we can do it in just two. Why?"

"Well, probably, as fast as you drive! But what would I do about my senior year of high school?"

"Oh, I never thought of that. Let's see…"

Kandy interrupted him saying, "I don't see why I should go to school anymore, do you? I mean, I won't need a job or anything. You, or should I say, *we* have plenty of money."

"You know everyone will think that is a bad idea, but you could just get a G.E.D. or something if you really wanted to. Right?" Jaybird said.

"Sure I could. Any old time. Besides it's our life now, not theirs. We are married. So I say, it's off to see America, then the rest of the world, like that guy…what's his name…um, Bloodhead!" All she could think about were lavish hotels, room service and gifts to remember the trip by. *Perfect,* she thought. She could finally see her mother's goal for her coming true.

"Great, but right now I think we should be off to see a restaurant for some food."

After showering off the suntan lotion, sand and sweat, they dressed and headed up the road on foot. There were a few shops and some small bars with all the regulars sitting in the best seats. They decided to have dinner in a place called Two Tails. Jaybird looked around and saw a table facing the ocean. He asked the hostess if they could sit at that one and before she could hem and haw, he handed her two one-hundred dollar bills. This seemed to make the table readily available. They sat down and began observing the interesting items that decorated the establishment. There was a six-foot blue sailfish mounted on one wall. A ten-foot shark on another. Upon closer scrutiny one could see the deformed tail, which surely was where the restaurant got its name. A large aquarium to their right held as many different colors of fish as you would find in a child's 100-piece crayon pack. Kandy was captivated by how each fish seemed to swim with a particular grace all its own. Jaybird pointed another one out and asked the hostess if she knew its name.

She answered as if she had been asked a thousand times.

"It's a Two-Striped Aphyosemion, sir."

There were many shark jaws, all different sizes, each stripped of its flesh. A wooden wheel from a very old ship had more lacquer coatings than it really needed. In one corner near the ceiling hung a fisherman's net complete with small buoys evenly spaced throughout its mesh. There were even a few old but workable heavy brass portholes that were in dire need of polishing with some brass cleaner. *Get the Brasso*. But the most intriguing article about the restaurant, in Jaybird's opinion, was the old rotting treasure chest by the waiting area. Atop the chest was an expertly dressed pirate dummy with one wooden peg leg and a hook for the left hand. It had a patch over one eye and even a gold tooth. In his good hand was a sword whose tip was lodged in the old rusty lock that secured the trunk, keeping the contents a mystery to all. He was quite a sight. *The children surely enjoyed him the most*, he thought.

After eating dinner they ordered drinks and cuddled closer together, commenting on the fabulous Mahi Mahi dish that was prepared just right. As they were enjoying their Singapore Slings, an old man with a cigar hanging out of his mouth and wearing an old military sailor's cap with yellow "scrambled eggs" on the brim, which were leaf swirls denoting an officer, swaggered toward their table from the right side of the restaurant. He had long white hair and a drawn, leathery-skinned face. He was wearing khaki shorts and a torn shirt with big unlaced Boon Dockers on his feet. The black patch on his eye stood out in contrast to his hair. He did look quite a bit like the dummy up front.

"Aye, thar, mateys. Mighten I ask ye 'bout the dinner ye just scarfed down?"

Kandy started to laugh as Jaybird said it was the best fish he had ever had. Kandy nodded affirmatively.

Exhaling a big cloud of smoke and sitting down, the old man introduced himself.

"Me name's Captain One-Eye. I owns this here joint. An' lemme tell ya, that thar fish ye had was from the biggest dolphin ever caught here off the Bora Bora coast. An' I's should know. I reeled 'im in just two days ago, meself."

"Captain, huh? Well you look like a pirate to me, except for the hat. Didn't pirates have a skull and crossbones on a triangle or pyramid-shaped hat that looked like a boat?" Jaybird asked teasingly as he took a sip of his drink.

"Ya got an eye for authenticity, mate and I's only gets one eye but I is a pirate Captain I are. Someone had to be the leader of them swash-bucklin' scallywags. Stole the hat from a man I skewered, I did!"

Kandy was looking at her empty plate and said squeamishly,

"Yuk...dolphin! I never knew you could eat dolphin."

"Well sure ye can. Fish is fish. Food is food. 'Twas good eating, weren't it?"

"Very," Jaybird said. Quite sure that Mahi Mahi was fish and not a mammal, as dolphins are, he asked, "Did you really catch this particular dolphin we just ate?"

"Surely did. Lemme tell ya a story. I's been fishin' these waters fer darn near thirty years. Ever since I's got retired. Two days ago I'm lookin' fer the catch of the day fer me customers. Ya know, they just love fresh fish. So's I had just put the line in the water when I gets a big hit. I grab me pole an' the fight was on. I fought her fer three hours. Never in me life did I ever fight so hard. She put up one helluva fight, I must say. But she weren't no match fer me. I gets her in the ship and I sees that she is carryin' young 'uns. Thar a squirming around her belly as she lay thar dyin'. So's I take me big knife and carefully split her open as not to harm the babies. One, two. Out they pop. I picked em up and tossed em back in the water. They were about to be born soon anyways, best I could tell. Filleted the mother and that's whatcha had tonight."

"Is any of that true?" Kandy asked.

"Aye, ev'ry word," the Captain said, inhaling a deep breath of cigar smoke.

Jaybird took a drink and said, "So what boat were you captain of?"

"*Ship*! She's a ship!" he bellowed. "Ye never call her a 'boat', matey. A row boat is a boat. But a ship, well, she's like a wife. She deserves respect. She's what makes a sailor a sailor."

Jaybird could see that he was avoiding that question so he asked, "What made you open up a restaurant?"

"I went round the world fer years. I seen ever' port thar was to put a ship into. Had me a cutie-pie in most of 'em, too. I was even better lookin' back then." He winked at Kandy and continued, "But I nev'r had the time to find me fortune. Me ships wouldn't stay long 'nuff at any port. So's I decided to make me landin' here when I hung up me Captain's cap and look fer me treasures around here."

"What kind of treasures, Mr. One-Eye?" Kandy asked.

"Capt'n. Call me Capt'n, missy. Them's pirate treasures, of course. Them crafty ol' pirates used to come down here even before the maps showed these here islands. Only sea stories to most people of the times, but they are true. They would find a place to unload all the plunderin's.

They sprinkled most every island with thar stashes. Some came back fer 'em. Others died before ever returnin', so them treasures are just waitin' to be found. As long as you don't get spooked about any pirate's curse thar might be attached to it."

Jaybird waited for him to continue but he was just puffing away and staring out into the moonlit night. So Jaybird prodded him on. "Did you ever find any pirate's treasures?"

"Aye, matey; I did at that. Found me a gold coin, I did. Still got it. Been told it's worth a least 10,000 dollars. So I's savin' it till I gets old."

Kandy and Jaybird both started to laugh. He already seemed very old to them. With them still laughing he stood up, excused himself, said farewell and swaggered over to the other side of the restaurant where a blond-haired woman was sitting. She had been looking in the direction of their table quite a lot during the Captain's visit with them. Jaybird figured she wanted to ensure she headed to the bathroom if he ever came her direction.

Kandy had noticed her also. She didn't like any woman looking at Jaybird and from where they were sitting she could tell the blond had been dining alone. Not anymore. Captain One Eye was closing in on her table.

"Do you believe there are treasures on every island, Jaybird?"

"No. But I believe he was on a ship once. The rest is probably just crap. Oh, and trust me, we didn't eat any dolphin tonight. Dolphins are protected by law. And what is it with that accent, huh? I mean, no offense, but why do all pirates sound like a bad cross between an Irishman and a drunken Australian? Pirates were from every established country, many were just good sailors who got into a bit of trouble and were mustered out of the service. They certainly didn't all sound like that."

Kandy smiled while stuffing in the last spoonful of her dessert, saying, "Movies, I would guess. Anyway he did look and talk like my idea of a pirate."

Jaybird wasn't listening; he was still contemplating a coin that was worth that much money. *A hundred of those coins and you'd have a million dollars,* he thought.

Shortly they walked out to the deck area, ordered a nightcap and started to plan the next day's events while watching the crabs on the beach scurry around under the moonlight every time the waves washed up onto the beach.

CHAPTER XIV

ROBIN SCURRIED to ensure none of his private body parts were showing as he heard his door open. *Why do hospital gowns all have open backs?* he wondered.

"Robin. Robin S. Duvall?"

"That's what my mom calls me, usually after I've done something wrong," Robin said stoically, looking up at the man in the three-piece suit walking toward him, holding a big black briefcase. He wasn't smiling.

The man held out his hand to shake Robin's and promptly told him that he was Mr. Bill Print, attorney-at-law.

"I sure wish I had just gotten insurance and I wouldn't be in this mess," Robin said. He thought it was to himself but·it wasn't.

"So you didn't secure insurance at the time you bought the car or beforehand?" Mr. Print asked.

"No. I paid cash for my car and I…forgot. I know there isn't any law that says you must have insurance. Even though I was going to get some, well, probably after someone reminded me."

"You are quite right. You don't have to have insurance, but you must have secured sufficient funds to defray the cost of any liabilities," the lawyer said.

"Well, I've got plenty of funds. I have over eight million dollars. That's why I am in this private hospital instead of the general hospital."

"Am I to assume that you are prepared to settle out of court and avoid a wrongful death lawsuit, Mr. Duvall?"

"Sure, I guess so. I don't want to be sued. But, aren't you supposed to help me, like, not have to pay any money?"

"No. That's not my job."

Robin thought that was quite a strange attitude for his lawyer to have right off the bat without much discussion. He sat there for a second wondering if all the drugs he had been requesting were making him not understand the situation fully. As he repositioned his pillow another man came in through his hospital room door.

"Robin Duvall?" Asked another man as he took a step into the room.

"Right you are, but I am busy with my lawyer here. Could you wait a second, Doc? I need some privacy for about ten more minutes."

"I'm not a doctor, I'm Rick Moss, Esq., attorney-at-law. Mr. Young, Jaybird's father, told me that you would be expecting me. I got here as soon as I could. But if you have been advised by other counsel, then I guess I'll be leaving," he said, stepping backward toward the door.

"Wait just a minute. If you're my lawyer," Robin said rather confusedly, "then I must ask Mr. Print here one question: Who the hell are you?"

Mr. Print sat back in his chair as he closed his briefcase. The smirk on his face would have made the most passive person want to stand up and knock it away.

"OK, I say again, who the hell are you, sir?" Robin asked, pointing toward Mr. Print.

"I represent Julie's mother."

Robin looked at Mr. Moss and said, "I think I may have made a tiny mistake. I...I...I'm on painkillers you know, and..."

"Just a minute," Mr. Moss said, interrupting him, "Don't say anything else." With that, the two lawyers exchanged business cards.

Mr. Print started out the door and without turning his head in their direction said, "I'll be in touch."

"I'm sure he will," Mr. Moss said as he put his briefcase down beside the chair. He opened a small note pad, grabbed a pen from his jacket and began asking what Robin had talked about with the other man.

After a few minutes Mr. Moss put down his pad and said, "Well, I wish you hadn't told him you had eight million dollars. That is not good. I doubt he ever would have thought an eighteen-year-old had access to that kind of money. But then again if he is any good he would have found out soon enough. Plus, if he is from around here, chances are he may have heard about you and Mr. Young anyway."

"Sorry, I didn't know who was coming over. Jaybird just mentioned he would have his dad send someone. I just assumed that guy was the someone. If you had been about ten minutes earlier everything would have been much better," Robin said.

"Be that as it may, I think I have everything I need from you. I will do some checking around with the hospital and the police station to see what they have in their reports. I should be getting back to you in a few days."

"I'll be right here. I don't…get around…much with this cast," Robin said in a somber tone. He knew that at any other time he could have made a joke out of the whole situation but nothing seemed funny to him anymore. He wished he didn't even have to talk to anyone. What was the point?

Mr. Moss walked out the door, thinking to himself about this new case. He hoped that he could stave off any kind of lawsuit and maybe just mediate a settlement out of court but from what Robin had told him, the other side knew he had plenty of money. That was not good. He thought to himself that it would be a challenge to ensure that his client retained his money…all except his own fee, of course.

Robin buzzed the nurse. More painkillers was the request. He liked this setup. He buzzed, someone came in and his mind was diverted from the pain and sorrow of Julie's death, if only for a while. He didn't have to deal with it until the drugs wore off and his mind became focused. He was getting very adapted to the feeling of being numb. He even thought about staying submerged in the drugs for the rest of his life.

CHAPTER XV

JAYBIRD SUBMERGED his head and started snorkeling along the reef below the veranda. He knew, somehow instinctively, that smaller sharks could swim in the depth of water he was in, so he stayed vigilant. The fish were varied, plentiful and he was impressed with the multitude of colors. He was astonished at how clear the water was for the 20th century. He had a fleeting recollection from a time long, long ago when all the oceans' waters were virgin and untouched by mankind's overuse. *What a shame,* he thought, *we humans have done so much polluting, especially around large coastal cities.*

Even though he had just arrived there, he had a nagging feeling that he needed to get going again. He truly hated that feeling. It seemed that no matter where he was at the moment, he always had an urge to be somewhere else. As he swam around taking in the wonderful scenery, he wished he could just take things slower. He had tried so many times to count to two or three before just blurting out the first thing that crossed his mind. It never stuck. He would only remember to do it after the fact.

Kandy didn't like water very much and had decided to go shopping. Getting away from him would become harder to do now that they were married. Once out of his sight though, she could be herself and not the perfect little wife. She walked up the street and into each shop along the road just to see if there was anything she might like to buy. Jaybird had given her a handful of bills and said to have fun. She thought how great it was to have her hands full of money. She found some souvenirs for her mother and even picked up a shark jaw for her dad. If they did go visit him, she hoped he wouldn't see the correlation between a shark and what she thought of him. There weren't many sharks on the reservation she figured as she laughed to herself. She would give it to him when or if they got around to driving to Montana.

With one sack full of trinkets, she decided to stop in and have a drink at the Two Tails. Even at seventeen she could pass easily for twenty-one. The bartender didn't even think about carding her. *No need to turn away good money.* As she sipped her drink she noticed a blond woman in glasses and a hat at the end of the bar. She thought it looked like the same woman that the old Captain One-Eye character had sat down with after he left their table the night before. She didn't make friends easily, especially with women, but she really wanted to know what the old guy had talked to her about. She assumed that the Captain always told the same story, but she was curious.

Kandy picked up her drink and walked over to introduce herself. She mentioned that she had seen the Captain talking with her the night before and started to relate some of the conversation he had with her and Jaybird.

Elizabeth started laughing and said, "Yes, he was quite a talker. But he seemed to be more interested in where I had been traveling than anything else. Although he did tell me a story about mermaids that were on some island out there somewhere. I didn't pay much attention after that."

"I wonder where he is. I don't see him here today," Kandy said, looking around.

Elizabeth took a drink and stated, "I'm glad he's not here. He would probably be bothering us again."

After two more drinks the women were having a great time chatting and getting to know each other. Kandy told her she had been with Jaybird for ten months or so and how she had just gotten engaged a week and a half ago and married a short time after that. Elizabeth ogled her engagement ring with the interlocking wedding ring, and then explained how she had met her Eddie. After a few more drinks they were fast becoming friends. With Jaybird nowhere in sight, Kandy could be herself. She laughed as she explained to Elizabeth how hard it was for her to make friends, until today, it seemed.

They were only five years apart in age, and they soon found out that they both really enjoyed strawberry daiquiris. Another amazing thing they discovered was that they had lived about twenty minutes from each other in Missouri. Kandy in St. Joseph and Elizabeth in Faucett.

As the afternoon progressed they shared some good stories, and never once though, did Edward's last name come up. Elizabeth at one point offered her account of the first time she made love and Kandy was going to tell her about her first time but never got a chance to tell her that she had just lost her virginity. Kandy was very interested to hear Elizabeth's story though.

"Oh, I can tell you we were so much in love. He was barely seventeen and I was sixteen. We went everywhere together. It was such a long relationship. Six months, you know. Well, long for me back then," Elizabeth said, laughing. "On this one special night he took me to see a movie, then to the mall to take pictures in this two minute photo booth. Then to a Stuckey's restaurant way out on highway 29, somewhere between Kansas City and Faucett. I mean, all that on the same date. I was so impressed! He even bought a pecan roll, to go."

Kandy giggled as she put her hand on Elizabeth's shoulder and said, "My God, he must have spent a full week's pay on you."

"Oh, I'm sure he did, but he was the Head Dishwasher, you know, so he could afford it."

They both started laughing.

"In Faucett, Missouri? I just can't believe I met someone in Tahiti, from right down the road where I live," Kandy said.

"Yeah. What a trip. Anyhow," Elizabeth continued, "I knew what I was getting primed for and I wanted to do it just as much as he did. We were both virgins, but neither of us wanted to be. Well, to make a long story short, when it finally did happened later that night, way out on a dark back road, well…it lasted all of about three minutes."

"You mean…"

"Yeah, I mean maybe three minutes from start to finish," Elizabeth laughed.

"What did you say to him, um…after?"

"Oh, I told him that it was great. What else did I know? He thought it was great, so I guess we both had a great time."

"So did you, well, you know…"

"I didn't even know what that was at that point. But I found out later when I started to date older, more experienced men. Believe me when I say that men need a lot of practice before they figure out how to use everything correctly. You never want to be with a virgin if you can help it. You know what I mean? It's no fun at all. You only want an experienced man or else *he'll* be the only one that has any fun. They can't please us till we tell them what we want and we as virgins don't know what we want! Right?"

"Oh yes, yes, you are right. Um, my first time was quick too," Kandy said, just to go along with Elizabeth, although she was now beginning to wonder about her first night with Jaybird.

As they continued to chat Kandy couldn't help but think that what Elizabeth had just said made perfect sense. She began to realize that Jaybird had obviously lied to her. There was no way he could have known what to do on their first night in bed. He had clearly been with other women, maybe even many other women.

Elizabeth started to order them both another drink but Kandy declined and made an excuse to leave. She exchanged room numbers with Elizabeth and began walking back to the hotel. Her mind was reeling. Jaybird had some explaining to do. She had always believed Jaybird when he told her she would be the first one and he would wait for their honeymoon. She had always believed that she could snare him into doing everything she wanted by making him wait till they got married. But now it was as if he was somehow aware of her game and had gone behind her back with other women. How could that have happened? She was seeing red. Her mother was obviously right. But how could he have covered up that secret so well?

CHAPTER XVI

"WE FOUND a trunk that is about three-quarters covered with silt, Mr. Bloodhead," a diver said, as he emerged from the water. "It is buried pretty good but we should be able to dig it out."

Edward's heart skipped a beat upon hearing that news.

"Well, it's about time," he said as he ran up the beach and grabbed one end of the thick long pile of coiled rope and gave it to the diver as he stepped out of the water onto the beach.

"Now what you need to do is tie this rope onto the handle and send the others up here to help pull it ashore. Didn't you find more than one?"

"Not yet, sir."

"OK, OK. Never mind. Just tie it tight and take that metal slab over there and use it like a sled. Keep it under the trunk and clear anything that might get in its way. You got that?"

"Yessir!" Everyone had been wondering what the large curved piece of metal was going to be used for. But without something like that, the trunk would be next to impossible to bring up unless they had more manpower or a winch.

The diver took the rope and grabbed the sixty-pound metal slab, dragging it to the water's edge. He put on his goggles, bit his breathing apparatus and re-submerged into the lagoon. As the rope slowly played out, Edward had a crew member tie the other end to the beginning of another pile of rope. It just kept uncoiling. Another leader was tied to the end of that one. Finally the rope stopped moving. Edward figured they were about seventy-five to eighty feet out and down from the shoreline.

Under the water, the first diver motioned all the others to head back to the beach. He then tied the rope around the handle with a blood loop dropper knot and started to dig the silt out from around the front of the metal trunk. Then he positioned the slab of metal so that when they pulled on the trunk it would ease right onto the sled.

On the beach the four divers got out of their gear. They and two of the crew started to pull on the rope. It didn't seem to move for a few seconds, then, as all six of them dug their feet in the sand for traction, they slowly pulled the rope back toward shore. Edward stood by the water and barked out commands to pull. They had six piles of the one-and-a-half-inch thick rope. Each pile was thirty feet long. This trunk hadn't been very far out in the lagoon.

As they labored to keep up with Edward's cadence, the trunk finally broke the surface of the water as the slight inland tide undulated over it. Edward knew the dimensions. Three feet by three feet by three feet. There, after more than 400 years, was one of his trunks.

All seven men began to look at the large chunk of metal that had become rusty and pitted from being underwater for so long. But the walls had not been breached as far as anyone could see.

"How much you think that weighs there?" a diver asked.

"I'd say about 500 pounds," another answered.

"How are we going to get this back to the launches, Mr. Bloodhead?" a deck hand asked.

"We're not. We will just leave this here. When we have all three up here, I will get a helicopter to carry them back to the deck of the '3 CANES'."

Everybody grabbed a drink from the cooler and sat in the shade. They had exhausted themselves by pulling so hard and long. One of the divers whispered to another, "What do you think is in there, eh?"

"I don't even care. I just want to find the other two and get away from this man."

"Are you worried about what kind of curse Voodoo may have put on him?"

"There is no 'may have' about it. Voodoo surely will get even. I wouldn't want to be this Bloodhead man. I really don't even want to be around him."

"It seems that everything is going smoothly so far, though."

The diver crossed his chest in the proper Catholic motion and kissed the cross hanging from his neck, repeating, "So far."

"You men about ready to go or what?" Edward asked impatiently.

Just then the diver who had tied off the trunk in the water poked his head out of the water about sixty feet out in the lagoon. He thought he had seen something as he followed the first trunk up the lagoon floor and had gone back to check it out.

"I have found another one, sir," he yelled, as he swam for the beach.

The other divers were very glad to hear this. The shorter their stay was with Edward, the better off they were, in their minds.

Edward quickly walked over and untied the rope. He told the men to roll the first trunk off the metal slab so they could get the other trunk.

"After the rope stops moving, we will give you three minutes before we start to pull it up. You can have those few minutes to dig out around it. I presume it, too, is buried in silt?"

"Yes, it is, sir. Three minutes then. No problem," the diver said, as he once again started toward the second trunk with rope and metal sled.

The other men waited around the rope. When Edward decided it was time to pull, they did so.

They got the second chest up on the beach. It looked exactly like the first one. By now the men were getting tired. Their forearms, backs and legs were really starting to feel the strain. Luckily for them the sun was sinking lower in the sky by the minute. It looked as if the third chest would have to wait for tomorrow. Edward ordered everyone back to the *3 CANES*.

When they got back, all the women had drinks in their hands for each man. The crew had a fine meal laid out. Edward told the first mate, Duke, to go below and get a case of Dom Perignon. Tonight was a night to celebrate. He felt like he could relax now. Only one more trunk to find. He hoped that tomorrow would bring an end to this search. The music was turned up loud and the evening party was in full swing. The divers seemed to be a bit more at ease now. They were eating and drinking and a few were dancing on the large forward deck.

One diver walked over to Edward and asked, "What is in the trunks, sir?"

Edward looked at him with a roguish grin and said, "Metal. Heavy metal."

"So they are just chunks of iron?"

"Well, it really isn't any of your business, now, is it? I think you will be paid quite well for doing this job. But I don't think knowing what is in the trunks will make much difference to you one way or another," Edward said, looking up at the woman who was running her fingers through his hair.

The diver thought to himself, *How insolent this Bloodhead guy is,* so he just turned and walked away. *He thinks he's so high and mighty,* the diver's thoughts continued. *He probably wouldn't give a drink to a dying man in the desert. Why couldn't he just tell me what was inside the trunks?* he wondered? He hoped that Voodoo had an excruciatingly painful way of killing Bloodhead.

CHAPTER XVII

WHEN KANDY got back inside the room she was still fuming. There were many ideas on how to painfully kill her cheating husband running through her head. She didn't see Jaybird and he wasn't outside the fare either so she flung herself on the bed. The alcohol, combined with the walk back under the hot sun, had burned her out. She thought about how she would confront Jaybird. There seemed to be no other way but to be blunt. She didn't want to be nice anyhow. She was mad as hell. He had beaten her to the punch, she figured. Then it came to her. What was she thinking? She could use this as an excuse to get a divorce. Now that she thought of it, she could still turn this to her advantage. She was sure it would work. It just came sooner than she had anticipated. She had to act furious. Not that she was acting anymore, she *was* furious. She fell asleep flat out on her back, thinking of things to throw at him.

Within twenty minutes Jaybird came in with a handful of shells, not to mention sand and salt all over his body, plus a sunburn. He headed for the shower, being careful not to wake Kandy. When he came out she was sitting up on the edge of the bed.

"Hello there, Mrs. Young; how was your day?"

"I did have some fun until I found out you have been with other women!" she snapped at him.

Jaybird was stopped in his tracks. He started to laugh but he could see that she had a stern look on her face.

"What on earth are you talking about, Kandy?"

"Why don't you just tell me who they were, Jaybird?" she demanded.

"I have no idea what you are talking about. What women? What do you mean you found out?"

"Well?"

"Well, what? Kandy, you know you were the first," he said, as he moved to sit next to her on the bed. But Kandy got up quickly.

"Don't lie to me. I was talking to a new friend of mine and she said that no man ever knows what to do the first time. But you did. How do you explain that, huh? Go ahead, try," she said, her voice becoming quite loud.

Jaybird realized that he couldn't really explain it but he tried anyway.

"I feel like I am defending myself and I haven't done anything wrong. I have never been with anyone else until last night. Honestly, I only did what came naturally to me. There wasn't anything hard about it."

"But you knew exactly what to do. I...I had no clue!"

"Kandy, I can't really explain it. I didn't know what to do either, I just did it."

"Well, my friend told me that she made sure she found men who had been with other women because virgins don't have any experience. She never wanted to be with another virgin, they were so, so...lame."

"So you believe everything *she* says now?"

"I believe some things that make sense to me. And that makes sense."

"Does your friend have a name?"

"Elizabeth...something."

"Have you been drinking?" he asked, knowing full well she had been.

"What if I have? That won't change a thing here."

"Kandy, I swear to you that you were the first. I promise you."

"You promise?"

"Yes."

Kandy paced the room in silence as Jaybird sat on the bed, bewildered. She knew he had never broken a promise, nor lied, at least not until the marriage license fiasco. Finally cooling down a bit, she said, "But how could you be so, so…. how could you last so long? And we did it like five times, too."

"Is that bad?"

"No, it wasn't bad, but Liz said the guy she did it with the first time was a virgin also and he only lasted three minutes. And could only do it once."

"Did you ever think that maybe the guy had a problem?"

"What kind of a problem?"

"I don't know. But we all can't be the same, I guess. Everybody must be different. Maybe I'm normal and he was abnormal."

"Oh. Well, I um…. I never thought of that."

Jaybird stood up saying, "I've loved you and only you for ten months now. I couldn't even think of being with anyone else but you." With that he started to sing *their* song: "Please, Please Me."

Kandy turned to face the wall and rethought the whole scenario. She really didn't want to believe Jaybird. She wanted to be angry. But he had never lied to *her* before, as far as she knew. Why would he start now? She started wondering if she was still acting or if she really cared. After a minute of contemplating she decided to apologize. She needed more time to figure out her feelings. She had to try and understand why all of a sudden she was getting such strong feelings. She felt confused.

"I'm sorry for this whole argument. It must just be my stupid insecurities. Can you forgive me?"

"I think it was the alcohol. But I will forgive you if you promise to rub Noxema on my back. I am really sore and sunburned from swimming around all day."

Kandy sauntered over to the bed and kissed his forehead. She was calming down. She told him to lie down on the bed. "I promise to cool your back off," she whispered in his ear, adding, "I will start right now." And with that she grabbed the blue jar on the night stand and began to lightly rub the cream on his back and arms, careful not to rub too hard on the red areas about his shoulders and neck. She seemed to actually like touching him. Her mind was as confused as it ever had been. She felt her plan slipping away somehow. She knew she needed more sleep. She needed to regroup and get her plan back on track.

Jaybird lay there wondering how she could even consider such an idea. She had shown some jealousy before but nothing to this extreme. Robin had tried a few times to discuss her behavior with him but Jaybird wouldn't hear of it. He was in love. Love conquers all. It must have been the liquor in Kandy doing the talking. They had never had more than a few beers before, at least when she was with him. Then again, maybe it wasn't the alcohol. A fleeting thought crossed his mind; maybe she would always be like this in their marriage. He didn't know if he liked that idea. They had only been married for a short time and he was already seeing a change in her behavior. He closed his eyes and tried to enjoy the coolness of the cream on his back. He knew he was getting tired of her jealousies. Maybe he *had* made another spur-of-the-moment decision by marrying her. He hoped it was the right decision.

After a nice long nap both were feeling better.

"Maybe I should ask my friend to go to dinner with us tonight. Then you could talk to her about this problem her first lover had," Kandy said, as she got up from the bed.

"I don't see any point in that. Besides it sounds like 'girl talk' to me."

"Come on, she's nice and I think she is lonely. Her boyfriend is off on a boat somewhere."

"Is her a boat or is her a ship?" Jaybird said gruffly, trying to sound like that old pirate.

She genuinely laughed and said, "Please? I have her room number right here."

"Whatever, I guess it's cool. Give her a call."

Kandy called room 33, but Elizabeth was not in, so she left a message with the concierge for her to meet them at Two Tails around eight o'clock for dinner if she wanted to.

About an hour later they got dressed and started walking toward the Two Tails restaurant. Standing inside, Kandy said, "Well, I don't see her. I guess we could have just gone over and knocked on her door."

"Yeah, but maybe she had something else planned," Jaybird said.

They were seated at the best table in the house and soon they had another excellent dinner. The service had picked up about five notches. It must have had something to do with the hundred-dollar tips Jaybird had given to everyone involved with their last dinner there the night before. He continued the tipping even against all of Kandy's objections.

After dinner back in the hotel room, as Jaybird waited for Kandy to get out of the bathroom, he wondered why the Captain character never showed up again. It didn't matter; he was ready to make love, but try as he might to stay awake, he just couldn't keep his eyes open. He was certainly high enough from all the drinks, not to mention tired from snorkeling; moments later he was asleep.

CHAPTER XVIII

"NURSE, ANOTHER shot, pretty please," Robin pleaded, after deciding that he wasn't high enough.

"Mr. Duvall, you are such a strong-looking young man. Are you sure your knee hurts so much all the time that you must resort to whining?" the nurse asked as she checked the chart for the last time he had been given painkillers.

"I have a bad injury here, Nurse Chapel; I believe you should just ask Doctor McCoy how bad this knee is.

"That's not the doctor's name and I'm not Nurse Chapel either."

"Oh yes, he's *Bones,* isn't he?" Robin said chuckling to himself as the nurse smiled, not really knowing in the least what he was referring to. She was sure he was not feeling any pain at the moment from the incoherent way he spoke. She also knew that everybody had a different threshold for pain. She provided him with another shot of morphine, as he asked.

He laid his head back on the pillow and looked at the TV. An instant rush shot through his body. He felt better. It wasn't the physical pain he was trying to ease; it was the mental pain. For now he didn't have to think about Julie being dead. He could just watch another rerun of *Gilligan's Island* and hope this time they would get rescued.

When the doctor came in a few hours later, Robin asked if he could go home soon.

"I believe you can leave on Saturday morning after we take those stitches out."

"Does that hurt much?" Robin asked.

"Not as much as having your face punched on inside the ring, I would presume."

"That never hurts until the next day. But I guess it does sound painful. Of course you *do* get used to it. So. Saturday. Good. I can't wait. You can prescribe more painkillers for me at home, right?"

"Of course, Mr. Duvall, but you know you will have to come back in three weeks for a check up?"

"Remind me again later, please. I'm not remembering too much today."

"Of course," the doctor said as he left.

Just then Robin did remember that he was supposed to have had another fight on Saturday. *That was completely shot to hell*, he thought. All his life he had been good at looking on the bright side of things. He always loved to make people laugh. Then he found boxing at Jaybird's coaxing. He found that he loved to be a winner. He could hit people as hard as he liked which served as a stress reliever actually, not that he really had much stress. *Laughter and pain. Strange combo*, he thought. As he changed the channel to the national news he wondered if he had the drive to get his knee back into tiptop shape or if the knee was going to cooperate. Right now he couldn't see trying very hard at rehab. He certainly had enough money to get the best physical therapist though. Although he would certainly need a job if he lost the lawsuit. But his drive seemed to be all gone at this point. *Could he live without boxing?* he wondered. *Did it matter?* He had killed a girl. There was no bright side to look forward to.

Just before visiting hours were over, his boxing coach, Adam, came by to visit. The coach tried to get Robin pumped up enough to at least *say* he wanted to fight again. Robin tried to be honest with him. He told the coach that he didn't know if he could do it. So the coach got down and dirty.

"You know your money won't last forever. You need an income or you will spend it all. It won't take long for a young man to spend what you've got. You need a goal: something to shoot for. Without that you will just get bored with life."

"I will never run out of money, coach. And I do have a goal: To walk. That's about the best outlook the doctor has given me. To walk. Pretty dim, don't you think?"

They talked for about fifteen minutes then the coach left. Adam had hoped to persuade Robin to set a goal for himself and put forth an effort into reaching it. He didn't have a warm and fuzzy feeling as he left Robin's room. He could feel Robin's pain. He feared he had not done much good.

CHAPTER XIX

MR. VAN Tangle didn't always have a warm and fuzzy feeling about calling his boss when he didn't have much to report, but this time he had plenty of stuff to talk about. He always tried to have enough information to warrant a call to his employer. Sometimes he felt like he would be fired if he didn't have much info, but Dr. Young always seemed satisfied with what ever he had to present, so he dialed the number anyway.

"Dr. Young?" asked the voice on the phone.

"Yes, this is Nicholas Young."

"This is Van Tangle."

"So, Mr. VT, what is the scoop on my nephew?"

"Well, sir, he is married now as you know, and was just in Tahiti for his honeymoon. His wife is a good-looking young lady too. They make a cute couple," Van Tangle reported.

"Far out. Yes, I knew all that from Nan's phone call. Does seem odd though. I mean, him being old enough to be married already."

"That isn't the half of it, sir."

"What are you talking about, VT?"

"Well, sir, I believe that Edward Bloodhead was in Tahiti also."

"Really? Well, I'll be an uncle's monkey! I wonder what the odds of that happening were? We lose leads on Edward, follow Jaybird and find

Edward again. Hmm."

"Yes, well, anyhow, I saw Elizabeth at the very same restaurant where Jaybird and his wife were. I checked it out and sure enough, Bloodhead's yacht had pulled into the bay briefly, but I don't think he was staying at the hotel."

"Did they bump into each other?" Nicholas asked.

"I don't think they ever crossed paths," Van Tangle said, not knowing of the encounter between Kandy and Elizabeth.

"Wow, this is very interesting, man. OK, go ahead and give me the whole scoop; break it down for me."

Van Tangle proceeded to brief Nicholas on the movements of Jaybird and the information he had been able to acquire about Edward, which was sparse. He provided him with times and places for the entire time Jaybird and his wife spent in Tahiti. Nicholas was making mental notes. After Van Tangle was done he asked him the same question he always did, "So, who were you this time?"

"I was a pirate who owned a seafood restaurant, sir," Van Tangle said, rather proudly.

"Oh, dude, you never cease to amaze me. Groovy job; thanks, man. Tell you what: I've changed my mind. Start keeping Edward under surveillance again. Hmm, yes, that's the idea. If you have anything…well, you know…interesting, don't hesitate to call me."

"Not a problem, sir. I'll stick by Edward as best I can. Oh, I did happen to find out from a longshoreman who had heard that the *3 CANES* was to set sail for Monaco next. I'll head there as soon as I can get a ticket out of here. I haven't seen his yacht here so they may have already headed out." With that said they both hung up.

Nicholas Young was a bio-scientist by trade. He worked in a research lab that conducted experiments on DNA, chromosomes and genes: a fascinating field of study for him. He had long silver hair, as if he just couldn't let go of the sixties. He was an ex-hippie who had a good job *in* the establishment but sometimes forgot it was the late seventies. He pretty much had the look of a mad scientist, but his personality made him a genuine pleasure to be around.

The information he had received on Jaybird and Edward needed to be given to the other members soon. The members of 'The Calm' would be excited to hear that these two men had almost crossed paths. There hadn't been much news to speak of recently in the meetings. It had been ten years since they discovered Edward was a 'Knower' and the group had been watching him ever since. He was very reclusive at times which made him difficult to track. Nicholas had asked Van Tangle to keep an eye on Jaybird in Tahiti after his sister-in-law, Nan, had called about her son's quick marriage and honeymoon plans. Since VT hadn't had a lead on Edward in months, Nicholas figured it would give him something to stay busy with. What luck it was that both of them were in Tahiti at the same time. *Or was it luck*, he pondered? Nicholas had known that Jaybird was a 'Knower' from the first time he held Jaybird as a youngster. He mused about what would happen if those two ever came in contact with each other. 'The Calm' members also would enjoy knowing what would happen if that occurred. Would there be fireworks or not? You just never knew how someone would act after becoming aware that the other one had killed him in a past life. It was always an eye-opener.

CHAPTER XX

TIME TO rise and shine, Edward thought as he opened his eyes. It was still dark out side and the air was humid. It would be another hot day. He decided to shower off the sweat and other body fluids from the night before. He was enjoying having three women to sleep with each night. But they were just whores. He thought of Elizabeth for a second. She loved him but he knew he would get caught someday cheating on her or something and her beautiful body would not be his any longer. No matter. There were others to be had. He was only biding time with her. He didn't love her anyway and the thrill of victory in just getting her for himself was all but over. He only loved money. Everything else came second. He just wanted to be the richest man in the world. He wanted to always be the richest man in the world. In every life from here on out, forever.

After showering, he drank his cappuccino and watched the sun start to peek over the horizon. The sunlight created long shadows on the deck. He thought how different his life had become since that strange day in San Francisco ten years earlier.

It was just another boring fashion show for some snot-nosed faggot designer, he thought. Oh, he didn't mind the money but the people around him were so often on the fringe of society. Drugs and back stabbing were just added courses to the slimy menu. For appetizers he could have lesbians, pedophiles or some religious cult freaks. For dessert there were fat people, foreigners or just plain old idiots. He hated *all* people that he thought were not like himself: white, blond, intelligent and perfect-looking. His conceit for himself and bigotry toward others was ancient and ran deep. He had no idea why. Things were about to change for him.

He took another sip from his cup as he remembered how he had been killing time that pivotal night. Killing time between shows, he had wandered over to a book exhibit inside the cramped booths at the convention center. Some man was explaining his book to a young woman of beauty. Edward had thought of an intriguing remark to get her attention focused on him. As he started towards her he brushed against the forearm of the author who had just finished signing his book for the young lady. The man was Dr. Nicholas Young.

Edward couldn't explain to his own satisfaction what had happened to him the moment he brushed against that man. It was as if he had been suddenly filled up with memories. Things he couldn't have known were now somehow sitting as facts in his mind; like they had always been there but he had just never needed to remember them. He laughed at how he had staggered back to the dressing room. He had barely gotten dressed in time for the next runway showing. After the gig he sat in his penthouse hotel room and started to write down on paper all the things he could remember, but that was a futile act; there were too many to even count. Edward knew suddenly, somehow *now* that he had been to many places; he had been many people; he knew many more things than a just a short while ago. He knew he had taken and hidden many things of value. He also realized that he had to recover them all. The decision to quit the modeling business had taken about ten minutes. His new goal was his old ancient goal and that was to find his own hidden treasures by whatever means necessary, no matter who stood in the way. Then he could begin work on eradicating the world of what he called the scum of the earth. To do that in today's world he had to be very rich and very powerful. Even though he had been many different nationalities, sizes, weights, and skin colors in past lives, he retained many of his current bigotries. He hated everyone!

As the divers started emerging from their rooms they quickly grabbed some breakfast. Within an hour they were heading back into the lagoon.

It didn't take long for the third trunk to be found. After they got it up on the beach, Edward felt totally relieved. He had the divers and deck hands load all the gear back on the launches. Once back on the *3 CANES* they weighed anchor and headed for the bay where they could drop off the workers. The first mate radioed ahead to see if anyone at harbor operations could locate Voodoo and inform him that they were returning. Everyone knew how to get hold of him. He was the local shaman.

When they approached the pier, Voodoo did have the same old bus waiting there. Once everything and everybody was off-loaded, Voodoo walked over to Edward and the first mate. All three stood glaring at one another for a short few seconds then Duke handed Voodoo the other half of the money he had been promised. As soon as Voodoo put it in his pocket he leaned toward Edward and sprayed the contents of his mouth all over his former employer. Duke quickly reached around and grabbed Voodoo by the neck of his shirt and was in the middle of what was sure to be the knockout punch when Edward reached for his arm, stopping him from completing the swing. Voodoo was smiling and giddy, saying something about how Edward had a short time to live. Edward was also laughing. He knew someone did only have a short time to live but it wasn't him; it was Voodoo.

As Edward grabbed his handkerchief and started wiping his face he said, "Oh, animal blood, now that's good. I haven't seen that for a while. Shall we find a virgin, too, or don't you like the taste of human blood?"

Voodoo shoved Duke's hand away and said, "You will die before the next full moon, Bloodhead." Then he walked back over to the bus. Edward was amused but he had more important things to do than worry about a man who thought he had some mystical powers. He knew Voodoo fancied himself to have such powers. Edward knew that Voodoo really had nothing at all. Edward actually had the power, because money was power. Voodoo had very little of it and Edward had too much. More than any thirty-year-old really needed.

Edward told Duke to forget Voodoo and go secure a helicopter, one with a heavy duty winch setup on it. He then walked mischievously toward the bus as it started to pull away. He could see all the heads inside turning to watch him. He knew what they were thinking. They most assuredly believed that what Voodoo had just done to him would surely kill him. Edward just laughed out loud.

He then told the captain to call the hotel on the short-wave radio and leave a message for Elizabeth to meet the helicopter at the airport charter services in three hours so she could rendezvous with the yacht before dark.

The deck hands met the helicopter at the beach and secured the trunks for transportation. After all three were on board the yacht, Duke went back to wait for Elizabeth. Edward had told Duke to wait for her 'til dark. Then, after he dropped her off on the yacht, he was to take the speed-boat back to Aratika. Duke was then to kill Voodoo for the three stupid mistakes he had made. Edward laughed as he thought of the scenario. Who would even suspect him of a murder when at least eight people saw Voodoo place a so-called evil curse on him three different times. Now all he had to do was wait for Elizabeth. If she didn't make the ride back before it got dark, he had ordered Duke to leave without her. He was growing so tired of her. He laughed as he took a sip of his drink and ordered dinner from the galley.

Elizabeth had gotten the message and was waiting at the pier early to be brought back on board. She was fast asleep now next to Edward.

It was three o'clock in the morning when Duke got back aboard.

Edward was awakened by the sound of the anchor being hoisted. He had told the captain to set a course for Monaco upon Duke's return. Edward could rest soundly now. His dirty work was taken care of and the ship was making its way out toward open waters.

CHAPTER XXI

MAKING HIS way back over to the porch swing, Robin began swinging and listening to his favorite music. He had strung two long wires from the stereo system to the speakers and moved them out on the porch. He had loaded up four LPs on the phonograph and felt he was good for about two hours. He was glad he had bought his parents a new house. He always wanted them to have more space. Just then his father, Donnelly, came out and sat by him on the wide wooden swing and said, "That was Mr. Moss on the phone. He is on his way over here to talk to you."

"OK. I was wondering what happened to him. It's been a week since I got out of the hospital."

"I hope for your sake he has some good news."

"At this point, Dad, anything would be good news. It couldn't get any worse."

"So, how is the knee feeling today, son?"

"Not bad, I just wish I could scratch it right here," Robin said as he pointed to the middle of the cast on his leg.

His father laughed, saying, "The next seven weeks will fly by, you just wait and see."

"I think that all I can do *is* wait, Dad."

Within forty-five minutes Mr. Moss drove up to the curb and proceeded to climb out of the Delta 88 with his black briefcase in hand.

After some pleasantries he got down to business.

"Well Robin, I checked with the police and they didn't cite you with any violation because it was a single car accident. They couldn't get you for drag-racing because they didn't even know that's what you were doing because everyone else bugged out on you, plus you didn't destroy any property so there will be no property damage claim to settle. You didn't have any insurance so there are no claims from your side to deal with. That is the good news."

"And the bad news, Mr. Moss?" Robin prodded.

"The bad news is that Mrs. Christina Volt, Julie's mom, is suing you for personal damages and wrongful death."

Donnelly had to ask; he could see Robin couldn't get the obvious question out.

"Suing for how much?"

"Eight million dollars, Mr. Duvall."

"But that's about all I have!" Robin said in disbelief.

"It could been worse," Mr. Moss said bluntly.

Robin looked at him in disbelief and asked, "What could make it worse?"

"She could be suing you for ten million."

"Is that supposed to be funny?"

"I'm a lawyer; I don't have a sense of humor. I just present the facts. At least if we lose, the worst-case scenario should be only eight million. But also remember that if this goes to trial, the jury could lower that amount or they could raise it. Oh, and all of that is excluding my fee."

Robin turned his head toward his dad and remembered that he hadn't asked the fee question yet. Now seemed like the time. "And what is your fee?"

"I am charging you 80,000 dollars if we lose and 100,000 if we win."

"That seems fair, Mr. Moss. Doesn't it, dad?"

"Quite," his dad answered.

Robin's mother, Marsha, came out with a pitcher of sun tea and poured everyone a glass. The day was very hot and muggy, which was normal for an early Missouri summer afternoon. There seemed to be a moment of silence that was broken by the sound of a chain saw cutting something down a few houses up the street.

"What are the chances of winning this…this wrongful death suit then?" Donnelly asked.

"I think I can prove that it was simply a case of engine malfunction and get a reduced settlement. I think eight million is a bit much for something that was unavoidable. That rod would have let go no matter where you were going or what you were doing. So I give our chances about sixty-forty in our favor."

As they discussed more *what-ifs*, Robin started to think of how quickly things seemed to come and go. One day he had a girl he liked, then she was gone. One day he had no money, then he had lots of it. Now it looked like it would be gone. One day he had a promising boxing career and now it, too, might be gone. Everything was always getting taken away from him. He remembered the same feelings from when he knew the flagman, whatever his name was then or is now. He knew that in a past life with the flagman, long before this time, he was confronted with great loss also. He pondered just how he was going to come to grips with all of these things rolling around in his head. He grabbed a few of the codeine pills the doctor prescribed and swallowed them, washing them down with the iced tea. These pills were not working as well as the shots of morphine though. He felt he must find something stronger. His happy world had fallen to pieces. He needed to relieve the pain. After Mr. Moss left, Robin daydreamed for a few hours on the porch swing, just listening to his music.

That night as Robin started to fall asleep, he decided to make himself a promise. If Jaybird could always keep a promise, then so could he. He knew he needed a goal in his life again but he needed to honor Julie's memory in some way also. Jaybird had always said, "Just make your mind up and don't look back." So Robin thought hard. He concluded that he needed something that would remind him daily of both what he had done and what he wanted to do. So, after hours of restless tossing and turning with the cast itching and his mind reeling, he finally decided. He promised himself that he would only talk in verse, just song lyrics, until he was the heavyweight champion of the world. He felt this sacrifice would enable him to somehow address, daily, the deep sorrow he would always have for Julie's death, yet put him on a path to his goal which should…someday, hopefully…make him feel good again and to be Number One. No one could change his mind now; he was making his mind up and he wasn't looking back. Hell, if Jaybird could always keep his promise then, damn it, so could he. He figured he might just be the first person to ever attempt this. He felt pleased with himself as he fell into a deep sleep at last.

CHAPTER XXII

JAYBIRD FELT pleased about how the Tahiti trip panned out. There were moments that were not so good, but that's life, he figured. He and Kandy hadn't even been back from the airport for two minutes before he called Robin to see how he was. Donnelly told him that he and Kandy should drop by whenever they felt like it the next day.

When Jaybird awoke, he had already decided to go out and buy a large motor home. Jaybird had fun talking the salesman down to his rock bottom price, a price that he just wouldn't budge from, then asking him what a person could get the vehicle for if they paid in cash. After the salesman stopped laughing, he said that if anyone had that kind of cash he could let it go for about ten thousand less. The look on his face was clearly a Kodak moment as Jaybird got out his checkbook and started writing. The salesman came back after clearing the amount with the bank and handed him the keys to their new Winnebago, along with an arm full of papers they had to fill out. They sat in the air-conditioned motor home finishing up the paper work. Kandy was just bored. She wanted to be buying things for herself.

Jaybird called the insurance man and secured his coverage. *Such a simple thing to do to stay out of any kind of trouble,* he mused. He wished he had been with Robin when he bought his Maserati. He would surely have reminded him of the insurance.

"Can you drive a big thing like this?" Kandy asked, as she sat down on the huge swiveling passenger seat. "I mean, they wouldn't even let us test-drive it. The salesman had to drive."

"Well, I guess we will just have to find out. Here goes. I mean what's a few trees between friends anyway?" Jaybird said as he started moving the giant wheeled house forward. Kandy just rolled her eyes. She did of course force a chuckle out for Jaybird's benefit. She really hated it when she caught herself wondering if she meant to laugh honestly or if she was putting on the act.

As they pulled up in front of his parents' house and climbed out of the front doors, Jaybird's dad and mom came out to see what kind of a monster had stopped next to their driveway.

"So, tell me this is a loaner," Harry said as he walked towards them.

"No. I bought it," Jaybird replied excitedly.

"We are going to see all the states and all the family. On both sides. Maybe go into Mexico later on down the road."

"Oh, now; that's a fine idea, Jaybird. I've got all the addresses in the roll-top desk," Nan said.

Harry was just shaking his head. He wondered if giving Jaybird all that money at eighteen was such a good idea after all. But it was Jaybird's to do with as he pleased. Harry decided to at least try and stop worrying about it. He knew he should let Jaybird handle his own life. It was just hard for him to watch his son make what he considered mistakes. He tried not to care, but he loved his son. He cared so much, but knew he had to let Jaybird go on his own, to make his own triumphs and mistakes. They all climbed inside for the grand tour.

The quest started on July second, after getting the family addresses from both their mothers. Jaybird and Kandy decided to go see her father in Montana first. Kandy hadn't seen him since she was ten and she really just wanted to get it out of the way as fast as possible. Jaybird thought he was being so nice by seeing her dad first. He didn't know how Kandy felt about her father.

Robin was going to ride along also after much prodding from everyone. Except Kandy of course. His cast would be on for six-and-a-half more weeks anyhow. There was no reason for him to be stuck in good ol' St. Joe the whole time. Kandy and Jaybird spent the two days prior buying things for the motor home. They bought a TV, a top-of-the-line cassette deck with a new gadget called auto reverse. No more stopping to flip the tape over right in the middle of "Free Bird". They bought loads of cassettes. They bought just about everything they saw. There was just so much stuff to have. Kandy wanted it all and Jaybird was buying it for her. They were enjoying each other but it was costing a bunch of money.

The trek to visit all the relatives started out very exciting for Jaybird but Kandy was ambivalent and Robin definitely wasn't his usual self. When Donnelly told Jaybird that Robin had written down his intentions and commitment to talking only in verse, Jaybird figured it was a joke. Besides he just hadn't had a chance to talk to Robin mano-a-mano lately. Surely Robin would talk to his best friend. He told Kandy that they should just play along with Robin for the time being.

The crash and all that had ensued did seem to Jaybird to have taken away Robin's zest for life. But this was a summer road trip with all the trimmings. Jaybird tried hard to get the other two excited. Yet Robin just listened and nodded when spoken to. No joke or comment could entice Robin to break his new vow. It was easier for Jaybird and Kandy to just not include him in any conversation. Unless a yes or no head motion would work. At least Robin would still do that.

On the evening of the fourth of July, after another full day of Robin not saying a word, there were fireworks lighting up the sky off in the distance. They pulled over to watch them when they found a clearing at the roadside. Jaybird remarked that it reminded him of Disneyland in the evening. His father had taken the family there when Jaybird was only five years old, but he could still remember the bumper car ride he loved so much.

Robin remembered back when his father also had splurged and taken their family to Disneyland prior to having marital problems with his wife, Marsha.

Robin suddenly, out of nowhere, started singing "Wish You Were Here," by Pink Floyd, quite a bit off pitch.

Kandy and Jaybird just sat there quietly and watched the spectacular light show without saying a word. Inside Jaybird knew what Robin was trying to relate. Just two lost souls, he repeated to himself. Robin must have really wanted to share this moment with Julie. *Maybe I am way off base with this interpretation*, he thought to himself. Then just as that thought crossed his mind, Jaybird knew he *was* off base and that he now truly understood what Robin meant. Robin must have been talking about the two of *them*. Jaybird knew he had been friends with Robin many times before in past lives. And although he didn't quite understand how he could know this, it was clear to him that they had seen and done so many things together. He also knew that in every life that they were together, he had died before Robin. Every single time. Well, on third thought, maybe he was being too narcissistic. Robin was probably talking about Julie. He wondered if Robin had been with her in a past life, also.

He wondered how long Robin could keep this strange personal quest going. At least he still had a voice; it had been a long while since they had heard Robin's voice. Jaybird missed the banter a best friend provided. He missed the fun. Kandy didn't seem to be filling the void in the fun department.

Jaybird looked at Kandy and decided to tell her a story about the *Pirates of the Caribbean* ride at Disneyland. It had broken down in the middle of the ride and they all had to get out and walk behind a wall to an exit. This totally deflated the excitement of the rest of the rides for him, since he was only five years old. After that, he was always thinking that the ride he was on could break down also. He found himself constantly looking for an exit on every ride, it took the magic out of the whole experience.

Kandy had rarely been out of the St. Joseph area. The farthest she had traveled, up to the beginning of this summer, was when she and Jaybird had gotten married. Her mom had taken her to Kansas City to an amusement park called Worlds of Fun once, but that was it.

In the beginning of their trek they listened to music and periodically Jaybird told stories. Although Robin didn't say anything, he did sing a few times, mostly he would just pop some painkillers in his mouth, fall silent and sleep for long periods of time.

Jaybird would stop at every historical site and at every "must see" place that the ever-present billboards advertised. Kandy, of course, kept badgering Jaybird about every female in sight. No matter how they looked, whether they were fifty feet away or behind a cashier's counter at a gas station in the middle of nowhere, she just had to act jealous. With only three days into the trip Jaybird was getting sick and tired of it. So was Robin. He couldn't for the life of him see what Jaybird found in her personality to like. At one point he sang out:

Happiness is a warm gun, yes it is,

Happiness is a warm gun, yes it is,

When I hold you in my hands,

I know nobody can do me no harm,

And I feel your hand on my trigger,

I know no one can do me no harm,

Happiness is a warm gun, yeah.

Jaybird got the personal hint, but Kandy didn't have a clue. She had tuned Robin out long ago.

During the long stretches when no one was talking, which were many, as the dirty yellow stripes just kept blinking by, each person became immersed in his or her own daydreams. With music always playing, Jaybird reflected on the place he first heard a particular song or who he was with or what he was doing when he first heard it. Robin was wondering if he could pen Rock and Roll as well as he had composed music while he was Beethoven. Kandy would remember what store she was in when she heard particular songs. There were lots of long stretches.

When Kandy wasn't deciding in her head on the place and time to leave Jaybird, she would wonder how she would react to her father. She had been so young when her parents got divorced. She had received only a few birthday cards from him and they had contained only small impersonal and unrevealing notes scribbled on them. She had been bombarded by her mother's views of her father and those views weren't particularly nice ones. She really didn't want to see him but then, he was her father. She wondered what she would say to him. She was getting nervous. He was the whole reason she was planning to screw Jaybird over. She got knots in the pit of her stomach just thinking of what her father had done to her mother.

Robin was watching the miles of corn fields go by as they went through northern Nebraska. Field after field. Farm after farm. The light golden stalks bending in the breeze, creating a mesmerizing ripple effect. He was stuck in a dazed stare. He didn't want to hear his favorite song but he knew sooner or later Jaybird would put it on, just for him. He just didn't want to tell Jaybird that it would remind him of Julie. So, he wouldn't. When "Little GTO" did come on, all Robin could think of was how much fun he had with Julie just cruising around in his new car and talking with her those few times. He was sure that that song would always make him think of her. Forever. He didn't know if he liked that thought. But he knew he had loved her. Puppy love? Who knows? All he knew was he hurt in a place that he couldn't really touch. He couldn't let her memory slip away.

Soon another song came on that he knew by heart. He sang along out loud since it seemed to match his mood perfectly. The song was "More Than a Feeling", by the group Boston. As he sang it he replaced the name Marianne with Julie and wondered how that song could have come on at that exact moment. How could Tom Scholz of Boston have penned just what he was feeling inside and how could the disc jockey have put it on the turn-table just then? He sat there contemplating something he had already thought to himself before. Everything has been said before. Nothing is really new. Nothing. Not even pain of the heart. There were no new feelings to hear about; there was only the act of experiencing them. Musicians had always tried to capture a feeling with words and merge them with, hopefully, the perfect melodic passage, perhaps preserving that magical combination forever in the listener's memory. Robin knew he consistently related songs to where he first heard them and usually the mood he was in at that moment. Composers were always very intuitive and creative people, he felt. Or did he Know? Yes, he Knew it! What puzzled Robin was why he still liked his Beethoven music but had developed an ear for rock and roll at the same time. He knew his, now, so called, classical music, had stood the test of time, but he was quite sure he could write equally appealing songs in the rock genre. He still got a kick out of stepping into an elevator and hearing his Beethoven music playing.

Jaybird was not pleased with Kandy at the moment. He hoped that he could be cordial to her father when they met. He kept hearing his own dad say "spur-of-the-moment, spur-of-the-moment." Now Jaybird understood what he was talking about. Maybe he did rush things. He had never been with Kandy constantly for long periods of time. Alone. Thoughts of divorce had already gone through his mind. More than once he was wondering how he would greet her father.

"Hey, what the hell did you do to your kid anyhow?" or "Here; she's yours. No tag backs." No, that was childish. What would he call him? Sir, Dad, Mr. Norton, Chief? Funny, but Norton didn't sound like an Indian name. No matter, he would try them all, he supposed.

A day later, everyone's patience had worn thin. Kandy and Jaybird were at each other's throats and Robin was almost incoherent. He paid no attention to their arguing anymore. He had planted himself in the back of the motor home and turned to face the back. They could have driven straight there but Jaybird had decided to take the scenic route. Finally they arrived, after almost turning around numerous times. Kandy grabbed the shark's jaw she had wrapped up and they all went into the trading post where her father had said he would meet them.

They walked around and looked at all the hand-made Indian goods. There was some remarkable silver and turquoise jewelry along with leather goods. There were all kinds of wonderful little knickknacks. They had been there about twenty minutes when a deep voice rang out from the direction of the entrance, "Kandy."

Kandy turned around to see her father. She was surprised to get butterflies in her stomach all of a sudden. Even more amazingly her eyes lit up as she said, "Daddy," and walked cautiously towards him. Jaybird was taken aback by the whole scene.

She didn't know why it felt somehow good to see him but he had his arms out wide and she hugged him with honesty.

He was a tall man with a dark complexion, probably in his mid-fifties with a weathered face. His eyes were just like Kandy's. Big. Dark. Intriguing. He had long graying black hair parted in the middle and braided in two thick braids each hanging down his chest.

Robin's first thought was that he looked like just like what an Indian chief should look like. And that pleased him.

"You look as beautiful as your mother, even more so," her father said, stepping back a few feet to look at her. She just smiled tucking her chin to her chest, blushing.

"I am Chief Eagleclaw. So who are these young men?" he queried.

"Oh, sorry. Daddy, this is Jaybird. He is…" she said, getting interrupted as she half-heartedly pointed to him.

"Jaybird!" her father exclaimed, "A bird name. One from the crow family. Very interesting. I am sorry, my daughter, please continue."

"Well, um Daddy, you see, he is my…husband," she said nervously, but without the kind of warm feeling one would expect. She didn't say it proudly, she just said it.

"Husband?" he asked. "My little girl is married?"

"Yes. We got married about a month ago," she said as she started to get butterflies in her stomach again.

"Are you not but seventeen years old?"

"Yes, but Mother signed a consent form." She stopped talking when she saw his eyes slowly move away from hers. He fixed a stone cold stare on Jaybird.

It felt like a very long time to Jaybird as her father looked him straight in the eyes. Uneasily Jaybird looked directly back at him. He had no idea what to say at that moment. He was readying himself for more questions; why they got married so young and so on and so on. *Parents*, he thought to himself. *They always question their children's decisions. When would it ever stop?* But to everyone's surprise the chief said, "Well then, congratulations to both of you!"

With that he stepped toward Jaybird and gave him a bear hug. A real bone-cracking bear hug. It wasn't the slight pain that he was thinking about at that moment, it was the disbelief over the feeling that had welled up inside his whole body and his mind. He was once again experiencing what he felt when he first shook Robin's hand. He became quite disoriented. The memories were crashing in so fast that he felt dizzy.

As her father let go of Jaybird he took a deep breath and a step backward, saying, "An 'Ancient Warrior'. This is very good. We may have a lot in common, you and I."

Nobody knew what he was talking about as he looked at Robin, leaving Jaybird to fend for himself with the rush of memories flooding his mind.

"You are a friend?" he asked looking at Robin.

"Daddy, this is his friend, um, Robin. He only sings. He won't talk to you," she said with disdain.

"You are named for a bird also. A very important bird. This bird is a good friend of the Indian people. And this bird has a broken limb but in time I'm sure it will heal well," he said, as he reached out to shake Robin's hand.

As they touched, Robin, too, felt strange new memories flood his mind. A wave of new thoughts expanded from the inside out. He was, for the third time in his life, trying to grasp the feeling. He dropped one crutch and leaned on a nearby barrel.

Kandy's father looked at both men, who were still clearly disoriented and said to Kandy, "Two 'Ancient Warriors'. A most rare omen. My daughter has been in good company on her journey to her homeland."

"What are you talking about? What is a, an 'Ancient Warrior'? What's wrong with them?" a very confused Kandy asked.

"Do not worry about them. They are fine. They have had a long day and are exhausted from meeting me, I would suppose. I can be intimidating at times. Come, we should get some food. Follow me in that large rolling house of yours to my land. You can ride with me, my daughter."

She felt nervous being alone with him but during the ride his demeanor somehow began to soothe her. She started losing the apprehensions that had built up.

After Robin and Jaybird regained their composure and were following his old truck down a rutted dirt road, Jaybird finally said to Robin, "You won't believe this, man, but it happened again."

Robin just shook his head up and down vigorously, as he swivelled the front passenger seat in Jaybird's direction.

"I wonder if he felt anything. He didn't look like he did, huh?" Jaybird continued.

Robin just looked at Jaybird's eyes and motioned "no."

"Whoa, man, I am beginning to wonder about our sanity here. But we couldn't be going insane...together. I don't feel crazy!" Jaybird said emphatically. "And what is all that 'Ancient Warrior' crap? What was that all about?"

Robin wasn't talking and Jaybird was tired of always asking yes or no questions, so he just drove and kept his thoughts to himself for the time being.

Robin on the other hand, Knew all about being a Warrior. That fit his demeanor, he thought. He liked the idea of being called a Warrior.

Ancient or otherwise. He could remember being victorious in battle many, many times. He looked forward to hearing Eagleclaw expand on the subject, if it ever came up again. Besides, how did the Chief seemingly know he had been a Warrior?

Both Robin and Jaybird were immersed in the wonder of the new memories that had just popped into their heads from very old lives they had lived with the Chief. They both wondered why they didn't remember these before they met him. And Jaybird wondered what the Chief had experienced during their handshake. He didn't seem as taken aback as he and Robin had been.

After they arrived at the Chief's home and had finished eating, they were sitting around what looked to Robin to be a huge old hand-carved table. He also noticed that there were many hand-made items all around. Chairs, shelves, pottery, paintings and now a shark's jaw that looked out of place. *The house looks very old yet it has a comfortable feeling to it*, Robin thought to himself, as he sat back after a filling meal of elk stew and cornbread.

As they relaxed, Kandy got her father caught up with what had been going on with her for the last seven years. They all took turns answering the questions the Chief had. Robin just nodded if questions were directed at him. After about two hours they had all become comfortable with each other. The chief had a very to-the-point way about himself; one always knew what he meant; there was no confusion.

Kandy started to yawn more frequently so her father suggested that she go to bed. He said he would entertain the young braves for a while longer. Jaybird knew this would be the perfect opportunity to talk to him about the 'Ancient Warrior' comment.

Kandy lightly, almost lovingly, kissed her dad on the cheek and waved at Jaybird and actually said goodnight to Robin as she headed for one of the bedrooms down the hall. *This was the nicest she has been since we left*, Jaybird thought to himself.

"Mr. Norton I…" Jaybird started.

"Chief Eagleclaw. Norton is the name Kandy's mother took after she and I divorced. You should just call me Chief."

Jaybird nodded and said, "All right. Chief, I was, well we were wondering about something and we hoped you could maybe help us in figuring it out."

"I will try. What are you wondering about?"

"Well, first of all, when you met us in the trading post you called us 'Ancient Warriors'. What exactly does that mean?"

The Chief got a slight grin on his face. He scanned the eyes of both young men, then said, "You don't have any idea?"

Jaybird shook his head and replied, "No sir. I haven't a clue. I doubt that Robin does either."

Robin was emphatically shaking his head "no."

The Chief sat up straight in his chair. The wood creaked with the weight shift. He clasped his hands together and said, "I, too, am an 'Ancient Warrior'. We have much in common, the three of us. Much more than you know. I can see that now. It is a great feat that you have found me when you had no idea that you were looking for me."

"Of course we weren't looking for you!" Jaybird stated bluntly, not knowing why he said it so boldly, adding, "We just came here because you are Kandy's father and my father in-law.... now."

"Oh, but you *were* looking for someone. You have both been looking. Looking for someone with the answers. Now you have asked one of the questions," the Chief countered.

Robin was just as confused. He wanted to ask, but he wouldn't.

Jaybird did ask, though, "What are you talking about? Can we get back to the 'Ancient Warrior' thing?"

The Chief rubbed his full belly and said with a mischievous grin, "Let me try to explain. You must have felt something in the trading post, the second you touched me. Both of you did, am I not right?" the Chief queried.

"Yes. You are right. But we don't know what the hell it is. We thought we were going crazy, well at least I did. It happened years ago when I first shook hands with Robin also. So do you know what is happening?" Jaybird asked.

"Yes."

There was a long pause. Robin and Jaybird were not even breathing. The suspense was tremendous.

"Chief! Please, please tell us!" Jaybird begged.

The Chief stood up, stretched and with a big smile said, "Both of you carry your old Warrior's Spirit with you. You still have all of the travels it has experienced locked up inside, just waiting to show you where you have been. I have felt it. I have remembered it. We three have crossed each other's paths many moons ago and a number of times, too. You also will remember more when you touch the other half of your 'Rib Maker'. For now you are what we call an 'Ancient Warrior'."

"What other half? What travels? Ribs? What spirits? I don't even believe in ghosts," Jaybird said. He started to feel tension in his chest. It was as if he was going to explode. He wanted to know more but he was also scared to know.

"You can not explain all the memories you have because you have not met the other half of the two spirits that created your spirit in the first place. It happened like this to us also. You are not alone. You are special," the Chief said and added, "There are no ghosts but spirits; yes. There is only you and your memories. Places you have been and *people* you have been."

Jaybird was silent for about twenty seconds until he had formulated a statement. Then he stated impatiently, "You know, we are positive that Robin and I were brothers once, back in like 1848. Robin and I hid that gold we told you about earlier tonight. We hid it together. In Colorado. We know we were brothers then, I knew just where to go to get the gold."

The chief sat back down and grabbed the braided hair on the left side of his head. He himself was wondering how to address Jaybird's statement.

"You may have been linked to each other many more times than I or anyone of the 'First Rib' have ever heard. No tales that I know have accounted for this kind of exact memory. At least not one that is so clear that you could have embarked on a journey to verify the memory. It would seem unlikely that you could remember something like that without coming in contact with your other 'Rib Maker'. And I know that you haven't experienced that yet."

"Robin," Jaybird asked, baffled, "Are you getting this?"

Robin raised one eyebrow and shook his head "no."

The Chief chuckled and said, "You two and I are of the 'First Rib'. It is a group of people that are like us three. We will have many stories to tell each other some day. You need to mingle with the rest of the members of the 'First Rib' to see if the other half of your 'Rib Maker' is among them. Normally you wouldn't be able to bring any memories into real focus. I have never heard of that from one who is just an 'Ancient Warrior.'"

"First Rib, Chief?" Jaybird asked.

"Yes. First we need to open up your mind to some new possibilities. You have an inherited gift. You may not understand it fully yet but you will. I shall call a meeting of the 'First Rib'. The others will be very excited to meet you two. You may even find your other 'Rib Maker', which would be grand. There has not been a 'First Rib' meeting in many years. There is much to explain. Tonight we sleep. We go to Warrior Cave tomorrow night."

Robin and Jaybird were not ready for sleep. They wanted more explanations but Chief Eagleclaw insisted they rest. He showed Robin his room and tapped and pointed on the door where Jaybird could find Kandy sleeping.

Later that night, as Robin lay on his back, he stared at the ceiling, trying to stop his mind from reeling. He was intrigued with the mystery of what Eagleclaw was talking about, but he was also perplexed. Could this Indian Chief have some answers for him? Could Eagleclaw explain the strange knowledge that just pops into his head, seemingly out of nowhere, just from shaking someone's hand? Robin couldn't sleep. He wondered if Jaybird was having as hard a time falling asleep.

He definitely was.

The morning came too slowly for Jaybird and Robin, they were too excited to sleep much. Kandy was refreshed. After breakfast Chief Eagleclaw told them he had been up with the sun and saddled three horses. "We should go riding," he said. After an hour of quick lessons in horsemanship and a special contraption for Robin's cast, they decided to go out and explore the surrounding area. The Chief told them he had to assemble that evening's participants. His old truck rumbled down the dirt road. The three novice horse riders headed off, with great trepidation, toward the great big open valley west of the house.

CHAPTER XXIII

IN THE Great Room in the west wing of the house, Nicholas motioned to the forty or so members of 'The Calm' to quiet down. As they took their seats, the room got very quiet.

"Well," Nicholas started, "I have some news to report with respect to ol' Bloodhead and Jaybird Young, my nephew." With that there was a low murmur.

"It is pretty groovy stuff, although no big revelation, I guess. Seems that my nephew and Mr. Bloodhead were both in Tahiti. They weren't together and it doesn't look like they ran across each other, but this has given us a chance to put the tail back on Bloodhead."

After Nicholas related everything that the P.I. Van Tangle had told him, he asked the members if they had any questions.

"It's great that you are back on the track of Bloodhead but does it look to you like he is making any attempts at any destruction anywhere?" one of the members asked.

Nicholas replied, "No. Not from what VT can tell. But historically Bloodhead has always been a crafty character. As you know, he has met both of his 'Rendering Parents', so he has all of his past memories to draw from. You just never know with him."

One of the new 'Knowers' then asked, "I know this is off the subject but where are you on your research, Dr. Young?"

"Hey, all right. Cool question," Nicholas said, as his eyes lit up and he smiled broadly. "Well, as far as my research goes, my team and I have been getting closer to finding smaller components of the human body's cell structure and the chemistry involved with life itself. We will eventually find a smaller *something* to measure and understand. We always do. I suppose we always will. That's why we try in the first place. We are always looking for the next discovery to aid our understanding the human body and how it functions. Hopefully we can unlock the reason that some of us can remember our past lives and who we were and determine what exactly causes us to remember. But until then we should remember that we are not to discuss our knowledge with 'non-Knowers'. It's a bummer, I know, but it would be much worse to be considered crazy and be sent away to the rubber room. Better that we just discuss things with the other members of 'The Calm'. Many of you know what it is like to try and express your knowledge to your parents, family members or others. They just don't have the capacity to understand. Yet. Seems they tend to want to fix you. They see you as being somewhat broken or crazy, as it were."

Dr. Young continued to explain in more detail to some of the other new members how to provide the instantly needed counseling to a person whom they have just touched, where both of them are experiencing a shared feeling.

"Of course," he said, "it's always a tricky topic of discussion to start up. Quite frankly, all you have to do is remember how you felt when you got that feeling the first time. Whether you are one of their 'Rendering Parents' or just a 'Knower' who has known them to be in your family in one or more of your past lives, they will be desperately looking for answers at that moment. For a 'Knower', most of the memories will be just out of reach. Where some may be clearer, you can give support. Remember, it isn't exactly the same for everyone. If you were their second 'Rendering Parent' to touch them you will have an easier discussion, since you will be making them a 'Complete Knower' with your touch. That, my friends, is a great moment. Normally they will want to join us in 'The Calm' after hearing there are others out there just like them. It will open many doors that before were not there for them. It should calm them down. That in itself was the reason the founding members and I named our little group 'The Calm'. Knowing there are others out there who '*Know*', does make the anxiety go away. It is a release of pent-up emotions and confusion caused by the knowledge and memories they just instantly received in a most unusual way, through just the touch of another person."

When Nicholas had finished his lengthy explanation, one of the new members stood up and asked a question.

"Could you explain 'The Tree', sir, for me?"

"Think I can't? Sure I can, but listen, don't ever call me sir, please! Any who, the most far-out thing I think we have ever attempted since our little group started about fifteen years ago, was the 'Family Tree of Knowers'. We just call it 'The Tree' for short . We have over 2000 folks world wide, who have touched both their 'Rendering Parents' which makes them 'Complete Knowers' and they have been steadily providing us with names to add to 'The Tree'. They are all writing down their past lives as they remember them. Who they were, when they lived, what they did and what they were. And I do mean what they *were*. Most of them can remember who they were so far back that there weren't even names to call themselves, 'cause there weren't any real languages yet. But we were aware of ourselves. So with the earth's population growing at about sixty million a year, there are some very old souls out there but also many first time souls. As far as the number of names of people who have been traced so far, I would put the number at nearly at two million. And that is a huge volume of paper to secretly store, let alone research through. Someday I hope to put all this info into a computer. But as of now I just don't have the means to get all this information into a mainframe computer. I mean, what would I say to my Board of Directors at Intertwine, 'Hey, I need to borrow the mainframe for my personal little project, etc. etc.' That ain't happening. But someday someone will make a smaller computer that will be inexpensive enough for you and me to buy, at least I hope it will happen."

"Doctor," the new member interrupted, "could you explain the 'Rendering Parent' thing for me a little better? I think I understand but..."

"Think I can't? Sure, be glad to, my new friend. The 'Rendering Parents' are the two souls that create, biologically, a new 'First Time Soul'. Some souls or 'O's' as I like to call them, since a circle is never ending and the 'O' is a circle and the soul never really dies, any who, you know, it fit. What was I saying? Oh, yes. Some 'O's' are reborn to biological parents but the soul has been around for two or more, even thousands of re-births. This, my friend, is not unlike what we all have come to understand the term 'reincarnation' to be. But we in 'The Calm' understand that each of us only has just one set of 'Rendering Parents', although many biological parents. So, the far out thing is that when you physically touch the body of a person who is one of your 'Rendering Parents' you become a 'Knower'. When you touch someone who has touched one or both of his or her 'Rendering Parents', you 'Know' that person is also a 'Knower'. You just *Know* you have been acquainted with them before. Good, bad or otherwise."

Nicholas stopped for a moment, looked toward the ceiling, cleared his throat, then continued, "How? We don't really know this, but we all assume there is a chemical reaction in the body. You usually can remember if you were biologically related to that person you just touched, before...um, in a previous life. So, like I said, how? No one knows that. That is exactly what my team of researchers is trying to discover. As you are aware, you get strange feelings and a rush of fuzzy memories and such, but you normally can't really piece everything together right then and there, but you just know. You recognize that there is a kinship between you. Most of you have related that you usually felt, shortly after that initial meeting, that you were on a search for an answer to an internal question but you didn't even know the question. It is pretty much an annoying and nagging feeling at that point. Then, and hold onto your britches now, my new young member, when you touch the other 'Rendering Parent' you are flooded with all the memories of *all* the lives you have ever lived before. You can remember everything you have ever experienced, learned or accomplished. Your question is finally answered. And like I said earlier, there are only about 2000 of those groovy folks that we know about and we call them 'Complete Knowers'.

So, for quite some time now, we in 'The Calm' have been trying to get all the lives and names that are remembered, put down on a huge grand list in the 'Family Tree of Knowers'. If we can do that, we feel we can better understand the human race. We know we all have been related to each other if you go far enough back, but seeing it on a gigantic list and following your particular birth line back to your 'O's' first life, which was created by your 'Rendering Parents', now that would be neat. Imagine if you could see where you intersect with everyone else in the world. I think it would be the just the coolest thing you could ever do."

When Nicholas said that, the whole room erupted in applause and handshakes. It didn't matter how many times the others had heard it, they loved the way the Doctor expressed it, and the way he said it just slightly different each time. *It was almost like an Amway meeting.*

After the room quieted down a bit, the new member asked, "So who would want to know that their 'O' was like, oh…I don't know, someone horrible like say, Jack the Ripper, in a life before or something? If I ever ran across that 'O' I am sure I would want to kill it, I mean if I knew it was a killer in previous life, it would be revolting! Wouldn't *you* want to kill him or her if you knew for sure?"

With that said, you could hear a pin drop in the room, as everyone waited for Dr. Young to answer quickly.

But this question made him pause longer than anyone had expected.

CHAPTER XXIV

AS THEY paused by a stream to get their bearings, Robin thought how quickly the day had gone by. *Well, for everyone but the horses,* he chuckled to himself. They had kept the Chief's house in view the whole day but still had acres upon acres left to explore. As the sun inched closer to the western horizon, they decided to go back.

Chief Eagleclaw met them by the stable as they arrived. He had a young man take the horses from them and they went inside to eat.

"You should eat your fill tonight. You will want to be strong for the event tonight," the Chief said.

"What event?" Kandy asked.

"You will have a treat tonight, my daughter. We are going to Chief Mountain to witness a grand event," her father said.

"Do I have to go?"

Chief Eagleclaw gave the room a swoop of his arm and said, "Unless you wish to stay here where there is no TV or radio to keep you entertained. It is your choice, of course."

"Kandy, it should be fun to see a real Indian Chief run a meeting," Jaybird said as he went toward her chair to pat her hand.

She quickly moved her hand before Jaybird touched it and stood up, saying, "OK, whatever, as long as I can bring a pillow for my butt. I am so sore from all the riding today."

"Of course, my little one," the Chief said as he noticed her actions toward her husband.

"There is not a cloud in the sky. The sun will shine brightly from behind the earth on the rising moon as dusk turns into night and then the moon will reflect its hidden glow. A most wonderful evening for a special ceremony," the Chief continued.

After supper they started out the door. Kandy headed for the old truck. After a few steps she heard Jaybird call to her,

"Kandy, I think we are going this way…um, on foot."

Kandy saw her father nod affirmatively, so she asked, "Are you guys trying to kill me or something? I mean how far are we going to have to walk for this ceremony thing?"

"It's only about a mile or so; that's why I wanted you to eat a good meal. Robin, you can handle this little walk, can't you?" Chief Eagleclaw asked as he led the way up a trail behind the house, never once looking back to Robin for any kind of acknowledgment. He had the feeling that Robin could conquer anything.

The moonlight was bright enough for them to see the trail clearly. When they reached the entrance of Warrior Cave they could see a group of people already standing in a circle under a big tree. Robin counted five women, one about the Chief's age; the other four were much older. There were also four very old men. They all wore what he thought to be traditional Indian attire. Robin wondered who the highest ranking chief was. Was it Eagleclaw or one of the older men?

After the Chief finished with some pleasantries, he explained that tonight they were joined by several other tribes. The representatives were members of the Crow, Salish, Kootenai, Gros Ventre, Assiniboine, Cheyenne, Cree, Chippewa. They all proceeded to a cave opening, about thirty-five feet away. Unusual for the area, the cave was a perfect place for holding this type of gathering. There was a large entrance and two other natural openings above the entrance, large enough for a person to crawl through. From where he was standing, Robin could see no other way in or out of the cave.

Eagleclaw addressed the group and then introduced Kandy as his daughter and Robin and Jaybird as 'Ancient Warriors'. The four of them sat down and one old man handed Eagleclaw a long hand-carved wooden pipe. The three-quarter-inch deep bowl had a half-dollar sized opening and looked, to Jaybird, to be filled with tobacco. Eagleclaw took the pipe and said, "I have waited for seven years to see my daughter again. This is a very special night. I wish for her to have the first taste of the pipe."

Kandy leaned over toward her father and whispered, "I don't know how to smoke. I mean, I never have tried pot. Are you sure this is a good thing for a father to show his daughter?"

All the Indians laughed. They could hear her very well, with the acoustics of the cave being what they were. Eagleclaw explained to her that it most certainly was not hemp. He told her it was a special herb that all Indians in his tribe used at these gatherings to attract spirits to the cave. It was a form of initiating a connection of one level of existence to another. She was told by the old woman sitting across from her that being the daughter of the Indian Chief, there was no more powerful way than that to start a wonderful event like this. Jaybird saw that every other head nodding up and down, so he leaned over and said, "Come on Kandy, it is probably an honor to get the first taste. Right, Chief?"

"You are correct, Jaybird," he said.

Begrudgingly Kandy held the pipe to her mouth as her father lit the dried herb. He told her to inhale slowly and to hold the breath in her lungs and exhale when the smoke decided to come out. She inhaled it as a rather bark-like taste filled her mouth and then her lungs. She held it in for about six seconds, that's when it felt like it wanted out so she opened her mouth. Nothing came out. She looked at her father and then at Jaybird in surprise and said, "That wasn't so bad. It kinda tasted like bark, though."

Eagleclaw took the pipe from her hand and laid it on the flat rock in the middle of the cave. He said that the first taste was complete and the rest of the dried herb in the pipe must burn out by itself.

Robin was a bit disappointed. He was quite ready for a taste of the herb. Jaybird glanced at Kandy and noticed that her eyes were starting to close. He was reaching over to shake her but the Chief stopped him and whispered in his ear, "In a few minutes she will be totally asleep. We must wait for that to happen."

Robin was as surprised as Jaybird. Both of them began to get nervous. Sure enough, within two minutes Kandy was asleep and had put up no resistance at all. Eagleclaw asked Jaybird to help him move her to a spot close to the front of the cave and they laid her head on the pillow she had brought. Jaybird followed Eagleclaw back to the circle of people.

"What's going on here, Chief?" Jaybird asked.

Eagleclaw stood back up and opened his arms to the entire group saying, "This is a time for only 'Ancient Warriors'. No others should see or hear what goes on in this cave but us. We have put my daughter into a deep slumber. She will wake up in the morning refreshed and ready to embrace the new day. But tonight we shall call upon the 'Old Ones'. Many questions will be asked and maybe some answers will be given. When the moonlight shines on the pipe, we will eat the buttons."

With that he sat down and opened a fist-sized leather pouch. He handed Jaybird and Robin something that looked like dried up rotten apricots. The Chief passed the pouch around to the others and then instructed them to put what he called buttons in their left hands and wait for the moonlight.

About ten minutes later the light from the moon started creeping in above the entrance to the cave. It illuminated the whole cave. Finally at one point it shown directly on the pipe. The Chief motioned for everyone to eat the buttons. Robin thought his tasted like a piece of old dirty carpet, with maybe some dog pee on it. Jaybird wasn't impressed by the taste either.

The Chief then said, "We have two 'Ancient Warriors' in front of us tonight. They are not of this tribe or culture but I have been with them before. You all are in the 'First Rib'. I ask you all to come and join hands with these men of bird names and see if you are a 'Rib Maker' for them or if they are a 'Rib Maker' for one of you.

The Indians stood up and, one at a time, grasped Jaybird's and Robin's hands. Each time each young man experienced an overwhelming rush of memories. It was like a tidal wave of memories, places, and faces once forgotten and now remembered. They shook the hand of each Indian. Then the Chief asked if any of them were their 'First Rib'. No one answered 'yes'.

Robin sat down and looked at the moonlight coming in the cave. At certain places it looked like silver threads of spider webs to him. The perception was so strange and foreign to him that all he could do was watch. One Indian woman started to chant something and the others soon joined in. Robin was immersed in one of his memories. He was in a place long ago, a grassy area, somewhere warm and sunny. He knew he was with the old Indian woman sitting across from him. But at that time and place he seemed to be older than she was. He was showing her how to dig a root out of the ground for eating. He felt a familiar feeling –he was proud of her. She was happy and playful. She ran around with complete abandon upon finding a root all by herself. Robin looked up at the old Indian woman. She smiled as she continued to chant with the others. He wondered if she was thinking about the root also, when his thoughts were diverted to listening to the words of the chant. It went like this:

Called again to the world surrounded by lightning and thunder
Arms reaching up trying to balance the terror with wonder
Memories come to light from the teachings of the old
Tales of knowledge begin to unfold
We know there are no survivors on the earth
But self pity is nothing in comparison to death
So with sober consciousness we keep ourselves whole
Time once again to replenish the soul

We are Warriors, some of the few
To live forever you must know what to do
Proud Warriors, humans they call you and me
The only difference is that we have learned of eternity
Long life is the goal; never succumb to its defeat
Life itself may seem so sufficient and complete
It dazzles us with its cunning and we lose all our reason
Still we know inside that the end can come anytime of the season
The old ones know the rules of life; we call and they hear
They know the body will soon disappear
Oh, but the memories will remain whole
We will remember again the one and only goal: replenish the soul
We are Ancient Warriors, some of the few
We have learned what to do to live beyond one million and two
There are no tricks or sleight of hand
Life just happens, you don't need any plan
We are Warriors, humans they call you and me
The only difference is we know we are free
Calling all knowledge, wisdom and will
We open our minds at the base of this hill
The spirits gather and replenish the empty with hope
Our lives are remembered and this helps us cope
We are Warriors; we will continue the strife
For this is an extravagant journey and we call it life
The lives beyond this one will have many a path
So we must look at the end of this one and laugh
For the Ancient Warriors know only one true destiny
That we have been and will always, just be.

There was a long pause before anyone said anything. Each person was deep in his own thoughts, reflecting on the new memories.

Robin was trying to grasp the meaning of the song but it was hard for him to concentrate. He had so many questions building up inside.

Jaybird was impressed at the way they all took turns singing a different verse. He marveled at how their words all flowed as each one chanted his verse at the exact spot, with the Chief adding in a chorus when they were through.

About ten minutes passed before the silence was broken.

"You should now ask all the questions that you have. We will do our best to answer them," the Chief said, looking toward Jaybird and Robin.

Robin of course didn't offer up any verbal question at this point.

But Jaybird had some. "What is the 'First Rib'?" he asked.

The Chief looked around and pointed at one of the Indians who proceeded to give Jaybird an answer.

"The 'First Rib' is simply a group of people who have experienced the touch of one or both of the 'Rib Makers' who are just the living parents who first made your spirit. Somewhere in your life you have touched the Spirit of one of your first parents. We call anyone who has done that, an 'Ancient Warrior'. This is the only way that one could ever have any half memories of earlier lives. The longing to know and to complete the other half of your spirit is only satisfied by touching both 'Rib Makers'. Each of us has only touched one 'Rib Maker'. You most assuredly would remember meeting that person unless you were very young when it happened. Even if you had been very young, when you finally came of age the knowledge would manifest itself at that time. Meeting both 'Rib Makers' is a very emotionally, wonderful feeling, we are told, greater than the feeling you have experienced tonight. This is why you can remember much of your past lives, but not all. You can see the places you have been but you can't get back there in your mind because the images are out of focus. You can feel that you have been with some of us before in certain times and places but you can't remember it all yet. Neither can we. But when you touch the other 'Rib Maker' you will remember all of yourself, like it was yesterday. The same will happen for us. Until then, we can only dream of the families that we have once had. For now we must live with only half a memory and vague feelings. It is like we are being teased.

We use peyote to open our thoughts. We believe there is a trigger inside everyone that will release the ancient memories by using peyote. We try to get closer to the distant places. Our ancestors have taught us this ritual, so we continue to practice it. But only 'Ancient Warriors' can be in the 'First Rib'; only they can know these things."

"Wow! But could everyone have this happen to them? It sounds like reincarnation to me," Jaybird stated.

The same Indian answered, "No. Some spirits are on but their first encounter with life. They have not yet learned to fly. Others have had many, many lives. Everything has a beginning, a middle and an end. We believe that the 'Ancient Warriors' of the 'First Rib' are only at the first part of their journey. We have tried to call them tonight, to have them all stop here and enlighten us."

Just then Robin began singing the first verse of "Shine on You Crazy Diamond" by Pink Floyd.

Chief Eagleclaw looked at Robin after he stopped singing and said, "It is good to know you still have a voice. I believe I understand a question in that song."

Everyone looked at the Chief as he took a few seconds and then stated, "Yes, there are many yesterday triumphs and you may have been a winner or a loser before in a past life. I think we all still mine for the truth. Robin, you have a grand perception. I think you are not crazy at all, nor are we."

Jaybird was starting to feel like he had never felt before. He did get one more question out, though. "Chief, it still sounds like reincarnation, you know? And like I said, I don't have just half memories. I have full-blown facts."

"There are many names for the same thing. We have told you what we believe, what has been taught to us by our forefathers. The people who claim to be re-incarnated seem to tell of memories of only one life before. They are surely special people, but they get no help or compassion from others with the same uniqueness. They feel ostracized. They usually end up being told to disregard the memories as only dreams. So they endure years of pain and suffering until they become brainwashed into *not* believing what is truly a memory. They could very well be 'Ancient Warriors', but just on their second life of remembrance, who knows? If they seek help from the memories, they will surely agree with any doctor, if it will keep them from being committed. I would laugh at modern day psychologists. They have not a clue and perhaps have chosen that field of study to figure out what is wrong with themselves. They continue to use man-made drugs to eliminate the feelings inside a person, instead of using Nature's herbs to enhance a person's feelings. Finding our 'Rib Maker' could be our entire purpose in life while here on the earth. To bring peace within has been our ancient goal from the beginning. To remember all that he or she has done may be part of that process. You could be your own best teacher. The Spirit is everlasting; it can guide you; it can never be ignored. We embrace our beliefs and always shall. You are informing us that you have facts in your head and not just half memories. Maybe *you* can enlighten *us* tonight!"

Jaybird shrugged his shoulders. He didn't know how he could help enlighten the group but he did feel that a huge question had been answered for him. There *were* others like Robin and himself.

Suddenly his thought process was interrupted by a very strange perception. He looked around and, to his eyes, everything looked red. There were no other colors in the cave. Just red. Even the fire was red instead of yellow. His mind knew that fire was yellow but it made no difference at this particular time. His field of vision only saw red. Somehow he got another question out. He hoped it wasn't a stupid one, but it had just popped into his head.

"I really doubt I can enlighten anyone, Chief, but let me ask you this; why did you call me and Robin men with bird names? Is that good or bad or what?"

"It is neither good nor bad. It is just the way it is. You see, many of us believe in omens. Both you and Robin have bird names. I also have a bird name. A Robin is a powerful image for the Indians. It is a strong omen when a 'First Rib' with a bird name crosses our path. Quite rare for us, really. Robin looks to be strong, although he is on the mend right now. And Jaybird is a bird name. But the Jaybird is known to the Indians as an egg killer. The Jaybird destroys the young of other birds. I am Eagleclaw, the father of young Kandy. I would hope you don't destroy my young: my daughter Kandy. That is my family's hope also."

Jaybird looked around and felt compelled to defend his name,

"Um –well you know Jaybird is not my given name. I was born with Jeffery. But ever since I can remember I have been called Jaybird. It came from…something, some story my dad told me but I forget right now. And I married Kandy so I am committed to taking care of her!" he said with as much conviction as he could muster.

One of the old Indian women who had been quiet spoke up and said, "There are reasons for everything in one's life, whether it is because of this life or carried over from another life. We can only accept what is put in front of us to view. Life continues, good or bad."

Jaybird leaned back to stretch his back and said in a rather matter-of-fact tone, "Everything is red in here."

As a low laughter went around the cave, Jaybird then added, "Every one of you has been in my family before."

"Maybe you have been in our family," an old woman said.

"Well, I don't feel Indian. But you look red, man. Um, no disrespect intended," he replied.

"There is no color of skin to a Spirit. There is only the essence of the Spirit inside the skin. The Spirit may stop anywhere on its journey. We know this now as the truth," she stated.

Jaybird wondered what journey she was talking about and he would have asked her, except Robin had just stood up, grabbing his attention. At least it looked like he had stood up.

"OK. OK. I got another one. Who was the first 'Ancient Warrior'?" Jaybird asked.

The oldest male Indian in the cave decided to answer his question, "The 'First Rib' story is told to all young Indians when they are old enough to grasp the meaning of the Spirit. We believe we all came from one great ancient couple. When they died their children took one rib from each body and buried it by a fruit-bearing tree. When the tree bore fruit and was eaten by the remaining tribe, the Spirits of the first couple were passed on, to forever be a part of us in our memories. Other tribes have the same story but have a different Spirit. Long ago we were all one tribe. As the moons passed, the 'Ancient Ones' tell us, the tribe grew very large. There was much fighting. The tribe broke up into two smaller groups. Then these groups kept splitting off. Different ways of life and different views. The Indian people evolved. But our tribe has stayed in contact with any and all of the 'Ancient Warrior' spirits it has come across. There is a bond there, so we ask them to join the 'First Rib' group. We, here now in this cave, are all 'Ancient Warriors' looking for their 'Rib Makers'. The Chief's daughter is not. Her spirit is young. It may be on its first stop. It may be a new spirit. Just because her father is an 'Ancient Warrior' in no way ensures that her spirit will be. Flesh is only a container for the Spirit. She must find her own path and her 'Rib Maker'."

Robin and Jaybird both began to comprehend what he had said. When he was done they seemed to exhale a breath that had been held in for years. Finally, an explanation.

Soon the peyote that they all had ingested was starting to have major effects on them. Robin at one point stood four feet away from the wall of the cave. He started throwing punches in the moonlight. He started laughing. Suddenly he saw a very strange thing. His shadow stopped emulating his exact moves and stood still for a few seconds as he stared in disbelief. Then it raised its hands straight up over its head and vanished, leaving Robin no shadow. He turned around to see if anyone else had seen the unusual event. One old man who was sitting close to Robin's feet, held his hands up in the air and then started flapping his hands like a bird. He started laughing and pointed to the wall behind Robin. When

Robin turned around his shadow had returned and was flapping its hands like a bird. He decided to sit down.

Jaybird was engaged in drawing figures on the ground with his fingers, which seemed to be forty feet long and made of rubber. His perception was that he had grown very tall but a nagging voice inside told him that the cave wasn't but fifteen feet high. Each finger was drawing in a different color in the dirt. That perception made the event all that much more interesting. At least everything still wasn't red. He wondered if everyone could see the colors. He was going to yell down to them and ask but he figured they were too far away to hear him. Jaybird was very amused since he had never even tried to paint before. He thought his dirt drawing was a wonderful likeness of the group in the cave and he wanted to put a name to each figure but for some reason the names sounded foreign to him so he just gave them cartoon names. Fred, Barney, Mickey, and so on. After painting in the dirt he took to rolling around the floor like a drunken gymnast.

The Indians sat and watched. Sometimes chanting. They, too, were engrossed in their new memories that were being enhanced by the effects of the peyote buttons. They had been in this state of mind before and had a better grasp of the sensations.

The night grew longer and the moon passed behind the hill, no longer shining in the cave. Jaybird kept trying to herd all the people together for a group picture until Eagleclaw reminded him that he had no camera.

Robin was immersed in his own world. He somehow felt he could call any Spirit he wanted with just his thoughts. So he tried calling Julie's Spirit, only to be disappointed when it did not make an appearance.

CHAPTER XXV

NOT ONE for making a grand appearance any longer, Edward had instructed the captain to put into port before dawn. Just about an hour before reaching Monaco, still far enough out that he couldn't see the lights of any shore line, Edward looked up at the full moon from the front of the yacht. Overhead, a row of low-lying thin clouds looked to him like rows of potato chips spread evenly across the pre-sunrise sky. The moonlight shown brightly through the clouds and into a port hole, making the piles of gold coins reflect a yellow gleam around the softly lit room. He peered into the room from the railing and laughed to himself. *Finally,* he thought, *after centuries, I have recovered my bounty.* It was a full moon and he wasn't dead. But Voodoo was! He chuckled to himself at the thought of that stupid man and his idiotic superstitions. Things were working out for Edward quite well. He was uncertain how he could know these things in his head, but it didn't matter. He could somehow feel his power growing. He took a deep breath and filled his chest with the salty smell of the ocean air. *Yes,* he thought, *I will succeed!*

The appearance of Mr. Bloodhead at the Monaco hotel caused the help to step up their service about two notches. Edward had a way of making people hop. He left Elizabeth in the plush suite at the two year old Monte Carlo Grand Hotel and swiftly headed to the shop of a coin dealer who one of his accountants had said was reputable.

When the owner of the coin shop came down from the office, at Edward's insistence, he asked if there was a problem with the clerk who was assisting him. Edward said he just wanted an expert's advice on some old coins and he felt better with the owner than with the hired help.

"I assure you that my clerk is quite capable of appraising any coins that you might have, sir."

"Nonetheless, as I said, I would prefer to do my business with management not the hired help," Edward stated bluntly.

"I see no point in taking anything away from the expertise of…"

"Gold Doubloons, Excelentes, circa mid 1500's!" Edward thundered, drowning out the owner's verbal exception.

The look on the owner's face was one of surprise and suspicion. He had deduced on appearance alone that this man was just another blue-nosed rich kid who was used to being waited on hand and foot and who had stolen some of daddy's coins for gambling money or drugs. He glanced at the clerk, gave him a wink and promptly held out his hand toward Edward saying, "Well now, sir; I am Liam McCallock and this is my best clerk, Mr. Rousseau."

Edward looked at his outstretched hand and smirked, then said, "Yeah, whatever. I see how it works in this establishment. If you say the right words then you become an instantly valued customer. I have half a mind to walk down the street and find another dealer."

The owner slowly placed his hand on the counter without receiving a handshake. He made a mental note of Bloodhead's refusal to shake hands then quickly managed to say, "I get all kinds of people in here and they all think they have the rarest of coins. Please excuse my trepidation, sir. I will be delighted to help you. Personally!"

"Very well," Edward said as he reached into his pocket. "Here is what I have."

He laid six coins on the counter.

The clerk looked as if he had never seen those particular coins before, except in pictures. He said nothing as Mr. McCallock put each one in order from the smallest denomination to the largest. He then took the smallest denomination coin and held it up, carefully scrutinizing it.

"What we have here are Excelente gold pieces from Spain. 1525. They have the Bajoire front and the Escudo back. And in extra fine condition for a coin so old. All of these are dated 1525. You've got a half, one, two, four, eight and a fifty-piece Excelente! Well, that's interesting. There must be some mistake here. I don't think there was ever a fifty-piece coined. Rousseau! Find that Spanish reference book!" McCallock ordered, motioning quite excitedly with his hand toward the left of the room in the back.

"Of course there was a fifty piece coined. There's one right there. Do you think I made these myself?" Edward asked, as he watched the clerk coming back with a large book.

Mr. McCallock riffled through the pages as he talked to himself aloud. "This coin has the Bajoire or busts that kiss each other on the front and the shield or Escudo on the back, but I just don't think…."

Quickly he kept turning pages while reading quickly. Everyone was silent. The clerk started to pick a coin up until he saw Edward give him the 'I wouldn't if I were you' look, with only the rise of an eyebrow and a tilt of his head.

"Well, I'll be damned! You know what you might have here, sir? A very, very rare, I mean extremely rare coin. As a matter of fact there has never been a single one of these turned up before. It says here that the King's edict allows for the fifty-piece but no one has ever come across one."

The clerk looked at his boss, puzzled, and asked, "How could there never have been one show up?"

"I'll tell you why," Edward said, "It's because King Ferdinand carried them around on his person everywhere he went. He only presented the fifty gold piece to very courageous high-ranking military officers, usually to captains of the ships in his fleet when they returned victorious from a sea battle. If the King promoted a ship's Captain to Admiral after some extraordinary battle, he could expect the fifty-piece. I'm sure each General in the King's army had at least one, also. Never would these be circulated or used. They were too prized a possession, as well as a status enhancer. They most assuredly became instant family heirlooms to be passed on to the next generation. Every Admiral I ever kill...ahh...rather, read about, had at least one on him. They sure were proud of those coins. Rubbed them for good luck, I would presume."

"It sounds like you know a lot about these people," McCallock stated. "Are you a history teacher?"

"No. But my parents were both history teachers so I am well-read in this period as well as others. I feel that I know a great deal about those times. Captains in the fleet at that time seemed to have been very good leaders but most lacked the harsh buccaneer's edge that would make them victorious in a hand to hand contest. I read that King Ferdinand had only a dozen of these coins pressed each year. Each one had Isabella's, his wife, and his own likeness pressed onto the front of the coin. Only the fifty-piece had his face on the right and her face on the left; the opposite of all the other coins during their reign. He was proud of this idea, since he had designed it himself. Now King Charles the Fifth was even more miserly with the fifty-piece. He didn't have many at all pressed with his head on it. But there are probably fifteen or twenty out there somewhere. Maybe a few more."

"Well, I am sure that King had his reasons for being miserly. He gave us something to be on the lookout for. Anyway, you know I will have to test this for authenticity," McCallock said.

"I'd expect nothing less."

With that, the dealer took all the coins into the backroom of the shop. The clerk started browsing the open page in the reference book and blurted, "It says that those other coins are worth between about $1,000 and $5,000 each. *If* they're real, that is."

"Oh, they're real, all right, Cousteau," Edward snipped.

"That's Rousseau."

"Whatever."

"There isn't even a price quote given for the fifty-piece though. It must be worth whatever a private investor is willing to pay just to have it in their collection. Surely this is a rare find."

"Oh, it was one hell of a find!" Edward boasted.

The owner came back about five minutes later. He placed the coins down on the counter in front of Edward. He told him that they were indeed real and that he would give him $5,000 for all of them right then and there.

Edward laughed at the man, saying, "Well, you see, your clerk here has already told me that they are worth about $1,000-$5,000 each with the exception of the fifty-piece, so I suggest you try again."

Mr. McCallock looked very displeased as he turned his head toward his clerk.

"Oh, did he now? Well, how unfortunate for me then. I guess bargaining is out of the question now."

Edward smiled devilishly and said, "I have another idea. I will allow you to auction off my coins to the highest bidder and I'll give you a commission of ten percent of the take."

"That would be fine, but I don't want to sell these coins to anyone else. I want them for my private collection. Especially the fifty-piece. Just name your price."

"Maybe I didn't make myself clear," Edward stated. "I have forty of the fifty-piece Excelentes and about 10,000 each of the other denominations."

"I find that impossible to believe," McCallock said, shaking his head as he puckered his lips and made a clicking sound with his tongue.

Edward motioned at Duke to put the suitcase on the counter. Duke's muscles bulged with the strain caused by the weight of the case. He managed to wrestle it up to the counter top. Thankfully, this end of the counter was wooden, not glass, as the rest was.

Duke opened the suitcase. And staring Mr. McCallock right in the face were more gold doubloons than he had ever seen in one place.

The clerk cleared his throat and meekly said, "That doesn't look like 50,000 coins to me."

"It's not, you jerk! Do you think I would bring all of them down here? Trust me, they would weigh a ton. Duke is strong but not that strong. This is just a sample of the quality and quantity of the coins I have in my possession," Edward said cuttingly. "The rest are in a safe place. So now what do you think of my proposal?"

Mr. McCallock sifted his hands through the pile of coins and said, "It would be my pleasure to auction these off to the highest bidders, Mister…what was your name?"

"Bloodhead. Edward Bloodhead."

"I do believe I can find some very interested private parties. And I expect they will gladly buy the whole lot. Just one thing, Mr. Bloodhead, may I have first choice on the fifty-piece Excelentes?"

"I'll tell you what, if you sell thirty-nine of them, I will give you one of the fifties along with the ten percent, for making this happen. Maybe you will try harder to get top dollar for them that way. Is it a deal, Mr. McCallock?"

The owner held out his hand and was again denied the customary handshake but said, "It's a deal, sir. I will set it up for a week from today. If that's alright with you, sir?"

"I see no problem with that. By the way, what do you think the fifty-pieces will go for?"

After a long pause and some internal figuring, Mr. McCallock stated, "No less than $750,000 and quite possibly as high as a million or more for each one. But once the word gets out, that price could double."

"Now remember, you get ten percent. The more you get for them, the higher your commission will be."

"To be perfectly honest with you, Mr. Bloodhead, that is *foremost* on my mind right now."

"Here is my accountant's phone number in Switzerland. Duke will call and let tell him know you are going to be handling the auction and you three can set up the transfer of money as needed. You just ensure the buyers credit whatever account is set up."

"Sounds fine."

With that Edward left the hotel switch-board number and started out the door. Duke closed the suitcase and quickly followed him.

"That's that American billionaire guy, Liam," the clerk said closing up the reference book. "The one who used to do the beer commercials. Remember those ones with all those female guest stars? He was very big in America first, I believe."

"Of course! Now I remember. I thought he looked familiar. Well, I guess my first impression was correct then. He *is* a blue-nosed, or more like a snot-nosed rich kid. He just isn't a kid anymore."

"No. He's a jerk," said Rousseau.

With that said, Mr. McCallock nodded and quickly started placing calls to all of his international contacts and was shortly on his way to setting up the private auction. He also called a friend of his who would be able to tell him if any gold doubloons had been stolen recently or if there was any record of a shipwreck having been looted. He knew that a government would try to collect the twenty percent sovereign tax for any and all salvaged wrecks that had been flying the flag of that country or had been located in waters claimed by that country, no matter when the ship had gone down. If the government could prove ownership, it could legally claim twenty percent of the find, leaving only eighty percent to the finder and the investors of the salvage operation. He didn't want to be the fence for stolen property, so he also called his lawyer and his banker. Mr. McCallock wasn't stupid. He wasn't going to set up an account in Bloodhead's name using all of Bloodhead's people. There would be too much room for deceit. This was the big time and big money. This was another big break that just fell into his lap. *This could set me up on easy street*, he thought.

Elizabeth was getting ready to go down to the casino when Edward came in the bedroom.

"Oh, Eddie…hello. Do you want to go gamble some tonight?" she asked as she gave him a peck on the cheek.

He thought for a second and then said, "Sure, Liz, let's go blow some money. Let me get ready. Fix me a drink will you? Give me a Captain Morgan and Coke. I'm feeling a bit swashbuckling tonight."

Elizabeth was surprised that he actually wanted to go out with her. Usually when it came to being in public he would make the excuse that he hated to be recognized, since people always wanted to touch him and get his autograph. He claimed he had had quite enough of that when he was a model and he wanted to be left alone now, to have a private life again. So she was pleasantly surprised when he agreed to step out. She certainly was ready for some fun since the long boring voyage to Monaco had involved only the counting of coins. Thousands and thousands of them. Putting them in the correct pile within each denomination. He had seemed very distant then. *Maybe things will start to get better between us*, she thought as she poured the spiced rum over some ice and then added the Coke.

As Edward shaved he imagined ways of leaving Elizabeth. She was a beautiful woman but he couldn't see spending much more time with her. She was just extra baggage. The challenge and excitement were over. He didn't think about her much when she wasn't around. Today his thoughts were all centered around the 250 million dollars or more he expected to make from selling the coins. And that was just the coins from one of the trunks. He was so excited that he nicked himself with the razor. As he stuck a small piece of tissue on the cut, he knew that adding this large influx of money to the nine billion dollars he had already amassed would enable his team of brokers and account managers to continue on the path toward achieving his dream. It was their sole task: to make him the world's first *trillionaire*. Someday, it wouldn't be just a dream.

CHAPTER XXVI

ROBIN WOKE up from what seemed like a dream, at the Chief's house. After thinking for a minute or two he knew the night before had been no dream at all. He couldn't remember walking back though. He looked at his watch and saw that it was four in the afternoon. As he hobbled out to the living room, he mused that he couldn't believe he had walked so far. A mile or more to and from the cave, all with crutches and a cast on his leg. But for some reason he enjoyed doing things the hard way. It was as if torturing himself made him feel better about Julie's death somehow. He plunked down on an old wooden rocking chair.

Jaybird came out a few minutes later and sat on the couch. After ten minutes of silence Jaybird finally said, "So, like what did you think about last night?"

With that question, Robin just said, "Timothy Leary's dead, no, no, no, no, he's outside looking in."

Not expecting a answer, a surprised Jaybird waited for more but Robin had stopped after that sentence. He thought about it for a second and then said, "You know, Robin, I'm sure that's from a song, although I don't recognize it, but I think I know what you are trying to say. I think I was on the outside looking in last night. I feel like I have come back from the dead, to tell you the truth!"

Robin just smiled and shook his head like he always did when Jaybird interpreted anything he sang. Many times Jaybird would paraphrase into words what Robin was singing and be totally off base. But Robin couldn't correct him. Robin knew that his friendship with Jaybird could endure anything. He knew that Jaybird would indulge him at every level. He was pretty lucky to have a friend like that. One who just accepted him. He had had other friends growing up, at school and parks and such, but they were just not as close as Jaybird. Someday he would have to explain himself better. For now he had to stick to his vow. His vow to Julie was all that mattered. It was his quest.

Jaybird, on the other hand, often wondered if Robin was actually thinking exactly what he thought he was or if he was just agreeing to be agreeable. It didn't matter. Jaybird's head was still foggy. They both sat there for a few more silent moments.

"Well, it sure was an eye opening experience," Jaybird said, finally breaking the silence and rubbing his eyes, adding, "but I don't remember much after I was painting with my fingers."

Jaybird yawned then said, "The Chief said he needed to open our minds. And that is exactly what he did. I was really impressed though with what the older Indians had to say earlier in the evening. They sure seemed to have many of the answers I was looking for. Pretty interesting stuff, huh, Robin?"

He looked at Robin who was nodding "yes."

Jaybird knew he needed to get Robin back to St. Joseph to have his leg checked. He decided they should head out sometime that evening before any other freaky stuff happened.

"Robin, hey, listen man, I think we will be leaving tonight. Sound good to you?"

As Robin again nodded his head, Kandy entered the room and asked, "Leaving? When?"

"Today. We have to get Robin back to the doctors so they can check on the leg and all," Jaybird said.

Chief Eagleclaw came in a second later and they all sat around the hand-carved tree trunk of wood that was the table, and talked while eating some delicious stew. Kandy and her father didn't have much else to say to each other so Jaybird and the Chief held the bulk of the conversations. They talked about everything except the previous night, for about an hour and then they loaded up the Winnebago and headed back to St. Joseph.

Kandy was pleased that they were going home. She had felt a bit out of place, not to mention ignored. Initially she felt like she could get to know her father but she resented the way both Jaybird and even the non-talking Robin had hit it off with her father. It had left little time for her to get reacquainted with him. She decided that her mother was right. Men had little time for women. She changed her mind again. She was going to squeeze whatever she could out of Jaybird and get out of this marriage.

CHAPTER XXVII

EDWARD WANTED to get out of the relationship, but tonight he would try to act like he still cared. As they got off the elevator in the lobby Edward handed the man selling flowers outside the entrance to the casino a fifty-dollar bill for one red rose. He passed the rose to Elizabeth and they entered the casino. They were dressed to the hilt. Every male who saw Elizabeth stared at her a bit longer than what was considered sociably acceptable. Taking a mental snapshot. Many of them were quite sure that they had seen her somewhere before. Was it the perfect figure or the long silky blond hair that flowed about her head and shoulders? It didn't matter; she was just stunningly gorgeous. Every female who gazed at Edward would feel her heart beat faster as she wondered if he was as romantic and caring as he was handsome. A few would be wishing they could be with him long enough to have the chance to undo his ponytail and feel his muscular arms around them. They were the perfect-looking couple. They commanded attention by just being together. But that was only what others could see, for Edward was planning to dump Elizabeth, while she was wondering what he would do next to surprise her. She knew that he had triumphed again with the coins, so she didn't know what to expect next. She hated this feeling. She was worried.

"What do you want to play tonight, Eddie?"

"I think it is a poker night."

"You know that if you play poker I can't stay up and wait for you. I get so bored just watching you."

"I know. But I haven't played for a while and I feel lucky. Let's go get some markers to play with."

"How much are you giving me then?" Elizabeth asked, resigning herself to another night out without him.

"Oh, I don't know. How about twenty grand?" he asked, hoping that amount would keep her out of his hair for the evening.

"Well, you *are* feeling good tonight," she said in amazement.

After getting the markers, Edward headed for the poker rooms and Elizabeth was left standing with twenty thousand dollars worth of chips. She walked around the casino and looked at the blackjack tables and slots but nothing jumped out at her. She didn't know how to play craps very well and poker was out of her league. She was constantly brushing off gentlemen with her patented line for every come-on they could conjure up. She would just tell them that her extremely jealous husband had just gone to the restroom and would be back shortly. That usually worked. If it didn't, she would point to the biggest man within sight and start walking in his direction.

After half an hour of meandering around the casino and losing half the money Edward had given her, she became bored and didn't feel like gambling any longer. She did feel like taking a hot bubble bath and relaxing, though. All the expectations of the night had vanished as quickly as they had come. Edward had spoiled her night again. She was getting tired of that. But she did have ten grand. Usually she would have stopped gambling when the money ran out, but tonight she decided to cash in her remaining markers. Back in the room, she ordered a late snack and got lost in the sweet smelling oils and bubbles in the large antique lion paw tub.

The stale smell of cigar could guide even a blind person to the poker tables. The layers of smoke were so thick in the poker room, as Edward walked in, that it reminded him of his grandfather's house when he was a child. He remembered that every Sunday his family would go there after Sunday school in their best dress clothes. His grandfather would be in his favorite reclining chair with a cigar hanging out of his mouth watching a football game on the big Zenith with the other men in the family. The only time he didn't have a lighted cigar was when he was eating or when he was at church. The smell of that house would be exactly what Edward smelled the following Sunday morning as he pulled out the same unwashed Sunday dress suit off the hanger to get ready for church again. That smell was always somehow…familiar. As for church, he thought, how ridiculous church was. Looking back to those days, he felt he had been brainwashed with religion, growing up. Eventually he discovered that most people were going to believe in the same religion as their parents, unless they were a little rebellious or had a horrible life-altering event happen to them and had picked up a religion out of desperation. He could laugh at it now, but back then he was so scared at just the thought of going to Hell that he did everything that the Bible said. He wouldn't ask any questions, even if he was confused by the teachings, for fear of reprisal or eternal damnation. He just blindly followed the leaders of the church.

That upbringing had actually fueled his rise to the top of the male modeling business. He was the golden boy. The goody-two-shoes kid. He was the epitome of good. *Funny how things change*, he thought. He loved cigars now and he didn't believe in any religion and he certainly wasn't a golden boy anymore. Meeting that one man changed his whole life. He laughed to himself as he sat down at a table that needed one more player. Boy, had his life changed!

For the next five days Edward repeated the same scenario. Dinner, buy her a rose, give her some money and head for the poker tables. Then he would come back to the room around 5 AM and sleep till early afternoon. Upon awaking he would make a few phone calls and get ready for the same routine. Elizabeth would get dressed and accompany him as far as the cashier's booth where Edward asked her if she had any money left and she would nervously reply with a "No." So he would give her another twenty thousand. He would head off for the poker rooms and she would stroll through the boutiques, maybe buying a trinket here and there; she would pocket the rest of the money and head up to their room.

Elizabeth had decided to save these large chunks of cash Edward was granting her. He had never given her that much cash at anyone time before, so she wasn't quite sure how to interpret this change in his behavior. Somewhere in the back of her mind she felt him slipping away. She was never really sure of how he felt about her but she had always thought he loved her. They had been together longer than any other relationship she had ever had during her brief twenty-two years. Due to her physical appearance, she had started having sex partners at sixteen. Most of them were older men. None lasted. She thought Edward was the one she would settle down with. In the beginning she was in awe of him. But things didn't seem to be going along like she had dreamed.

On the sixth morning Edward did not return to the room. She was all alone.

Edward walked into the coin shop and said, "How much have we made so far, Mr. McCallock?"

"I am very surprised, Mr. Bloodhead. I have been able to sell all of the smaller denominations of doubloons in lots of five thousand. The bidding was much livelier than I had anticipated. It seemed that I almost could name my price. So actually I did precisely that with the first lot. They went so fast that I started the next lot at a price that I never dreamed anyone would agree to pay, but they also went within minutes. I then sold the rest of the coins, minus the fifty-pieces, in a few hours."

"What is the grand total then? That is all I am concerned about."

"Well, sir, you have a little over…one half billion dollars in the account I set up for you for this transaction. That's billion with a big fat "B.""

Edward rubbed his hands together like a greedy little kid in a candy store. His eyes lit up as he said, "And that is without the fifty-pieces?"

"Yes, sir. But the bids in for those right now are up to four million each."

"It seems the initial amount you quoted me was a very conservative one. You are becoming a very important person in my life, Mr. McCallock."

"And you, sir, are very important to me. About fifty million dollars worth of importance!"

"I may just have to find a job for you somewhere on my staff. We will have to talk further when this is all over. Speaking of that, when do you think this bidding will end?"

"I would say sometime in the next few hours," Mr. McCallock said, as one of the phones rang.

"Keep on doing what you're doing and I'll be back later this afternoon."

As Edward got into the back of a taxi and headed for a restaurant, he could only think of the other two trunks full of coins. If he was going to clear over a half billion from just one of them, he knew he must decide when and where to unload the other two. Maybe he should wait for ten years. Maybe he should sell them all now. The latter would allow him to have that much more money to invest. *Would this flood the market and bring the prices down?* he wondered. No matter, he was sure to be the world's richest man soon enough. He was so excited that he forgot to tell Duke to follow up with the accountants to ensure all the transactions were proceeding as planned. He was more elated than he had ever been. With this new money he would be able to do anything. Anything he wanted. And he knew what he wanted to do next. To look for the paintings he had secretly hidden in Italy during the 1600's. He went back to the hotel room to find it empty. He was actually relieved.

Elizabeth had had enough. Earlier that morning she had taken the nearly ninety thousand dollars cash she had and deposited it in a bank. She had also picked up some traveler's checks and booked a flight for New York with a connecting flight to Kansas City.

As the plane leveled out and the passengers started to turn off their overhead lights, she allowed herself to think about Edward. Elizabeth felt as if she had just turned off the TV after a long movie that wasn't really that good but one couldn't just quit in the middle of it. At the end you were mad at yourself for not stopping it sooner. She knew he couldn't love her the same way she loved him, but she had always felt that over time he would grow out of his restless stage. She wanted to be there when he did finally grow out of it. But that wasn't to be. He was so passionate, powerful and unpredictable. She was drawn to that. Even now she knew what *not* to fall for in the next relationship, if she would ever let herself have another one. Her eyes began to tear up as the emotions finally came to the surface. They weren't tears for the loss of Edward as much as they were tears for her bad judgment. She was a young, beautiful, bright eyed twenty-year-old when she had met him. Now she was twenty-two and heading home to her parents' house where she could do some soul-searching in the wide open spaces of the Midwest.

The next day Edward and Duke walked into the coin shop.

"Well, how is my favorite coin dealer doing?" Edward asked.

"I sold all the coins. The grand total is…let's see here, six hundred and sixty-six million, or so," Mr. McCallock said, shaking his head in near disbelief.

"Now that is just wonderful. I will be back tomorrow morning and we will head down to the bank and transfer your ten percent into your account." Reaching into his pocket, Edward pulled out the last fifty-piece and laid it on the counter saying, "You truly deserve this coin. I hope it is the centerpiece of your collection."

Mr. McCallock picked up the coin and let out a heavy sigh, "It could be nothing else but that, sir, I can assure you."

"So around ten tomorrow morning, I will come by for you in a car. Sleep well tonight, Mr. McCallock."

"I am sure that I will have a hard time sleeping tonight, Mr. Blood-head. But I will be here when you come by in the morning."

"You better be or I will just have to keep that money!" Edward said as he turned and winked at Duke. Duke knew what *he* would be doing very early in the morning and it wouldn't be sleeping, either.

Around midnight Duke went to case the coin shop. From an alley across the street he waited patiently. He waited another hour after the last light had gone out. He knew his target was inside; he had seen McCallock walking in front of the windows of his modest flat that sat directly on top of the coin shop. *This will be an easy kill,* Duke thought to himself. McCallock wasn't a big man. Just another slit throat. Trash the place to make it look like a burglary and take a few valuables, like the fifty-piece doubloon, which he imagined would be right by the bed. No problem. He had done scores of these. This job was going to be an easy one compared to the search-and-destroy missions he had been on in Vietnam some ten or more years ago. Those were real kills. This was more like amateur-night kill. He didn't get the same kind of rush he got from war killings though. Civilians never put up much of a fight. They just weren't trained to be prepared. But then again, he was paid well for these kills. All he got in the Special Forces was three squares a day and a denial from his government that any covert operation was ever carried out by his country. Well, that and a medal to prove that he did something that none of them could ever prove or talk about "on the record." Still, he figured, he couldn't have an easier job. Travel the world and kill people. *Put that in your resume.*

He climbed the back trellis up to the window farthest from the bedroom and slipped in quietly. As he tiptoed toward the bedroom door he drew the eight-inch knife out of the sleeve fastened to his belt. Upon crossing through the doorway into the bedroom, he raised his hand over his head ready to plunge the knife deep into the chest or back of the blanket-covered figure lying on the bed. All of a sudden a light came on, blinding him momentarily. Sitting in a chair on the other side of the bed was Liam McCallock. And he had a gun pointing straight at Duke.

"Don't make any kind of a move or I will cap your ass!" the coin dealer said with a force that was totally unexpected, even to himself.

Duke was frozen in his tracks. His eyes darted left to right. Instinctively looking for a way out. But this seemed to be a no-win situation. He reluctantly dropped the knife.

"What you have here is a problem, I would say. Don't you think so, Duke?" McCallock asked, standing up but never taking his eyes or the gun off Duke. "I thought this whole thing was too good to be true as soon as you two walked into my shop. Let me cut to the chase. I have the entire proceeds from the auction, in my name! I never called Bloodhead's accountants. I have only to just *not* show up tomorrow at the bank by eleven and your boss Mr. *Bighead* will be quickly located by the police. He'll be out his half billion and brought up on accessory to murder charges, since I am sure I would be dead if your little scenario had played out as planned. I will assume that you aren't dumb enough to blow this deal for him, I suggest that you go back and tell him all about this little change of events. I will be waiting out front at ten, as we agreed."

"No problem," Duke said begrudgingly, as he slowly backed up to the door. He turned and walked down the steps and out the front door. As he headed for the hotel, he didn't know what made him madder: the fact that he had been out-maneuvered or the fact that he had let his guard down. He has seriously underestimated McCallock. The first rule of killing was to never underestimate the enemy. This would be the last time he would make that mistake.

At exactly 10 AM a limo pulled up in front of the coin shop. Mr. McCallock got in the seat facing the rear. Edward and Duke were sitting opposite him.

"Well, I see that you are quite an excellent businessman. I like that in a person. Let's start this acquaintance over. You can call me Edward."

"My name is still Mr. McCallock. You can just call me that!" he said as he caressed the gun in the pocket of his overcoat.

"There is no need to get gruff here. You have all the cards in your hand. You called my bluff, so I will be up front with you from now on."

Mr. McCallock looked at him and smirked, saying, "My percentage has gone up since last night, Bloodhead. You will give me twenty percent instead of ten."

"You are one tough cookie, aren't you? Well, I guess that's fair enough."

"Fair would be to have attempted murder charges brought against you, but then you would probably get out of it with all your money. And Duke there would just disappear, I suppose. Better I should play on your turf, I figure."

"You sure talk a lot. You also let too much of your hand be seen. That's to my advantage, though," Edward said as they pulled up to the bank.

Reluctantly, Edward completed the transaction that left McCallock with just under one hundred and thirty million dollars and a bitter taste in Duke's mouth.

Later, as the *3 CANES* set sail, Edward had a one-sided conversation with Duke. Duke had made his first mistake.

CHAPTER XXVIII

IT WOULD be a mistake for Dr. Young to force his deepest personal opinions onto this group, so he slowly scanned the faces in the room as he thought about how to answer the question posed to him. "Wouldn't you want to kill a person who you knew was an evil-doer in a past life?" Yes, was the quick and true answer in his heart, but he knew that he should use some restraint, given this day and age, this society and its laws. He knew how he felt about it but also knew it was a touchy subject even if only within this small group of 'Knowers'. He had always thought that if you were able to know that an 'O' was a bad 'O' in previous lives, you should terminate it. Then again, just maybe there are so many seemingly incomprehensible killings in the world because a 'Knower' is doing the killings. Maybe, just maybe, there were many more 'Knowers' out there engaging in personal vigilante killings and taking the consequences that came with getting caught. They might be sacrificing their own freedoms if they were caught, just to rid the world of an evil 'O' or two. Since they were 'Knowers', they would understand that they themselves would be coming back anyway in a future life. He decided to ponder that thought later over a barley pop.

His whole research was based on the idea that there should be a way to measure memories. He had guided his research team toward finding smaller and smaller building-blocks in the human body. But he really wanted to find out how the 'Knowers' could remember past lives and then find a way to rid the world of the evil 'O's, before they became evil …again. Abortion was legal at this time, so who would want to be the parents of another Hitler or Jack the Ripper type…if they actually could know of their past tendencies? A simple test could be performed on an embryo and then there would be the option to terminate it or have it tracked from birth, to ensure it stayed on the straight and narrow. Then again, maybe his research would find a way to locate the so-called "evil gene" and remove it altogether. It was working in cancer research. The hardest part was working with non-'Knowers' who really didn't see where he was truly heading in his research. It always seemed so simple, he thought. Harmony, just simple human harmony.

"Let me see…would I want to kill it? Well, wouldn't I be put in jail for murder? There are lots of things to consider in answering that question, my friend. Morally, ethically and personally."

"OK, could we hear your personal feelings then?

"Ding, ding, ding, personally –then the answer is yes! And you are right. It is revolting to know that someone you have just touched was evil in a past life, but you have to understand the rules of the times in which you are currently living. I can remember way back to a time when there weren't laws to follow and if I touched an 'O' whom I knew was evil, I killed him right then and there, if I was able to. It seemed morally correct even though I had no idea what a moral was. It felt right. But at that juncture in evolution only the strong survived. If you were strong and good you could get rid of the bad; equally so, if you were strong and bad, you could get rid of the good. It was an even playing field in that respect."

Nicholas heard his phone ringing and excused himself, saying to the group, "You know my feelings, go ahead and discuss it among your-selves."

He was grateful for the phone interruption; this particular topic always made his head hurt.

This conversation would be a good one for a change, Van Tangle thought as he waited for someone to answer the phone.

"Goodbye!" a voice said surprisingly, after a dozen rings.

"Dr. Young?"

"Yes...is this VT?" Dr. Young asked.

"Yes, sir, it is...um...did you just answer with a 'Goodbye'?" Van Tangle queried, thinking that he never really did understand his employer's eccentric lingo.

"I guess I did at that. I figure if you are really paying attention to what I am saying you will question my words. If you don't question me, then you ain't hearing me."

"OK. Well anyhow, I have some news from Monte Carlo for you."

"Sock it to me, baby!"

"Pardon me?"

"OK, VT, what do you have for me?"

"Well, it seems that Bloodhead made a significant treasure find and was over here pawning the goods."

"What was he selling this time?"

"Gold coins, as far as I can tell."

Nicholas paused for a moment and then asked, "Was anyone else there who we know?"

"No, sir, just him. Elizabeth left by plane before he set sail. I am hanging around long enough to talk to a coin dealer at a coin shop where Bloodhead made some transactions. Then I will be trying to find out where the 3 CANES is heading."

"Hmm. I wonder what gives with Elizabeth not going by boat. OK, no matter, dude, keep an eye on him and keep me posted. Thanks. Good...whoops, wait, hang on there. Go ahead and tell me what you were this time. Hell, I almost forgot to ask."

"I was a florist," Van Tangle said, grinning from ear to ear.

"Simple and unassuming. Cool! You are the best. Just the best. OK then, until next time, VT. Goodbye."

The next day at Intertwine, Nicholas meandered around the lab and started up a conversation with one of his workmates about the possibility of ever mapping the entire human genome. Shop talk

He had always felt if that could be done, he would be so much closer to where he needed to be in his own quest toward unlocking the chemical reaction that must be present when a 'Knower' touches another 'Knower' or a 'Rendering Parent'. They just didn't have the tools yet to register the smallest particles of the body. They most assuredly were there. It had to be a chemical reaction related to memories and how they are stored, he thought. If only the company had more funding, they could surely begin that awesome trek down the road to what would probably lead to a Nobel Prize.

CHAPTER XXIX

KANDY AND Jaybird had dropped by to see Robin at his parents' house before they continued on their trek. Kandy had decided to remain with her husband only due to the fact that Robin wouldn't be traveling with them. He was undergoing physical therapy for his leg. Kandy had promised herself to stop the petty bickering. That decision came after Jaybird had bought her a pair of very expensive pearl earrings. She didn't really want to go back on the road in the Winnebago but she couldn't find an excuse good enough to stay in St. Joseph. Besides, she decided she should get him to buy her more jewelry and stuff before she made the final cut away from him. She figured she could play her game for a little longer.

Robin was sitting at home when Mr. Moss called to inform Donnelly that his court date was the following Monday. Robin tried to be optimistic about it but there was a part of him that knew he owed something to Julie's mom. He really didn't care what the outcome was. The accident *had* been his fault. He knew he should be man enough to do the honorable thing instead of hiding behind the technicalities of the law.

That Monday the jury awarded Julie's mother eight million dollars in total damages. Mr. Moss told Robin that they could appeal and that he would get right to work on that paperwork. But Robin stopped him from running on and on with all his legal gibberish with a finger to his mouth. He then got out his checkbook and wrote a check for the entire amount. He still hadn't put any of his money in a tax shelter, mutual fund or savings account. It had been just sitting in his checking account.

Mr. Moss tried to explain to Robin what the appeal process could do for him in terms of lowering the settlement. But Robin scribbled on a piece of paper, "give it a rest!" He grabbed his cane, limped over to Mrs. Volt, who was talking to her lawyer, Mr. Print, and handed her the check for eight million dollars. He also gave her a copy of the poem that he had written for Julie before that fatal night. He hadn't found the right moment to give it to Julie the night of their second date. So he figured her mother should have it. He would have explained how he felt but he had endured so much criticism during the litigation that he was just drained. He wanted to move on. This part of his life was finally over. He had done the honorable thing and paid his debt.

Robin remembered a time in 1251 in Ireland when his horse-drawn cart had accidentally run over and killed a young boy who had darted onto the dirt road in front of him. He went to see the father of the boy and told him that he could have his land and belongings as reparations. Then he left the village on foot. Again, his debt paid! *Why did these things happen to him over and over?* he wondered.

The next day, sitting on the porch swing Robin remembered that Chief Eagleclaw had said he could come back anytime. Now seemed like the best time to get away and decide what his next steps would be. He still had some money left after paying Mrs. Volt, the lawyer and court costs. He had also bought an old car. No need for a fancy speed-demon car anymore. *Speed kills.* He bought an old on-the-dash push-button-transmission Rambler. It was a piece of crap car. Just something to get him to where he was going. And Montana was his next stop. His parents tried to persuade him to stay home and rehab the leg, as they were very worried about his state of mind. He had lost his sense of humor, had become withdrawn, and he still talked only in verse. They knew he was taking painkillers but were sure the pain was not just in his leg. They also knew he was depressed but they couldn't get him to seek professional help.

Robin though, felt he would be able to sort things out and ease the pain inside him while he was out in Montana. He felt drawn to visit that quiet space by a strong nagging feeling inside. So he assured his parents that he would be fine and left the next day with little more than a back seat full of clothes, a cooler full of soda and olive loaf and cheese sandwiches, his favorite.

CHAPTER XXX

"**OLIVE LOAF** and cheese! Nobody but Robin likes that crap. Can I have a ham and cheese, please? Who packed this cooler anyway?" Jaybird asked, as he spit out the bite he just took.

"Oh. Sorry. I thought you liked those also," Kandy said, trying to sound apologetic.

"No problem, we'll just hit the next Stuckey's and get a pecan roll or something to munch on. So, who's next on the list of relatives?" Jaybird asked as he took a drink of his soda.

"My aunt and uncle in Wauconda, Illinois, are next up."

Early the next morning they backed out of Aunt May and Uncle Dale's huge driveway in a suburb of Chicago. They had stayed overnight after taking her aunt, uncle, two cousins and three second-cousins out to dinner. The kids liked the Winnebago. They entertained themselves by opening every door and cabinet drawer there was. Kandy had seen her aunt and uncle only once before, when she was a first-grader. She and her mother weren't in a financial position to take any vacations, even if it was to see relatives, so she had missed out on getting to know most of her family. She found them to be wonderful people to talk to. Since they had a lot of catching up to do, conversation and small-talk rambled on at break-neck speed until midnight when Jaybird suggested they all hit the hay. Her aunt invited the both of them back anytime they ever passed by the area again.

Kandy had actually been nice around them. Since they were her relatives and not Jaybird's, she didn't need to put on an act for them.

Once they got on the main highway and headed east, Jaybird asked, "OK, cross them off. Now, who is next on the list?"

"Your Uncle Nicholas is next. He lives in Mullica Hill, New Jersey," Kandy replied.

Jaybird thought for a moment and said, "Great, I can't wait to meet him. He is one of the few people in our family who wasn't around for holidays. But he always sent me big money for my birthdays. My mom always said my dad's brother was forever away somewhere getting stuff for his books and doing research that would save the world. He probably won't even be home."

"What does he do?"

"Well, Mom said he works for…Intertwine, and writes history books or something on the side," Jaybird said, recalling what his mother had called from the kitchen.

"Never heard of it. Sounds boring. And I always hated history," Kandy said as she marked the map with a yellow line depicting the quickest way to their next stop.

"Your grades showed that to be true," Jaybird said as he saw the sneer come across Kandy's face. He paid no attention to that now oh-so-familiar look.

Kandy continued, "Well, your uncle can have his history. I want to see things that are here and now. Like that, that…um, McDonald's College!" Kandy said as she got the camera out to take a quick picture.

Jaybird thought she was joking until he glanced over and saw the big sign. Sure enough, there was a huge McDonald's College sign.

"Hey, we can go get a PhD in burger-making. And a minor in fries!" Jaybird chuckled.

Kandy forced out a "Yeah, right," as she clicked off another picture.

Many states later as dusk was falling, Jaybird turned off the radio. Kandy looked at him with one of those "what now" looks.

"Did my mom have a phone number for my uncle?" Jaybird asked, as they drove across the Walt Whitman Bridge from Pennsylvania into New Jersey.

"I don't know."

"Could you check the address book or are you too busy driving?"

She looked at him as if that would be the biggest chore in the world. Begrudgingly she dug the notebook out from under the seat. She had heard his smart-alecky, sarcastic tone before addressed to other people but never had he talked to her like that. Never. She wondered what was causing it. Jaybird had always said his sarcasm was how he made jokes: by making fun of how people act and talk since they usually don't see themselves as others do. He said if he talked back to people just like they talked to him, maybe they would see how stupid they sometimes sounded. But she had always felt it to be a biting, insincere wit. If you didn't know him well enough, it would hurt because he would say things with a straight face. If you weren't strong enough to laugh at yourself, you would never hear him say that he was just kidding. Some folks never got the joke and took it personally. *I take it personally*.

"Let's see," Kandy said as she flipped through the pages. "Yes, there is a phone number for him. I guess you should stop and see if he will be home, huh?"

Jaybird looked at her and said, "Yeah, we should do that. Say, how big is this Mullica Hill town?"

"How should I know?"

"Take a look on the map and see if it has a star, a black dot or a clear dot for the town marker."

"It has nothing by it, does that help you?"

"A star in a circle means it is the state capitol and…never mind. If there isn't anything by the town name it is really small."

"Where did you learn that?"

"I was reading the legend on the map when you were at the last pit stop going to the bathroom."

"Think you're pretty smart, don'tcha?" Kandy said. She was getting tired of the game she was playing again. She just wanted to get the divorce and be on her way. She had to find the right time and place to get away from him. She felt that possibly he was growing tired of her too. She knew that was a very good sign. Why else would he start being sarcastic with her?

"You betcha," Jaybird replied.

They drove for another half hour as Kandy peered out the window at the acres of orchards along the highway. *New Jersey looks as boring as all the other states we have driven through*, she thought. *When I get all of Jaybird's money I will never drive anywhere for vacation. First class will be my only mode of travel.*

Jaybird stopped at a gas station and called the number in the address book from a pay phone. He was surprised but glad to get his uncle on the phone. Nicholas gave him quick directions to his home and told Jaybird they were only a few minutes away. two lefts, second street on the right and half-mile up to the gate.

So he climbed up onto the plush, swiveling, high-back driver's seat and headed up the road.

Shortly, they drew to a halt in the driveway of a large house sitting on top of a hill about two miles from the main road. Jaybird wondered if this was *the* Mullica Hill namesake hill. The driveway circled around a neatly trimmed chunk of yard that had a large assortment of granite statues in it and was wide enough for the Winnebago to traverse easily. Jaybird turned off the engine and remarked that he didn't know how much money a bio-scientist or history book writer made but from the size of the house it looked like Uncle Nicholas was doing very well indeed.

Kandy thought the house was a mansion and couldn't wait to see the inside of it, although she was extremely tired and didn't particularly want to meet any of *his* relatives. She was so weary of putting on a fake smile and engaging in conversations that she could not care less about. She knew it was time to get away from Jaybird. She couldn't pretend to love him any longer no matter how hard she tried. And the joy of sex had worn off for her. *Maybe it was true what they say: you have to be in love to make love.*

Once inside the gates, Jaybird parked by a broad expanse of steps. The entrance was under a huge archway flanked by two massive stone lions. The large wooden double doors opened and standing in the doorway was a man's figure back-lighted from the hallway beyond. Jaybird assumed it was his uncle. The man waved at them as they continued to stretch a bit.

Nicholas Young was a thirty-six-year-old man who stood five-feet ten. He had an average build and looked healthy. His long blond hair hung over his shoulders. He had a small amount of silver around the temples, but Jaybird could not see that easily, since the long hair mostly covered the gray. He wore faded blue jeans and a short sleeve tie-dyed T-shirt with the face of Jimi Hendrix on it. His attire didn't match the opulence of the house.

He motioned them to hurry for no reason whatsoever, so Jaybird grabbed two suitcases and followed Kandy up the granite steps.

Dr. Young greeted Kandy first with a nod and a smile then asked who she was.

"I'm Kandy…Young, and you *are* Nicholas, right?" she asked.

"You got that right. So, Mrs. Young. My nephew, married you, did?" Sounding as much like the character Yoda as he could, from a recent movie he had seen. This made no sense to either Kandy or Jaybird.

"Wonderful, just wonderful, you make a good-looking couple. Listen, you both can just call me Uncle Nick."

"Hello, Uncle Nick," Jaybird said as he set the suitcases down. He laughed to himself as he thought that just a few short months ago he would have agreed with Nicholas on the good-looking couple remark, but now somehow he just didn't really feel it.

"Howdy, Nephew. Good to see you in person," Nicholas said as he grabbed the two suitcases and headed into the foyer, adding, "All I ever had was a photograph of you when you were in the eighth grade. I only got to hold you once for a little bit on my lap one summer when you were little as I happened through your town on a book-signing tour. Never got out to visit Harry's side of the family after that. College, then work, book deadlines. Life has always kept me busy and away. Your mom did call me up, out of nowhere, just after you got married. She said you were heading out to see me sometime this summer after you did that honeymoon thing in Tahiti but she never told me your wife's name...um, at least I don't think she did."

"Oh, I was wondering why it sounded like you were expecting me when we spoke on the phone. Well, anyway, I sure am glad to get here and meet you. We have been zooming along the highways, seeing the sights between Chicago and here. Sleeping in a house will feel good for a change," Jaybird said as he shut the huge door behind him.

"Groovy little trip. I'll bet you're hungry and tired then. I will put you up in a guest room and you can crash or raid the refrigerator, whatever you want to do. My house is your house."

Kandy said that she would love to tour the house but that sleep would be her first choice, so Nicholas placed their luggage inside the first large bedroom at the top of the grand staircase on the left side of the huge room.

As Kandy entered the room, Jaybird motioned to her that he was going to follow Nicholas who was heading down the right side staircase. She was relieved that he wasn't coming to bed. That part of the relationship was hard for her to fake at this point. The sex had been great in the beginning because it was new to her. That had made it easier for her to put up with being around him, but that, too, was getting old. She just didn't care for sex that much anymore. She nodded to him with heavy eyes and put both her hands together, tilting her head to one side in a gesture of sleep. Jaybird turned around quickly to follow his uncle down the stairs and into a long hallway. After about twenty feet and several more doors, they came to some wide stairs that went down a few steps into another large open room.

"I think Kandy will be out until late morning, Uncle Nick," Jaybird said as he looked at the wall ahead of him.

"Right on. If you feel up to it we can just bullshit for a while and get to know each other."

"Sure. Sounds good to me."

"Want a barley pop?" Nick asked.

"A what?"

"A beer. Sorry, I have always called them that."

"Beer, now that sounds good," Jaybird replied, remembering it had been about five hours since he had anything to drink.

"But how do you get the name barley pop from beer?"

"Well…beer is made from barley hops and it ain't no *soda* pop, so I just hooked them together and got barely pop. I think I coined that phrase in college.

"That hasn't caught on out in Missouri yet, Uncle Nick," Jaybird said as he followed along.

Nicholas started to go around the corner but Jaybird stopped at the bottom of the steps. In front of him was a huge open area. Inset into the convex wall on his left was the largest fish tank he had ever seen, in a house at least. It went from one side of the room and followed the curve of the wall to the other side of the room. It was at least forty feet long. All along the base of the tank was a long couch. Since this base was three feet above the floor, the couch was perfect for placing your knees on and staring into the tank at the multitude of fish swimming ever so gracefully.

"This way, Jaybird," Nick said from around the corner.

As Jaybird followed his uncle's voice around the corner, he was again taken aback when he saw the giant eighty by eighty foot room. There was a bar that ran the length of the other side of the fish tank and followed the inverse curve of it. When he looked hard he could see the stairs through the water. It was an awesome sight, complete with mirrors, barstools and four tapped kegs, from one of which his uncle was drawing beer into a frosty glass. In the middle of this huge room was a sunken area that held an antique pool table. It was two more steps down, providing seating all around for on-lookers or hecklers. Along the far back wall was another sunken area in front of a huge fireplace. Jaybird thought that would be perfect for a quiet, romantic evening with the wife.

"Here. A Missouri beer. The King of Beers," Nicholas said, setting the glass down on the bar in front of Jaybird.

All Jaybird could mutter was a "Thanks," as he took the glass. He was still absorbing the interesting items the house had to offer. It seemed very eclectic. There were some stunning antique furniture pieces around but the walls were covered with black light posters; each one having its own small black light over it. There were large tapestries hanging on other walls along with a few tribal masks. The interior didn't seem to have any particular theme.

"Pretty nice pad, if I do say so myself. You think so?" Nicholas asked as he took a drink of beer.

"Yes, it is a nice place. Very …big. Your books must make a lot of money to pay for all this."

"Well, I guess they do keep the little green paper stuff coming in. I have a few other money-making resources. Have a seat there, Jaybird."

"Thanks. So you write books, Nick?" he said settling onto a bar stool.

"Sometimes. I am a bio-scientist by day but the book writing is an outlet, I guess. I play with DNA, genes, chromosomes and boring stuff at work but I've written five books since getting my doctorate."

"Interesting."

"Think it ain't! Life is made up of all those things and I *like* to see what life is made of. Ah, life; learn to enjoy it. Yup, the here and now and the past. There's really not much else out there. Except what you have upstairs."

"Upstairs?"

"In your noggin," Nicholas said, tapping his temple.

"I suppose you're right. But no future though?" Jaybird asked, not really expecting an answer.

"Hey…let's get deep right off the bat here! OK, I say that the future hasn't happened yet so it can be changed, but the past is cast in stone. It can't be changed; it can only be known and verified. I try to let some of the truth be known through my books. Everyone can learn from the truth."

"I see, sure, with history books, right?" Jaybird asked.

"Yup."

"OK."

"Is that it? No further deep discussions?"

They sat there in silence for a moment. Jaybird was busy looking around the room at the furniture, paintings and odd designs in the architecture. He thought that his uncle had an unusual eye for things and hadn't really heard his last question. Nicholas on the other hand, was waiting for a moment just like this one. He reached over the bar and nudged Jaybird on the arm and sat back to watch.

As soon as Nicholas touched his arm, that strange feeling started to happen to Jaybird again, only this time it was a much stronger flood of memories.

He *knew!!* He *knew* every time he had been acquainted with Nicholas. All of his past lives with Nicholas. Everything he had ever done and learned. The good, the bad and the ugly.

It was not the same feeling he had when he touched Robin that first time or the old man or all the Indians; it was different somehow. More clear initially. The knowledge came over him like waves on a beach, each wave totally different from the others. He dropped the glass of beer and closed his eyes. He couldn't have moved if he had wanted to. There was no way of stopping the onslaught of feelings and thoughts.

He was consumed by memories of his own past lives with this man. He felt elated, then pained; there were volumes of feelings he had never felt before. Names, dates, places and faces. Other times had no dates, no names, only faces, feelings and actions. The emotions he was feeling were like a roller-coaster ride. Highs and lows, good and bad. Justification, indignation and vindication. Laughter, love, tenderness, embarrassment, pain and suffering. All at the speed of thought.

Nicholas stood up and started backing up slowly to a closet where the broom and dust pan were. He had seen this quite a few times before in this life and in his past lives. It was always an event to behold. He smiled as he empathized with his nephew. He knew sooner or later Jaybird would snap out of it and be able to talk again. Nicholas would have the monu-mental task of explaining to Jaybird what had just happened to him. In the meantime he swept up the broken beer glass and watched Jaybird from behind the bar after putting the glass shards in the trash can.

Jaybird was holding onto the bar with one hand and trying to catch his breath. His head turned toward Nicholas once but he couldn't get any words out. He was fully engrossed in the moment.

After what seemed like an hour to Jaybird, but was in fact only five minutes, he inhaled deeply and said with great surprise, "I know you!"

"Think you don't!"

"No. I mean I really know who you were, um, even before today. But…I just met you!"

"Yes, you have known me many times, am I right?"

Jaybird shook his head up and down saying, "Yes, you are in my memories quite a number of times, from what I can remember now. You are in one of my oldest and most crusty memories. The first time I remember you…you were…my father…well…I…it was so long ago…that I can't…" Jaybird was grappling with the thought of no time or dates, when Nicholas asked, "What was my name then that first, very important time?"

"I…I…don't know. But you were my father."

"Funny, isn't it?"

"Not really. More like unnerving, or maybe interesting, I haven't decided yet."

"So why can't you remember my name that particular time, eh? Focus, Jaybird!" Nicholas said, laughing.

"Well, I…ah…you didn't have one," Jaybird said, not really sure why he even knew that.

"What year was it?" his uncle prodded.

"I don't know! I can't remember the year. Why are you asking me these things? Do you know the answers? Do you have any clue as to what just happened to me?"

"I most certainly do. And you are right; I didn't have a name then and I was your father. You can't remember a year because it wasn't invented yet."

"What wasn't invented?"

"The measure of time hadn't been thought up yet. Survival, eating and reproducing were about all there was then. Are you confused yet?"

"Absolutely! Hey where did my beer go? I need a drink," Jaybird said looking at the bar and on the floor.

"Well, you lost that beer when you regained your memories. I swept it up."

As Nicholas handed him another glass with a fresh draw of beer in it, Jaybird looked at him strangely and continued, "You invented beer, didn't you?"

"Think I didn't? About 9000 years ago in what they now call China. Way before any current historian would place the beginning of a good thing like a barley pop. But someday they'll dig up something and bookmark my nice rice and fruit drink as originating in China."

Jaybird just shook his head saying, "OK, well, sorry about the glass. I feel like I just woke up from a coma or something. It feels like I have been dreaming and now I am awake and everything I dreamt was actually true, but there is so much to think about. What is…I mean, how did you know what I was remembering?"

"Well, conjunction junction what's my function," Nicholas said singing a bit off key, "I didn't know what you were remembering but I knew that you were a 'Knower', because I held you when you were little, remember? I Knew at that moment that...well, I made you...um...the very first time. I made your soul, that is. That first touch from me made you a 'Knower' but since you hadn't hit puberty yet you didn't get any of the feelings or memories. So yes, we have run across each other often, over the ages of mankind. What is so cool is that we have had this little conversation before. You have already remembered that I was your very first biological father. We call that a 'Rendering Parent'. I was the first to capture your 'O'."

"You captured my what? A 'Knower'? Can you clarify things a little bit better?"

Those ideas sounded somehow familiar but Jaybird couldn't put his finger on the meaning of the words.

"Well, a 'Knower' is someone who has regained some glimpses and partial continuity of his memories from his past lives. The 'O'? That's what we in 'The Calm' call the soul, your essence, spirit or whatever. Capturing your 'O' just refers to the very first time your soul is born into this world and into a body. We really just named it that because the soul, once made, is never-ending, hence the 'O' or circle. We call someone who has touched both 'Rendering Parents' a 'Complete Knower'."

"Oh, right, you are my 'Other thingy'! From the...the um...'First Rib' right?"

"Huh...well, I'll be. Leapin' lizards! Sounds like you have been talking to some Indians. A particular small group of Indians. Am I correct?"

"Yeah, Kandy's father, Chief Eagleclaw is Indian. We went to see him and he had a little get together thing and...well it's a long story. But he said we were from the 'First Rib' and we hadn't touched the Other...um...half...'Rib Maker' yet or something like that."

"We? You and Kandy?" Nicholas asked.

"No, me and my friend, Robin. Well, Kandy was there but she was asleep."

"So this Robin, is she a member of the 'First Rib' too?"

"Oh, Robin is a guy. My next door neighbor and best friend, Well, he used to live next door. Anyway, he was my brother in the mid 1800's. He was my dad before that time also…and you…you were his father that first time also! Hey this is so weird. We all have the same problem …memory problem thing."

Nicholas laughed and said, "You don't have anything and it definitely isn't a problem per se. Man, you make it sound like a disease. I think we have a lot to talk about. Let me get you another barley pop. Be sure to hang onto this one!"

CHAPTER XXXI

EDWARD HUNG onto the railing as his yacht lightly bumped the pier in Trieste, Italy. It was a nice little port that could support larger ships and the *3 CANES* had tied up pier-side there many times before. It was a quiet town. He could hop on a train and go over to Milan from there. He was glad that he had Elizabeth out of his hair. And he knew that Duke wouldn't make another mistake. He was sure that Duke would eliminate her and meet him back here in Trieste. He felt no remorse in having her killed. She had been with him too long. She knew too much about his whereabouts. *There are so many other women to have*, he thought. He definitely wouldn't allow the next woman he was infatuated with hang around for such a long length of time. He had known better, but she was such a beauty. Better to remain detached from the females from now on, he decided.

On the train Edward sipped some wine as he remembered the farm house in Milan. He had stored many of his paintings there while he lived life as Michelangelo Merisi da Caravaggio from 1571-1610.

Edward had finally received confirmation from his Italian business liaison that the estate was now legally his. It was time to collect the goods. *These times are so much like living a game*, he mused. *The rules and laws of every country are different; it's all about how you use them to your benefit.*

If he wasn't so wealthy he might never have been able to purchase the estate that was once his small little world of inspiration, while at the same time his prison. It was such a long time ago but he could remember it vividly. He had read what the history books said about Caravaggio. They had always classified him as a revolutionary painter who had about fifty or so paintings to his credit. But he died penniless. Truth be known, he was left to rot in a hell-hole of a jail for an old crime that hadn't been expunged from his records, The Pope had actually granted him a pardon, but the local authorities never bothered to investigate his claim. When he finally was released, he missed the ship that was to take him away to a new start on life. He watched it set sail early with his goods and all his hope, which was the only thing keeping him alive. He died from a fever on the beach.

When Edward remembered he had been Caravaggio, he could recall having many horrible years as a youngster painting from inside his small bedroom up in the corner of the main house that his father owned in Milan. Many of his works were inspired by writings of the day. Others were pure fantasy. Still other inspirations came from the pain inside him that was bursting to get out. He had hidden countless canvas attempts at beauty in an underground cubbyhole at the servants' quarters in the west acres of the estate. A false floor under the boards in the back corner of the pantry had been his and the senior servants' little secret. After he became a teenager and had escaped from his father's iron control, he had traveled to Rome. Many times he was able to sell his work. He had done a few consignment paintings which had made his reputation. But it was the two hundred other paintings that he had completed and taken back to Milan to hide in that cubbyhole that would make Edward even richer in this life. If the canvas paintings were still there after four hundred plus years, they would fetch as much as forty million dollars each on the open market. But to private collectors…he could name his price. One hundred million would not be out of the question for just one of them.

The thought of who he was during that life made him laugh. How could a mentally ill man with so much angst and confusion inside himself be a world-renowned painter and function within that society? He could remember that he liked to paint religious scenes because he had constantly read the Bible as a very young boy. He tried to bring the stories to life. As he grew he would read anything he could get his hands on. When an idea struck him, he would use whoever was near him as a subject for his painting. When he got older, after running away from his family, he became prone to violent outbursts of emotion, which usually got him into trouble. He even killed a man once. The man was trying to welch out of paying him what was rightfully his after losing a bet. Edward always seemed to be killing someone at sometime in his past lives.

Edward thought to himself, *Isn't it ironic that I could have had such a religious foundation during that time, yet still been able to kill another human being? Religion, such a silly outdated concept.*

During that life as Michelangelo Caravaggio, Edward had never gained the knowledge of any of his other past lives. He only hid the paintings initially to keep them away from his father who was trying to sell them, claiming they were his own work. After his father died, Edward continued to go back to the family estate and hide his paintings.

Caravaggio would paint an ear on the canvas and go from there. He always started with the ears because of the constant barrage of voices he heard. The voices would tell him what to paint, what colors to use and what size canvas. He thought the suggestions were coming from invisible external people, when of course it was really his own internal thoughts. But he could not understand the difference, because of his schizophrenia.

The train pulled into the station at Milan. Edward exited, jumped into a taxi and headed for the estate. Once there he met his Italian business manager and the estate curator who had been waiting for almost an hour already. They signed some final papers and the curator left, briskly. Edward noticed that he seemed to be in quite a hurry. The small flatbed truck that Edward had requested was there with a driver, along with the

ten large empty trunks. As Edward entered the severely unkempt property, he motioned for the driver to follow him as he headed for the old
servants' buildings in the most distant area of the property.

As they approached the smaller buildings, Edward could see that there
was a camp fire of sorts outside one of the cottages and people sitting
near the heat. Edward instantly knew why the curator had been in such
a hurry to leave. He had obviously known these people were there all
along. *They must be squatters. They will just have to go; this is my land now,*
he thought to himself.

As the two approached the group of five people, a man of about fifty,
wearing raggedy clothes, stood up and came towards him. He informed
Edward that he was the father of the Etruscan Haruspex who was seated
over by the fire. He extended his hand in the customary manner but
Edward, as always, did not shake his hand.

"The Haruspex…hmm, now why does that sound familiar?" Edward
asked as he walked past the man toward the others.

When he got to the fire he asked mockingly, "So, who is the High
Priest prophet child here who thinks he can tell the future by sacrificing
animals, gutting them and reading their, oh, well now, what is it, livers?"

"That would be me, sir," A lanky teenaged boy said as he stood up.
The man beside him tried to pull him back down in an attempt at being
inconspicuous, but the attempt was useless. The boy was proud of his
status.

"So you think you can read livers, eh?" Edward asked.

"I have recently seen and advised my people that a tall American man
would come and try to take our people's rightful land away from us. My
reading seems to be correct, was it not?" he asked with a deep Italian
accent.

Edward scratched his head and laughed out loud, saying, "Listen you
bunch of…squatters, I could not care less about your second-century
esoteric religion, your little *Tagetic Book* and your sacred traditions of
killing animals and what-not. I *am* quite surprised that there are any of

you still around though. It amuses me that anybody in this day and age would buy into the notion that this boy here could read a *liver* to get that information. It is very clear to me that he has been talking to the curator of this estate and got his *divine* reading from him, not some God or immortal deity. Talk about pulling the wool over your eyes, come on now."

The boy smiled and said, "Well, I almost always must explain the deep religious beliefs of my people. It is not often that a foreigner happens upon us, let alone one who has any knowledge of our ways."

"Listen kid, Haruspex, or what ever they call you. I'm not here to bash your beliefs, even though there were new religions popping up all around about the same time that yours did. Mind you, these little cult religions were only created in opposition to the growing popularity of Christianity. Lots of folks didn't want to follow the pack, so to speak. A lot of you were killed for practicing your own particular kind of rites."

Edward remembered another life he lived a long time ago. It was about 110 years after Jesus had been crucified. Edward was named Mark, son of John, the builder. He was a mason by trade, as was his father. His father had always told him to believe in what he wanted, but believing with the majority would surely keep you alive. Everyone in that time knew that Christianity was rapidly spreading and anyone who didn't like those teachings could rest assured of being run out of their particular hamlet, or worse, being stoned to death. He had listened to his father and kept his beliefs to himself. Edward mused at the enormous number of times he could remember being a mason in his past lives. *I am very good at building things,* he thought, knowing he would eventually embark on recovering some of the many valuable treasures he and his mason brethren had encased inside structures they built.

"Yes," the boy's father said, "We were killed in the name of *their* Lord."

"Yeah, what a bitch," Edward scoffed. "Listen, what I want is in that old cottage back there. After I get it and leave, you can...hell, you can read all the pig livers you want as far as I'm concerned. I'll never come back here, that's for sure. You can live here forever for all I care."

With that Edward and the truck driver went into the pantry in the back of the cottage. The boards had been nailed carefully and firmly to the floor. Edward pulled up enough boards to allow him to wiggle down into the dark, dry smelling dirt crawl space. He was pleasantly surprised to fine his old paintings still there. As he began pulling the canvases out, he ordered the truck driver to bring the truck closer to the door. He chuckled at how the servants had always hidden their liquor bottles in that hole and covered the boards with a table.

The group from the fire milled around outside but they didn't present a problem to Edward. They were trying to ascertain if Edward was going to actually let them stay there without a fight for the rights to the land.

After all the paintings were loaded into the trunks on the bed of the truck, Edward climbed in and had the driver head to Trieste. That would be the last he ever wanted to deal with that land and estate and the Etruscans. He had his goods. He was satisfied. Now to find some buyers. He knew he couldn't flood the market with all the paintings at once. He had to be patient selling these works of art to garner the value that he wanted from them. Patience was not something he had much of, but he knew might have to hang on to these for a longer time and parcel them out slowly.

CHAPTER XXXII

"WHOOPS, HANG on, just a second while I grab another pen; this one just ran out on me," the journalist said.

He had been asking Mr. McCallock about all the intricate details from start to finish of his brief, yet profitable, if not actually lucky, acquaintance with Edward Bloodhead.

He was not in the least bit surprised by anything Mr. McCallock was telling him of his dealings with Mr. Bloodhead. He was impressed with the forethought the man had shown. He ascertained that the coin dealer was a very intelligent and calculating thinker. He gave Mr. McCallock his card and left after about three hours of conversation. His advice was to find another place of residence for at least the near future. He tried to impress upon Mr. McCallock how, during his *journalistic investigating*, he had concluded that Bloodhead was a thorough and tidy person. Loose ends were made to be tied up and not just forgotten. Being finagled out of sixty million dollars left a very large loose end. He was certain that Mr. Bloodhead would see McCallock as a loose end.

The journalist then quickly headed for the hotel where a woman had been found dead, to see if the killing fit the same Bloodhead M.O. as the others he had run across over the years. He had learned to see a pattern associated with these killings. Professional. Very professional.

There seemed to always be a murder in the area when Van Tangle was tailing Bloodhead. Now, if his disguise worked the way it should, maybe he could gather some important information.

The local authorities offered no help as he pressed them for anything useful. Thankfully they just believed him to be another foreign journalist looking for a sensational story that he could blow out of proportion for some ragtag magazine. They paid him no mind as he meandered around.

As the coroner was taking the body out, the sheet covering the victim's face slid off just enough for the journalist to get a good look at the older dark-skinned woman lying there. He wondered if she was in any way connected to Bloodhead. If not, the trail would be getting cold again.

Duke got out of the taxi and went to the pier in Trieste. After finding the launch and returning to the yacht, he sat down on a nicely cushioned chair to relax. He was quite pleased with himself for what he thought would make up for his previous mistake of not killing McCallock. Killing a woman was not as difficult as killing a man because of the female's physical limitations. She was weak; it was dark; no problems. He had enjoyed killing Elizabeth. She had just been one more thing for Edward to worry about. No more worries now. *She won't be talking to anyone ever again,* he thought. All he had to do was be patient until Edward returned with the paintings. He couldn't wait to brag.

Before he fell asleep he read the latest telegram from the U.S. accountant. Normally Edward kept his business information out of sight or locked away. This paper was in plain view on the table next to the couch. It made interesting reading. Seems the oil recovery business was making profits exponentially. That little venture was proving to be very valuable for Edward. Fifteen million dollars a month now. Duke figured it was time he asked for a raise.

"You didn't do anything stupid like go find that McCallock bastard and snuff him too, did you?" Edward asked after he shook Duke awake.

"No, sir. I did just what you told me to: I put Elizabeth out of your hair forever. Fast and clean. No struggle. No surprises," Duke said, smirking somewhat as he rubbed his eyes.

"Good. You already have one strike against you. You don't need another. I'll get that *Mc Scoundrel* one day myself. I'll get him good. My lawyers will ruin him first. Then it will be my turn to totally devastate his pathetic little life. Death would be too good for him anyway. He took my money and I'm going to make him pay."

Looks like I will have to put an asterisk by the coin dealer's name, Duke thought to himself. *Of course I'll be the one doing all the work.* As he glanced at the clock that showed midnight he decided that it was definitely time for a raise. He then quickly fell back asleep.

CHAPTER XXXIII

IT WAS already after midnight but Nicholas told Jaybird to hang onto his seat and listen carefully, there was much more to understand.

"OK, now first of all, you have to realize that this whole conversation can't be explained to anyone else except another 'Knower'. You would be hauled off for a psychological evaluation if you ever tried. Believe me, you could end up never getting free of that sector of society. And I am talking from experience here, OK? They have their own set of rules and if you don't play by them, they label you nuts, crazy, schizoid even! No, it isn't time for non-'Knowers' to wrestle with this particular facet of life just yet. You only discuss this with other 'Knowers' in 'The Calm' or a 'Knower' who asks for clarification. And that goes for wives also, understand?"

"Yes…well, no, not totally, but I gather I am a 'Knower' and I kinda get the idea of the 'O'. Just tell me what 'The Calm' is."

"Right, good question, easy answer. 'The Calm' is a group of 'Knowers' who get together and tell stories and talk about life in general, really. Whether it is consciously or subconsciously they *know* more than a person who has not touched one or both of their 'Rendering Parents'. 'Knowers' are just people like you. You are more aware of yourself now, with your regained memories of your past lives. Your friend Robin and those Indians of the 'First Rib' are also in this category. Rest assured you will be dying to meet the members of 'The Calm'. Any 'Knower' can be part of the group. No dues, initiations, or charters. You just come and talk if you feel like it and are in the area. When those of us that are 'Complete Knowers' touch someone, we can instantly tell if they are 'Knowers' or 'Complete Knowers' or neither. If we touch someone to whom we know we have been related in the past but aren't 'Knowers', then we don't say anything. Of course they don't feel anything unusual. But if there was a good relationship back then in a past life, it usually means we get along well in this life. We hope they get to touch one or both of their 'Rendering Parents' so they can get that grand feeling of recognition of their past memories."

Jaybird was engrossed with everything Nicholas was saying. It was such a huge relief to him to finally validate his feelings and ease his bewilderment.

Nicholas continued, "So: 'Knowers' usually can't remember names or exact places with their memories though. It is more like deja vu, a really strong insight, or a gut feeling of sorts. Some memories do seem stronger than others though; yet it is like only half of what is stored up in the head actually gets released. A teaser of sorts. But if they touch their other 'Rendering Parent', things become crystal clear as all the memories of all that person's past lives are released. Those lucky folks, who we call 'Complete Knowers', for obvious reasons, tend to be really calm. We in 'The Calm' believe that is why scientists have said that we only use ten percent of our brains. The rest of the brain's capacity is actually reserved for future memories, or it is already full of stored-up memories, just waiting to be remembered. But damned if I know what exactly causes the remembering process, aside from the touch. Must be chemical though. Weird, just weird."

With that, Nicholas took a drink of his beer and waited for a response from Jaybird.

"Weird is an understatement, Uncle Nick," Jaybird said.

"Think it ain't? The Indians that I have had the pleasure to talk with are close to the mark with their traditional stories of how their tribes got started and all, but they won't budge from their story line or their rituals. And I don't know if they ever will, 'cause it is a religion *and* a way of life to them. That is, until someone in their group meets the 'Other Half' of their 'Rendering Parents', or 'First Rib Maker' as they call it. To my knowledge they haven't, and I have talked to many of them. They are still waiting to experience that moment, right there in the security of the reservation. But they will only have those vague, half memories until someone comes along by chance to meet them. They should get out more. Shake some hands."

"So they are not from the 'First Rib'?" Jaybird asked.

"Well, that is just a name. They *are* descendants from me…and *you*, as a matter of fact, but they have a different story to tell. The 'Other Half' they describe is right on track though. I understand some of their other meanings, but we in 'The Calm' have different views and terminology. We are saying the same thing basically. But we *know* for a fact that we were actually in a particular time and place because we have talked to many of the 'Complete Knowers', of whom, I am one, like I said. We are remembering the facts, not just believing in some myth or placing our hope on some belief system. They only believe in what they have been taught and what has been handed down through eons of story telling. I don't think they have anyone who has touched both sides of their so called 'Rib-Maker' yet. That act could change their whole belief system. Quite gnarly, man."

"OK, OK, back up, what do you mean they are descendants from you and me?"

"Well…put your beer down, I don't want you to break another glass," Nicholas said as he took a deep breath. "Are you ready for this?"

As Jaybird put his glass down he said, "Um…I guess so."

"Let me give you a brief overview here, man. Basically I was the person who the Indians would call the 'First Ancient Warrior', the man they took the first rib from and also who the Christian Bible would call Adam. None of those sects think it is the same story or person they are referring to, but it is. Every religion and or belief system has taken something from a perceived starting point and expanded it to fit their story line. Religion is man-made, as you may know."

"Get out of here. You're going to Hell if you keep talking like that!" Jaybird said, trying to make a joke.

"Hear me out before you pass judgment on me. Search your memories a bit, dude. There are many different legends, myths, and religions. All of them try to make fact out of stories that have been handed down by word of mouth and they always get distorted greatly. And you, my nephew, were once, long, long ago, the second son born to my first mate. I was the first to capture your 'O', along with my mate of course. So we became your 'Rendering Parents'."

"Whoa now…slow down, back up, rewind. I am getting lost here."

Nicholas chuckled as he took a sip from his glass, "This is going to be long night."

"I'm sure," Jaybird said, standing up to stretch his back.

"Think it ain't?"

"OK, for some reason I clearly remember you and that I was your second-born son, way back; actually, it is one of the earliest memories I have, I think. There is nothing before it. If that's the one you are talking about, then…and I…that…hey, Robin was my big brother. Your first-born. I had a lot of brothers and sisters. Oh, man, the third brother…he was…" Jaybird's words trailed off as his mind went back to a time long ago. He shook his head back and forth, looking at the bottom of the glass he was holding. A disturbing image came into focus.

"He was what, Jaybird? Your third brother, what was he, man?" Nicholas asked excitedly, egging him on.

"He was bad. Very bad," he said as he looked up at Nicholas.

"Think he wasn't! You have a great memory now, don't you?"

"I guess so, but he was my brother and he…he…was beating me! He beat me to…death!" Jaybird said, in disbelief at what he now knew was fact.

"Far out, man. That is what I have been trying to tell you. I was the one on whom the Christians base their Old Testament. They refer to me, the first man, as Adam in the Bible, and you were Abel and that bad big bro was Cain. He actually slew you. He killed you. Snuff city, man. And it was over the fact that you ate a few of the roots that he had just dug up. Boy, was he mad. Hungry, too, I presume."

"I remember that whole scene now. I *was* hungry and he had some roots lying there behind him. He had just picked a bunch of stuff when I grabbed some and started eating. He saw me and chased me around for the longest time and then when he caught me, he started bashing me in the head with a branch or a log or something. That's all I remember from that life. There was pain and then darkness. How weird."

"Think it ain't?"

"Why do you keep saying that?" Jaybird asked.

"Oh, um…it just means…I agree with you. Sorry, it's a bad habit I've had for some time now."

Jaybird shook his head, knocking some cobwebs off his memories and stated, "Let me get this straight. Correct me if I'm wrong. You were Adam and I was Abel and…hey…Robin would have been the oldest brother, Seth! But that's not how the Bible goes. I think they got the birth orders mixed up. Plus we didn't have names back then. Where did they come up with that? Yet, if we use the names the Bible does for the three of us…then Cain was…who was Cain, my brother that…well…killed me? How could a brother kill another brother? Do you know who that was, Uncle Nick?"

Nicholas decided that it wouldn't be a good idea to tell Jaybird who Cain was at this point. He knew that getting that knowledge right now might just freak him out more. Telling him who in *this* life had killed him once before just didn't have any value, so he tried to change the subject, stating somberly,

"Yes, I do know. I ran into his 'O' in this life about ten years ago. Never mind that. Now I am curious, did you say that your friend Robin was, for this discussion, the Biblical Seth, my first son?"

"Yes. He was there. As a matter of fact he was right there running behind me and Cain. He surely saw Cain kill me. You know I can remember the pain of dying?"

"Think you can't? Sucks, don't it? They always say you can never remember dying but they are wrong most of the time. If you lived it, you can remember it, if it had an impact."

"What do you mean, 'if it had an impact'?" Jaybird asked.

"You usually only remember things that were important. I mean, can you remember what you ate for lunch three weeks ago Monday?"

"Um, no, I can't."

"But you probably did eat lunch that day, it just wasn't important enough to remember. But you can remember that very first life with me and being killed. I would say that had quite an impact. We tend to always remember our deaths. It's usually painful, that death thing. But listen, this is a monumental event, you know."

"What is?"

"Well, first off, you and I shouldn't use the names from the Bible. It is kinda cool when you can place yourself in any current historical document, but the Bible has more embellishments in it than historical facts. It is just a collection of stories from the power brokers of the time who decided to gather together and make a book. Most of the stories were culled from word-of-mouth and had been repeated wrongly or exaggerated for ages. Many stories were either so far-fetched or so boring that they didn't even get placed in the Bible. But, dude, you are so correct when you said we didn't have names. That time was before everything. It was the very beginning. We just knew how to eat and sleep and reproduce. We were living on our instincts for survival. Now, you say Robin is a friend you can contact right now, if you wanted to? You are sure he was your older brother at that time?"

"I am positive. And he was my brother in the 1800's when we buried the gold. Oh, and we have been family many times, over…like hundreds of times. And friends…tons of times," Jaybird said amazed at his new-found clarity of thought. Nicholas went around the bar to get another draft beer, saying, "This is unreal. I figured it would happen some day but I thought a few thousand years down the road, when more of this knowledge became…well, mainstream and people actually wanted to Know and were trying to find their…"

Jaybird had to interrupt. "What do you think is so unreal? Everything is pretty unreal to me, although in contrast, easy to accept for some reason."

"Well, for so many of the first family to be gathered so closely together now by chance, is monumental, I would think."

Jaybird did not understand everything so he asked, "What is so monumental? And what first family, Nick?"

Nicholas took out his comb and started running it through his long locks, he himself searching for the answer,

"The first family was large and I have now met every one of my eighteen offspring from that time, in this time, except for your friend Robin. What's monumental is that you and he ended up so close to each other as next door neighbors. I wonder what the odds are on that happening?"

"Really? Is that unusual?"

"Totally, dude. I wonder…" Nicholas' words faded as he paced behind the bar, deep in analytical thought.

Jaybird was thinking how interesting it was for him to have such a friendly conversation with someone of Nicholas' age, who he had just met and actually enjoy it. It felt like he was talking to his own dad, Harry. Well, family is family, he figured.

Jaybird gulped down a couple of swallows from his beer and after a few moments he asked Nicholas, "If you held me when I was younger, then…why did I have such a reaction when I touched you tonight? Does that happen every time you touch a 'Knower' or 'Rendering Parent'?"

"No, it doesn't. Only the first time will produce that huge all-consuming rush. You see, when you are an infant you don't have the full capacity to remember yet. Your memories are up there waiting to be released but at a later time in life. Puberty! Thought we talked about this? No matter. The body goes through some freaky chemical changes during those times, as you know. No one is able to remember before his own puberty."

"Oh…well, I guess that makes sense. Couldn't have a baby with memories and stuff before they can even talk."

"There you go, Nephew. Now you are getting it, but I Knew I was your 'Rendering Parent' back then, as you will know whose 'O' you helped make also. After the initial touch, every time you shake their hand or touch their skin, it will be like greeting your family; you never forget them and you will have familiar thoughts bombard you. Of course they are not always good or bad, just thoughts of the two of you interacting whenever or wherever you did, usually about whatever had an impact on the two of you. Consequently since you were about five I think when I touched you the first time, it was just delayed until now."

"Wow…that helps me understand better! But I have another question," Jaybird said. "If you have met most of that whole first family then…where is my other 'Rendering Parent' or do you know that?"

"Course I do. She's in California and works at Disneyland. She gets to dance around Disneyland all day in a Minnie Mouse costume; done it for almost twenty-five years now," Nicholas said as he paused and scratched his chin, "I myself met her there when I was on a summer trip between my junior and senior year in high school, in ahh…um…1958. That was an interesting time for me after that, well at least after I made it through some personal strife. Then I did the college thing, wrote a few books and got some serious cash. Hell, by 1965 I had my PhD. I was only twenty-five. I found that academia was easy, so I had a fast track to my doctorate. Then I kinda took 1966 off. Didn't get my head together till I was about twenty-six. Man, it's kind of a blur to me now, 'cause of all the drugs we were taking, but that was the thing to do back in those days, you know. The Beatles, Stones, Leary and Castaneda were into that stuff, so we all had to be hip, you know. Like the hippies. Hey…it just occurred to me that that's where they got that term! Or did the hippies come first? Anyhow, I was going through my money pretty fast so I got a job at Intertwine. Made a bucket of money off a couple of new books and…well, there have been other sources of money …Any who, I digress. Yup; she's still out there in Anaheim at Disneyland."

"I went to Disneyland once but I never saw Minnie Mouse," Jaybird stated.

Nicholas thought for a second and asked, "Are you sure, Jaybird?"

"I'm sure. I was pretty disappointed about it. You know, 'cause I was young and we just loved the Mickey cartoons and all. But I guess Minnie was off in the bathroom or something. Never saw that character."

"Hmm…very interesting! No, you must have met her, you must have touched her at some point or else you couldn't have the full knowledge of all your lives," Nicholas said, as he pondered the ramifications of Jaybird not having met his other 'Rendering Parent', yet seemingly having all his complete memories intact. *It couldn't be*, he thought. *I would have felt differently when I touched Jaybird.* He was certain that he made Jaybird a 'Complete Knower' earlier.

Nicholas' mind was racing. He knew that he was Jaybird's 'Rendering Parent' and he knew that Evelynn was his other one. What he couldn't understand was how Jaybird could seemingly have unlocked all his memories without touching Eve. And how could Robin have them? This Robin lad hasn't even shaken my hand yet. Well, maybe Robin has touched Eve. That must be the answer; he probably went to Disneyland. But still, the rule doesn't seem to fit either one of them. Quite interesting, he mused.

"Eighteen offspring with your first mate there, Nick? But the Bible only talks about the first three sons," Jaybird said, nudging Nicholas out of his deep reverie.

"Well, um…I guess you haven't read that book as thoroughly as you could have. It's in there somewhere. You know they called it the Kingdom of Nod and all, which was like, just a valley over the next hill where my other children and their offspring lived. Look, forget the Bible. Fairy tales and fluff. Morally inclined good intentions, tales of intrigue, spiced up just enough to fit the times and updated whenever needed or as needed. Not so much historical truth in it. Especially the Old Testament. Any who…me and Minnie Mouse, well her name is Evelynn Jackson actually, back in that particular lifetime, had quite an offspring-filled existence. Besides how do you think the human race could continue without females? Remember we were little removed from the animal kingdom, so there was much inbreeding to get the line going."

"Yuk!" Jaybird said, almost choking on his beer,

"But then…hmm…I suppose that would explain how Cain went to the kingdom of Nod and found a wife. You gotta wonder where she came from if you were the only two producing offspring."

"Hey, what have I been telling you? And it wasn't a kingdom. It wasn't even named at that time. They call it Africa now. But it's not like he actually got married or anything. No priests yet. He mated; that's all. Perpetuating the race was what we did back then. That, along with eating and sleeping, was pretty much it. Of course, staying alive was also a huge part of life. There really isn't much factual stuff in the Bible, the Koran, or the Hare Krishna's Akadvadvidaad. The values and morals that all religions try to teach are exactly what humans needed at the time their books were written. It seems they need morals and values even more nowadays. Trust me. We can put things in their rightful place in history, though. 'The Calm' can get to the truth of things. Besides, I was there, man. Yet, I can't really write a book about that time and place in history…not just yet."

"Which place and time are we talking about now, Uncle Nick?" Jaybird asked.

"Dude, I was around when they were putting together the Bible. Both times. See, they messed up the first one so the sequel was developed. Couldn't have this God entity, Supreme Being guy, being so mean to the very creatures he supposedly had made in the first place. You know, with the flood killing most everyone and all."

Jaybird looked at Nicholas and let out a sigh saying, "So you are going to Hell for sure." Somehow Jaybird knew Nicholas wasn't saying anything untruthful. He was also quite sure there was no heaven or hell.

"Oh well, Hell, schmell, that is just a figment of someone's imagination. Say, are you religious?"

"No, not really. I had to read the Bible when I was younger and I went to church, but as I got older my parents gave me and all us kids a choice and I chose not to go. They never went to church either except on Christmas or Easter Sunday. But most people believe in Heaven and Hell, Uncle Nick."

"Think they don't? Well, Christians do. They certainly are not the majority of the world's religious peoples though. Anyhow, take your place called Hell. You would either be stupid or crazy to actually want to go there, so it seems to me that the freedom of choice really isn't there. I mean, isn't this how it goes; 'be good and repent and go to Heaven or else go to Hell'. Where's the choice?"

"I see your point, but isn't that the idea: religion teaches people to be good by using the punishment of burning in Hell as a deterrent?" Jaybird asked.

"Look," Nicholas said, "All I am saying is that these Heaven and Hell things are relatively new places, made up to scare the folks into believing. A control thing for the masses. Where did they think people went before Heaven and Hell? My experience has been that some religions were created to keep the less intellectually developed sector of the human race, well…in line, so to speak. There were followers and there were leaders. Most of the religious icons were just leaders with ideas on how to be in charge. So whatever doctrine they came up with was *the* word of their God. The followers needed leadership and it was provided. Not all religions were started at the same time, you know. There are quite a lot of different ones out there. Hinduism started 3000 years before that Jesus dude was walking the earth. The Muslims got it going in the 1600's. You can just pick the religion you like the best. What kind of a deal is that? Pick your fate in the afterlife. To me it's like picking a color. If you like blue, then you tell everyone you like blue. Does that make it the best color? No! It's just what makes you happy. So that is how I see religions. You pick the one that makes you happy, if you don't like the one you were born into. Or you could decide to do without it. Now there is the choice. You don't really get anything in the end from being as good as you can be while you're alive, because there isn't really an end to your soul."

"But there are people who go to church all the time; they are pretty religious. What if any of them became 'Knowers'?"

"Well, Jaybird, going into a church doesn't make you religious any more than going into a garage makes you an automobile. I know a few 'Knowers' that used to be very devout believers in their religious faith. But once they Knew about themselves and what they had done in previous lives, they made their own choices. They all stopped attending church because they understood that there was no Heaven to go to. Plus Knowing puts everything in perspective."

"What do you mean, Uncle Nick?"

"Well, for one thing, they understood that if the Christians were right then the Jews were going to Hell. But if the Muslims were right then all the Christians and Jews were going to Hell. And if the Hindus were right we could come back as a cow. You get my drift? There is no single right God. There is only nature, the here and now and where and what you have been. That is all. Plus, when you can remember your own deaths, it makes you see the futility of hoping for anything else."

"No God, hmm, why doesn't that scare me as much as it probably should?"

On some level Jaybird knew that Nicholas was telling him the facts as he knew them. And Jaybird also knew what was in his head was fact. Somehow he had lost the fright that was usually attached to even thinking about any blasphemy, such as there being no God. His change of view on the religion his parents had taught the family had actually started manifesting after meeting Robin. After their initial handshake, he had just taken his and all religion at face value. If someone liked it and believed in it then that was fine with him. He just didn't find it particularly necessary.

"Because you know it's true!" Nicholas erupted. "Each 'O' or soul of a person has to make the best of what he has to work with while alive in each life. The knowledge you have is all you have. Your whole life is based upon what you have learned. You will make all your personal decisions from your personal history. All your trials and errors. Whether you are an old man when you remember, or a Hare Krishna, a monk, a nun or a post puberty boy or girl. Once you remember all your past lives, you have so much more to work with that you know is factual, from that point on. Sometimes it causes personal conflict and pain, but that is life. Not everyone can handle it. Some do become even more confused than before they got their memories, of course. But it is rare as far as I have seen. That's pretty much why we are called 'Knowers'. Usually once you Know, you become calmer."

"'Knowers', eh?" Jay said softly.

"Yes. Like I said we in 'The Calm' call ourselves 'Knowers' because we know about ourselves and what happened during our other lives and times. And once you touch both the 'Rendering Parents' you must decide what it is you want to do in this life and how you can prepare for the next life or whatever you think is best for yourself."

Jaybird thought a moment and then said, "Let me play devil's advocate for a bit. That sounds like what most religions do anyway, sort of. They try to guide you into doing good or whatnot, to prepare you for Heaven which is the afterlife, which is really another life here on earth. So is 'The Calm' really a religion?"

"No, of course not! It's just a group of like souls. And listen, there isn't any actual place called Heaven. And the earth is neither Heaven nor Hell. I have been around for eons and through so many lives that I can tell you there just isn't anything but this place. The here and now and where you have been. No afterlife as most folks think of it. The afterlife is just another life, right here. It is a continuation of your life in a different container, so to speak."

"It's just a bit hard to…to say it out loud, though," Jaybird said as he motioned with his glass for another beer. He had never had this many beers in such a short time before tonight; so he deduced that the time of the night and the number of beers was starting to affect him some.

"Think it ain't?" Nicholas said as he filled it up again. Then he continued, "I know this is all very hard to grasp. It was hard for me when I first came to Know, but I know I was around many times before. So were you. I can remember back before there were languages, before alphabets, before morals, and values. There was a time when all that mattered was survival. We have progressed and evolved. Non-Knowing humans are a funny bunch. They are so full of themselves but then they want to give all the credit to a higher source. It makes them feel better. What a dichotomy. Even when something goes bad they place blame with their God. They have devised a system of religions that allows them to take no responsibility for their actions. How quaint."

"I never thought of it that way."

"Well…maybe you should. It makes them feel secure and satisfied. What a bunch of hypocrites. No one can follow the teachings of the Bible, or any other religious doctrine, to the letter. It would be impossible. It is designed to be unattainable. If it could be attained, then I suppose you would have too many God-like, perfect people, running around, moving mountains at will. They would have to find something else to believe in 'cause the mystery would be gone. All belief systems create a mystery. Then they make you afraid of not playing by the rules while you search for the mystery which is designed to keep you in line, while waiting for the big payoff: Eternity in Heaven, or seventy-two virgins, take your pick. But being perfect is so unattainable. Most religions have some kind of unreachable goal. That's what keeps them around. By the way, if the Muslim's knew that the Aramaic prize for martyrdom, called 'Hur', meant white grapes, and not the Arabic meaning of 'Hur' which is loosely, enchantress virgin, I doubt there would be such a rush to kill the infidels. You have to ask why new religions keep popping up. Look at Scientology. Hey, the guy who started that one used to write science fiction books. Come on. Get real. But they have succeeded in scaring the masses into believing that they need faith to survive. And the faiths need their money. People are just as scared to even speak out against religion now as they were 2000 years ago. So I guess it works in keeping the masses in order. There are many times in history when the whole picture gets reversed though; when a normal everyday average person could look at a book like the Bible and see it for what it really was. They would know what it really was."

"And what's that?" Jaybird asked.

"Just another book."

"You sure wouldn't get much podium time in the South or the Bible Belt, Uncle Nick."

"Think I wouldn't? No, of course not, dude, and I wouldn't even try to push what I know to be true onto non-'Knowers'. I'm not going to try to destroy the only thing that holds some people, families, or communities together, or much of the human race for that matter. They can do what they want for now. It doesn't hurt anything. But eventually their 'O' will come back to a new body and sooner or later they will bump into a 'Knower' or one of their 'Rendering Parents' or both and presto, bingo, they will have to deal with all the memories, and their personal truths. They may go nuts trying to deal with them or they may have complete understanding of the truth in their new memories and feel calm about it. It can go both ways. If another 'Knower' explains it to them at the time of enlightenment, they usually handle it fine. It's kinda like when you are told the correct answer on a test. You got it wrong on the test but as soon as the teacher tells you the right answer, you just say, Oh yeah! Because it was in there all along; you just couldn't pull it up in your head. That, or you talked yourself out of the right answer."

"Presto, bingo?" Jaybird queried, thinking that his uncle sounded like Robin every now and then. And noticing how he could ramble on and on at times.

"Ahh…presto change-o; yeah, that's it."

Jaybird took another sip and began, "You know, I was talking to Robin awhile back when he was, um…talking…I had to read a book once and this author thought the schizos were not as developed or as evolved as much as other humans. It was interesting. I kind of thought, after reading that book, that Robin and I were more evolved than them or something."

"Hey, man, I know the book and I met the author. I went to graduate school with him. He is so close to the mark on some points but he isn't a 'Knower'. His 'O' probably hasn't been around long enough yet, so he will keep trying to persuade people to believe him as long as he has not touched one of his 'Rendering Parents' in this life. He has a hard time getting people to follow his particular train of thought, though. It doesn't have any prize at the end. People need that. Something to strive for. As a matter of fact, now that I think of it, that's where I met another of your very first brothers: my third-born from my first family. He was modeling clothes for some big uppity fashion designer and I was trying to sell my first effort at a book. And he was striving for the top spot in the modeling world, I guess. I've got no clue what their trip is all about. Any who, there was this big trade show thing in Vegas and we bumped into each other and I knew he was who he was. I just left there as quickly as I could. He has been bad all down through the ages. His 'O' is just no good."

"You bumped into him; I thought you had to shake hands?"

"No, no, it's just a touch of the skin anywhere, that will do it."

"OK. So who is he? What's his name?" Jaybird asked, quite curious now.

"Oh, never mind his name. It really isn't worth knowing. You wouldn't want to get to know his type of 'O'."

"Why not?" Jaybird asked.

"'Cause he is still a bad person in this life. I had always hoped that he hadn't been to Disneyland. But, I know he has already touched Eve."

"Eve?"

"Short for Evelynn. Nice name for the first 'O' bearing woman, huh?" Nicholas said, smiling.

"Yeah, sure is. Would her name be a coincidence?"

"Think it ain't? Over such a long period of time the chances for things happening just keep going up. You know, the averages even out, so to speak. Then again I may have some other theories developing on that very issue," Nicholas said, chuckling.

Jaybird swivelled in his chair for a moment trying to grasp all of what was happening to him. Shortly, he thought of a question.

"So you people in 'The Calm' try to get people to believe you?"

"No way. Don't have to. We just know who is a 'Knower' when we touch them; along with knowing if we made their 'O' or not or if we have been biological family somewhere down through the ages. When you know, there is no need for persuading usually. And when you touch both the 'Rendering Parents' the complete knowledge is just there. After assimilating the initial rush of remembering, you just know. Everyone who doesn't know is guessing, hoping, wishing, or trying to believe in something. It seems like that's what humans always try to do. They are searching for something. Never satisfied. Great philosophers have built whole cultures around thinking that there must be more. Devising ways to make the masses feel better, comfortable or enlightened. But there ain't no more, man. So, I say the non-'Knowers' are just in their infant growing phase."

"Growing phase? Why?" Jaybird asked.

"Well, non-'Knowers' just haven't had the good fortune of meeting either of their 'Rendering Parents'. But then there are some people like say…a palm reader or…or psychics who exploit their own good fortune of having touched both 'Rendering Parents'. They are 'Knowers' but no one has explained it to them, so they handle it as best they can. I mean, it must be pretty easy to read someone's past when you just hold their hand and you actually get the knowledge of when you personally had interaction with them, from the touch, if it is there, you know. Then they just pick a nice life and incident out of their mutual experiences and relate that to the gullible customer and he or she feels like the psychic has magic powers or talks to ghosts or spirits or whatever nonsense they peddle their goods with."

"I guess that makes sense. A palm reader has to hold your hand to read it and a psychic always makes you hold hands," Jaybird said, quite proud of that analogy.

"See dude, now you are understanding some things a little better. Things we really don't take any time to think about normally. And let's not forget a séance. Hold hands, please! Am I right?"

"Right. So what is the 'O's purpose then, Nick? Do we have a purpose in life?"

"To enjoy life!" Nicholas said matter-of-factly.

"That's it?"

"Think it ain't?" Nicholas said with a smile on his face.

"Sounds too simple…and a bit of a let down too, I might add."

"That sounds so very civilized of you. Making much more out of something so basic and simple. To live is all there ever was to do. That's more than enough; why make it harder? What we really need to do is focus on making our lives better and with less pain from those evil 'O's. But we just don't pay attention to the instincts we already have as much as we should nowadays."

"What do you mean, Uncle Nick?"

"Well, like I said: I have a theory…so here it is. Take some things like say, a…a feeling for example. A feeling is what I like to call a leak of information. A leak from your memory of factual info. I mean, let's be real here, man, how could our species have survived if we didn't have some kind of knowledge passed on to ourselves in each life? How would we ever learn if every generation had to start learning from scratch? So the big whoop-tee-do scientists say we have innate instincts or involuntary bodily actions that allow us to do these things from birth. True enough, but I think it is also a leak of informational knowledge from things we have lived through and learned. Those things that we have learned are being stored in our brains over the eons of lives we have lived and come to us as a feeling."

"I could use an example, Uncle Nick."

"OK, dig this. Some babies learn to talk earlier than others; some learn more quickly not to touch a hot stove. Their 'O' has been around longer and they have retained that particular feeling or knowledge, if you will, of knowing that touching that stove or red glowing thing will hurt. Others, who are brand new or younger 'O's, get burnt over and over again. I mean, we have feelings all the time but we tend to not act on them as we should. Haven't you ever heard someone say, "I have a bad feeling about this or that?" In reality it is one of their very own memories or lessons leaking out and trying to tell them something. We just don't usually pay any attention to such feelings. We may have the answer stored in our heads, but without the needed chemical reaction of being a 'Knower', we don't seem to pay any attention to the idea that we really should listen to our feelings, up front. And some feelings are far stronger than others."

"I can see that. You know, I have had those thoughts. I somehow get the feeling that I know exactly what is right and or wrong and I don't feel like I am guessing at it," Jaybird said.

"Think you ain't! Plus, the more lives you have had means there is so much more information you have stored up, or memories as we call them. And this leaks out earlier and earlier. So all those child prodigies, they are all old souls whose memories are leaking, providing them with valuable info they have gathered over their other lives. Only their information is focused on one thing more than others. Things like math, music and such."

"OK," Jaybird said, nodding his head.

After a short silence, Nicholas said, "Many of the things we remember have no meaning and are not important to us, like brushing our teeth and going to the bathroom on any given day. I bet you can't remember brushing your teeth on February second, 1968?"

"Can't say that I can," Jaybird responded, not able to recall that date in his life.

"But you do remember where you put that gold."

"Of course, because it was very important!" Jaybird said

"Right and you can remember your deaths, I bet?"

"Oh my, my, my; yes, I can. Every one of them."

"Right on! That's because they were very important. Now, take a gut feeling. I mean how many times have you heard a person say, "Hey, I had a gut feeling that was going to happen" or whatever. They usually didn't act on it when they actually had the gut feeling. I think humans need to pay more attention to their bodies. The body is telling us stuff but we ain't listening."

Jaybird nodded in agreement and said, "That also makes sense to me."

"Think it don't? I bet you did extremely well in school, am I right?"

"You know, Uncle Nick; I never had to study a day in my life. Neither did Robin. We always got straight A's, even before we met."

"And you say you haven't even touched your other 'Rendering Parent'. Very groovy man. Way out. Yup. It's leakage. Knowledge leakage. Or better yet memory leakage. Memories themselves must have mass and weight and they all get carried over with the 'O' to the next life. We in 'The Calm' know that there is a chemical reaction when you touch another 'Knower' or your 'Rendering Parents'...I have been trying to measure that very thing for years. The actual chemical makeup of a memory must be smaller than anything we have measured so far in the lab. But I know it's just waiting there to be discovered, measured and deciphered. If you keep adding to the memories over eons, there must be a saturation point, hence the leaks of info. And your particular leak seems to be giving you about the same information as a 'Complete Knower' would have. This is fitting well into my working theory."

Nicholas was just rambling now, off on a tangent, pacing behind the bar, caught up in his own new quickly developing theory.

"Yes, memories must have weight. Memories have to weigh something if they are…something; everything weighs something," Nicholas muttered softly into his drink.

"The weight of memories. Kinda sounds like a book title," Jaybird said aloud.

"OK, Nephew, that's enough beer for you. You've had a long day. Let's call it a night. Follow me and I'll show you where Kandy is sleeping. I know you're ready for bed."

CHAPTER XXXIV

"I DON'T care if you were just going to bed, listen to me. It's another three billion dollars...no, not million, billion with a B, as in Blood-head...Yes, that's right.... It was easy...don't worry about how I got it, just access those accounts and make them grow even more! Goodbye," Edward said, as he hung up the phone at his Marian office. He had been talking to his account manager in Switzerland. It had taken quite a while, but it was worth it. He had just received word of the deposits from selling one third of the paintings via his various brokers worldwide and had been updated on his total net worth: 369 billion dollars. His senior accountant had assured him that in no more than three years' time he would be a trillionaire. The first person to accomplish that feat.

Edward was so proud of himself. The oil recovery company was storing hoards of oil, plus making tons of money from the byproducts of the various ores. But being the richest man in the world wasn't enough. He still just had to have more. He knew there would be more if his next treasure recovery would pan out like he assumed it would. Then he could put his devious plan into action.

He had advised his east coast account manager to distribute the annual three million dollars to his favorite white supremacist militias, funneled accordingly through their legal fronts, of course. Edward had been outfitting them in Massachusetts and neighboring states for a number of years. They were going to be his private army when he felt the time was right to use them in his best interests. The groups had grown to over 10,000 strong. All they did was practice on the weekends in their own little towns. Practice for war. Weekend warriors. They were a close-knit secretive bunch and Edward knew that when the social climate was right, he would make his move. And he would be the man holding their strings. The richest man in the world with his own little army.

Once on the *3 CANES*, Edward informed his captain to set sail for Cape Cod Canal, USA. Edward had always liked that area. There were so many rich white assholes there. He was also a rich white asshole but he was young with new money and they were all old with family money that was sure to run out. For some reason he got a kick out of irritating them every chance he got. He was totally focused on always having the biggest, best, newest; everything.

CHAPTER XXXV

WHAT I need to do is focus on making everything in my life better now, I need to be the Heavy-Weight Champion of the World, Robin thought to himself, remembering his old desire and dream. He was finding life on the reservation very much to his liking, but he drifted back and forth from that very positive thought to the very negative extreme by taking drugs constantly. He was still torn between the agony of losing a girlfriend and his dream. When he needed an escape to numb his pain, he used the drugs.

He truly liked the reservation. Nobody ever bothered him about his 'not talking' vow. Most of the Indians wouldn't even look him in the eyes, or anyone else for that matter. *It must be a cultural thing.* But Robin had often wondered if it was because of his scarred-up face or his unusual limp; until someone told him otherwise.

Eagleclaw had told him that the Indians had been herded like cattle into small areas of land that dotted the United States. They had been granted enough money to barely live and little hope of ever making it off the reservation. Yet there was an unspoken social attitude that they would someday regroup as a unified nation and win back the land that was originally theirs. They continued to practice the traditional ways of life from before the white man came, sometimes with ceremonies and other times with rites of passage with the young as if there were no technology at all. The Indians tried to stay in harmony with all of Nature. They used everything around them to help them live, rarely wasting anything.

The part of their culture Robin was most attracted to was their use of plant life. Eagleclaw had introduced him to the medicine man. With his guidance they had taken numerous trips into the unknown regions of his mind. The sheer fact that Robin didn't have to think about causing Julie's death, while feeling the effects of these plants and herbs, was enough for him to want to partake of them most every day. He had found a place to hide from the reality of life. It was in Montana and in his own mind. Every now and then, in a moment of lucidity, he knew this way of life couldn't last forever.

One day Eagleclaw told Robin that they were going to pick mushrooms from the far end of the reservation. They packed enough gear for three days and rode the horses toward the west.

Around noon of the third day as they crested an embankment, Eagleclaw stopped his horse and dismounted. When Robin joined him at the top he was impressed with the magnificent view. His eyes scanned the area in front of him. He could see mountain ranges on the left, the right and straight ahead. There was nothing taller beyond them. Since they were standing on a ridge, he saw that this was a huge valley, a perfectly hidden valley. He saw a small river, lush grassy areas, thick woods and small rolling hills throughout the low-lying parts. It was a picturesque view. All he could do was marvel at its beauty. Knowing that the valley was formed by glaciers and the melting water that came from them, he could picture the valley filled with water when there surely would have been a beautiful raging river flowing to the ocean, long ago.

"This is the end of the reservation. This place we stand on now," the Chief said as he drew in a deep breath and exhaled. "Over that next ridge, past this valley, we will find the Cree. They are and have been the keepers of the gate from the west since the treaties were signed."

Robin stood looking at the awesome view and sang the whole song written by the band America called 'Horse with No Name'.

Chief Eagleclaw was getting used to interpreting the sentiment that Robin was periodically expressing aloud. He thought Robin had a wonderful way of presenting his feelings in song. He thought it to be a gift. What a quick mind he must have to come up with them so fast; the lyrics always seemed to fit the situation or mood and were easily inferred.

"Yes, the white man wanted all the best land for himself, even if he didn't need it or wasn't planning to use it as we did. We Indians gave it love though. But this land is so far out of the way that the government has been trying to sell it for many years. There are no takers. It is now just part of the Glacier National Park. There are close to 20,000 acres. There are few paved roads out there. It is bordered by this reservation, Canada and a river that make up the other three bordering sides. On the other side of the river are thousands of acres of national forest land. My tribe has been trying to get this valley annexed as reservation land, but that just hasn't happened. What a beautiful sight to behold, though. I come out here many times a year just to see it," the Chief said, remounting his horse.

Agreeing, Robin nodded his head.

They rode around the large rocks and followed the switch-back trail about another 300 feet. Then they went up a small bank. Upon reaching the flat area atop the bench, Robin could see a sconce built into the side of the hill. He wondered who needed such a fortified dwelling so far from any well traveled path. He also saw a totem pole ten feet directly in front of the entrance. As he was staring at it, a young man came out and stood beside the totem pole. He put his hand in the air with his palms facing forward and said, with obvious recognition in his voice, "Welcome. We are the Cree. Please dismount and I shall get you a drink of water."

At that moment Robin had an image flash through his mind. This scene was somehow very familiar to him. Then it hit him. The flagman!

He stumbled as he got off his horse, forgetting the still tender and healing leg. He was certain that this was the same person who had shaken his hand the night of the wreck.

The Chief was tying up the horses as Robin walked slowly toward the young man.

"I'm Hawk."

He and Robin shook hands and a smile came across each of their faces.

"I am Hawk Longwing. And I believe you were in that car that crashed during a drag race in Missouri, weren't you?"

Robin nodded affirmatively, feeling the familiarity of some memories again.

"What happened? What made your car veer off the road like that? Man, some of us were going to run and help but we heard police sirens and...well, we bugged out of there," Hawk said, obviously feeling ashamed of himself.

"Hawk," said the Chief, "Robin has vowed to only speak in song verse since that very accident, I believe."

Hawk just looked over at Robin, not knowing what to say to that.

Eagleclaw continued, "He has made this commitment to the loving memory of the young lady that was taken from him in that car wreck. What I am told of this story, from my new son-in-law, Jaybird, is that a rod shot through the engine block. Robin pushed the car past its limits, evidently. It was a brand new car and only had 100 miles or so on it. The engine wasn't ready for that kind of abuse."

Robin, of course, had a song for the moment and he began singing a macabre song called "D.O.A." by the group Bloodrock.

Hawk squinted his left eye as he turned his head to the right, saying to Robin, "I think I understand. You must have experienced so much pain...inside and out. And I also now know you are of the 'First Rib'."

Robin again nodded his head up and down.

"Then I bet you had as much of a hard time accepting that flood of memories as I did that night. No wonder you couldn't maintain the wheel. It got pretty distracting for me, too. It always will, I suppose."

Eagleclaw listened with amazement, stating, "This is a very interesting omen. I would like to hear all about it. Where is your father, Hawk?"

"He went to catch the evening meal. He should be back before night-fall."

They went inside and Hawk began to tell the Chief of their chance meeting.

They talked until early evening.

CHAPTER XXXVI

EARLY IN the morning Kandy found her way through the house to the kitchen where Jaybird and Nicholas were already sipping coffee. She grabbed a carton of orange juice from the refrigerator and sat down, without even acknowledging the two men. Nicholas smiled as he handed her a glass. Jaybird informed her that he and his uncle were going to look up Robin. Jaybird had called Robin's father earlier and found out that Robin had gone back to the reservation.

Kandy decided, after about two seconds of thought, that she was not going back to Montana. She was going to her mom's house. She knew this was definitely the time to get away from Jaybird. She could go back and start the divorce paperwork while he was off on some wild goose chase. She saw herself telling a lawyer how her husband had left her, deserted her no less, and had gone off on some silly trek without her. The winning move to her little game was forming up just grand. She would explain how he had abandoned her and was obviously chasing other women. She had finally grown tired of the whole facade. It was time to end it.

There was no disagreement at all. Kandy wanted to go home and Jaybird wanted her to leave. He had come to the conclusion that the whole marriage was a mistake. He *had* rushed into another situation and it had turned out to be a bad one. He had fallen out of love with her just as fast as he had fallen in love. But today with his new-found knowledge, it seemed less painful to think about. He could remember countless relationships in his many past lives and they had all turned out to be short-lived for some reason.

The next day Kandy left Philadelphia by plane for Kansas City while Nicholas and Jaybird left for Montana by Winnebago.

The phone rang and rang. There was no answer. Van Tangle had been trying to reach his employer for twenty-four hours now, with no luck. The trail on Bloodhead had grown cold again. He had hoped to get some guidance from the man who hired him. Since Nicholas was not available, he decided to relax in his all-expenses-paid hotel room in Monaco a bit longer. He would get up later and go gamble a few hundred bucks. These kinds of dry spells were just part of the game. He had learned to be patient and submit to the lulls that this kind of surveillance often presented. *Sometimes they just get away from you for a while,* he thought. But he knew he would find a clue sooner or later. He would scour the papers and check out the port logs and continue to talk to people. Something would come up.

He remembered a year or so ago back in Salem, Massachusetts, when the trail had dried up as he was following Edward and Elizabeth. He had been keeping close tabs on Edward when there was a news bulletin on the radio about what the local media was calling a witch-burning ritual killing on the outskirts of Salem. Van Tangle had decided to go check it out.

When he got there, all that was left was the ashes of what looked like an old ceremonial witch burning platform. Something you would only read about in books on the occult or history books or see in horror movies. There were also three sets of bones that the local police had pulled from the water-soaked ashes. There didn't seem to be any witnesses around but there were men and dogs searching the woods anyway. Van Tangle found out from the lead detective on the scene that some crazy things usually happened on Halloween in these parts but this one had the officer baffled. "Who in their right minds would burn anyone at the stake? It's the late 1970's for God's sake," the officer grumbled.

Upon reflection Van Tangle reminded himself of how evil he knew Edward Bloodhead was. What a strange name, too. It seemed to fit his personality though. So with that in mind he always kept open the possibility of Edward being involved in whatever murder or wrong-doings might pop up in the vicinity of Edward's whereabouts. With all his training and experience, he just couldn't place Edward at the scene of this or any other crime. He couldn't make any clear connections. If and when he did, he wondered if Nicholas would actually want him to proceed with presenting the evidence to the authorities. He knew his job was to just follow Edward and report back to Dr. Young, but he feared that sooner or later he would have undeniable evidence linking Edward to a vicious crime and his moral duty would take precedence over the wishes of the good Doctor and 'The Calm'. Another murder and another town; he knew he would find a connection sooner or later.

CHAPTER XXXVII

"HEY, ANOTHER town. What did that sign say?" Nicholas asked as the Winnebago lumbered past the "Welcome to Dixon" sign.

"We are in Dixon, Illinois. Do you know someone here?" Jaybird asked.

"Thought that's what the sign said. Think I don't know someone here? His name was Franklin T. Night."

"Was?"

"Yup, he's dead," Nicholas said, sounding rather cheerful considering the moment.

"Oh, well, sorry to hear…"

"Not to worry, he's back."

"What are you talking about?"

"He was me. I mean I was him back then in the late 1700's. Look, we gotta find someone who knows where the old cemetery, on top of a hill is. Or…I guess if we keep looking we'll find the graveyard eventually, huh?"

"OK…I think I'll just pull off the highway and into the next gas station and ask a local. Hopefully it won't be too hard to find."

After getting the directions and arriving at the cemetery, they started looking for Franklin's grave. After a short time Nicholas stumbled across the tombstone he was looking for.

"Here I am, Jaybird, over here," Nicholas said to Jaybird who was about twenty feet away to his left.

"Man this is weird, Uncle Nick," Jaybird said as he hopped over a few graves to get to Nicholas.

"Think it ain't?"

As Jaybird read the inscription, he just had to laugh. He read it again, this time out loud, "Franklin T. Night 1799-1829 Killed in a bar fight. Could have been right could have been wrong. Don't matter; he's gone."

"Now that's funny, Uncle Nick."

"Yup. And I was right, you know," Nicholas said chuckling.

"OK, I've got to hear this one. What were you right about?"

"I told this fella that one day we were all going to ride around in wagons that would be powered by something other than horses. He had way too much whisky and we got to fighting and well, he popped me in the stomach with a bullet."

"Ouch," Jaybird said.

"You got that right. A gut-shot man died a slow death in those days. I sure remember it hurt for a long time. Took me about six hours to kick the bucket."

"And you remember it, don't you? Jaybird asked.

"You betcha."

"You know, I really wish the old saying was true," Jaybird said.

"You mean the one that claims you don't remember your death and it doesn't hurt, 'cause you're dead?"

"That's the one. Boy are *they* wrong."

"They are wrong more often than they are right. But remembering your death tends to make you a bit more cautious, don't you think? I mean dying really does hurt, a lot," Nicholas said

"You know, I'm getting kinda freaked out here. Can we go now?"

"Sure, but I bet you will do this yourself when the situation presents itself to you."

"It's pretty macabre though, Uncle Nick," Jaybird said shaking his head as if he could make the memories of a few of his own deaths, now bubbling to the surface, go away.

"It's validation, my boy. Validation! It's easy to tell a good story, but to prove it, now that's what gets folks to repeat it. That is how legends are made. Good or bad, right or wrong, that doesn't matter, but if it's true, that's what will perpetuate any story."

As they headed back to the Winnebago, Jaybird asked, "Say, Uncle Nick, we have gone through a bunch of towns on this trip. Is this the first time you remembered something like that or does it happen a lot when you travel?"

"Well, you know, in the big picture of countries, America is really a very new country. So I personally I have been alive before in the U.S.A. only a few times, three to be exact."

As they climbed onto the plush swivel chairs Jaybird said, "You know what? I think I'll drive the speed limit. We don't need any more deaths."

"You do drive fast. I never thought a thing this size could do 85 mph. But hey, I ain't your daddy. I'm just along for the ride."

After arriving in Montana, Nicholas and Jaybird rode a pair of beautiful horses up to the Cree land; leading them was Eagleclaw. After Nicholas stopped rambling long enough for someone else to talk, Jaybird explained to the Chief that he and Kandy hadn't been getting along lately and she had decided to go back to stay with her mother. The Chief mumbled something about destroying the nest of his family, but after Jaybird recited a few instances of her behavior to him, the Chief concluded there was much more of her mother in her than he had hoped.

Jaybird told the Chief he suspected it had something to do with the fact that he had cheated on Kandy's mother while they were married. Maybe that's why Kandy acted so jealous and was on the look-out all the time.

A very perplexed Chief explained that he had never cheated on his wife. He said that Kandy's mother had been jealous herself toward any woman that he came into contact with. The reason he had gotten divorced was the cruel and unjust way she had treated *him* over their eight-year marriage.

Jaybird was surprised to hear that, but he knew there were always two sides to every story. He pondered for a moment as to whether or not he should attempt to explain that later on to Kandy. Would it make a difference in her attitude? Would she believe him or even her father? Did he really even care at this point?

Once at the Cree land, Jaybird looked at the totem pole while dismounting and thought about what Robin had said to him in the hospital. Was this the totem pole he had remembered? Just then Hawk and Robin came out of the shelter to greet them, following them was Chief Longwing. Pleasantly surprised, Robin said, "Welcome back, my friend, to the show that never ends, come inside, come inside."

Jaybird once again didn't know if that was from a song but assuming it was, and since Robin sang it, he just smiled and asked, "Been thinking of me huh, Robin?"

Robin limped straight over to Jaybird with his scarred face beaming and gave Jaybird a firm handshake.

Robin *was* glad to see Jaybird. His best friend had always been there for him. He knew he should start being there for Jaybird again. Robin felt like he had to protect Jaybird for some reason. When he wasn't around him, it was like he wasn't fulfilling his obligations. He couldn't understand why he felt the need to protect Jaybird. It was just the feeling he got. It was a mutual unspoken understanding between them. Jaybird provided stability and direction for Robin, who in turn paid him back with the security of acceptance and gratitude. Robin remembered the many times he had stood up for Jaybird when a bigger guy was picking on him during their school days. There were many times he was forced to punch someone in the nose. Even if Jaybird felt he could handle the situation himself, Robin was there to settle things. Quickly. He had Jaybird's back covered at all times.

As they tied up the horses, Chief Eagleclaw introduced Nicholas as an 'Ancient Warrior' to Chief Longwing and his son, Hawk. Nicholas just smiled and nodded at the Chief's use of the term 'Ancient Warrior'. They all seemed to get a twinkle in their eyes as they reached out for the customary handshake. Expecting the memories was a bit different from being caught off-guard by them. The men sat down right where they were and began dealing with the influx of memories. All except Eagleclaw, who had already experienced the memories Nicholas had brought forward in him as they shook hands back at the house.

Robin though, was consumed. After shaking Nicholas' hand he had another rush of knowledge. He Knew! He knew every time he had ever been a part of Nicholas' life. He could remember meaningful conversations that were centuries old. Things he had learned, eaten, bought and loved. He knew that Dr. Young had been a very important influence in his lives, many times before. He could even remember back to his very first life, which was eons ago. That memory seemed so old that it was as if it was stored in his brain in black and white versus color. This handshake was different from any he had ever experienced.

The others were watching Robin as he took more time to get back to the present. It wasn't like they were waiting for him to say something, but maybe, just maybe, he would.

Jaybird decided to explain what he thought his friend was going through. "Nicholas is one of Robin's 'Rendering Parents' or what you in the 'First Rib' call the 'Rib Maker'. Robin was his first-born and I was his second-born, many, many lives ago. We both have now met one of the two that made our 'O' the first time. But Robin and I have always had, um …pretty much…all our full memories for whatever reason. We just didn't know what to do with them. And with every touch of another 'Knower' or 'Ancient Warrior' we grew better at refining the knowledge. For me, coming in contact with one-half of my 'Rendering Parents' was the little extra push I needed to remember everything. You can't believe what it feels like to let others know that!"

Hawk looked at him and asked, "What *does* it feel like…to you, I mean?"

"Well, I can tell you that it is like a sobering feeling or maybe even a calming feeling of sorts, to use Uncle Nick's term. First off I was so happy to find out that I was not crazy. That was such a relief! Because I have always known things about myself, all the people that I have been, places and names and such. Things I had learned, did or felt, but I concealed it and never talked of it. Even Robin and I wouldn't bring it up to each other until recently. But since meeting Uncle Nick here, it is like I am, well…more relaxed or something. It finally makes sense to me. And I guess I'm not alone. You can't imagine what a relief that is!"

"Think it ain't?" Nicholas interjected, "Plus you have so much life behind you to draw from. I believe your 'O' is complete. Your bewilderment is over. You are aware of so many more personal experiences than the rest of the population. You now know *why* you know everything you have experienced. Bonus, dudes! The big question is why you two, seemingly, have your full knowledge without ever touching *both* 'Rendering Parents'…or 'Rib Makers' as you folks here would say. We may need to change our understanding of the rules just for you. Or rather; just *because* of you! I guess your brain can't hold all the memories it has stored up there and consequently you don't need both 'Rendering Parents' touch to release your knowledge. Ah, man, that still baffles me!"

Robin was content to just sit there and peruse his newly-enhanced memories. He understood the whole thing now. He understood that in all of his lives, he lived to be very old and everyone he knew and loved died before him. That was why he always had a huge feeling of loss for every 'Knower' he met. There was such a great loss in outliving everyone you ever loved or cared for. But it was just his lot in all his lives. With only a few exceptions he had always grown old, very old. That must be why he had always tried to protect those whom he loved, so they would be safe and not die. It was a bit futile, but what else could he do?

The afternoon turned into night as they sat there and related back and forth to one another the similarities between what the Indians believed and what Nicholas believed. To Nicholas it was what he knew to be true from having lived it. To the Indians it was what they had been taught to believe, with only the hope of ever finding their 'Rib Makers'. It was *their* truth to believe in. Yet as Nicholas talked and explained the way of 'The Calm' and the terminology they used within 'The Calm', it became clear to the three Indians that there may indeed be a need to re-evaluate their stories of how the first Indians came into being. Nicholas had been with each of them many times. Touching Nicholas had brought some of their memories to the very edge of their perception. A 'Knower' touching a 'Knower' is still quite an experience. But without them actually touching their other 'Rendering Parent' or 'Rib Maker', there could be no full memory realization for them.

Both chiefs found this extremely unusual since they weren't ingesting any kind of mind-expanding plants. All of their previous insights had been revealed only under the use of the special ceremonial plants. No one had ever accounted for any of the stories without them.

Nicholas continued telling them stories of old. Times when they had played a game or done a good deed together or had a moment of glory or shared an emotional experience due to some important act. But he was only making them long for a feeling that just wasn't there. Not yet.

Chief Longwing was making a fire as Robin thought to himself how strange it was to know that Hawk had been his father in the late 1400's. Hawk had stood right there in front of the totem pole and given him advice before letting Robin embark on a long journey. He was to seek out the so-called 'pale face' and bring back news of what they looked like and how they acted, etc. The scene that Robin had been so engrossed with the night of his car wreck was of Hawk telling his son, long ago, to never forget this moment, this place and this feeling. Hawk reminded him that any tribe that he might run across in his journey would surely welcome him in from the elements. Hawk never saw his son again in that life. Hawk had died before Robin had returned home, more than six months later.

They all watched the sun set behind the mountains in the west as Chief Eagleclaw stood up. He stated that he would have to talk to all the other members of the 'First Rib' and try to persuade them to meet with Nicholas and get their reaction to the idea of altering some of the stories of old.

Nicholas emphasized that only the Indians of the 'First Rib' should be informed of any changes since the whole idea would be foreign to the others without experiencing either of the 'Rib Makers' touching them. Chief Longwing agreed.

They ate some antelope steaks, sipped boot-leg whisky, and talked until two in the morning, after which they fell asleep by the fire.

CHAPTER XXXVIII

ELIZABETH SIPPED her coffee and looked out over the patio at the rolling pasture behind her parents' house. It was a brisk Missouri morning. She loved to sit there and gaze at the field. She could see the old hickory nut tree at the back edge of their property where her brothers had built a tree house when they were younger. It was still there just waiting to be enjoyed by hordes of children again. She remembered how much courage it took for her to climb up to the top limbs. In the summer they would sit up there and watch the drive-in movie from the big outdoor theater a block away. If the wind was right they could even hear it. Her brothers and their friends had always talked about running a speaker wire from the tree up to the last window speaker in the back row, so they could hear better, but that never came to fruition. She laughed to herself at how the neighborhood boys would all want to be friends with her brothers just so they could spend the night and maybe get a glimpse through a bedroom window of her in a nightgown. Life was so much simpler then. All she had to worry about was which boy would be her new boyfriend that week or month. She could always change her mind. She had known she was pretty from an early age but never dreamed where her looks would take her. It was pure luck that she was at the hottest disco club in Kansas City, where a Playboy photographer also happened to be. He had seen her from across the dance floor and managed to start a conversation with her. Although she didn't believe his story, she decided to take a few friends and go to his hotel room anyway. After seeing all the camera equipment and being put at ease from the female assistant, she posed for some tasteful but nonetheless revealing pictures. Two months later she was in Chicago doing a full-blown photo shoot. Winning the Playmate of the Year title was something she had never even dreamed about, but it had happened. The fifty thousand dollar prize had vanished faster than she had expected, even though Edward had picked up the tab for everything. She just frittered her money on trinkets for herself. But the 1975 Trans Am she had also won was still parked in the garage. It only had 900 miles on it.

Just a few years back she had fully believed all the hype around her. They had said she would be given commercial spots and product endorsements and maybe even guest shots on soap operas or *The Love Boat*, like all the other fledgling actresses. So what did she do? She ran off with the first handsome man who came along and went sailing all over the world for almost two years, virtually hiding from everyone.

She knew that everything about her relationship with Edward was a bad thing and a mistake. Sometimes she felt good about hoarding the hundred grand he had handed her to spend. Other times she had to fight the feeling inside her that said she had stolen it. *No, he gave it to me and I just didn't gamble it away. Thank God I'm not a hard core gambler*, she thought. Some things about the relationship were good, she concluded. She did get to see many countries from all the traveling they did. *But what will I do now?* she wondered.

Hours went by as she just sat there and stared out into the green grass and overgrown underbrush of the field. Then her gaze was broken when a neighbor's dog started chasing a blue racer snake across the yard. Funny thing, she had imagined Edward as a snake...often. She continued to daydream for a while, as she noticed a large storm front of dark clouds start to slowly move across the sky. She then had an idea. It came across her like a wave. She decided it was a great idea even if it was her own. It would keep her busy, too. As the dog caught the snake and batted it around mercilessly with its paws, a new excitement came over her. She grabbed her empty coffee cup and headed inside.

"I'm going to start right now. I'm going to write a book!" she said aloud.

The more she thought about it, the better she liked the idea. *Hmm…a book about my travels and experiences with the…well, eccentric Mr. E. Bloodhead*, she said to herself. *I guess eccentric is a word I could use. Or a better word would be snake!* She instantly thought of a title for her book. The Snake and the Playmate. *My book could make millions, even billions. No, of course it won't, but at least there will be a cleansing effect in getting everything down on paper and off my chest*, she thought.

Four hours later Elizabeth was putting the last period on her first chapter as another late summer Missouri storm raged outside. She had just pulled the last page out of the electric typewriter when the power went out. With it, went all the lights. Perfect, she thought. I finished not a second too soon. She got up from the desk and walked over to the window between the flashes of lightning. The storm brought back a memory of when she and Edward had just set sail from Cape Cod Canal in Massachusetts. He had said they needed to outrun a big storm front and had to sail quickly. He was in such a rush and very adamant about leaving right then. His actions seemed very odd. *I'll put that in my book*, she thought. She had almost forgotten about that day.

"The weirdest thing happened at that Halloween party" she said, aloud, as she counted the seconds between the lightning and the boom of the thunder. The storm was about ten miles off she calculated, starting the count over again. One one thousand, two one thousand, three…

Just a few miles up the highway in St. Joseph, Kandy jumped out of the car and ran into the office building across the Belt highway from the Frog Hop Ballroom as quickly as she could to avoid the downpour. Her mother headed off to the mall.

Kandy stepped up to the desk dripping wet and said, "I'm here to see about getting a divorce."

"And you are?" the receptionist inquired.

"I'm Kandy Young."

"All right, Mrs. Young, you're a bit early. Please have a seat. It will be just a few minutes."

"Thanks," Kandy said as she picked up the 'Yachting' magazine and started nervously flipping through the pages. She imagined which yacht she would get for herself after she took all of Jaybird's money in the divorce. She was still searching for the most expensive one when a man's voice asked, "Mrs. Young?"

Looking up, she saw the lawyer holding his hand out. She answered, "Yes. That's me."

As they shook hands he said, "I'm Mr. Print, Bill Print. A pleasure to meet you."

In his art deco office they talked about why, when and how much. After that short conversation, Mr. Print knew that this girl was out to take her husband for everything he had. He thought to himself how young she was to show such disdain for just one man and after such a short time with him. He took from his past experiences that she was just another 'gold-digger.' No matter, he thought. The more she gets from her husband, the more I get for myself. He laughed to himself for thinking that he was just like her: constantly making a living off other people's personal problems. Well, that's what lawyers do. They kick you when you're down.

He told her that it would be an open-and-shut case. She would get half of his money and a substantial monthly alimony check. He explained that there wasn't much Jaybird could do to fight back. He said he would get the paperwork going right away. Kandy thanked him and left. She went back to her mother's house. They began looking through the previous Sunday's newspaper section titled 'New homes, farms and undeveloped land.'

CHAPTER XXXIX

THIS EXPANSE *of undeveloped land is beautiful to look at,* Jaybird thought as he strolled out to the edge of the rise. He watched the long shadows creep slowly back toward the rising sun. He started humming a Beatles' song called "Good Morning". He stopped himself as he laughed and thought that the song thing was Robin's deal. He wondered what song Robin would have in store for the beautiful sight stretched out before him.

Nicholas wandered out and stood beside him saying, "That's got to be the most beautiful valley in the world, right there."

"Glorious," Jaybird said, yawning.

"Think it ain't?"

Jaybird smiled and took a deep breath. Nicholas did the same. There was no need for other words. The scene in front of them was all that was needed.

A few minutes later all six men were standing in silence looking at the beautiful early morning, a wonderful crack-of-dawn view.

Sure enough, Robin broke the silence by singing the first six lines of the song "Way Over Yonder" by Carole King.

After the men stood there for a few silent minutes, each one mulling over the words Robin had sung, Longwing asked, "So, I hear you and

Robin are wealthy, Jaybird?"

Before Jaybird answered, Robin remembered that he hadn't told him that he had paid out the eight million to Julie's mother. He would have to write that out on some paper in the near future.

"Tell him how you got your wealth," Eagleclaw urged.

Jaybird looked at Robin, knowing that Robin surely could tell a better story, he begrudgingly began,

"Well, Robin was a rich businessman in California in the mid-1800's and we hid some gold in a cave in 1849 for future use."

Longwing looked at Jaybird and asked, "So you mean to say that you were his brother back then?"

"Yes. He was Sam Brannan and I was William Brannan.

"Are you saying that you knew you would be alive again in another time and that you would be aware of the gold you hid?" Hawk questioned.

Jaybird nodded his head affirmatively.

"Well, we hoped we would remember again sometime in the future. And since we had remembered past lives before, we could only assume we would again."

"They met their 'Rendering Parents' at that time also," Nicholas said, nodding his head up and down in agreement.

"Then you knew them in that life, didn't you, Nick?" Eagleclaw asked.

"Think I didn't?" Nicholas replied with a smile.

"Yes, we did know him back then! That's how we knew that we would make better use of the gold at a later date versus cashing it all in there in 1849. Old Nick here was a Pony Express rider from St. Joseph, Misery. Right, Uncle Nick?" Jaybird asked.

"Yep. I was 'Cyclone' Thompson. Well, Charlie, was my real name. And misery was how my butt felt after riding twelve hours on those horses at break-neck speeds. Then had to get up and do it again the next day on the return trip," Nicholas said, continuing, "I answered a newspaper ad which read, 'Wiry, young single men needed to ride mail through dangerous territory. Orphans preferred. Three dollars a week.'"

Jaybird laughed as he said, "I remember when we were talking to him at the horse trough outside the general store in 'Frisco that day. We thanked him for bringing a letter from St. Joseph in such a short time and as we each shook his hand…well, we *Knew*. It had only been about a week since we had shaken Evelynn's hand at the stables. Well, she wasn't named Evelynn at that time. Anyhow we both had been struggling with the funky memories we had…but as soon as we touched ol' Cyclone…we had a much better understanding of everything."

"So this is what we have to look forward to when we, too, find our 'Other'…I mean…'Rendering Parents'?" Chief Longwing asked, hopefully.

"Yes," Jaybird stated, "And it is an interesting feeling to get. I never understood it until recently though. I was very scared of it when I was younger. I couldn't handle the knowledge, or didn't know what to do with it. I think talking to my Uncle Nick here has definitely given me the understanding I needed all along to appreciate it for the gift that it is."

"What did you expect would happen when you found your 'Other Half', Chief Eagleclaw?" Jaybird asked.

The Chief paused for a long time, and then he said, "We were taught to believe that we would remember only Indian lives. It never occurred to us that our spirit would have been in the body of a non-Indian. I think now that having and maintaining that view is a very narrow-minded one. I hope we can learn more as time goes on. I also hope some of our people will find their 'Rendering Parents'. Then the skies will open and the knowledge will fall upon us. We thought the peyote and herbs were bringing the knowledge to us."

"Why do you appreciate this growing knowledge so much, only now, Jaybird?" Eagleclaw asked, walking over to stand beside his son-in-law.

"I guess it gives me the feeling of being with my…well, my family. Any 'O' I know who has at one time or another been related to me, I am sure would feel the same. Families belong together. There is such a bond there. Plus, think of all the stories you could reminisce about with each other."

"Think you couldn't!" Nicholas said, continuing, "Just think of the resources you could tap into if you had a civilization of people who could relate exactly what went on years, even centuries ago. A whole new concept in book writing would take place."

"Yeah, it would be like a diary of people's pasts which could be verified by another person from 'The Calm' who was actually there with them," Jaybird said.

"Yes, verification is the key to the facts," Nicholas stated.

They talked amongst themselves for a few more hours, discussing many things. The Indians were all very excited about the concept of gathering and meeting others in 'The Calm'. The chiefs decided to call a gathering of the 'First Rib' and explain what they had learned from Nicholas. Eagleclaw knew that the Indian traditions went back many generations and would be hard to break. He wondered to himself if the elders were going to be able to handle a change of view in such an old Indian belief. Some elders may not agree now, but knowledge seemed to favor 'The Calm'.

Robin was thinking to himself about how he wanted to just break out and speak with everyone around him. He longed for the interaction of conversation. But he had made a promise to himself and to Julie. As he recalled his promise, he knew that he was no closer to achieving his dream of being the heavy-weight champion today than three months ago. He had to change his attitude. He had to find the inner strength to accomplish his goal. He was failing himself right now. That was losing, and he hated losing. Just as that thought crossed his mind, he got his renewed motivation. He was not a loser. He was a winner. He had some overriding desire to be first…number one at something, anything. His mind was made up. He was going to start his training. Now!

"You know what, I feel different somehow today. Sort of like a bridge was crossed. I feel at ease or something," Jaybird said, to no one in particular.

Nicholas answered his lament anyway, saying, "You are at ease. Knowledge is wisdom. Wisdom creates calm. You are wiser today than you were before touching me…You are more at peace within yourself due to the knowledge and experiences you have been able to remember. You now have so much more to draw from and to reason things out from. That's why we call it 'The Calm'. Everything is up there in the noggin just waiting to be remembered. There aren't really many surprises when you finally come to terms with that notion. Knowledge has quite a calming affect on humans. Everything has been said and done before. Hopefully, if we get lucky, we will be able to learn from our many pasts and not make the same dumb mistakes over again in this or the next life. But then again, we are just human."

When Robin heard Nicholas say that, he felt validated with his own thoughts about life and feelings and emotions. That very premise, that everything had been said and done before, that sentiment and Julie were exactly why he had started his vow of only talking in verse. He always had respect for Nicholas in each life when they crossed paths. He knew Nicholas was a wise man.

CHAPTER XL

1980

THE WISE old Indians of the 'First Rib' and 'The Calm' members had been integrating their ideas and knowledge on a regular basis. They had begun the process of validating various lives from the growing number of members they had met. Three years had passed and now in late December, 1980, the members were learning that history was not always told with truth as its guiding factor. They were working on the dream that Nicholas had, which they adopted: to document the true history of man. To corroborate the true facts of all the lives that had ever lived on this earth and create the real family tree for all humans. Nicholas hoped that the new knowledge of relationships would end bigotry and racism forever. Human harmony. He felt that if you knew that you had lived past lives as an Eskimo or an Asian or a Jewish or Anglo person, there would be no way you could hold on to your prejudices. Initially to some, it seemed like maybe he spent too much time down on Haight-Ashbury street during his college days but the hope was intriguing to everyone who heard it. Upon reflection they understood what he was striving for; harmony and truth for all.

Robin had started boxing again after a grueling leg rehabilitation regime led by his new coach, Hawk. His record was now at thirteen wins and no losses. He had quickly become the number one contender and the title fight was in two days.

Kandy had seen her bid for a divorce turn into an annulment of the entire marriage. This was what the judge had decided, after it was discovered that the old man had falsified the consent form for Jaybird. A marriage really never existed, technically. Getting the old man to tell the judge the truth had cost Jaybird twenty grand. His lawyer made a plea-bargain for the old man. He pled guilty to a misdemeanor and Jaybird paid the small fine for him also. After that whole ordeal was over, Jaybird offered to pay off Kandy's mother's mortgage if she would enter rehabilitation. She accepted both terms. The communications Kandy had with her father over the last three years had made her understand that her mother was not all there upstairs, she was a couple of chips shy of a full bag. The grudge she had for her father and all men was replaced by a loving relationship with her new boyfriend. She also was writing her father letters about once a month. She had her GED and was in her second year of college. Jaybird had often wondered if he had made the right decision in divorcing her. Maybe he could have stuck it out longer and made it work. But something inside him told him to just keep going forward; don't look back. No time for regrets.

Nicholas had just finished another book and had flown to California and explained to Evelynn that he felt it was time for her to quit the Disneyland gig and live with him in New Jersey. He felt there was an undercurrent of angst in America and he feared another civil war was brewing. Since Evelynn had always been his best friend or wife throughout the eons every time they met up, she happily agreed. The only reason they didn't marry in this life was because of the age difference.

She completely understood his concern with what he called 'the direction of the immediate populace'. She too knew the present social structure was being chipped away from its core. Moral values were losing ground to more liberal views. She loved his analogy: the melting pot was full and some of the pot is spilling over, causing fires. Nicholas had consistently reminded everyone who would listen, that all great civilizations eventually fall. All this was nothing new to the older 'O's. These social attitude shifts were common throughout human history. Like peoples always grouped together. When you think alike, you gravitate to others who think as you do. 'That's why there are groups', Nicholas had always said. Even if the goal of 'The Calm' was to enlighten all humans to the possibility of actually being just one group that was completely in harmony with itself, Evelynn knew they had to start out slowly. This small group called 'The Calm' was only in its grass-roots phase.

'The Calm Land', which was what everyone was calling the 20,000 acres of land Robin had bought in Montana, had a small group of Knowers homesteading on it already. He had used almost every cent of his boxing winnings to purchase the land. It bordered the Indian reservation and anyone in 'The Calm' was allowed to homestead there on any one acre plot they chose that was available.

The Indians were showing the trickle of 'Calm' homesteaders how to hunt, fish, cook and live off the land if they wanted to learn. Some had money and some didn't; there was a diverse range of social and financial status within the group. The Indians had a renewed sense of purpose while teaching and practicing the ways of the old with their new-found knowledge. A number of the Indians had become 'Complete Knowers' which served to enhance their culture greatly.

The private investigator Van Tangle had lost and found Edward numerous times. As of this moment Van Tangle was staking out the *3 CANES*, which was moored at the Coronado Yacht Club pier at North Island, San Diego, California. The last time he had found it in port was over five months ago. No telling what Edward was doing or where he had been during that time.

Jaybird was still traveling around both the North and South Americas, with his new wife, Cinnamon. They had just left some of

Jaybird's family who lived in Idaho, completing a long overdue visit. Cinnamon was a very bright young woman, fresh out of college, where she had just graduated as Valedictorian. The tall half African-American and half Irish young lady was as beautiful as she was smart. Jaybird had bumped into her at a convenience store. They had begun a conversation which led to lunch and eventually a year-long courtship and, finally, marriage. Cinnamon had been excited to have a chance to travel around the continent after putting so much effort into school for four years. She had planned to head to Europe and hop around from country to country by train for a year or so, but Jaybird's plan was just as enticing. They spent most of their days shaking hands with everyone they met. They were being friendly, getting to know a little about each person with whom they came in contact . When Jaybird *knew* they were 'Knowers' he would explain to them that they would always have a place to go if they wanted to or if life took a turn for the worse for them. Most were just grateful to finally have someone who understood their half-memories. Each and every one of them was overjoyed to find out he was not alone with the mysteries upstairs in his head. A few were content at where they were at in life, yet promised to make 'The Calm Land' a 'must go to' stop on their vacation time, just to see if they might find a 'Rendering Parent' there.

Elizabeth had finished her book, which had turned out to be a block-buster. It had consumed her life for the past two-and-a-half years. She had put every ounce of heart and thought into it and now she could reap the rewards. Her book-signing tour would start in Las Vegas tomorrow, the day before the big Heavyweight Championship fight at the hotel where she was staying. The MGM had also given her complimentary ringside tickets. The owners always liked to put celebrities and female beauties up front to show them off and to subliminally entice fans with the idea that *this* hotel should be their hotel of choice, too. She was going to be a bigger celebrity this time around. First with the Playmate of the Year and now with her number one best-selling fiction book titled, *Bloodhead, Sweat and Fears*. She was glad she had changed the title and made it a work of fiction and not an autobiography.

Edward had sent Duke out to find a bar or hotel that was showing the big fight on a closed-circuit TV. Duke had found that the Coronado Hotel lounge was the nearest and most adequate place to view the match as per Edward's request. Duke had no idea why his boss was always so interested in boxing.

In the next state east, Elizabeth was entering the arena. She smiled as she thanked the young usher, who was thoroughly thrilled to be so close to such a gorgeous woman. She sat down in the chair the usher had directed her to in the front row. There were about twenty seats behind her that were empty. *I must be early*, she thought. The security men were sneaking glances at her. Maybe she should have worn the gown that showed a little less cleavage. *No matter*, she thought. That's why she had been given a front row seat anyway, she assumed. Besides, anyone who still had a copy of the 1975 'Playboy Magazine' she was in, had seen more of her than this little red dress was showing. She was alone for only a few seconds when the reporters started to stick their microphones and cameras in her face. She put on a smile and began answering the barrage of questions, most of which she had answered a hundred times before, just to different reporters. *This is what I wanted: fame and fortune. Better late than never*, she thought. She would survive this frenzy. No problem.

Robin 'The Silent' Duvall, as he was now known, was a five-to-one underdog to take the title away from the Champ, Larry Holmes. And to add to it, he was a white man. There hadn't been a Caucasian heavy-weight champ for many years. Robin had captured the hearts of boxing enthusiasts, not to mention all the short white men in the world. He was their spokesperson of sorts, without ever uttering a word. "It's not what you say; it's what you do that counts." Robin had that as his motto on his robe, his tee-shirts, hats and anything else the promoters could find to sew it on. His unusual vow of silence had served to only boost his popularity; it was a source of intrigue and definitely added to his drawing power.

Jaybird and Cinnamon were escorted to their seats, right next to Elizabeth in the front row. The rest of the seats were filled up shortly by some of 'The Calm' members who came to root for Robin. The flash-bulbs were still going off around Elizabeth as the first pair of boxers on the event fight card took to the ring for their match. Jaybird whispered to his wife that he was sure he had seen the woman seated next to her before. He just couldn't place the face. Cinnamon said she was the woman they had passed in the pavilion earlier in the day. She had been signing books at an author's table set up by the hotel. Jaybird figured that must be where he had seen her. As they looked around the ring, there were quite a few faces that looked familiar but they were unable to match a name to very many of them.

One state west, Edward sat down on a soft-cushioned, high-back chair and sipped his whisky while the fighters were being introduced. Van Tangle was at the bar on a swiveling wooden stool, licking the salt from the rim of his margarita glass. He was keeping just far enough away from Edward to assure that he could not be distinguished from any other mailman. Van Tangle didn't really blend in at the ritzy Del Coronado Hotel, but no one was bothering him to leave either.

As soon as the camera panned the audience, Edward sat up straight in his chair. He stared at the TV until it panned again over the same section of seats at ringside. When he was sure that he had seen Elizabeth, he slammed his drink down on the table and stormed out the door to the parking lot.

Van Tangle was caught off guard at Edward's swift departure. As he was paying for his drink he managed to see the direction Edward took as he sped away in his rented Corvette. Van Tangle quickly jumped into his own rent-a-car and luckily caught up to the very noticeable red Corvette convertible. He followed at a safe distance. He removed the long-hair wig that was making him extremely hot. The pier was only a few blocks away from the hotel and shortly Van Tangle knew Bloodhead was heading back towards the *3 CANES*. What could have made Edward leave an event like that so fast was beyond Van Tangle. Most men sat glued to the TV when a big fight like that was on.

Edward quickly walked down the dock to the yacht and climbed on board. The "mailman" positioned himself about twenty yards away on a bench by the pier with a three-day-old paper in hand. Although he couldn't hear anything they were saying, he did take notice of the agitated mannerisms of each man as he pretended to read.

"Come here, Duke. I need you to tell me something," Edward bellowed.

From the fantail of the yacht where he was scanning a "*Soldier of Fortune*" magazine, Duke looked up. *What now?* he wondered.

"What do you need to know, Mr. Bloodhead?"

Edward reached into his pocket and pulled out a gun and pointed it at Duke saying, "I need to know why I just saw Elizabeth sitting at ringside in Las Vegas!"

"You must be mistaken..." Duke said with an air of confidence.

"I am not one to forget a pretty face and believe me, she is pretty. You didn't kill her! You idiot!"

"I assure you sir, she was dead. I killed her. The knife went right through the base of the skull. There was no movement after that. None!"

"I think you missed. Or maybe she wasn't the one you killed. I just saw her and I am very pissed off! Do you know what kind of crap she could tell the authorities? She went everywhere with us for two years."

"There is no way she survived. I can promise you that."

"I don't think your promise is worth much, Duke, my boy. You screwed up. That makes two mistakes!"

"If she's still alive, then I will find her and finish the job," Duke said as he watched Edward's hand. He tried to explain how he would kill her this time, but Edward was tired of listening. Duke's boss quickly pulled the small ivory handled Derringer from his pants pocket and shot Duke in the lower leg, which dropped him to the deck. Then Edward quickly walked over to Duke and stuck the gun to his head.

Duke, still wincing in pain, exclaimed as he grabbed his leg, "But… that's only two mistakes!"

"Employees only get two. Oh, did I forget to tell you that rule? Everyone else gets three chances. But I expect more from my own people. The ones I pay good money to *not* make mistakes." With that said, he fired a life-ending shot to the head. Duke's body fell by the deep-sea fishing chair bolted to the deck.

Van Tangle was heading for a phone booth after the first gunshot. He could only assume that Bloodhead had been thorough when he heard the second shot.

By the time the police arrived the *3 CANES'* had weighed anchor, left the harbor and was rounding Point Loma. At that point the police had to call the Harbor Police. They were on their way via boat. Someone was about to be in some serious trouble.

CHAPTER XLI

IT WAS the first round and the Champ was in serious trouble. Never had he been hit with so many perfectly-placed punches to the mid-section nor with such force. These punches were hurting him. The Champ wondered if his trainers had kept that little bit of scouting information from him, just to keep him focused. He had been given the impression that Duvall was just a flash-in-the-pan kid. Duvall was the first fighter to ever have a noticeable limp also. The Champ had been told that was a handicap he should exploit. Besides, a cripple couldn't possibly be a contender for the Heavyweight Championship of the World. The Champ and his entire entourage had obviously underestimated this kid.

Half a minute before the fifth round would end, Robin had battered the Champ around and had him leaning on the ropes, stunned. Robin glanced at Jaybird, between a few hard-pounding blows. Jaybird was on his feet with the rest of the crowd, yelling and screaming. In that split-second he saw Jaybird put his hands palm up to the ceiling and shrug his shoulders. It was *the* signal. Four hard-hitting combinations later, the Champ was on the canvas for the first time in his career. He was knocked out. A fifth round KO for the winner and new Heavyweight Champion of the World! Robin "The Silent" Duvall. It was an unprecedented win.

Jaybird hugged Cinnamon as the crowd exploded in a frenzy. At one point Elizabeth was pushed into Cinnamon, who was holding onto Jaybird.

"Oh, I'm so sorry," Elizabeth said.

"Don't worry," Cinnamon yelled. "We should feel lucky we are able to stand, unlike the guy on the floor up there!"

Elizabeth grinned as she applauded with the same fervor as the rest of the mob.

Robin was just standing there in the middle of the ring looking to the ceiling. Julie was the only thing on his mind. *I did it for you*, he thought to himself. Then he felt the weight lifting off his shoulders. It most certainly was the beginning of a new phase in his life. He could finally let go of his self-induced burden. He had kept his vow to Julie and now he was Number One. He scurried over to the area where Jaybird and Cinnamon were, ignoring everyone in his path. Elizabeth also looked up at Robin, thinking that he was picking her out of the crowd. She thought it was a flattering gesture. But Robin extended his still-gloved hands to Jaybird, who banged down on his fists. Cinnamon also joined in with a few hits of her own. Elizabeth felt a bit embarrassed with her newly-surfacing pretentiousness as Robin went back to the ring for the official announcement of victory and his acceptance of the Championship Belt.

The ring reporters were ready for the 'non-interview' that had always followed any of Robin's wins. Since Robin had first burst onto the scene, they had gotten used to him never talking. But they still struggled to ask yes or no questions.

Cinnamon turned to Elizabeth out of pure excitement and told her that Robin was her husband's best friend. Elizabeth's eyes lit up as she smiled and said, "Wow! Really? Do you think I could meet him sometime? I think he is quite a...an interesting man."

"I don't see why not. Come to the penthouse suite eleven in about two hours. We will be having a big ol' party there. Tell the guard, 'Jaybird sent me'," Cinnamon said, as she looked at Jaybird for confirmation. He was nodding his head in agreement, still smiling and clapping.

As the TV commentator muscled his way over to Robin for what he thought was going to be a hard interview, he grabbed Robin by the arm and asked the first yes or no question,"

"So, do you feel like the Champion of the World?"

Then to everyone's surprise Robin said, aloud, into the microphone, "Julie, this was for you!"

Much of the arena didn't hear him but those who did were trying to hush everyone else. A weird silence quickly came over the crowd. In utter amazement, the commentator said, "Well, um, you didn't answer the question but we are pleased to know that you *can* actually talk. Could you let us all know what it feels like to be the undisputed Heavyweight Champion of the World, in your own words…um…now?"

"Julie, this was for you!" he said again, as loud as he could. Then he said something no one could have predicted. "It feels great to be the Champion. I'll be enjoying it as long as I can, which ain't long because I am hereby retiring from fighting. There is nowhere else to go but down, so I am leaving while on the top."

The arena became so silent at that moment that you could have heard a pin drop, but it only took about five seconds for a full crescendo to build. The reporter knew he had to make the most out of the unusual moment, but since he had been caught off-guard, the only thing he could think of to say was, "Well, of course you…you could always defend your title and make some more money, but never mind that. Who is Julie? I am sure we all want to know," the interviewer said. But Robin was heading to the locker-room, with the biggest smile on his scarred-up face. The burden had been lifted. It was an enormous personal relief that his pledge had finally come to fruition. He felt seven feet tall.

Hours later the penthouse suite was full of many people. Robin didn't see anyone except Elizabeth. Since Cinnamon had introduced her to him they had been involved in uninterrupted conversation. Robin was waving off anyone who would try to say any more than 'Congratulations.' He was very attracted to Elizabeth, but there was more to the attraction than her physical beauty. He was talking to her as if he knew her. It was easy for him. The only other time he had felt this was during the short time he had spent with Julie. Of course, he hadn't talked to anyone in three years, but he was glad he could speak now, finally.

Elizabeth was also having a wonderful time getting to know Robin. She could see through the scars that creased his face, not to mention the swelling by his left eye from the fight. She thought the scars gave him a worn, survivor look, not an ugly appearance at all. His humor had her in stitches at times. She found his attentiveness very attractive.

Those two never saw the friends, acquaintances and entourage trickle out the door, leaving just the two of them in the suite. The late evening became the early morning as they continued to revel in each other's presence.

CHAPTER XLII

THE PRESENCE of the Harbor Patrol boat that had pulled along the starboard side of the *3 CANES*'made the captain of the yacht throttle back to a full stop. They had caught up with the *3 CANES* about twenty miles out of the San Diego harbor. They proceeded to board her. The yacht was well beyond the horizon if you were standing on the beach looking toward the ocean. Van Tangle was on deck with his long-hair wig back on, watching intently. The Harbor Marshall and two armed men cautiously stepped onto the yacht. Van Tangle could hear bits of conversation from the Patrol boat, but wasn't able to put anything together. He had given a very precise description of Duke's appearance and told them that he believed they would find a bloody body on board, if not a dead one. After about twenty minutes the Harbor Patrol men re-boarded their boat and pulled away from the yacht. They explained to Van Tangle that there was no blood, no body and no one was wounded on board the yacht. The crew didn't volunteer any concerns or problems to the officers. The patrolmen seemed very perturbed as they headed back to the pier to drop Van Tangle off.

Van Tangle was not really upset. He was just trying to interlock these latest events. He knew there was something puzzling going on but he didn't have all the pieces yet. He felt so close to nailing Bloodhead that he could taste it. *All these years on one subject,* he thought. How elated he would feel to finally get it some kind of closure. Maybe a body would show up that matched the Bloodhead M.O. Then he would have enough evidence to make a case out of all his findings. But would that be what Dr. Young wanted? Maybe getting Bloodhead arrested was the moral thing to do but he knew he should respect the wishes of his current employer.

He went back to his hotel room and flipped on the TV. The news was on. He watched, wondering, no, hoping to see a local story on a shooting or murder, but there wasn't one. The big story was the large group of militia men that had marched in Boston, rallying support for the U.S. to bomb Iran and disband the United Nations. *What a bunch of fanatics,* he thought. As he pondered his next move as opposed to Bloodhead's movement he saw the sports clip on the Heavyweight fight he had not been able to see at the hotel. The split-screen beside the commentator's head was all they had of the fight, since it was only carried on HBO. That screen picture was all Van Tangle needed to see.

Leaning forward in his chair he let out a bellowing, "Yes! That's why he left! It must have something to do with her. Elizabeth was watching the fight from the arena and Bloodhead had seen her. That would explain his behavior."

Van Tangle had always held onto a theory that the black woman who was killed in Monaco was supposed to have been Elizabeth. She was unfortunately in the room Elizabeth had occupied. It was just so odd for Elizabeth to drop out of sight alone and then a murder of someone in that very room...yes, it had to be related. Van Tangle grabbed a beer from the mini-bar and sat down to ponder his conclusions.

In the still picture on TV was a view of Robin in the middle of a left uppercut punch. But more importantly to Van Tangle was that he saw a full frontal face shot of Elizabeth Lewis and a somehow familiar male face sitting one seat over from her through the ropes of the ring. He found it unusually funny how she just popped up out of nowhere.

How did she fit into this scenario? he wondered. And the guy next to her looked very familiar. The last place he had seen Elizabeth was in Monaco. But where had he seen that young man before? He pressed the mute button so he could concentrate better. After a few minutes it came to him. The man was at the Two Tails restaurant in Tahiti. It was the nephew of Nicholas Young: Jaybird. He had only seen him once in a picture since that encounter and that was a few years ago, but he was sure of it. Van Tangle wondered if Jaybird knew Elizabeth. Could he have been involved with Bloodhead somehow? They were in Tahiti at the same time. A conspiracy theory was growing in his head. No matter, he had already decided to take the next flight to Vegas and hope that he could track down Ms. Elizabeth Lewis. He felt she might be in danger.

Late the next day, Elizabeth was signing books and smiling graciously for each photo. She was enjoying herself immensely, although she was very tired from staying up all night talking with Robin. There seemed to be only a few more people in line and it looked as if she would be able to make her dinner date with Robin without any problem. She noticed that the last man in line was the same one who had been sitting in the chairs by the Keno area for about two hours, reading her book. She smiled as he came up to the table, hoping that he wasn't a stalker or something.

"Well, what did you think of my book?" she asked him, reaching out to shake his hand, just as she had done at least 300 other times already that day.

"I think it is chock-full of very interesting information," Van Tangle said, smiling.

"So how did you like the ending?" she asked, having heard so many different answers all day that she had actually stopped listening to them.

"I don't think it's over yet. You never found those mermaids on that deserted island," he said.

"Well, thank you…I am…glad…What did you say?"

"You never found those mermaids."

"Well, that was just a story that one of my characters made up," she laughed as she dotted her 'i's. "Funny, that's the first time anyone mentioned that part of the book."

With a smile Van Tangle asked, "Was that character made up, or was he a real person?"

"That depends. Are you a lawyer or a real person?" she countered jokingly.

"Very funny, Ms. Lewis. You and I both know that lawyers are not real people!"

"So…which are you?" she asked, laughing along with him.

Pulling a business card out of his pocket and handing it to her he said, "Well, I am a private investigator and I think you are going to be a very important piece of a puzzle that I have been working on for a long time."

"Really, now," she said, standing up.

"Yes. I would like to talk to you, if I could, about some particular dates and places that I read in your book."

Grabbing her light jacket and purse, she remarked that she was heading for a very important dinner engagement but she could make plans to meet him for lunch the next day. She further explained that she was leaving for the next city tomorrow on her month-long book-signing tour and that was the only free time she had on her schedule. They set a place and time to meet. He also thanked her for the signature and for her time.

The next day at lunch, Elizabeth, Robin, Cinnamon and Jaybird were greeted by a man in quite a unique outfit.

"Captain One-Eye!" Elizabeth and Jaybird said almost in unison as they both looked at each other, totally surprised.

"Aye, Mateys, is yer waitn' fer me? Or is this here char taken?" the man asked, as he lifted the eye-patch from his eye.

Elizabeth and Jaybird were still laughing as he proceeded to remove his scraggly wig. Robin and Cinnamon just stared at the de-cloaking man in bewilderment.

"I am Kristopher Van Tangle. You can call me VT!" he said, without the fake coarse voice.

The five of them had a very entertaining and enlightening lunch.

CHAPTER XLIII

EDWARD WAS entertaining himself with a waitress at the bar, having landed in Las Vegas the night before via a private jet. He had just missed seeing the book-signing booth where Elizabeth had been. It had been taken down just a few minutes prior to his walking into the casino area. With his ponytail tucked up under a hat and dark sunglasses on, he headed upstairs to check out the maid services at the MGM Grand Hotel. Within ten minutes and using only 2000 dollars of hush money, he had the suite number and a passkey to the room of a one E. Lewis. He laughed at how easy it was to get anything he wanted. Money was such an *eye-closer*. Telling the maid that he was going to 'pop the question' to his girlfriend, had made the whole situation seem so 'sweet' to the maid, not to mention the huge six carat cubic zirconium that Edward flashed before her eyes.

He sat in his room and pondered the situation. He wasn't nervous at all; he was actually excited. He hadn't killed in a long time and he definitely wanted Elizabeth dead. He usually let Duke handle these kinds of things in this life, unlike his past lives. But this time he had to do it himself, just as he had had to make Duke into fish food. This one he was doing for spite.

Edward waited until three in the morning. Then he took the elevator up to the third floor. He strolled down the hallway, making sure no one saw him. As he came up to her room he took out the key and a very long and sharp knife. Entering the room very quietly, then closing the door behind him just as quietly, he waited for a second for his eyes to get acclimated to the dark. From where he was, he could make out his ex-lover sleeping on the bed, face down. *As usual,* he mused. *This is just too easy. Why would I pay someone else to do this?*

Tip-toeing with a measured pace, he reached the bed, jumped on top of the body and delivered a powerful knife thrust. He tried to withdraw the knife, but it felt as if wasn't going to come out. Then the lights came on. Squinting from the unexpected brightness and noticing the guns pointing at him, Edward slowly put his hands in the air. He looked down and eyed the mannequin he had tried to kill. With their guns still aimed at him, the police led him out of the room into the hallway. On his way out Edward caught a glimpse of the camera on a tripod in the bathroom. It had obviously filmed the event from a hole in the wall. A smirk came over his face as he thought how his lawyers would have a field day with this blatant case of entrapment.

The police hand-cuffed him and hauled him away. Further down the hallway, in the opposite direction, Robin shook the P.I.'s hand. Van Tangle was relieved that the situation went off as planned without any foul-ups. Then they all went to the police station to fill out some paperwork. They picked up Elizabeth on the way. She had been waiting with Cinnamon, out of harm's way, in Robin's room.

Van Tangle was feeling especially proud of himself for piecing the whole thing together. The pattern that Bloodhead had shown over the years was that he was quick and efficient. *At least this time I was one step ahead of him,* Van Tangle thought to himself. He deduced that the justice system would have a very hard time acquitting Bloodhead. All the data Van Tangle had collected over the years, along with the new evidence the police had on Bloodhead, made quite a convincing package for the Las Vegas District Attorney. Now if he could just find the coin dealer, Mr.

McCallock. That surprise witness would surely nail the coffin closed on the Bloodhead saga. *Finally,* he thought.

CHAPTER XLIV

1982

"FINALLY, IT'S over," Elizabeth said with a heavy sigh. "Now let's relax and take it easy on our way to 'The Calm Land', I am really tired of signing my name. It has been far too long since we had any time for ourselves. Let's take the rest of the trip slowly."

The other three agreed. Of course, Jaybird didn't like to do anything slowly, but he could drive slower when someone mentioned it. They all had enjoyed the sights along the way. It had been an exhausting month, driving from town to town finding the book stores and radio stations, etc.

Elizabeth Lewis' second book had become a top twenty best-seller. Hollywood was going to make a movie out of her first book. She had invited Jaybird and Cinnamon to be the tour guides as well as chauffeurs on a month-long book-signing trek with her and Robin. She had to drag Robin away from his new recording studio. Seems the public wanted to see more of the man who had given up the Heavyweight title within five minutes of winning it. He was doing more commercial endorsements than he could keep track of. They were lucrative, too.

Elizabeth's last stop on the book tour was in New York, Jaybird had asked her if he could ask Nicholas and Evelynn to tag along; they were right down the road in New Jersey. Robin had talked about them but she had never met them, so she agreed.

Nicholas had said he needed a vacation from his work at Intertwine and wanted to see how the folks on 'The Calm Land' were getting along anyway. Since it had been two years since he and Evelynn had had a real vacation, both were ready.

So the Winnebago picked them up in Mullica Hill and the six headed across the northern states toward Montana, slowly.

During the ride, Cinnamon asked Nicholas if he could expound on a conversation he had with Evelynn and herself once about the start of the collapse of this society, since it clearly hadn't collapsed yet.

"Think it won't collapse? Sure, I remember that conversation. I have related that story a few times before for sure. You see, Cinnamon, I have seen many a civilization collapse. The Egyptians, the Mayans, the Romans, just to name a few. Even before languages, we humans ran in packs that had simplistic versions of unspoken moral and ethical law. Things everyone did and things no one would ever do, mainly for fear of being ostracized or even killed off by the majority of the others. That was where natural selection and morals all originated. But for some reason everything just starts to erode after a while. You're right; it hasn't happened yet but you just keep watching," Nicholas said.

"So you can pinpoint a start to your so-called moral decline?" Elizabeth asked, thinking that maybe she could find some inspiration for her next book with this discussion.

"Think I can't? It seems to be realized slowly by people who are living life for the first time. You know, a first time 'O'. Anyone who *knows* can see it coming a mile away; this prompts us to start discussing it within our little social groups."

"I would tend to agree with you there, Uncle," Jaybird said from the driver's seat.

"I have seen it before also, my dear," Robin commented, hugging his girlfriend's shoulders.

Nicholas continued, "You see, we humans do strange things over what seems like long periods of time. But they really aren't so long in terms of the length of your memories. Once you touch the 'Rendering Parents' and the chemical reaction triggers the memories of all your lives, you can see that time is not so long. You can live over and over again and continue to make the same social mistakes, or try to help correct them. It is always your choice, of course. But it isn't always just you and what you think. Many things are accepted and OK in one life and totally unacceptable in another life at a different time. And some things stay the same."

"Isn't that a fact!" Robin exclaimed.

"OK...could you give me an example?" Elizabeth asked.

"Sure," Robin continued. "Take the old Roman gladiator games. I can't, I mean you can't just go into a ring or arena and kill someone nowadays for the pure entertainment of the audience. That was the sport of the day in 200 BC. And I know, because I lived it, but you *can* enter a ring and fight someone. Even though we have more rules today, it's the same kind of entertainment. See how it changes over time? It gets more sophisticated. From swords and knives to no swords or knives; from no gloves to gloves; from no time limit to fifteen rounds. Now they want to make it only twelve rounds. That would be an example of how we took something and fit it into the laws of today. Some of the rules changed, but the fighting is still there."

"But if you did kill your opponent, you wouldn't go to jail," Jaybird interjected.

"Good point, Jaybird," Nicholas said, continuing. "Then again we have seen that there are some 'O's that are forever going to do horrible things no matter what the rules or laws are. They just can't be helped or taught to be good, as it were. Which brings us to our current history. For a while in the recent past we were making strong laws that protected society, now we see laws that are becoming quite liberal."

"Like what do you mean, Nick?" Elizabeth asked.

"Oh like…well, drugs were legal up until about 1913. Cocaine was in Coke. Morphine was widely used during the Civil War. Hell, you could buy opium pills at Sears! Then they made a law that prohibited most drugs from being bought or sold. Instantly you had a class of folks who became criminals overnight just by having a specific drug in their possession, which just the day before had been legal. One day earlier, they had a legal way to get rid of a bad toothache or a back ache and such. But now you have a big movement that wants to make some drugs legal again. Look at alcohol prohibition. What a roller-coaster ride. Was that so important to society that they had to change the Constitution of the United States? The group with the most votes won. The majority usually wins out. They wanted to drink, so the majority got what it wanted. But they had to change the Constitution again. I would surmise that when there is a majority of folks who think sugar causes obesity and that it is so bad for you physically, that they will pass a law making sugar an illegal drug. But you will be able to smoke pot 'cause the majority of the population wants it. Of course there would be no Twinkies to satiate your munchies. You'd have to get your neighborhood druggie to supply you with a mouth-watering Twinkie that you would gladly pay five bucks for!"

"It *is* getting kinda crazy out there," Robin stated.

"You sound like you are all for creating your own little group and segregating yourself from everyone else," Elizabeth said.

"Well, is that so terrible? If the majority of folks have all their past memories and can effect change and rid the world of all the bad, then I say yes, join my group. Listen to the wisdom of the 'O'," Nicholas said.

He knew Elizabeth was getting riled up. He had seen it before when talking to a non-'Knower'. Now he wished he hadn't even started this line of conversation.

"Sometimes though," Evelynn interjected, "you have long stretches of time where humans, as a race, get close to living in harmony but then a first time 'O' or an evil 'O', like Bloodhead, rises up to be in charge.

Somehow they turn enough opinions to their way of horrible social thinking and doing bad things, just enough, to mess the whole thing up all over again. Other bad 'O's get elected to positions of power and the lawmakers begin passing bad laws which protect the bad folks instead of good laws to protect the good folks and the whole thing just gets all messed up."

"What whole thing gets messed up?" Cinnamon asked her.

"The whole human race or the society," she replied.

Robin saw the perplexed look on Cinnamon's face and said, "You see, Nicholas believes there *can* be one great harmony to everything and everybody. Everything has a place in life, humans included. But all the chemicals have to be combined exactly right in us humans. Take Jaybird up there, driving his little heart out. He was Nicholas' second-born during Jaybird's very first life. He was a food-gatherer, not a hunter; he was killed early in his life by his brother at the time, who is Bloodhead in this life. All Jaybird's lives since, have him doing pretty much the same thing. Trying to get things done fast or on the spur of the moment because he is subconsciously, or as Nicholas says, genetically aware of his predilection to an early death."

"I don't understand, Robin," Cinnamon said as Elizabeth nodded emphatically.

"Well, we don't usually talk about certain things to non-'Knowers'. Nicholas thought it was best to not discuss that subject to any non-'Knowers' until recently," Jaybird interjected from the driver's seat.

"Correct-a-mundo," Nicholas said. "I just didn't think the current society milieu was ready for this information, but I must concede that letting some non-'Knowers' hear some of our knowledge may be a good thing now. And it is pretty hard to have secrets from your spouse. But maybe they are ready for it. Hey, we tried in the sixties…but the drugs got in the way. Maybe the advances in technology will help us prove it to them also. So perhaps the time has come to tell all humans of their own impending future capabilities and or doom. It seems like a crapshoot to me though."

"Future capabilities, Nick?" Elizabeth asked.

"Sure! Let's take Jaybird up there for example. He has always been sort of a gatherer. He gathers us up and drives us everywhere. He also came up with 'The Calm Land' idea and organized a meeting with all the 'Knowers' from 'The Calm' and offered them a place to homestead, which Robin paid for of course. He likes to do things right now and he likes organization. He seems to be like a–a leader of sorts, to be sure. He never looks back, no time for him to do that. 'Go forward' is his motto. Make that decision and run with it. So even though he has this weird leadership air about him, it certainly doesn't make his decisions always correct. But he shows such confidence in his beliefs and opinions that it is infectious and consequently if you follow his advice, well…that's the road you choose to travel down, right or wrong. And nobody is always right."

"Course my dad has always said it is just a spur-of-the-moment thing," Jaybird said nodding his head.

"Think Jaybird could change? No way. His type of 'O' is just that way. Ain't it a funny thing?" Nicholas continued. "He needs a regulator of sorts. And that would be Robin. Someone who can hear what Jaybird has to say but will put on the brakes if need be. Then there are Jaybird's many associations with two's."

Suddenly Jaybird turned up the radio, drowning out the conversation. Luckily, the voice repeated the news, saying that jury selection was to begin in the trial of billionaire Edward Bloodhead for attempted murder.

"Good grief," Cinnamon said, looking at Elizabeth. "What takes so long with these trials anyway?"

"And to think Jaybird wanted to be like him once," Robin said, shaking his head from side to side.

"Yeah, he turned out to be a bad role model, for sure," Jaybird mumbled.

"These things do drag on. I just hope justice prevails and I don't have to spend too much time in court. But Nicholas, back to Jaybird's acquaintances with two's," Elizabeth said.

"Yes, two's!" Nicholas said emphatically, "He was my groovy second-born little dude and let's see, he has had two wives, he usually stays on the second floor of a hotel or a room number with lots of two's in it. This seems like a coincidence. Over a long period of lives you tend to notice it more, because the two's just seem to come up over and over again that way for him. Given a choice, he will lean in the two's direction. He probably doesn't pay any attention to it yet, but it's always been there."

Cinnamon thought for a second and excitedly said, "Two's? Hmm, let me see…two, two-carat diamond rings, one for each of my hands. We were married on February 22. His two names start with J's…Jeffery Jason. Wow. That is interesting to a numerologist!"

"Lest we forget that he married two women who had names like sweet stuff: Kandy and Cinnamon. It goes on and on, my friends. Everything has a meaning and you really don't have to go far to connect the dots. Then again, does it really matter?" Nicholas bluntly stated, adding, "Quite frankly, a numerologist could find a pattern in anything, so I guess they would be interested in this."

"But his parents named him. He didn't have anything to do with that," Elizabeth said confidently.

"Think he didn't? Of course he didn't have anything to do with his name verbally, but it is all about the chemicals in the body. The body remembers because the soul keeps all its memories and it passes information along, even in the womb. Of course his biological mother birthed him but Evelynn and I made his 'O' the first time, remember? And sure the dad does his part but the mother shares her body with the baby. I believe the 'O' has a great influence during pregnancy. We just don't pay attention to it yet. Although I am sure you have heard a pregnant mother say something like…'he's going to be a football player'…or the like. Since we know we have memories of old past lives, it would be safe to say that the chemicals from the memories in Jaybird were crossing in the womb and maybe that is why his mom, Nan, felt compelled to give him the name Jeffery Jason and a nickname of Jaybird. She could have named him David, but she didn't! She felt something, or maybe she was being told internally via some un-measurable DNA code or chromosome or some other tiny particle inside her, to do such and such. I mean if a woman can pass on her genes to her child, why can't it go the other way during pregnancy? From child to the parent?"

"Seems like quite a stretch there, Nicholas, but…OK, whatever. Now what about Robin?" Elizabeth asked.

"Hmm. Robin was my first-born," Nicholas said. "He was always the strongest. That's why he won the Heavyweight title and was the youngest person to do so; a first. Then he promptly retired; another first of its kind. He was always somewhat like a protector of the meek humans and he had to be strong to do that and to always come in first. Of course he had his first real girlfriend taken from him. I don't mean to embarrass you but he told me he never had sex until you came along, Elizabeth. His first longtime girlfriend."

She blushed as she heard everyone laugh. She glanced at Robin who was hanging his head down laughing also. *Must have been guy talk*, she thought.

"Well, he sure could have fooled me! I had a hard time believing that he was a virgin after our first night together myself."

"Hey, I had a huge argument with my first wife over that very same thing," Jaybird said over his shoulder.

"Some knowledge just sticks with you over the eons, that's for sure and procreation has always been there!" Nicholas said with a twinkle in his eye as he glanced towards Evelynn.

"And Bloodhead, Nick?" Robin asked, although he already knew the answer.

Nicholas flipped his long hair back and looked at the faces of the two non-'Knowers' looking intently back at him, waiting impatiently for the answer.

"He has always been evil; this is just his lot in all his lives. He has always been an evil-doer. It's genetic. He really can't help it. He has almost always been the most avaricious of people too. His desire for material things is unquenchable. Some of the names you would instantly recognize that he lived were as Genghis Khan, Ivan Vasilyevich or Ivan the Terrible, and Hitler. Now there was a man who wanted…well, the whole world to himself. There are so many others that I could go on and on for hours."

"Is he the only evil person?" Cinnamon asked.

"Sakes alive, no. There are many 'O's who are genetically bad. That's why we have so many laws to catch the bad people. Why do you think we have all the shrinks out there trying to fix 'em after others put them in jail? Oh, some can conform or be rehabilitated into society if they are borderline bad, but you just can't change the genetic condition of a soul," Nicholas said.

"That's pretty heavy," Cinnamon said somberly.

"Think it ain't?" Nicholas quipped.

"Suffice to say that everything in the world is made up of chemicals. When put in certain orders and mixed together, you get life. Nicky is on a quest to identify and quantify this order. Then maybe he can find the problem 'O's via a test or something," Evelynn said.

"But…where would technology help our society, Nick? Cinnamon asked, wondering if anyone else had been wondering the same thing.

"Aha! Finally someone asked me that! You see, since everything is a chemical combination of some kind, memories also must be made up of chemicals. So, thoughts are made up of particles. The scientific community hasn't been able to break everything down to the smallest of particles yet. They always find something smaller to measure, probably always will," Nicholas said, holding his thumb and forefinger together.

Elizabeth was intrigued with the whole conversation. She thought Cinnamon had some great questions.

"But…" Cinnamon started.

"Technology, yes, I know, I know. Hold your pocket protected smock on, young 'un. Currently we can measure things down to about a yoctometer but I believe that technology will allow us to eventually measure even our memories as a substance with a weight or pattern or something we can't even imagine just yet. Then you could surely know who is who. Or should I say who *was* who...like from before birth, by matching up memory measurements, patterns or whatever, to some kind of a database. It would be just like a fingerprint. In the near future we should be able to track a signature if you will, of the evil 'O's. We'll put that information in a huge database and...well, eliminate them before they grow. On the other hand we will be able to know who will grow up to be another great leader or painter, etc. I am already on that track with my current research. Plus, with these new personal computers, I have been able to make inroads on our 'Family Tree' of names."

"Hold on there," Elizabeth said, "Are you talking about killing... like...embryos after tests are run on them or something, and they test out to be bad souls?"

"Think I ain't!"

Elizabeth didn't like the sound of that at all. It made her sick to her stomach, as if she had breathed in a noxious smell. She quickly retorted, "Isn't that playing God?"

Nicholas drew a deep breath and began, "Until everything is scientifically proven, there will always be the religious believers and their hope in their God. That sector has placed everything on a hope and a prayer. They have to cling to their religion because there aren't answers yet to everything and their faith helps them feel better about that mystery. But we 'Knowers' *know* some of the answers to who was who and what they did previously, right now. My belief is that when everyone *knows* certain common answers, everyone will agree that we don't want another 'O' growing up in the world, who was Hitler the last time around. We *can* make society better. We can have harmony and world peace, just like every Miss America and I want. We can be an intellectual society instead of a semi-barbaric one. Why do you think I started the whole handshaking thing way back when anyhow? Course it was easier when there weren't so many hands to shake. You tended to run into 'Knowers' more often when there weren't so many folks on the earth. Anyhow, once you know you are coming back for another life, you realize there is no need for religion."

Elizabeth looked at Nicholas and asked, "Wait a dog-gone minute here; you're saying no religion, so...no God, Nick?"

"Well, religion really doesn't have anything to do with God per se, but nope, no God. Remember *man* makes up religions," he replied.

"You sound so matter-of-fact," Elizabeth said as she felt herself getting quite angry.

"Think it ain't a fact? I only know what I know and it is all factual."

"How can you be so sure? You keep using the term 'I believe', isn't that a religious connotation; the belief in faith?" Elizabeth retorted.

"Look, 'believe' is just a word. But I am sure there isn't any God or Gods. You are the one with reservations. I *know* and you don't. You wouldn't have to ask it you already knew. You don't question that the earth is round anymore, right?"

"Right, but how can so many people be wrong about their God?" Cinnamon asked. She was feeling a bit uneasy with the conversation herself.

As Nicholas looked at Cinnamon then at Evelynn, he took another deep breath and said,

"You see folks; this is why I really don't think non-'Knowers' are ready for this kind of conversation. This higher source thing is burned into their psyche. Listen my friends, most everyone has been taught to believe whatever their parents believe. Oh sure, some people change religions and even your environment can have a lot to do with your beliefs, but normally you are brought into a certain way of life via your family upbringing and that is what you practice. Much of the time it is just where you live that decides your religion. Like peoples tend to stick together. Then again some folks have life-changing events or near-death events that make them seek out a religion that...well, makes them feel better or helps them through some horrible experience. 'Course they never had a religion before; they just heard it would help them, so they started believing, basically to save their own soul," Nicholas stated.

"Besides, most religions scare you into thinking you *have* to believe or you'll live an eternity somewhere vile," Evelynn said.

"Right, I mean what would be the difference between a devil-worshiper and let's say…a Christian, to you Liz?" Nicholas asked.

"Good and bad for one thing. Right?" Elizabeth said, with Cinnamon nodding in agreement.

"Good call. But what's the difference between the rituals they practice?" Nicholas asked.

"One is for the Devil and one is for God, duh!" Elizabeth said smirking a bit.

"That *sounds* right, yet neither God or the Devil exists. So both actions are useless," Nicholas said then continued, "So, you tell me what the difference is between devil-worshipers sacrificing a human and drinking the fresh blood and the Christians simulating the very same thing with the dried crackers or wafers and grape juice or red wine simulating the body and blood of Jesus? Every Sunday at church, people partake of this. Both rituals initially came from a like idea. A sacrifice to appease um…some supreme entity. Christians just don't use live humans or live animals anymore, but they used to use goats and sheep, and they still justify the ritual by saying it is in remembrance of one man's body and blood. It is all gross to me. Hey that's what they want to believe. It makes them feel better, thinking that there is something better than this, later on in heaven. It holds them together inside. Yet we 'Complete Knowers' *know* we come back again and again right here on earth…forever."

There was a long pause in the conversation and since no one was speaking up, Nicholas continued on with his ramble, "We could for instance create a panel that had oversight on say…"red-flagged" embryos and if an embryo was a person or an 'O' who had received a sentence of five consecutive life terms in jail for some horrible crime he committed… well, you could ensure he served out the entire five life sentences. Why give multiple life sentences when you only have one life to serve? But then maybe there are already 'Knowers' in the system; already making laws for just that eventuality? Kinda makes you wonder, huh? Let's extrapolate here. If they had captured, let's say, Hitler, before he killed himself, and put him on trial for crimes against humanity, you could rest assured his 'O' would be incarcerated for a very, very long time."

"Wait a minute! You started the handshake?" Elizabeth asked. She really wanted to just change the subject as she felt herself growing very disgusted with the current topic of conversation but didn't want to show it. *My Midwest religious upbringing is showing through,* she thought.

She had had a few topical conversations with Robin before about 'The Calm' group but he would never go into it in detail for whatever reason. *Now* she knew why. She had a strange feeling that if this was going to be the cornerstone of her boyfriend's life, she might have to re-evaluate their relationship. *And fast*, she thought.

"Think I didn't? How else was I to embark upon finding out who was a 'Knower' and who wasn't? I had to touch everyone I met, so I figured instead of holding up your hand to show everyone you didn't have any weapons, as was the custom in those early days, I just started reaching out and shaking the arm. Needless to say, it caught on," Nicholas said with a big grin on his face.

After a long pause in the conversation, Cinnamon asked, "So Jaybird says you were like…Adam and Evelynn was Eve. Like the Bible states, is that so, Nicholas?"

"Sort of. You see, all religions have a starting point. We seem to be what the Christians are referring to in their Bible. But we are also connected to many other religious beginnings. You see, many events in the Bible are based on actual events but most of it is just however the story-teller decided to tell it. Once it got transferred over to print, after being passed down again and again, verbally over long periods of time, things got embellished. Believe me, there were many more stories that didn't make the 'cut' as it were, into the Bible," Nicholas said.

There was a short silence then Evelynn began, "Yes, there were people, civilizations and so-called Gods way before Christianity came along. The Bible was a way of legitimizing the social thoughts of the times into a common script for the masses in that geographical area to read and hold sacred. Droves of people liked those ideas and teachings. It started out small but then it gelled with an ever-growing group of people and after some oppressive times, it became mainstream. But the idea of a single God actually talking to just one human and delivering some guiding commandments is…well, a bit far fetched, as most of the stories are from that time, if you really think about it. We have the same things in print today but we call them fiction writings. You can't *believe in* everything you read."

"Think you can't?" Nicholas continued. "Plus, Christianity didn't catch on right off the bat. It took a while. It eventually took on a great following of its own. Religions pop up all the time in our history. Always have. Sometimes a way of life doesn't actually start out as a religion but it may end up as one. That's what a belief system is. It is a far-out, groovy belief in something that you can relate to or connect deeply with and it makes you feel secure. But that just doesn't make it reality. I have always seen religion more like a co-dependency thing than anything else. If it helps you, then use it, but once you know, you won't be dependent on it. There ain't no prize at the end. Actually, at the end is just another beginning!"

"But I thought you and Evelynn said you actually were the so-called Adam and Eve that the Bible mentions. So you were the first two humans, right?" Elizabeth asked, thinking this could be the whole conceptual basis for her next book. *These folks are nuts*, she thought to herself! She decided that she would have to gather more of this crazy talk and start another book.

Nicholas scratched his chin and brushed his hair back and stated, "Let me just say that humans had been around for about ten thousand years by the time Jesus was walking the earth, which was not made in six days, mind you. We didn't start out in any garden and Eve here didn't eat any apple. Hell, we couldn't even talk in the beginning, but we had memories. I know this because I can remember it. I was there!"

Cinnamon sounded confused as she asked, "But if you agree that you were what the Bible is referring to as Adam and Eve and we all…um the entire human race came from you two, then you being the first two…why don't you let everyone know that…"

"Oh, we have never said we were the first two humans," Evelynn said, with a twinkle in her eye.

Jaybird had never heard this line of discussion before, so he asked, "Then what *are* you saying?"

"Well," Evelynn continued, "since neither Nick nor I have any 'Rendering Parents', we know that we…"

Nicholas quickly grabbed her arm gently while putting a finger to her lips. Smiling like a child holding in a secret, he said, "Please, Eve, not now, my little flower. I know they are definitely not ready for that particular bit of knowledge!"

To Be Continued………

Printed in the United States
By Bookmasters